Annabel

and the

Boy

in the

Window

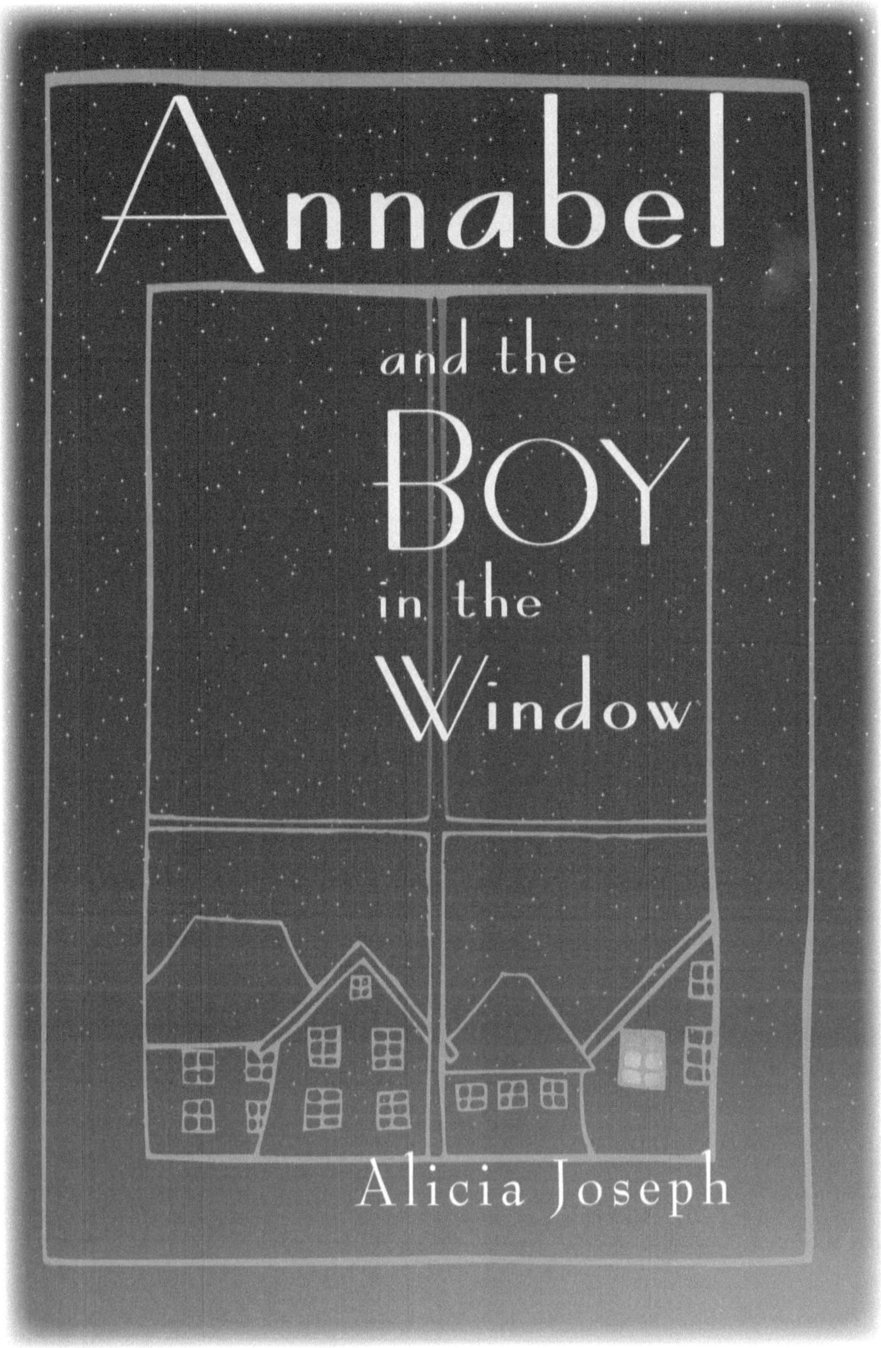

Annabel

and the

BOY

in the

Window

Alicia Joseph

Bink Books
Bedazzled Ink Publishing Company • Fairfield, California

978-1-949290-93-6 paperback

Cover Design
by

Bink Books
a division of
Bedazzled Ink Publishing, LLC
Fairfield, California
http://www.bedazzledink.com

Chapter One

THE SUN SHONE brightly on that early September day when, underneath clear skies, families celebrated the holiday weekend that brought an end to summer break. Children played in yards, as fathers charred hot dogs and burgers on backyard grills. Black smoke rose above the houses, dispersing the smell of barbeque throughout the neighborhood.

Annabel Turner poked her head outside her bedroom door and listened for any sounds coming from downstairs, but the music playing loudly in her room made it difficult to hear. She leaned farther into the hallway until she heard the sound of dishes being washed. She closed her bedroom door and turned to her friends.

"We can keep looking," she announced. "My mom's still in the kitchen."

"What's the big deal if she sees us?" Donna Parker asked, her nose pressed against the window.

"She doesn't like it when we snoop," Annabel said.

"You need a lock on your door." Molly Stenson leaned her skinny, twig-like arms against the ledge and peered out the window.

"They won't let me have a lock." Annabel dropped to her knees, between her friends, and set her gaze onto her alluring neighbors. "What're they doing now?"

Buddy Holly's "Rave On" played on the radio as Annabel and her friends watched the appealing couple through her bedroom window.

"Sylvia's still in her garden and Henry's still cutting the grass." Donna scooted her husky body over to give Annabel more room.

"That woman is sure gonna miss her garden when the season's over," Annabel said. "She's in there every day."

"He's coming around again!" Molly perked up.

"He's gonna pinch her butt again. I just know it." Donna stated with certainty.

"He's pinched her butt three times already. Twice when he passed her with the lawnmower and once when she walked by him." Molly turned to Annabel. "Your new neighbors are really something. Watching them was the best part of my summer."

"Mine too." Donna said.

Sylvia and Henry Chapman had moved into the neighborhood a month after Christmas, and Annabel was instantly drawn to them, especially Sylvia. The woman wasn't like any other woman Annabel had ever known. Sylvia didn't dress like the other housewives in town. She didn't talk like the other housewives in town. And she certainly didn't behave like the other housewives in town.

"I've never seen my father pinch my mother's butt, and they've been married for twenty-five years," Molly said.

"Yeah, but you've only been around for fifteen of those twenty-five years. Maybe he pinched your mom's butt before you came around," Donna pointed out.

"Forget I mentioned it. I don't want to picture my father pinching any part of my mother's body." Molly turned her attention back to Annabel's neighbors.

"Look," Donna shouted. "Sylvia's moving to a different spot."

"Do you think she's purposely moving to the places where Henry will pass with the mower? Like she wants him to pinch her butt?" Annabel inquired.

"Of course." Donna rolled her eyes. "That's what I would do if a hunk like Henry wanted to pinch my butt."

Annabel looked at her friend. "You really think Henry's a hunk?"

"Sure. Don't you?"

Annabel cast a gaze at her neighbor and sized him up. "He's tall and kind of skinny."

"But he has a lot of muscle." Donna intently watched the man she was describing. "You can see them on his arms when he pushes the lawnmower. You can tell he's strong. He has wide shoulders."

"Wide shoulders?" Molly laughed. "That's what you like about him?"

"Yes and he's cute in a nerdy kind of way because he wears glasses," Donna explained.

"I wear glasses. What are you saying? I can't be cute because I wear glasses?" Molly scowled at Donna.

"You can be cute, but only in a nerdy kind of way," Donna answered frankly.

"Oh . . . I swear, Donna. Sometimes I just don't know why I stay friends with you."

"What? I still said you can be cute."

Annabel laughed and turned back to Henry. "There's something devilish about him, though. He looks innocent, almost boyish, but he's the boy you're afraid to take your eyes off of because you don't know the trouble he'll get into."

"He grabs his wife's butt in public. What do you think he grabs in private?" A naughty grin spread across Donna's face.

"Oh, Donna." Molly smacked Donna in the arm. "You're so bad."

"I know." Donna giggled. "Ohhh . . . look! Here he comes again." She leaned her forehead against the window and watched as Henry pushed the lawnmower toward Sylvia who was bent over her garden.

Henry approached the spot where Sylvia stood over her array of colorful vegetables. As he came up to her, he dropped his hand against his side, slid it underneath her buttocks, and gave it a squeeze.

"I knew it," Donna screamed. "I knew it. He pinched her butt again."

"That's four times," Molly yelled. "I can't believe it. The man is relentless."

"Look at her. She doesn't seem to mind," Annabel said.

Wearing dark-blue Capri pants and a sleeveless white collared shirt, Sylvia straightened her body, and while laughing in a silly way, gave Henry a playful slap on the arm.

"She's enjoying the attention," Annabel said.

"Who wouldn't?" Donna continued to stare out the window.

"I suppose." Molly took off her glasses and wiped the lenses with her shirt. "But I can't believe they act that way in public. I don't think I could."

"Don't you ever want to do something outrageous, something that makes other people squirm just a little bit?" Annabel asked.

"I'm not sure," Molly replied.

"I would," Donna answered emphatically.

"Of course you would," Molly said.

A knock at the door halted the girls' conversation.

"Can I come in?" Joan, Annabel's mom, asked after knocking on the door.

"Hang on!" Annabel yelled and gestured for her friends to get up off their knees and move away from the window. "Come in."

Joan Turner entered the room where walls were plastered with pictures of Elvis Presley, James Dean, and Buddy Holly. She wore a dark-red housedress over her slender figure and her hair was pinned up in a bun. She was attractive in a natural way, wearing little makeup.

"What is the commotion? I could hear your screams from all the way downstairs." Jerry Lee Lewis's "Great Balls of Fire" blasted from the radio, and Joan switched it off on her way to the girls. "I can't stand that Jerry Lee." She stood in front of Annabel and her friends. "So? What is it? What's happened?"

"We were just"—Annabel glanced at her friends—"talking about school, and I guess we got a little over-excited because we can't wait for it to start."

Donna gave her an incredulous look.

Molly nudged Donna's arm.

Donna rubbed her arm. "Yes, that's right. We were talking about school and got a little too excited, happy not to be lowly freshmen anymore."

"Looking forward to school you tell me. That would be a first." Joan lifted her gaze and looked out the window to where Henry was playfully chasing Sylvia with the same hose she had used to water her garden.

Sylvia's screams, mixed with laughter, carried into Annabel's room as Henry lifted her up and spun her around. Joan walked to the window and closed the curtains, a stoic expression on her face. She turned to Annabel. "Your father will be back soon from his hunting trip. It's time for your friends to go home."

"That's okay. I had to leave soon anyway." Donna stood up. "My dad's barbequing. Annabel, you can come over if you want. Molly's coming. But warning, my dad always burns the burgers."

Annabel looked to her mother for permission.

"Go on. Enjoy your last days before school starts," Joan said.

"Oh gosh. Don't remind us." Donna scowled.

"But I thought only moments ago you girls were so thrilled that school was starting you could hardly contain your excitement." Joan raised her eyebrows.

"Oh . . . right . . . um . . ." Donna stammered.

Joan smiled and placed a hand on Donna's shoulder. "Go on. Have fun." She led them out of the room and down the stairs.

Minutes after they left for Donna's barbeque, Joan went back to Annabel's window and pulled back the curtain. She watched the free-loving couple, who were just a few years younger than herself, carry on with their public displays of affection with no regard to whoever may be watching.

THE BELL RANG loudly and classroom doors burst open. Students poured into the hallways. Annabel shuffled through the crowded corridors and searched for her friends. She saw faces of classmates she'd missed seeing during the summer vacation and quickly caught up with their summer adventures, while ignoring the faces she hadn't missed seeing at all.

Molly and Donna were to meet Annabel at her locker right after third period, a routine they'd started the previous school year, to catch up on hallway gossip, but when Annabel got to her locker, her friends weren't there.

She sifted through her locker for the next period's books when high-piercing screams made her jump, and she dropped her books to the floor. She turned around and the hallway was filled with teenage girls, shrieking and yelling out questions like, "How'd he ask you?" "Where'd he do it?" "How big is the ring?" "You're so lucky!" "Do you have a date set?"

Jane Byrne, a senior with long brown hair wrapped in a blue-ribbon ponytail, proudly held out her left hand to a swarm of ogling girls craning their necks to catch a peek of the ring. Basking in the attention, Jane took great satisfaction at being the envy of all her peers.

"We're gonna get married right after grad. Edward's father already has a job lined up for him in manufacturing. He's so smart. He'll be the boss someday. I just know it." Jane rested a hand against her chest and leaned her head back in sweet bliss. "He's gonna be so successful and we're gonna have a big house with a television set in every room and have lots of kids. You'll see."

"That's swell," a petite pimple-faced freshman girl with messy hair said.

Jane glared at the unkempt freshman. "It's better than swell. I'm *engaged.* Who's gonna wanna marry you?"

The unpopular girl pressed her books tightly against her skinny body and retreated to the other end of the hall. Jane shifted her attention back to her worthy admirers as they followed her to their next class.

Annabel picked her books off the floor, waited as the halls cleared, and scanned the corridor for the belittled freshman. She wanted to tell the girl that there was more to life than getting married, but the girl was gone.

Annabel didn't see her friends until after the next class when Donna yelled out to her and waved her chubby arms wildly in the air. She made a beeline for Annabel, with Molly trailing close behind.

"Annabel. Annabel! Did you hear the news? Did you?" Donna breathed heavily.

"What news? What's happened?" Annabel gripped her books at her side.

"Jane Byrne got engaged. Edward proposed to her last night. He even asked her father for permission first, like a real man."

"That's surprising for the moron that he is." Molly pushed her glasses up her pointed nose.

"Who cares if he's a moron? Jane's getting married. At this time next year she'll be a wife and have a home of her own with her own husband, living her own life."

"And we'll still be here trapped to our desks, doing stupid assignments and reading books I'd rather throw in a fire." Molly raised her hand to brush her bangs from her eyes, and the sleeve of her loose sweater slid down her slender arm.

"Oh, that. I saw her before last period showing off her ring to a bunch of gawking girls. It's pathetic, really." Annabel turned away and started for her locker.

"What do you mean it's pathetic?" Molly asked.

"Yeah, what do you mean it's pathetic?" Donna echoed.

Annabel tossed her books in her locker and pulled out two others. "It's pathetic because all they want is to get married. Don't you think we're too young? I wouldn't want to be married in a year, or two years, or even ten years. Besides, I like it here. I like school. I like reading the books you'd rather burn. I like learning new things."

"I like boys," Molly said.

"I like boys, too." Donna smiled.

"There's more to life than just liking boys. It's preposterous for teenage girls to only want to get married. I'll be just fine if I never get married."

Molly and Donna let out gasps.

Annabel cocked her head as she looked at her friends, and her long brown ponytail bopped in the air. "Oh, come on, guys. Don't be like Jane Byrne, flashing your engagement ring all over the halls and acting like getting engaged is the biggest achievement in your life."

"Getting engaged wouldn't be my biggest achievement," Donna said.

"I'm glad to hear you say that," Annabel replied.

"Getting *married* would be my biggest achievement." Donna giggled loudly, and Molly quickly joined in.

Annabel rolled her eyes. "Boys aren't everything. Most of them are a nuisance I just don't need right . . ." She stared straight ahead.

Danny Winfield was walking in her direction and he was looking right at her.

JOAN POKED THE roast with a fork while the meat cooked in the oven. Bloody juices spilled from the tender and slightly rare piece of meat—just the way George liked it. She snatched up a dish towel, pulled the hot pan of searing beef from the oven, and wrapped the dish with foil.

George Turner would be home from work soon, and Joan strived for the house to be in its most perfect order by the time he walked through the door, even though he never acknowledged her effort.

Joan took a feather duster from underneath the sink and busied herself with wiping every speck of dust, on every nook and cranny, in every room. When she finished, she wiped her hands against the apron tied tightly around her slender waist. She picked up a stack of George's favorite magazines with images of men holding large rifles and pictures of fancy, shiny cars on the covers. She piled the publications neatly across the coffee table beside George's favorite chair.

A commercial playing on the television caught Joan's eye.

A man entered the house and cheerfully yelled, "I'm home!"

His wife hurried into the room and greeted her husband with a kiss.

"How was your day?" she asked brightly.

He scowled. "It wasn't so great."

"Well," the jolly woman said with a smile, while straightening the man's tie. "I have something that will make it all better."

"That sounds swell." The man grinned broadly.

In the kitchen, the family gathered around the dinner table where a chocolate cake sat in the center. The merry wife placed a big slice of a perfectly cut piece of dessert onto a plate. She handed it to her husband and said, "Didn't I tell you I had something that would make it all better?"

The husband took the plate, and a wide smile beamed across his face. "You sure did." He looked down at the cake, and his smile quickly turned into a frown. "But how come you didn't make enough for you and the kids?"

The woman playfully slapped her husband on the shoulder, and the children giggled in their seats as they patiently waited for their slice of chocolate cake.

The happy wife then smiled into the camera and asked, "Do you love your family enough to bake with Betty Crocker?"

The slam of a car door turned Joan's attention away from the perfect TV family. She rushed to the front window, remembering Annabel still had friends over and worried it was George coming home early from work.

Relieved, Joan saw it was just Sylvia Chapman returning from a day of shopping. Sylvia carried bags from at least five different department stores. She wore a red curve-hugging pencil skirt with white polka dots. Her full lips were colored with bright red lipstick and her cheeks flushed with a soft pinkish glow. False eyelashes engulfed her blue eyes, and the way she applied her eyeliner to slightly wing out at the corner of her eyes gave them a cat's-eye look.

From the extravagant way Sylvia was dressed, it was apparent she didn't plan on doing much housework that day. Although Joan always tried to keep an attractive appearance, her style of dress was more practical for daily chores, consisting mostly of long-sleeved, buttoned-down shirts tucked into knee-length skirts, or sometimes a simple wrap dress.

Although some women in the neighborhood strived to look like domestic goddesses, even while they cleaned toilets, none accomplished this look as easily as Sylvia Chapman. Some rationalized that because Sylvia had no children to wear her down, it was easy for her to be glamorous all the time.

Joan didn't share the same jealousy over her neighbor's beauty as others did, but she was, at times, taken aback by the woman's free-spirited ways. Sylvia's public displays of affection with her husband disturbed Joan more than her seductive style of dress or the way her perfectly styled curls brushed neatly against her shoulders did.

Noticing Joan at the window, Sylvia smiled and waved, and while holding up one of her bags, she yelled, "Another busy day!"

Joan acknowledged her with a nod and a casual grin, and watched her struggle to open the front door while holding her packages before finally entering her house. Joan turned away from the window, and the clock on the wall reminded her that George would be home soon.

She hurried to the staircase and yelled for Annabel. When she got no response she yelled louder. "Annabel! Annabel!"

She hurried up the stairs, frustrated because Annabel knew it was better that her friends be out of the house by the time George got home. She headed toward Annabel's room as Elvis Presley's "That's All Right" blasted into the hallway. She knocked three times before Annabel whipped open the door while panting heavily.

"I've been calling for you." Joan looked sternly at Annabel.

Annabel caught her breath. "Sorry." She went back into the room and switched off the music. "We're practicing for the school's Sock Hop." She motioned toward Molly and Donna, who were standing near the bed looking equally as winded as Annabel.

Joan smiled at the girls. "A Sock Hop? That sounds like fun." Her tone softened.

"We hope so." Donna could hardly withhold her excitement. "We want to be ready when a boy asks us to dance." She clasped her hands together.

"I don't even know why I'm wasting my time." Molly pushed her long dark hair away from her face. "It's not like any boy's gonna ask me to dance."

"Now why would you say something like that?" Joan frowned.

Molly collapsed onto Annabel's bed. "Because I'm a square."

Joan eyed her curiously. "A what?"

"A square. I'm just not cool."

Annabel rolled her eyes. "Gosh, Molly. You don't have to be so dramatic."

Molly propped herself up on her elbows. "Easy for you to say. You only had the cutest boy in school talk to you today."

"I can't believe Danny Winfield talked to you today. If Danny Winfield ever talked to me I would just die," Donna screamed.

"He's so dreamy," Molly yelled and both girls pretended to faint onto Annabel's bed.

Annabel acted nonchalant in front of her mother, insisting it was nothing.

"Who is this Danny boy?" Joan asked, her curiosity about this boy made her forget the time.

Annabel's eyes were everywhere but on her.

"Danny Winfield is only the cutest boy in school," Molly explained.

"Yes, you've already said that, but is that it? Is there nothing else you can tell me about him?"

"He's the school quarterback," Donna answered. "And sooooo cute."

"But is he a nice boy?" Joan eyed the girls as she waited for an answer.

Donna wrinkled her brow. "How should I know? I've never talked to him before. But Annabel has."

Annabel blushed. "He asked me a question about an assignment. That's all."

"No, I think he likes her," Donna teased. "He thinks she's keen."

Annabel threw one of the stuffed bears sitting on her mantle at her friend. "Hush!" She glanced at her mother as her face burned bright red.

Donna caught the bear and cradled it in her arms, as she and Molly danced around the room belting out Elvis' song "Teddy Bear." Their skirts twirled loosely in the air and their ponytails bopped up and down as they spun around the room.

Molly and Donna sang out loud about tigers playing too rough and not loving lions enough. Then, while laughing hysterically, the girls collapsed onto Annabel's bed.

"Maybe Danny wants to be your teddy bear," Molly yelled, and the girls shrieked loudly in a way that only teenage girls can.

Annabel glared at her friends and tilted her head toward her mother to remind them that she was still in the room.

Molly quickly sat up. "I'm sorry Mrs. Turner, but you're just not like the rest of the mothers. My mother would *die* if she saw me acting so silly."

"But you're teenagers. You're supposed to act silly." Joan sat down at the edge of the bed.

"Tell that to my mom. It's as if I'm supposed to act like I'm in church every second of the day, and if I even mention a boy's name she'll accuse me of being boy crazy and tell me that it isn't lady-like."

Joan thought for a second. "Well, I do agree that a girl should present herself as a lady and not develop a reputation as being boy crazy, but that doesn't mean a girl shouldn't have fun with her friends."

Donna slid closer to Joan on the bed. "I wish my mom were more like you. We're always telling Annabel how lucky she is to have you for a mom."

Joan glanced at Annabel, but Annabel looked the other way, and Joan forced a smile. "Girls, I'm sorry, but you're going to have to excuse Annabel. It's time for supper. I'm sure your mothers are expecting you home soon, too."

"Yes, Mrs. Turner," Molly said. "Bye, Bel."

"Be sure to tell us if Danny talks to you again," Donna yelled on her way out.

JOAN LED THE girls out of Annabel's room, and Annabel closed the door behind them. She turned the radio back on and Fats Dominos' "Ain't that a Shame" played.

Annabel stood in front of the mirror above her small wooden dresser and stared at her reflection. Her thick brown hair was pulled back in a smooth ponytail. The light blue sweater didn't hug her tightly in the chest the way Donna's sweater did, but it also didn't hang off her body as loosely as Molly's. Annabel pulled her skirt over her knees, up to her thighs. Turning her head side to side, she critiqued her body while cursing its lack of shape. She couldn't compete with Marilyn's curves.

Annabel let her skirt fall back to its usual length just below her knees and continued to scrutinize herself. She knew she wasn't a skag or anything like that, but she never thought of herself as pretty. Though she wasn't as developed as Donna, she also wasn't as inept as Molly. She was somewhere in between, and she mostly felt insecure about her body.

With a heavy sigh, she lay across her bed. Even though she wasn't nearly as boy crazy as Molly and Donna were, Danny was always on her mind. She thought about their brief exchange in the school hall that day when Danny smiled that smile she loved so much. As if on cue, the radio DJ announced the next song and "A Teenager in Love" by Dion and the Belmonts played. Annabel didn't know if she was in love, having never been in love before, but she thought about Danny more than she thought about any other boy.

A knock at the door shook Annabel out of her reverie, and seconds later, Joan walked into the room. Annabel sat up just as the song about the heartaches of being a teenager in love was ending and was replaced with the smooth croon of Sam Cooke's elegant voice.

"I'm sorry I had to send your friends home. But you know . . ." Joan said.

Annabel nodded because of course she knew. She looked in the mirror at her and her mother's reflections, and couldn't ignore their similarities. She didn't doubt she'd end up looking just like her mother. Annabel was fine with that. She just didn't want to end up being like her, docile and conformed.

"We're going to have to tell your father about the dance," Joan said.

"What?" Annabel shot to her feet. "Why?"

Joan raised her eyebrows and looked intently at Annabel. "Because you'll need his permission, that's why."

"But he won't even notice I'm gone."

"Of course he will. How could you say that?"

Annabel turned away from her mother. She gazed out her bedroom window just as a man who lived across the street was coming home from work. She watched as he pulled a briefcase from the backseat of his car, and before he even made it to the front door, his toddler daughter rushed down the driveway to greet him. The man dropped to his knees and scooped up the little girl into a wide embrace as she wrapped her tiny arms around his neck.

Annabel would have given anything to be that little girl.

Joan smoothed her hands over her apron. "So we'll mention it to your father at dinner then."

Annabel held her breath, and with a slumped composure that screamed defeat, she nodded while still looking out the window. The loved father and cherished daughter were now tucked away inside their house.

Chapter Two

"I'M HOME!" GEORGE Turner roared as he entered the house to the aroma of a meal ready to be served and to the sound of utensils clinking against each other, as Annabel set the dining room table.

George was a stout man with a deep receding hairline. His face showed signs of aging usually seen in men ten years his senior, but years of hard drinking and living with a past he struggled to forget had taken its toll.

He was an old man before his time.

Joan hurried to the door to greet him. Her slender figure and perky composure in great contrast to George's stocky physique and somber mood. "How was your day?"

George took off his suit coat and hat, and hung them on a hook beside the door. "Busy. Everyone wants a damn loan. Houses. Cars. Everyone's buying something."

"Isn't that good for the bank?" Joan asked.

George was the manager of the local bank, a job he got through a well-connected friend he served with in the army, Bobby Hanley. George was admired and respected in town as a World War II hero, yet showed no sense of pride for his role. He disregarded the adulation altogether and was content to never speak of the war to anyone.

Because he managed a bank, George was seen as a man of power because he decided who received a piece of the American dream and who didn't. Old-time war buddies looked out for each other, and Bobby made sure George was well-taken care of.

"Of course it is, but we can't approve everybody," he blurted impatiently as he sat down in his favorite chair and wearily loosened his tie.

He brushed the back of his sleeve across his forehead and wiped away a blot of perspiration, staining his shirt with sweat marks. He ripped open the top buttons of his shirt. "I hate wearing this goddamn suit."

"George. The language. Annabel's right in the dining room," Joan warned.

"Please, Joan." George grimaced. "I hear how these kids today talk with their filthy mouths."

"Well, not our Annabel. Now go wash up. Supper's ready."

JOAN SLICED TWO thick pieces of roast beef and placed them onto George's plate. "Cooked just the way you like it, tender with a little pink inside." She smiled as brightly as the woman in the commercial holding the chocolate cake.

"Mashed potatoes," George snarled.

Annabel quickly handed him the bowl of potatoes, and he scooped two big helpings onto his plate. He leaned back and just before reaching for his fork, he slowly pulled each of his fingers back one at a time.

Crack. Crack. Crack.

The sound echoed in the quiet room. It was a nerve-wrecking sound that forced Annabel to close her eyes and hold her breath until it was over. It reminded her of when she was little, and how her father would slowly crack each knuckle right before he'd grab her and force her across his lap for a horrifying round of spankings.

Though she remembered her mother begging him not to punish her in this cruel way, Annabel had needed her mother to do more to make him stop because the spankings hurt. But all Joan did was clasp her hands over her face and close her eyes as Annabel cried hot tears. Annabel didn't remember the things she'd done to deserve such brutal discipline, but it never took much to set off her father's ire.

George's behavior at dinner was always unpredictable. Sometimes he was talkative, mostly berating his customers or the people who worked for him, and other times, like that night, he didn't want to talk at all. Work had been especially stressful that day, and he was already on his third glass of Scotch.

"More salad, George?" Joan held out a large bowl to him.

He shook his head and took a long, deep gulp of his drink.

In her peripheral vision, Annabel noticed her mother tapping the table and snapping her fingers in an attempt to get Annabel's attention, but Annabel kept her focus on her plate. She knew what her mother wanted, but there was no way she was going to bring up the dance at that moment. She avoided interacting with her father when he was drinking, which was most of the time, so their conversations were limited.

Being that George was mildly drunk and not blind, he also noticed Joan's strange behavior. "What the hell are you doing?" His wild eyes pored over Joan.

Joan sucked in a breath. "I . . . I . . . was just . . ."

"Well. What is it?" George barked.

Annabel snatched up the fork and knife and dug into her food, keeping her focus on cutting her meat.

"It's nothing, really, George," Joan answered in an extra cheerful tone. "Just a little dance at the school Annabel wants to attend. It sounds like it'll be a lot of fun. All of her friends will be there."

Annabel caught her breath. Being extra cheerful wasn't going to have any effect on her father's dour mood that night. She was sure of that.

George glared at Annabel for a few seconds. "And when were you going to tell me about this social event?"

Annabel dragged her fork across her plate. "After dinner I suppose."

"In the middle of the news?"

Annabel laid down her fork. "Maybe tomorrow I was gonna tell you."

"Gonna isn't a word."

"*Going* to tell you," Annabel quickly corrected.

George placed an elbow on the table and leaned his body forward. "I don't like these boys today with their long hair and all that grease. I see them walk past the bank. They strut around like they own the town. They got mouths on them, too."

"George, Annabel knows better than to go out with a boy like that. In fact, today the high school quarterback talked to Annabel. The *quarterback*, George. You played quarterback in high school, didn't you?"

George waved an impatient hand at Joan and concentrated his attention on Annabel. "This boy. What'd he want?"

"Just . . . just some help with school work," Annabel stammered.

George creased his forehead. "School work? Why would a boy ask a girl for help with school work?"

"Annabel gets good grades, George," Joan said.

"No boy, and I mean *no* boy, wants a girl who's smarter than him." George pointed a thick finger at Annabel and without taking his eyes off her, added, "You best remember that."

Annabel wanted to yell back to her father that Danny didn't mind a smart girl because he wasn't like the other boys, and he was certainly nothing like him, but she wouldn't say that to her father. She wouldn't dare say that to her father. As with everything he had ever said to berate her, Annabel kept her mouth shut and absorbed his harsh words.

Joan placed a hand on Annabel's arm. "We can't ignore the fact that Annabel does really well in school, George. She'll get a good job someday. Many women work."

George dropped his fork and it crashed on the plate. "The war is over. The boys are back. A woman's place is in the home."

Annabel was so disgusted with her mother, she didn't have the stomach to even look at her. The only thing Joan was supposed to bring up was the dance, one silly dance—not Danny and certainly not Annabel's grades.

George finished off his scotch. "She'll get married and have children and it won't matter what grades she got in school." He shot up from the table. "Her job, like yours, is right here." He glared at Joan, his eyes madder than before.

"Okay, George. Okay. I'm sorry. Now sit back down and let's finish this nice dinner." Joan reached out to calm him, but he shoved her hand away.

"You don't appreciate a thing I do for you. Neither of you do. You want a job? Go then. Get the hell out of here. See how easy it is out there."

Peering down at the floor, Annabel pushed herself away from the table. She sat frozen in her seat even though she wanted to run far away. She stole a glance at Joan, who, under any circumstances acted like everything was okay. No matter how many drunken outbursts George had, Joan always found a way to excuse them.

George reloaded his glass with ice from a small ice-bucket on the table and filled his drink with more Scotch. He took his plate into the living room and slumped into his favorite chair in front of the television.

Once he was out of the room, Annabel let out a breath she felt like she had been holding for a week.

Joan began clearing the table. "Your father had a hard day at work. He's under a lot of stress."

"Why do you always do that?"

"Do what?"

"Make excuses for him?"

"I don't always make . . ."

"And why did you have to tell him about Danny and my grades? What made you think he'd have any interest in my grades?"

"Because he's your father."

"So?"

"Fathers care about those things."

"Not mine," Annabel stated flatly.

"Deep down he does. He can be a good father."

"I know you think so."

"Come with me." Joan took Annabel by the arm and dragged her to the kitchen. She went to the refrigerator and pulled out a big chocolate cake, just like the one from the commercial. "Here." She held out the cake. "I made chocolate cake. Sit down. We can eat it together."

Joan set the cake on the table and took two small plates from the cupboards. She cut two pieces and slid them onto the plates.

Annabel stared dumbfoundedly at the dessert. "Cake? You're offering me cake?"

"Please have some cake with me. Let's have one good thing about tonight."

Annabel ignored the desperation in her mother's eyes and the pleading tone in her voice. It was the most pathetic thing she'd seen and heard. She pushed away the dish meant for her. "Tonight wasn't good, and chocolate cake can't make it better."

Chapter Three

THE MOONLIGHT BREAKING through the white curtains was the only light in the otherwise dark room, as a cool breeze blew through the open window. Annabel switched on the radio and lay across her bed. She closed her eyes and let the music take her away from her life and to a place where everything was different from what it really was.

Annabel drifted to sleep and was awakened hours later by a dog barking loudly outside her window. She propped herself onto a pillow and checked the clock beside her bed.

It was just past eight o'clock.

Still in the clothes she wore to school that day, a blue skirt and a white sweater, she went to the open window and pushed aside the curtain. The streets outside her house were usually quiet this time of night, especially on a weeknight, and that Tuesday night was no different.

Annabel sat on the windowsill, pulled her skirt over her knees, and watched the glare of the headlights of passing cars. She wondered about the life of the people inside those cars. Were they happy with their lives? Did they feel trapped and scared like she did?

As she always did when she gazed out her bedroom window and into the streets of the only town she ever knew, Annabel considered life and brooded over what else was out there in the world she desperately longed to see. She imagined the lives of people living in places she'd never been, what they were doing at that exact moment, and wondered how the sky, the moon, and the stars looked hanging over another street, in another town, from a different window.

Annabel opened the window as high as it would go and grabbed hold of a sturdy branch hanging just outside. With the ease of someone who had done something many times before, she pushed herself out the window and climbed down the tree, knowing exactly which branches were strong enough to clamp onto and which ones would crack under her weight.

Nearing the bottom of the tree, Annabel held down her skirt and jumped to the ground. She landed firmly on her feet and pulled the sleeves of her sweater to her wrists and started off on her walk.

The first time Annabel had snuck out her window at night, she'd only made it a couple blocks. Jumping at every sound—a cricket, a car door, a cat's meow—she was certain someone was creeping up behind her and looked back every couple paces.

She'd let her imagination get the best of her, but eventually she realized her bravery by reminding herself why she was sneaking out of the house in the first place. She convinced herself that anything the night offered couldn't be any more dangerous than living under the same roof as her father. That simple thought gave her enough reason to end any fear she harbored about walking alone after dark.

Annabel walked with no destination, only to get away. It was an attempt to escape things she could no longer live with, even if the getaway was a short stroll in her cookie-cutter neighborhood.

Walking at night made her feel safe, and she was well aware of the irony in a young girl feeling more protected outside alone at night than she did living in her own home. She had heard different versions of a story about a girl who had disappeared one night after walking home from a friend's house. Some kids at school claimed the girl was kidnapped, while others gossiped that she'd gotten caught "in the family way" and was sent to live with an aunt in another state.

Either way, the story didn't change the fact that Annabel loved to walk at night. There was freedom in it. She could see the world yet still hide from it. Though she knew the little suburban town she lived in was far from being the world, the place was all she had. Some nights she would find a spot on a stranger's lawn, tucked close to a tree where she couldn't be seen, and sit and gaze at the stars.

She wondered what Earth looked like from a place so far away. Maybe up there, in space, her problems would seem small and insignificant, but down here, they were vast and consumed every inch of her.

Most boys at school obsessed about going to space and fantasized about carrying out their dreams of becoming astronauts and walking on the moon. Though Annabel had no aspiration to fly to the moon, she did dream of leaving the suffocating town she lived in. To do what exactly, she didn't yet know, but she did know girls weren't supposed to dream that high.

By the time they graduated from high school, getting married was the main ambition for most girls, followed by having children. Annabel wasn't even certain she wanted to be a mother, while Molly and Donna already knew the names of their first-born children.

What Annabel really wanted was to go to college and experience the world, but for now, her worldly experiences were limited to her little town, and her curiosity was satisfied by looking through people's windows and imagining the life being lived behind those four walls.

From the outside, those walls looked the same—typical suburban ranch or two-story houses with white picket fences. The homogeneity of it all bored Annabel, but she knew despite the similarities on the outside, what happened inside each home was different.

Evenings were the perfect time for Annabel to walk the streets and observe how other people lived because families were together, home from work or school, and real life was beginning.

At school and work, people changed their personalities in order to fit the role expected of them. But only in the privacy of their homes were people truly themselves, and Annabel wanted to see the lives people lived after work, curious if she'd see any resemblance to her own life.

She never did.

Annabel had visited her father's workplace only once, when he had forgotten paperwork he needed, and the bank was close enough for Annabel to walk. In the short time she was there, it was obvious her father was the boss.

When George walked out from his office, tucked away in the back, all employees' eyes followed him. In the distance George had taken to walk from his office to meet Annabel near the front doors, multiple people had hurried to him and asked if he needed anything—coffee, tea—*anything*. Annabel didn't know if the urgency to meet her father's needs was done out of genuine respect for him and who he was as a person, or simply because he was the boss. She assumed it was the latter because she couldn't imagine anyone respecting her father based solely on his character.

Annabel didn't confide to Molly and Donna about her situation at home. It was a secret she shared with no one. Sometimes kids at school would shout at her in the halls about the cool new car their family bought thanks to her dad. Annabel would smile and let herself believe just for a moment that her father was a great man, but she knew better.

Annabel couldn't pretend things were different, but the respite she felt in escaping from her room and walking the streets of her quiet town, away from it all for just a little while, helped her manage the reality she struggled to accept was her own.

The silence of the streets relaxed her to the point where she felt like the night belonged only to her. It was the only time she ever felt powerful.

Annabel watched through windows as families gathered around dinner tables and engaged in sweet, calm conversation that invoked laughter. She'd once seen a young girl talking to her father, and as the girl spoke the father laid down his fork and listened intently to what she had to say.

It was nothing like the dinners she knew. Fathers weren't devouring drink after drink while tending only to their plates and ignoring those around them. Nor had Annabel ever seen a father stand in the midst of a drunken rage and scream at anyone who dared to talk back to him. Maybe it happened somewhere, but she had never seen it happen at anyone's dinner table but her own.

She envied the moments lived by other people she desperately wished were her own. Like the time two young boys were engaged in a game of tug of war over a small fire truck and burst into tears when their mother snapped the toy away and left the room, holding tightly to the coveted truck, or when two little girls pouted to their mother because they didn't want to clear the dinner table and were sent to their room for throwing food in protest.

All of those moments Annabel had witnessed were special and beautiful. They were special because they were spent with family, and they were beautiful because they were innocent.

Annabel's favorite time to watch families was after dinner when they huddled together on sofas and ate snacks while watching their favorite TV shows—something she'd never done with her own family. Her walks showed her what she was missing by not having the normal life most people in her neighborhood seemed to be living. She was the only person walking at night, hiding from her own life.

It was an isolating feeling.

Annabel felt so alone, but that loneliness eased a bit the first night she'd stood outside Danny Winfield's house and watched him through his front window. He was sitting on the couch, having a conversation with his mother. He'd just told her something that made the woman excitedly throw her arms around his neck and hug him tightly. She stood up, motioned that she'd be right back, and hurried out of the room.

Danny waited patiently with a gentle smile on his face and reached beside him, picked up a book, and started reading. Annabel had never seen someone so content and satisfied with their life. The image was comforting to her.

Though Annabel had already been familiar with Danny from school, she'd never spoken to him. He was two years older than her, and they were part of different social circles. Danny was a popular athlete and was someone Annabel could admire only from afar, and she did, every night she went on one of her walks and watched him through his window.

He'd captivated her with his dark brown hair, brown eyes, and his dimple that appeared on the right side of his cheek every time he smiled—and he smiled a lot. His features were pleasant, and his mannerisms were calm and relaxing. Annabel imagined she'd feel safe lying curled up in his arms, with her head resting against his strong chest.

The first night she saw Danny through his window, Annabel had stood alone in the night, mesmerized by a boy she barely knew. Even though she felt foolish, from that night on she never went on one of her walks again without stopping at the house with the boy in the window.

For all the nights she'd spent watching him, Annabel never thought she'd speak face to face with him. Though their exchange at school was only about schoolwork, their brief dialogue was more than she ever expected and made it harder for her to get Danny out of her mind.

Annabel was anxious to get to Danny's house that night because seeing him gave her hope that life didn't have to be the only way she knew it, but when she got there, the house was dark with no sign that anyone was home.

Although it was the last place she wanted to be, Annabel headed back home. On her way, she passed a house where an elderly couple lived. It was a house she had watched for so long that the old man and old woman hardly seemed strangers to her anymore. At this time of night, the old man was always reading the paper in his rocking chair, while his wife sat crocheting on the sofa beside him. The old woman always looked happy and content.

Annabel wondered if the elderly woman, like most of the girls in her school, had accepted her preordained station in life to be a wife, a mother, a homemaker. Was this the life she chose or did it choose her? Despite the fact that she looked happy, Annabel was curious if the woman had ever wanted more. Had the aged woman ever been curious about the universe, the stars, or walking on the moon?

Annabel went home that night worried her life would leave her wanting more.

JOAN CALLED FOR Annabel to come to breakfast. "Annabel? What are you doing? Your breakfast is getting cold."

Annabel jumped out of bed. She'd forgotten to set her alarm and had to be at school in half an hour.

"I'm coming!" Annabel scampered around her room and dressed quickly.

She hurried across the hall to the bathroom, and in record time she brushed her teeth, combed her hair, and quickly smeared gloss over her lips—the only makeup she was allowed to wear. Back in her room, she snatched her books off her dresser and ran down the stairs.

"You'll have to eat your breakfast quickly." Joan set a plate of scrambled eggs, toast, and bacon on the table.

"No time." Annabel blazed past her mother and ran out the door.

"Wait! We still need to talk about last night," Joan yelled after her.

Annabel pretended not to hear her mother as she ran all the way to school and made it before the first bell rang. She rushed through the corridor and found Molly and Donna standing at her locker, waiting for her.

"Hurry, Bel, we're gonna miss first period." Donna held her books against her chest.

Molly leaned against the lockers and casually examined a strand of her hair. "So what? Maybe we should ditch for once."

While Annabel gathered the books she needed for first period, Donna tapped her on her shoulder. "Bel. Hey, Bel."

"I'm moving as fast as I can." Annabel spun around, and Danny was standing in front of her in his Varsity letterman jacket. The beautiful smile that brought out the adorable dimple on his right cheek that Annabel loved so much, adorned his face.

Annabel's face burned.

Donna leaned into her. "I tried to tell you."

Annabel looked away from Danny and tried to regain her breath, but it was hard with Danny standing so close.

Danny shoved his hands into his jacket pockets and shifted nervously. His lack of composure was completely opposite from the confident competitor he was on the football field.

"Hi, Annabel. How are you?" he asked.

"I'm . . . I'm okay. How . . . how are you?" Annabel lowered her head and gave her friends a side-eye glance. They were as captivated by Danny's sudden presence at Annabel's locker as she was.

"I'm good. There's . . . there's something I need to ask you." He dipped his head in the direction of the other side of the hall. "Do you have a second to talk?"

"Sure," Annabel responded as casually as she could, even though there was nothing casual about talking to Danny.

The first bell rang, and the hall became crowded with students rushing to their classes, but Molly and Donna egged her on.

"Ignore the bell and go with him," Molly whispered to her.

"Yeah, Annabel. Go with him," Donna urged.

Annabel followed Danny to a vacant spot across the hall. He turned to her with a sweet, but nervous smile, and just as he opened his mouth to say something, a group of raucous greasers showed up.

Their hair was long and slicked back at the sides. They wore tight jeans and leather jackets, and swaggered around school like they were the coolest cats in town. One of the greasers, Brett Dante, snuck up behind Molly and yanked on her skirt.

"Hey!" Molly spun around. "Stop that."

"Yeah. Stop that." Donna stepped between Molly and the rough greaser.

He gave Donna a nasty smirk. "Well, looky here. The sweat hog has something to say." He slowly gazed up and down Donna's plump body, and his eyes lingered at her chest. "You're stacked higher than any girl in this rotten school, too bad it's wasted on such a skag."

His buddies standing around him laughed wildly.

Donna's face turned red, and she backed away from the insolent greaser with her head down.

Annabel took a step to help Donna, but Danny held her back and put himself between Brett and the girls.

"What's your problem?" Danny asked.

Brett stepped back to get a better look at Danny in his letterman jacket. "Who rattled your cage, pantywaist?" He turned to his chuckling buddies. "Have you ever seen anything so cherry and pristine? It's as if I'm standing in front of Ricky Nelson himself." He grabbed the sleeve of Danny's jacket. "Gee, what do I have to do to get me a pretty jacket like this, golden boy?"

"You have to be good at something," Annabel yelled. "And you're not good at anything."

"How would you know what I'm good at?" Brett arched an eyebrow. "You haven't had the pleasure of being in my backseat yet, but you're welcome anytime." He aimed his crooked smile at her.

Brett stepped closer to Annabel, but Danny grabbed his leather jacket and yanked him back. "Leave her alone."

"Get off me." Brett pushed Danny, but Danny pushed him harder, and Brett stumbled back.

Brett's face filled with rage, but he didn't make a move.

Danny stood as firm as a statue between the greasers and the girls.

"Come on." Brett's best pal, Ricky Slate, slung an arm around his shoulders. "The chick isn't worth it. She's probably all show and no go anyway."

Brett shrugged his buddy's arm off his shoulder, walked toward Annabel, and slowly gazed up and down her body as his lips curled into a devilish grin. "Maybe I should take you to the passion pit and find out how far you'll go. I ain't had a chick say no yet." He winked at her.

Danny clenched his fists.

Annabel dropped her books and grabbed hold of Danny's arm. "Stop! Danny, please."

She hated violence, and by now the boys had created a spectacle. Heads popped out of classrooms to catch a glimpse of the drama unfolding in the corridors. Students lingered around, watching in anticipation of a fight breaking out.

The first bell had already rung and soon the second bell would ring, too.

Danny didn't resist as Annabel pulled him away from the greasers.

The greasers taunted Danny with dog barks. "Good boy! Good boy!" one yelled. "Wanna treat?" another asked.

Annabel held tightly onto Danny, expecting him to react to their teasing, but instead, he lowered his arms to his sides.

"Come on," Ricky said. "Let's flee the scene. They're a bunch of wet rags."

While being pulled away by one of his gang friends, Brett pointed a finger at Danny. "Stay outta my way."

Danny watched the unruly group leave, and the crowd quickly dispersed while muttering their disappointment that there wasn't a show.

Danny turned to Annabel, Molly, and Donna. "Are you girls okay?"

Molly stared at Danny in a dream-like trance. "Yyyes. We're fine."

"I'm not fine. Did you hear what they called me? The whole school heard." Donna hung her head while her cheeks flared red.

"Hey." Danny lightly nudged her shoulder. "Don't let those rats get you down. They're scum and not half as cool as they think they are. They won't bother you again. I'll make sure of it."

"Thanks." Donna's sad expression lifted into a subtle smile.

Annabel realized she was still holding Danny's arm and let go. He picked her books off the floor and handed them to her. The second bell rang, but neither Danny nor Annabel took their eyes off each other.

"We have to go," Molly said. "We're gonna be in so much trouble."

"Weren't you the one who wanted to ditch?" Donna pointed out, and Molly made a face at her.

"I better get going," Annabel said. "Thanks for sticking up for us. That was
. . ."

"Come to the dance with me," Danny blurted.

Annabel's eyes widened. "What?"

"He said go to the dance with him," Donna said loudly.

Annabel let out a nervous laugh and looked away from the boy who was making her heart beat so hard that she was sure it would pop right out of her chest.

"Well?" Danny asked, sounding a bit anxious. "Will you go with me?"

"She'll go!" Molly shouted.

Annabel laughed again and with a shy smile, said, "Yes, Danny. I'll go to the dance with you."

Molly and Donna swooned in unison, and Annabel playfully hit them with her books. "Come on. We need to get to class."

Chapter Four

"SHAKE, RATTLE AND Roll" played on the radio, and Annabel swayed to the music as she searched her closet for the perfect outfit for the dance.

She pulled her favorite pink poodle skirt off its hanger and held it against herself in front of the mirror. She traced her finger along the small red rose patched near the hem of the skirt. She only wore the skirt on special occasions and she couldn't think of a more special occasion than going to a dance with Danny Winfield.

From downstairs, Joan called for Annabel to set the table.

"I'm coming!" Annabel hung up the skirt and turned off the radio. She hurried down the stairs, and with an extra bounce in her step, walked into the kitchen.

Joan was standing over the oven, stirring a large pot.

"Something smells really good. What is it?" Annabel swiped a piece of cucumber from the salad in a large wooden bowl on the counter and popped it into her mouth.

"Stew," Joan replied.

"Hmmm, smells good." Annabel placed the utensils on top of the stacked plates and carried them through the swinging door, into the dining room.

Annabel couldn't help smiling as she set the table.

"What's going on with you?"

Annebel looked up at Joan in the doorway. Joan narrowed her eyes.

Annabel stopped setting the table. "What do you mean?"

"I . . . I haven't seen you like this in a while."

"Like what?"

Joan hesitated. "Happy."

Annabel composed herself and went back to setting the table. "Am I? I mean . . . I don't know."

Joan kept her eyes on Annabel. "Yes, you are. It's . . . it's nice to see." She paused. "Listen, I'm sorry about mentioning your grades to your father. I just wanted your father to know."

"That's right. *You* wanted him to know about my grades, but *he* didn't want to know, and I don't know why that's so hard for you to understand."

"When you become a mother you'll understand why." Joan drew in a breath and smiled. "Things will get better. I promise. It won't be like this forever."

Annabel wanted to scream at her mother's hopeless need to make their family normal. She'd been making that promise for a long time.

"Will you at least tell me what's making you so happy?" Joan asked.

Annabel stopped smiling. "Do I still look happy?" She wanted to run to her room, turn on her music, and hide in the dream world she created for herself.

It was a place she could pretend her life wasn't what it really was. Her fantasy was a world filled with the affectionate moments she knew from watching people through their windows. The images she stole on her walks she imagined to be her own made her feel safe.

"You did look happy," Joan answered.

"Not anymore."

Joan pulled a chair out from under the table and scooted closer to where Annabel stood. She dropped her hands into her lap. "I want to see that smile more often. I wish you'd talk with me like you do your friends . . . and . . . and dance and act silly with me."

"Nobody does that with their mothers."

Joan smiled. "Okay, maybe the dancing was too much, but is it too much to want to know what or *who* is making my daughter so happy?"

Annabel gave a slight shrug.

"Is this about last night? Annabel, I don't know what you want me to do when he's like that."

"Just make chocolate cake," Annabel said in a harsh and unforgiving tone. She knew her words hurt her mother.

In a stiff and controlled manner, a grim-faced Joan stood up and returned to the kitchen. The swinging door swayed to a close. Annabel stood alone in the dining room and dropped down onto the seat her mother had sat only seconds ago. She closed her eyes, and when she opened them, she was looking at a large-framed family portrait hanging on the wall. She was three years old in the picture. George and Joan were sitting beside each other, their shoulders touching, with Annabel sitting between them on their laps.

George was wearing his army uniform. Since he didn't talk much about the war or what he did over there, what Annabel knew about the Second World War was only what she learned in school. A teacher had asked Annabel about inviting her father to class to talk about his experience in the war. She knew her father would never do that so she never asked.

Annabel hadn't noticed before how happy she looked in that portrait. Her eyes were big and wide, and she smiled with the excitement of a child who was just about to open the biggest present under the Christmas tree.

George wore the appearance of a protective father, with his arm hugged around Annabel's shoulder and his hand splayed across her lap, but Annabel knew better. His smile was small and his lips clamped tightly. It was a pathetic expression of warmth in a family portrait.

GEORGE TURNER PULLED into the driveway, got out of the car, and meticulously wiped a smear mark off the hood of his black Cadillac Coup De Ville with his coat sleeve. The spot had been bothering him since he noticed it at the stoplight on Sixth Avenue. The highly polished, chrome-plated vehicle glistened under the streetlights as George worked to clear the smudge. The car, with its large tailfins, resembled a wartime aircraft.

After he finished, he did a quick inspection of the rest of the car for any other imperfections, but didn't find any. With the briefcase he retrieved from the passenger seat, he walked the front path up to his house, the stress of the day weighing on his mind.

"Mr. Turner! Mr. Turner!" a voice behind him yelled out.

George turned stiffly around to see Henry following him eagerly up the front walk. Despite the fact that Henry and George were the same age, Henry never addressed George by his first name. Not many people referred to George Turner by his first name only. George was a respected man in town for being a war hero, as well as for the position of power he held at the bank.

Henry was tall and lean, wore round wire-rimmed glasses, and sported a full head of blond hair.

"How are you doing, Mr. Turner?" Henry asked.

"Fine, just fine." George held his suitcase in front of him and waited impatiently for Henry to get on with his business.

"I know you're a very busy man, Mr. Turner, but I just wanted to thank you again for approving the loan for my car. Look at her. Isn't she a beauty?"

George followed Henry's gaze to a shiny red Chevy convertible sitting in Henry's driveway. He gave the car a quick look. "It's very nice."

Henry continued to admire his prized possession, oblivious to George's disinterest. "She's not as pretty as yours, of course," Henry declared. "But I sure do love her, and I have you to thank for that, Mr. Turner. I can't remember the last time my wife's eyes lit up as much as they did when she first saw this car." He chuckled and leaned into George. "And you know how important it is to keep the little lady happy."

"Yes, yes. Very important," George mumbled and turned away from his chatty neighbor, but Henry stepped in front of him with a concerned expression on his face.

"Hey there, Mr. Turner. Are you okay?" He peered closely into George's face. "You don't look so good."

George frowned, and deep lines creased across his forehead. "What? What's that you say, Henry?"

Henry backed away. "Nothing . . . I . . . I said nothing."

"Henry! Henry!" Sylvia yelled from her front porch while holding a freshly baked apple pie. "Hello, Mr. Turner." She smiled brightly and held out the pie in one hand as she walked over to Henry and George. "This is for you and your family. We love the new car." She pressed a hand against her chest. "*I* love the new car.

"And I'm not the only one. Doris from down the block took one look at the car and decided she just had to have one, too. Her husband will be in to see you next week." Sylvia stared at George, waiting for a response, and her enthusiastic smile faded. "You don't look so good," she said with concern. "Are you feeling all right?"

George scowled at her, and Henry quickly pulled his wife away. "Come on, honey. Mr. Turner's just getting home from work. Let's let him be."

"Yes, of course. Here you go." She shoved the apple pie into George's hands. "Enjoy."

George took the pie in one hand while holding his briefcase in the other and quickly turned away from his pesky neighbors. He barreled up the front porch steps and burst into the house.

"I'm home!"

THE TURNER FAMILY ate dinner in silence, but Annabel was unfazed by the usual tension in the room as George guzzled down glass after glass of his favorite liquor. She was going to a dance with Danny. Not even her father could ruin the perfect mood that put her in.

Annabel stared at her plate, and while she dragged her fork over her food, she remembered how bravely Danny had stood up to those rotten greasers. He made her feel safe, the way she'd always fantasized that he would.

She didn't realize she was smiling until her father barked, "What's so funny?"

Annabel stopped smiling.

George, towering over his plate, lowered his fork that was filled with food. "What . . . is . . . so . . . funny?"

Annabel looked down at her plate, wanting to get through one dinner without an incident.

"George, it's nothing," Joan interjected. "She's probably just remembering a joke someone told at school."

"Oh really?" George raised his eyebrows and shoved the forkful of food into his mouth. He nodded slowly as he chewed with his mouth open. "Tell me the joke." He swallowed the food and then drained what was left of his drink in one gulp.

"What?" Joan laid her fork down and tapped her fingers nervously against the table. "George, I don't really know what she was smi . . ."

George slammed the empty glass on the table. "I want to hear the damn joke."

Annabel felt her father's gaze burn through her, but she kept her focus on her plate, and her mind scrambled to remember any jokes she knew, but she was too nervous to think clearly. Then the sounds that reminded her of her childhood punishments echoed throughout the room—crack, crack, crack of her father's knuckles. She dropped her fork, and food splattered across her plate, onto the table, and into her lap.

George stopped popping his knuckles and glared at her. "What the hell are you doing? You're making a mess."

Joan jumped up, grabbed a towel, and started cleaning up the spill. "Are you okay, Annabel?"

"She's fine!" George yelled impatiently. "She's just clumsy. Always was."

Joan finished wiping up the spilled food. "No, she's not, George. Why would you say something like that?"

"Shut up!" he screamed and bits of chewed food flew from his mouth. He grabbed the near-empty bottle of Scotch. "Get me another bottle!"

Joan hurried out of the room leaving Annabel alone with her father. She avoided looking at his face and instead concentrated on his hands. George's fingers were thick with big knuckles. His fork practically disappeared in the palm of his chunky hand. She noticed a mark on his hand, between his thumb and index finger. It was an ugly, but familiar scar.

When Annabel was tossed over her father's knee for a round of spankings, she had noticed the scar while he'd held her down. Sometimes the scar was all she'd look at as she endured the pain he whipped upon her.

"What are you starin' at!" he roared.

"Nothing." Annabel swallowed. "I was just . . ."

He tossed his napkin onto the table and with a deep grunt, picked up his plate and carried it to his chair in the next room.

Annabel let out a slow sigh of relief as she pushed herself away from the table. She glanced at the family portrait hanging on the wall, the one where she sat comfortably on her father's lap, and couldn't imagine sitting that comfortably close to him again.

She left the room before Joan came back.

ANNABEL WAS ABOUT to sneak out her bedroom window when a knock at the door pulled her back into the room.

"Annabel," Joan's voice called out. "May I come in?"

With a deep sigh, Annabel closed the window. "Come in."

Joan stepped into the room. "I'm sorry about what happened, but you have to try to understand."

"Understand? Understand what? Understand that I hate him, because I do. I *hate* him!"

"You don't mean that." Joan's tone was more hopeful than confident.

"Yes I do." Annabel's tone was crystal-clear.

Joan briefly closed her tired eyes. "I'm trying to make this house as normal for you as I can. I don't know what else to do. He's not perfect, but he works hard every day."

Annabel raised her arms at her side. "Why do you keep making excuses for him? I don't care how hard he works. Look at how we have to live. We can't eat dinner together like a normal family. I can't talk to him. I can barely look at him. And I can't even have my friends over."

"Your friends come over all the time."

"Not when he's here. They have to be rushed out no matter how much fun we're having because you're so scared he might come home early and God help us if he's in a sour mood, which is always. I'm so sick of making excuses about why they have to leave early or why they can never spend the night."

"What do you want me to do?"

"I want you to stand up to him. I want to be a normal teenage girl. I want to have friends over whenever I want. I want to have sleepovers. And I *want* to go to that dance." Annabel raised her voice.

"I can't tell him what to do." Joan raised her voice back. "He won't listen. All he'll do is lose his temper and scream."

"Then you've got to stop telling him stuff. Especially stuff about dances and boys and what grades I get in school. He doesn't need to know anything. Let him come home and drink till he passes out. I don't care anymore. But I'm going to that dance with Danny and I don't care what he says."

Joan's eyes widened. "You're going with Danny?"

Annabel gazed at the floor, and she stepped back, suddenly embarrassed. Her mother now knew that a boy liked her and that she liked him.

When Annabel had accepted Danny's invitation, she hadn't considered her father hadn't even given her permission to go to the dance, let alone to go with a boy.

"That's why you were so happy earlier," Joan stated.

Annabel nodded.

"How'd he ask you?"

Annabel glanced anxiously toward the door, wishing her mother would leave. "I don't feel like talking anymore."

"Don't worry. He's passed out," Joan said.

"I don't care. I just don't wanna talk about it."

Joan held onto Annabel's arm. "Please. I've seen all the bad parts of your life. Let me see the good. Let me see the ones that make you smile."

Annabel couldn't ignore the need in her mother's voice to know all about that special moment. She was hesitant to share it with her, but then relented, partly to make her mother happy, but mostly because it was a great story.

They sat on Annabel's bed, and Joan listened intently as Annabel told her story, looking horrified when she got to the part about the greasers.

"It is terrible the way boys act," Joan said.

"Not all boys," Annabel corrected. "Not Danny. I asked him not to fight and he didn't. He took their taunts without retaliating because I asked him to. He could have beaten them all up, and believe me, they had it coming. But he didn't fight because of me. Me! He actually listened to *me*. Has a boy ever listened to a girl and turned down a fight?"

"None that I ever knew," Joan said.

"Kids laughed and called him chicken. Mom, they called the high school quarterback a chicken. But he didn't care. He only cared about me and how *I* felt. He's nothing like . . ." Annabel stared at the floor.

"Your father," Joan finished, and Annabel nodded.

"Good," Joan whispered and kissed Annabel's forehead. "Thank you for sharing this with me."

"You're welcome," Annabel replied softly.

"Well." Joan stood up. "I'll let you get back to what you were doing. Studying, I imagine?"

"Yes," Annabel lied.

Joan walked to the door and looked back at her. "Some day, you'll have everything you want. Your life won't be like this forever."

Annabel wanted her mother to promise her that, but knew it wasn't a promise she could make. She went back to the window after Joan left the room, but she no longer felt like walking. She sat on the windowsill instead and gazed into the nearly starless sky and wondered what Danny was doing at that moment.

Muffled voices broke Annabel's attention. She looked down and saw Henry and Sylvia Chapman sitting together on their porch swing, uttering words to each other only they could hear. They cuddled affectionately close to each other while giggling like teenagers. Henry slung his arm around Sylvia's neck and squeezed her tightly against him and kissed the top of her head.

Annabel watched her neighbors a short while longer before deciding to give them the privacy she and her friends didn't give them over the summer. She slid off the sill and shut the window.

ANNABEL ATE BREAKFAST alone at the kitchen table. George almost always left for work before she was even out of bed, so at the very least she was assured one meal at home could be eaten in peace.

Joan washed the dishes as Annabel ate her oatmeal. When she finished, Joan snatched a hand towel hanging from a hook next to the sink and sat beside Annabel. She wiped her hands until they were dry. "Your father informed me he's going hunting this weekend with his buddies from the war."

Annabel looked up from her bowl of oatmeal. "Really?"

"So . . ." Joan continued. "I've decided there'd be no use in telling your father about you going to the dance since he won't—"

Annabel jumped out of her seat and threw her arms around her neck. "Thank you. Thank you. Thank you. This is the best news ever," Annabel yelled, and seconds later she pulled back and blurted, "But I would've climbed out my window if you didn't let me go."

"You would have what?"

"Nothing." Annabel swiped her books off the counter. "I gotta tell Molly and Donna." She hurried to the door.

"Hold it," Joan yelled.

Annabel halted and turned around.

Joan went to her, a stern expression on her face. "Listen to me. Your father can never know about this dance. I don't even want to begin to imagine what he would do if he found out you went to a dance without his permission. The only reason I'm letting you go is because he won't be here and I don't see how he'll find out as long as we never slip. You can't ever talk about this in the house. Even when you think he isn't here. Understand?"

Annabel understood very well.

"I want you to have some semblance of a normal childhood," Joan said. "And I see how important going to this dance is to you. It's worth letting you go even without your father's permission."

"But I have your permission. Shouldn't that count for something?"

Joan's thin lips pressed into a straight line. "It should, but it doesn't . . . at least not in this house. Go on now. Don't be late for school."

Chapter Five

THERE WAS A knock at Annabel's bedroom door late Saturday morning. She hurried across her room and flung the door open. "Is he gone? Did he leave?"

"He's gone," Joan replied.

Annabel's anxiety subsided. She had been waiting all morning for news of her father's departure.

"He's gone for good? Are you sure?"

"I watched him get into his car and drive away with my own two eyes."

"Did he forget anything?"

"I don't think so."

"Remember that one time he went hunting and he had to come back for his fishing poles because he forgot they were fishing, too?"

"Yes, I remember. But they're only hunting this time."

"How can you be so sure?"

"Because I asked him." Joan grasped Annabel's hands. "Relax."

"But what if . . ."

Joan pulled Annabel onto the bed. "Take a breath. Your father's not coming back until late tomorrow. Okay?"

Annabel did as Joan instructed and breathed slow, deep breaths. She understood the risk her mother was taking by allowing her to go to the dance without her father's permission, and she couldn't remember the last time she felt grateful to her mother for anything.

"Thanks for letting me go tonight," Annabel said softly.

"You're welcome." Joan smiled. "What time is this boy picking you up?"

"Six o'clock."

"I won't make you do all your normal Saturday chores this afternoon, but you be sure to have them finished before your father gets home tomorrow."

"I'll be sure," Annabel said.

"I'm heading to the grocery store. Is there anything special you'd like for dinner?"

"I'm too nervous to eat."

"You need to eat something. I know what. I'll buy a couple of those TV dinners they advertise on the television that your father won't let me buy. Says they remind him of the meals they served in the military. It must have been really bad over there to not want any memory of it."

Annabel wondered what part of her childhood her future self will reject because she doesn't want any memory of it. Joan left the room, and Annabel switched on the radio. "Runaround Sue" played as she twirled around her room before dropping onto her bed. She lay her head on the pillow, closed her eyes, and fantasized what it would feel like to dance with Danny.

She fell asleep without meaning to and woke up frantic she'd slept through the dance. She relaxed once she saw that only two hours had passed. She didn't usually fall asleep in the middle of the day, but the excitement of the dance had made it difficult for her to get much sleep the night before.

"Annabel!" Joan called from downstairs. "Come down and eat."

Annabel still wasn't hungry, but knew her mother wouldn't leave her alone until she ate something. She went downstairs, poured herself a glass of milk, and sat down at the table.

Joan set a TV dinner of fried chicken, mashed potatoes, and corn sectioned off in an aluminum tray in front of Annabel. "Be careful. It just came out of the oven and it's very hot."

Annabel stared at her plate of hefty proportions. "I can't eat all of this."

"You don't have to eat all of it, just some." Joan settled into her own aluminum tray of food and dug her fork into the potatoes.

Since it was just the two of them, they ate in the kitchen instead of the dining room. Supper was a lot less tense without George there.

Annabel picked at her food while taking small bites.

"Do I know this boy's parents?" Joan asked.

"I don't think so."

"They must not go to our church then."

Annabel shoved a piece of chicken into her mouth and shook her head. "They're Methodist. His parents are very involved with their church."

Joan chewed a bite of her food. "That's nice to hear."

Annabel glanced at the clock. Danny would be at her house in two hours. "I gotta get ready." She pushed herself away from the table so fast the chair squeaked loudly against the floor.

"You've got time. You barely touched your food."

"Not hungry." Annabel swiped the napkin over her mouth and tossed it onto the table. She had no idea how long it would take to get ready for her first date.

ANNABEL BOPPED AROUND the room to the beat of Buddy Holly's "Oh Boy" and pulled the pink poodle skirt and a white cardigan sweater from her closet. She changed into the outfit while singing to the music.

Standing in front of the mirror, she brushed her hair back in a high ponytail and tied a pink and white ribbon around it. She brushed her bangs over her forehead, just above her eyebrows, until they looked smooth and tidy.

Lastly, she smeared a thick coat of lip gloss across her lips and pinched her cheeks to give them color. She took a step back, twirled, and watched as her skirt flew loose and free in the air.

It was close to the time Danny was supposed to pick her up, when Annabel made her way down the stairs.

Joan rushed to greet her. "Oh my. Don't you look beautiful?"

Annabel glanced down at her outfit, suddenly uncertain of herself. "Are you sure I look okay? Is my ponytail high enough?"

"Everything about you is perfect."

"He should be coming soon." Annabel went to the front window.

"You look nervous," Joan said.

"I am nervous." Annabel sat on the edge of the couch.

Joan sat beside her and placed a hand on Annabel's lap. "I'm sure you're not the only one. He's probably just as nervous as you are."

"I don't think so. He's been on dates with lots of girls."

Joan gave Annabel's hand a squeeze. "But never with you. Trust me, he's nervous."

Annabel knew her mother had just given her a great compliment, but she didn't know what to say, so she said nothing at all.

Joan crossed her legs and let out a deep, thoughtful exhale. "Annabel . . . what did you mean when you said Danny's been on dates with lots of girls?"

Annabel shrugged. "I don't know. Just that he's been out with girls before."

Joan faced Annabel and wagged a finger at her. "No, no. You specifically said he's been out with *lots* of girls. Not just girls, but *lots* of girls. What constitutes lots of girls?"

Annabel thought for a bit, frowning. "I . . . I don't know. I just mean this isn't his first date."

"Do you know how many dates he's been on?"

"Of course not. I mean, he's a senior so how should I know?"

"A *senior*? Did . . . did I know he was a senior?"

"How should I know what you know?"

"I mean, did you tell me he was a senior?"

Annabel stood and walked to the window. "You never asked." She pulled back the curtain, but there was no sign of Danny.

"I didn't know I had to ask something like that." Joan went to Annabel. "I'd have expected you would tell me if the boy you were going out with was a senior. You're only a sophomore."

"So?" Annabel walked away from her mother, but Joan followed close behind.

"So . . . it's just as you said. He's dated lots of girls and you haven't dated anyone."

"I have to start somewhere," Annabel reasoned as she circled the room, Joan at her heels.

"True, but did you have to start with someone so . . . experienced?"

"Did you expect me to say no to him? He's the only boy I wanted to go to the dance with," Annabel said.

"Your father would . . ."

"My father's not here." Annabel faced her mother. "You're here and you gave me permission to go to this dance."

"But there are some things that a young girl is naïve about, and I don't want any boy taking advantage of that."

Annabel knew what her mother thought she was naïve about, but sex was not something she wanted to discuss with her mother. "I don't want to talk about this."

"I don't want to talk about this either and I wasn't expecting I'd have to, but I didn't know your date was a senior."

"So what?"

"So boys are different at that age."

"But Danny isn't like that. He isn't."

Joan looked unconvinced. "I want to believe that. I really do, but I don't want to regret letting you go to this dance."

Annabel threw her hands up in the air. "Why would you regret letting me go to the dance? It's a dance! Molly and Donna will be there. You said you wanted me to do normal things kids do. Dances are normal things kids go to."

"I just wish your father were here."

Annabel's body stiffened, and she looked her mother in her eyes. "Do you really wish that?"

Joan hesitated. "No, I suppose not. But I need someone to help me make these decisions. You'll understand when you have children and all the worrying and second-guessing every decision you make. It's enough to drive a person mad."

"I promise you won't regret this decision."

Joan squeezed Annabel's hand. "You make sure of it."

The doorbell rang, and Annabel let out a piercingly high-pitched squeal, a sound that had never come out of her mouth before. The only time she had heard anything resembling the sound was at the zoo, watching monkeys play.

Joan made a strange face at Annabel as she went to answer the door.

"I don't know what that was," Annabel said. "I'm just really nervous."

Joan turned to Annabel before she opened the door. "Remember . . . he's the lucky one. Don't forget that."

"I'll try." Annabel closed her eyes, took a deep breath, and chanted quietly to herself, "Don't make any noises that sound like zoo animals. Don't make any noises that sound like zoo animals."

Joan opened the door to find a handsome young man standing on her porch, appropriately dressed in black slacks, a white long-sleeved shirt, and a black suit coat and tie.

"Hello, I'm Danny Winfield. I'm here to pick up Annabel." Danny held a bouquet of pink carnations.

"I'm Joan Turner, Annabel's mother." Joan smiled and extended her hand.

"Nice to meet you, Mrs. Turner." Danny shook her hand.

"Please come in."

"Wow." Danny glanced around the living room and saw Annabel. "You look swell. I mean pretty . . . you look . . . pretty." He held out the flowers with a slight quiver in his usually steady hands. "These are for you."

"Thank you." Annabel took the first flowers she'd ever received from a boy, but didn't know what to do or say next. Danny Winfield was standing in her living room, about to take her to a dance where the whole school would see them. It was a scenario she never dreamed she'd be living.

Joan took the bouquet from Annabel. "I'll put these in a vase for you when you leave."

"Thanks," Annabel said, and Danny stood beside her looking equally as uneasy as she felt.

"Annabel tells me you play football," Joan said.

"Yes ma'am. That's right." Danny straightened. "I'm the quarterback."

"Yes, I remember Annabel telling me that. You know her fa . . ." Joan forced a smile. "Would you like something to drink, Danny?"

"No, thank you, ma'am."

"How about something to eat? I made chocolate chip cookies."

"We should probably get going. The dance has already started." Annabel wanted to leave before something unexpected happened that would prevent her from going to the dance with Danny, like her father suddenly coming home.

"Of course. You kids need to get to that dance." Joan walked Annabel and Danny to the door.

Annabel gave Joan a quick hug goodbye, and Joan whispered in her ear to have fun. Danny held the door open for Annabel. He turned back to Joan and stumbled a little on the front porch steps.

"Careful," Joan said. "Are you okay?"

"I'm fine, Mrs. Turner." Danny appeared flustered. "What time would you like Annabel home?"

"Oh." Joan blinked. "Um . . . well, what time does the dance end?"

"Nine o'clock. Is this okay?" Danny asked.

Standing behind Danny on the front porch, Annabel nodded for her mother to say yes.

"Yes. Nine o'clock will be fine," she replied.

"Wait, the dance ends at nine," Annabel said. "So I won't be home right at nine."

Joan eyed Annabel. "Fine. But I better not see you walk through this door a second past nine-thirty."

"Okay," Annabel said.

"Wait. Maybe nine-fifteen," Joan said.

"Mother." Annabel widened her eyes at Joan with an expression that begged for reconsideration.

"Fine. Nine-thirty," Joan relented.

"So . . . nine-thirty?" Danny looked between Annabel and Joan.

"Yes. Nine-thirty and this time I mean it." Joan smiled, but there was still a tone of uncertainty in her voice, and Annabel wished her mother wasn't so bad at making decisions.

"Okay. It was nice meeting you, Mrs. Turner."

"You too, Danny. Have fun tonight." Joan winked at Annabel.

Annabel smiled and followed Danny down the pathway.

He opened the car door for her. She got in and waited, her heart pounding, as Danny made his way to the other side of the car.

She peered out her window, and an elderly neighbor stood at her front door, watching them with a thoughtful expression. Annabel wondered if the aged woman was remembering the night of her first date and the first time a boy opened the car door for her, and many of the other first moments the woman remembered even as the decades had passed. Annabel was certain she'd never forget this night with Danny.

The old woman waved at Annabel, and Annabel waved back.

The car ride to the school was only seven minutes, but it was the first time Annabel was alone with Danny so the minutes felt like hours. She could tell Danny was jumpy too because he kept fidgeting with the radio.

"Let me know if you hear a song you like."

"It doesn't matter," Annabel replied. "You can put whatever you want on."

Annabel didn't care about songs on a radio. She was going to a dance with Danny, the boy in the window.

Chapter Six

COUPLES FILLED THE dance floor as Big Bopper's voice burst loudly from the speakers. The usually dull gym was adorned with bright streamers hanging from high beams, and colorful balloons and handmade posters decked the bare walls. The array of decorations made a place that mostly stunk of sweat and stinky feet appear charming.

Annabel was standing underneath the basketball hoop while Danny got them drinks, when she caught sight of Molly and Donna standing awkwardly in a corner of the gym. She quickly waved them over.

The girls hurried across the dance floor, snaking around couples to get to Annabel as fast as they could. Molly's indigo skirt, like most of her clothes, hung big on her and brushed against the dancing couples she rushed past, while Donna's snug-fitting olive-green skirt and white sweater clung tightly to her body.

"Where is he?" Donna craned her neck to get a better look around the gym.

"Getting us punch." Annabel motioned toward the refreshment table.

"I bet he looks so cute," Molly said.

"Of course he looks cute. He's Danny Winfield." Donna gazed to where Danny stood and pressed a hand against her chest. "Oh my gosh. He's beyond cute. He's dreamy."

"What'd your parents think of him?" Molly asked.

"My mom liked him. My dad wasn't home," Annabel answered quickly, hoping her friends didn't catch the tension in her voice.

"What's not to like? It's my mother's fantasy for me to bring home a boy like Danny," Molly said.

"He brought me flowers. No boy has ever done that."

"Truly? What kind?" Molly asked.

"Carnations."

"What color?"

"Pink."

"Ohhhh. Those are my favorite," Molly said.

"I can't wait till a boy buys me flowers. That must have felt really good," Donna said.

Annabel thought about it and smiled. "Yeah. It did." She glanced across the gym to Danny and watched as he scooped the red drink into two paper cups.

Molly followed Annabel's gaze at the refreshment stand. "You two look like the perfect couple."

"You think so?" Annabel asked.

"Sure. Don't you?"

Danny made his way back to Annabel, stealing the attention of all the girls he passed along the way. Annabel watched him while still in awe that it was she he had asked to the dance.

Donna tugged at Annabel's arm and leaned closer to her. "What was it like being alone in a car with him?"

"I don't have the words." Annabel smiled.

"You're so lucky," Donna replied.

Danny walked up to them with two white plastic cups in his hands and handed one to Annabel. "Hi, Molly. Hi, Donna. Would you girls like me to get you some punch?"

Neither Donna nor Molly could take their googly eyes off Danny.

"Umm . . . no . . . I'm . . . I'm okay," Molly stammered.

"Yeah, I'm okay too," Donna nervously replied.

Annabel's own nervousness wasn't as obvious as her friends'. She made a conscious effort to be as composed as a teenage girl could be while attending her first dance with a boy she'd been secretly watching through his window at night.

"Let's find a table," Danny said.

Annabel followed and urged her friends along, and Molly and Donna trailed close behind as Danny led them to an empty table.

"I can't believe we're at a dance with Danny Winfield. It's like a dream," Donna whispered excitedly to Molly.

BRETT CRUISED THE quiet streets with his rowdy gang while "Smokey Joe's Café" blasted on the radio. He took the cigarette trapped behind his ear and slipped it between his fingers. He cocked his head, sparked the cigarette, and drew in a deep drag. Exhaling a cloud of smoke, he relaxed into the driver's seat and said, "This chick was primo. First class all the way, baby."

"Then what the hell was she doing with you?" Dennis yelled from the backseat.

Brett reached behind the driver's seat and grabbed the back of Dennis's neck with one hand, while steering with the other. "Because, smartass, she knows the goods when she sees it." He tightened his grip around Dennis's neck.

"Okay. Okay." Dennis surrendered, and Brett let him go.

"You didn't have to grab me so hard," Dennis said, rubbing his neck.

"You didn't have to grab me so hard," Ricky mocked in a little girl's voice.

Dennis kicked the back of Ricky's seat. Ricky twisted around to grab him, and Dennis screamed like a girl.

The guys howled in laughter and teased Dennis without mercy.

"I knew you were a sissy." Ricky dismissed Dennis with a flick of his hand, as though he were no longer worth his time, faced the front, and lit a cigarette.

Dennis Hubert was the least intimidating of the rebellious crew. With a soft midsection and a round, pudgy face, Dennis could have easily passed for a choir boy—sans the leather jacket and greasy hair—but Dennis used his bad behavior to revolt against his innocent looks.

"Did this primo chick let you cop a feel?" Ricky took a swig of a bottle of beer and dragged his cigarette.

The sleeves of his white T-shirt were rolled tightly around his shoulders to show off his lean muscles. Always riding shotgun, he hung his elbow nonchalantly out the window as he eyed the streets for action. He was the most popular among the girls interested in bad boys. Though Ricky shared the same tough look as Brett, he had the dreamy eyes and soft smile of a teen idol, and was an expert at using both to his advantage.

"You ain't gonna see no virgin pin on that dolly anytime soon." Brett displayed a cocky grin as his cigarette dangled from his lips.

The boys roared loudly, and Curtis, who was sitting next to Dennis in the backseat, poked his scrawny body between Brett and Ricky. "Can I have her when you're done with her?"

"When I'm done with her there ain't gonna be nothin' left of her," Brett said with an even tone.

"Come on, man. You can leave just a little bit. I'll take anything." Curtis leaned deeper into the front seat and bumped Ricky's shoulder, making him spill beer all over his shirt.

"Watch it, asshole!" Ricky shoved Curtis hard into the backseat, and Curtis gave a solid kick to Ricky's seat.

"Do it again and see what happens," Ricky warned.

"Oh . . . I'm so scared." Curtis raised his hands in mocked fear and kicked the seat again.

Curtis Tanner was the skinniest of the gang, but he was also the wildest. His maniacal behavior was in great contrast to his delicate, gaunt look. Curtis knew no boundaries. It was what made him crazy.

"Goddamn it!" Ricky tossed his cigarette out the window, passed Brett his bottle, and threw himself into the backseat. "Maybe if you weren't such a candy ass you'd be able to get your own chic." Ricky wrestled with Curtis, his legs dangled over the front seat as he easily overtook his weaker counterpart.

"If you kick me in the face, I'm bustin' both your heads," Brett warned. "This ain't no playground. Cool it."

To make his point, Ricky punched Curtis one last time in the shoulder and then pushed himself back into the front seat.

"Are you girls done fighting now?" Brett asked calmly. "Save some of that energy for later."

"Why? What's happening later?" Ricky pulled a comb from his back jeans pocket and raked it through his greasy hair.

"You'll see." Brett gripped the steering wheel tightly and punched the gas. With a loud squeal of the tires the car took off—much to the amusement of his buddies.

"ROCK AROUND THE Clock" blasted throughout the gym as Danny spun Annabel around the dance floor. Just as on the football field, Danny was smooth in his moves on the dance floor. It was what separated him from the rest of the players. The natural way his body moved—whether he was dropping back for a pass or cradling the ball for a tight run up the middle—Danny had cunning instincts on the field and the dance floor.

The only dancing Annabel had done was goofing around in her bedroom with Molly and Donna. She followed Danny's lead and felt like Ginger Rogers to Danny's Fred Astaire. Danny had the ability to make anyone look good.

Despite Molly and Donna's initial concerns of not having anyone to dance with, the girls had no problems finding dancing partners, but they weren't half as excited about their partners as Annabel was about hers.

Three songs later, Danny and Annabel made their way back to their table. As they sat down, Danny nodded in acknowledgment to someone across the room. Annabel followed his gaze to a raucous table near the back of the gym filled with football players and cheerleaders, talking and laughing loudly.

"It's okay if you want to go over there," Annabel said.

"Why would I want to leave you to go over there? I see those guys all the time," Danny replied.

"I don't want you to feel like you have to stay by me."

"I wouldn't have asked you to be my date if I didn't want to stay by you."

Steve Pierce, one of Danny's teammates, waved at them and quickly made his way to their table. "Hey, Danny, we're gonna head out to Marvin's after this. You guys in?" He looked at Danny and then laid his eyes on Annabel.

Marvin's was a diner where the cool kids hung out. It was usually reserved for the older crowds of juniors and seniors, but if you were an athlete and you were good, you were allowed. Annabel had heard Danny had been going there since he was a freshman.

Annabel turned away from Steve's gaze because she had to be home right after the dance.

"Some other time," Danny replied.

THE GREASERS POUNDED through the school doors and made their way through the entrance of the gym where an elder teacher, Mrs. Higgins, sat behind a long wooden table, scattered with papers.

"Hold on just a minute, boys," the woman instructed. "I need to know your names."

"What for?" Curtis shouted.

"I need to check you on the school list and make sure you go here. This event is for students only." Mrs. Higgins fingered her way through the stacks of paper across the desk. "So what are your names?"

Ricky pushed himself to the front of the gang. "You tellin' me people who don't go here actually try sneakin' into one of these things?"

Mrs. Higgins tapped her fingers against the table. "Are you going to tell me your names or not?"

Brett stepped up. "I do have a name. I just can't remember it right now, but lucky for me I have ID. Hang on. Let me get it."

He stood directly in front of Mrs. Higgins so her face was at the same level as his groin. He dug his hand in the pocket of his tight jeans as though he were frantically searching for something.

His buddies behind him laughed as Brett wiggled his body obnoxiously inside his jeans. "I know it's in here somewhere. Wait, maybe it's in the other pocket."

Mrs. Higgins pushed her chair away from the table, her face like stone, as Brett took his left hand out of his pocket and held up his right hand.

"This is my strong hand. I'm really good with this hand." He winked.

The gang hooted even louder as Brett shoved his right hand into his pocket and simulated obscene gestures with his hand stuffed inside his jeans. He feigned frustration and freed his hand. "I just can't seem to find it, but maybe you can. Wanna give it a whirl?" He offered Mrs. Higgins his pocket.

Mrs. Higgins raised herself to her feet and looked Brett in the eyes. "You are a vile, *vile* young man." She looked over Brett's shoulder, to the rest of his crew. "All of you are just vile."

"Please stop, old lady. You're hurtin' my feelings," Dennis cried out.

Slipping on the pair of glasses that were dangling around her neck, Mrs. Higgins called out, "Who said that?"

Each greaser raised a hand, one at a time. "I did." "No, I did!" "No, it was me!"

With her glasses on, Mrs. Higgins inspected them more closely, and her eyes widened. "None of you even fit the dress code. You need a shirt, a tie, *and* a proper jacket to attend this social event."

Mr. Felder approached the table. He eyed the greasers suspiciously. "Is everything all right, Mrs. Higgins?"

"No, Mr. Felder. Everything is *not* all right. These despicable, inappropriately dressed boys are trying to get into the dance, but they can't. They must leave."

Mr. Felder looked at the greasers. "Okay, fellas. You heard her. You're not allowed to be here. Time to go."

Mr. Felder placed a hand on Brett's shoulder.

Brett ripped his shoulder out of Mr. Felder's grip. "Hands off!"

Mr. Felder stepped back. "Fine. Just get out."

Ricky glared at him. "No sweat. Ain't sure why we came here in the first place. This place is a drag. We need something more exciting. What's Mrs. Felder doing while you're here chaperoning?" He offered a twisted smile.

Mr. Felder pointed toward the door. "Go!"

The greasers howled loudly and tore down decorations taped to the walls as they made their way to the doors.

ANNABEL SAT WITH Molly and Donna at the table while she waited for Danny, who'd been pulled away by his teammates insisting they needed him outside. The girls took the opportunity alone to talk about the dance.

"You two looked so cool on the dance floor, like you've been a couple forever," Donna said.

"I didn't feel cool," Annabel said. "I felt crazy nervous."

"You pulled it off. Don't worry," Donna assured her.

"Thanks. I saw the two of you dancing. You guys were good too."

"Yeah right," Molly yelled and angrily crossed her legs, and her over-sized blue poodle skirt lifted briefly in the air. "Skip was such a spaz. He kept stepping on my toes." She held up a foot. "I bet I'm gonna wake up with bruises all over my feet." She slumped into her seat.

"My dancing partner almost dropped me to the floor when he tried to spin me. Everyone saw and laughed." Donna folded her arms over her plump body.

"I'm sorry about that. I didn't know," Annabel said.

Donna shrugged her rounded shoulders. "What could you have done about it?"

Molly glanced at the gymnasium clock and sighed. "My dad'll be coming soon."

"Already?" Donna propped up in her seat. "It feels like we just got here."

"What time does Danny have to bring you home?" Molly asked Annabel.

"Nine-thirty."

"Nine-thirty? Gosh, Bel, you're so lucky. My dad's picking us up at eight-thirty—on the dot. It's so unfair. How'd you get to stay out so late?"

"I don't know. I just did," Annabel said, even though she knew exactly why she got to stay later than her friends. Her father wasn't home. If her father had been home, she wouldn't have been able to go to the dance at all.

"If we were staying at my house we probably could have gotten till nine," Donna pointed out with a bit of an attitude.

"Maybe I would have been able to stay over at your house if someone had done her chores on time," Molly shot back. "Oh, and also if you hadn't broken your father's radio."

"It wasn't my fault," Donna insisted.

Molly rolled her eyes. "It never is."

"He really loved that radio," Donna said. "I don't even remember how I broke it. I suppose I'm lucky he let me come at all. But I really don't even know what the big deal is. I mean, we have a TV."

"You're just clumsy. Always were, always will be," Molly said flippantly.

"Gosh Molly. You don't have to be so mean," Donna yelled.

Molly shrugged. "You know it's true."

Annabel watched her friends, knowing that Molly was right. Donna was very heavy-handed, always dropping her books and knocking things over. Images of her father's angry expressions when he screamed at Annabel for dropping little things like a fork burned through her mind.

Donna wouldn't have lasted an hour in Annabel's house with George as her father. Donna's father never yelled at her the way George yelled at Annabel. Being that the only punishment Donna received for breaking her father's coveted radio was not being able to have a friend sleep over, Donna had never known anger like George's ire.

Annabel couldn't imagine breaking anything her father loved. Aside from his car, there wasn't anything the man loved more than the bottles filled with his favorite drink. If she ever broke one of those, she'd have a whole lot more to worry about than not being able to sleep over at a friend's house or to go to some dance.

She couldn't envision either of her friends' fathers behaving the way hers did. Maybe it was because she had never seen that side of them, or maybe, it was because that side didn't exist in them and only her father possessed that kind of rage.

Annabel had no idea what made her father so tumultuous. She'd spent a lot of time thinking about it, desperate to find a reason why her father was so angry, but it was hard to decipher because George was already agitated when he walked through the door. He came home that way. Neither Annabel nor Joan needed to give him a reason to be irritated, he just was.

Annabel thought most men would have been happy and satisfied with the homelife her father had. As far as she could tell, her mother fulfilled every expectation of a housewife. She cooked, she cleaned, she ironed, she washed, and she sewed, and did everything else that needed getting done. What more her father could want, Annabel had no idea. She only knew that she wasn't going to spend her life struggling to please someone so undeserving.

It was close to the time Molly and Donna were getting picked up and Danny hadn't come back yet.

"Come on." Annabel stood up from the table. "I'll wait with you outside."

THE GREASERS LEANED coolly against Brett's car in the school parking lot as they smoked cigarettes and stood in the toughest stances they knew. They were over-practiced poses stolen straight out of a James Dean movie, and Danny had seen this flick before.

"Look at those scumbags." Jimmy Leeds folded his beefy arms over his thick chest. "We should pop 'em right now."

Danny and his teammates stood shoulder to shoulder across the pavement, watching the greasers.

"Forget it," Danny said. "Let's get back inside."

Jimmy grabbed Danny by the arm as he started to walk away. "Hang on. We're not afraid of those guys. Why should we back off as if we are?"

Danny peered over Jimmy's shoulder to where the greasers stood in blue jeans, tight T-shirts, and black leather jackets, watching Danny and the rest of the team. Like a showdown, both groups showcased their bravest front as they waited for someone from the other side to make the first move.

"This is supposed to be a good time." Danny pulled his arm out of his teammate's grip. "You've got Sherry and I've got Annabel. This isn't the place to settle any score. Fighting on school property? What's that gonna do except get us suspended and into a whole heap of trouble with Coach?"

Jimmy continued to glare at the greasers as though he wanted to kill them.

"We want State this year, right?" Danny continued.

"Hell yeah," Jimmy yelled.

"Well, we can't do that with half the team suspended."

Jimmy, looking unconvinced, finally relented. "Fine. But I swear to God the next time they start with us, I don't care where we are, we're bustin' heads."

"Okay. Sure. We'll get 'em next time, but not on school property and *not* when the girls are around." Danny called for the rest of the players to follow him back into the gym.

They weren't happy about the retreat, but like Jimmy, they slowly fell in line while ignoring the taunts of "chicken-shits" and "candy-asses" from the greasers.

Danny saw Annabel standing in the parking lot with Molly and Donna. If he wasn't sure he'd made the right call by not fighting, one look at Annabel had reassured him that he had.

He stopped and watched her while his teammates shuffled past him, muttering to each other what they'll do to the greasers the next time they see them. But Danny didn't take his eyes off Annabel, and when she saw him watching her, she didn't take her eyes off him either.

They smiled at each other.

A car horn sounded, taking Annabel's attention away from Danny. Molly's father's blue Ford Thunderbird pulled up to the curb. Annabel walked with her friends to the car and hugged them goodbye.

Danny approached them as Donna got into the backseat and whispered to Annabel, "Come over tomorrow. I want to know everything."

Danny smiled.

Annabel shut the car door and stepped away from the curb. She and Danny watched the car pull away. When the vehicle faded from their sights, Annabel asked Danny if everything was all right.

Danny looked across the parking lot at the greasers, lingering outside Brett's polished black Chevy convertible while yelling insults to anyone who passed by.

It occurred to Danny that this fight wasn't personal for them. They didn't care who they messed with. They just wanted to mess with somebody. Their only goal was to jump bad on someone, and anyone would do.

"I'm sorry I left you in the gym," Danny said. "I should have stayed with you."

"If you'd stayed, there definitely would have been a fight tonight. I saw how much your teammates wanted to fight." She peered at the greasers. "And who knows what would have happened then."

Danny took Annabel's hand. It was cold. He slipped off his suit jacket and wrapped it around her shoulders. "Let's get you inside."

Chapter Seven

THE GYM BECAME less crowded as the night wore on. Those with early curfews, like Molly and Donna, had long gone, and the older kids with cars skipped out early to cruise the streets.

Annabel sat at a table with Danny. She still wore his coat even though she was no longer cold, but the coat smelled like him, and she wanted to keep his scent close to her.

"I'm glad you came with me tonight," Danny said. "I . . . I wasn't sure you would."

"Why would you think that?"

"I thought since I'd waited so long to ask you somebody else might have beaten me to it. But mostly, I was afraid you'd say no."

"Why would you think I'd say no?"

Danny gave a short shrug. "Because I've never seen you out with other boys. Heck, I don't think I've even seen you talking to other boys."

As the date of the dance had gotten closer and no boy had asked Annabel to the dance, she worried there must be something horribly wrong with her. But given that the star quarterback and captain of the football team was nervous to ask her out because he feared rejection, the regular boys at school may have had the same reservations, though she didn't understand why. She felt she was nothing special, just another girl at school.

"I talk to boys," Annabel said. "I have lots of friends who are boys."

"I'm not talking about boys who are friends." Danny looked Annabel straight in the eyes, and she was suddenly embarrassed because even Danny had noticed her lack of experience when it came to dating.

"I didn't mean it as a bad thing," Danny quickly said. "Most girls are so boy-crazy they'll parade around the halls on the arm of any guy who asks. I don't . . . I don't like girls like that." He paused. "I like you."

Annabel didn't know what to say, but her cheeks felt like they were on fire. She tugged Danny's jacket tighter around her body and looked away from him.

"I didn't mean to embarrass you," he said.

"Well you did," Annabel replied softly.

"I'm sorry about that, but it's true." Danny's gentle tone comforted Annabel as the gym lights dimmed and the last dance was announced.

The night was coming to an end.

Danny stood and offered his hand to Annabel. "Dance with me."

Annabel slid Danny's jacket off her shoulders and slung it over the back of the chair. She put her tiny hand in his and they walked to the dance floor as the beginning chords of "The Great Pretender" filled the gym. They brushed past couples swaying slowly to the music and made their way to the middle of the floor.

Danny placed the palm of his right hand against Annabel's lower back and took her hand with the other. Annabel followed Danny's lead as they moved to the slow beat of the music.

Danny was strong, yet he touched Annabel with the tenderness of a person handling a delicate flower. There were couples all around them, yet when Annabel looked at Danny, everyone disappeared.

Danny let go of Annabel's hand and interlaced his fingers at her lower back. The space between them grew smaller as their bodies touched. Annabel was physically closer to Danny than she had ever been to a boy before. She closed her eyes and laid her head on Danny's shoulder. With each passing moment, she became more comfortable in his arms, and they swayed slowly together until the last note faded out.

DANNY HELD ANNABEL'S hand on the short drive back and didn't let go until he parked the car in front of her house.

"Did you have fun tonight?" Danny asked.

"You really think you have to ask?" Annabel responded.

"I . . . I think you did. I just want to be sure." He looked at her with an anxious expression, waiting for her reassurance.

"Danny, you're used to going to dances and parties, but I'm not. Tonight was better than any dream I could ever have."

Danny softly touched Annabel's face and leaned down until his lips were close to hers, and whispered, "I may be used to going to dances and parties, but that doesn't mean that I've had nights like this before. Okay?"

Danny's gaze at Annabel was intense, so intense it made her shift uncomfortably in her seat, yet she couldn't look away from those brown eyes she loved so much. Even though Annabel had fantasized about being with Danny and having him look at her exactly the way he was looking at her at that moment, she lacked the experience to know what to say or what to do when it finally happened.

When her rapidly beating heart felt like it was going to burst out of her chest, she turned her head away from him and looked out the passenger window. Danny whispered her name, as though begging her to reconsider, but when Annabel kept her eyes away from him, he said her name again until she finally relented, and turned her gaze back to him.

"Danny, I don't know what I'm supposed to do. I'm an idiot when it comes to this."

"You're perfect. You should know that." Danny swallowed and his Adam's apple bopped in his throat. His hot breath brushed against her face and he traced his thumb gently across her cheek. "Would it be all right if I kissed you?"

Danny's lips were only inches away from Annabel's. She nodded and closed her eyes as Danny pressed his lips against hers. His kiss was soft and slow—the kind of kiss Annabel fantasized her first kiss to be.

"Oh no." Danny suddenly pulled away from her.

"What is it?" Annabel asked, worried he stopped because she was a bad kisser.

"Your mom's standing at the door."

Annabel looked out the car window and saw her mother waving at her from the front door. "Oh my God." She fell back into her seat. "I gotta go." She threw open the door and jumped out of Danny's car.

"Wait. I'll walk you to the door," Danny yelled.

"No need." Annabel rushed to the front porch where Joan stood with a smile across her face.

"Did you have fun?"

"Mother, what are you doing?" Annabel took Joan by the arm and pulled her inside the house.

"What? I wasn't doing anything? I came out to check if you were home because it's nine-thirty and there the two of you were, sitting in front of the house right on time. Thank you for that. I had this horrible feeling all night that your father was going to come home. I must have looked at the clock a hundred and ten times."

"So you didn't see anything?" Annabel asked.

"See? See what?" Joan stepped back and gave Annabel a long look. "What was there to see?"

Annabel let out a short sigh of relief.

"Annabel . . ." Joan began.

"Nothing. There was nothing to see. I'm tired. I'm going to bed." Annabel headed for the stairs.

"Will you at least tell me if you had fun tonight?" Joan asked.

Annabel faced her mother and smiled. "The night was perfect. Thank you for letting me go. Goodnight."

Before she went to her room, she collected her bouquet of flowers and carried the vase carefully up the stairs. She kept the flowers on her dresser and admired them often until they wilted, and then she tucked them away in a scrapbook to keep.

JOAN CHECKED FOR the third time to make sure the back door was locked. She then checked the front door too. When George was away, she was compulsive about locked doors. Even though George wasn't the protective husband and father most husbands and fathers were, Joan still preferred that he be home should an intruder break into the house.

She stood in the foyer and peeked through the small glass window on the door and settled her eyes on the quiet and dimly lit street. Faint breezes swayed the branches, and she relaxed in the calmness the scene invoked in her. She couldn't fathom anything bad happening on such a serene night, with its gentle winds, but that didn't stop her from making sure all the doors were locked.

She headed upstairs and checked on Annabel. She was sound asleep in her bed. Joan stood by her side and listened to the steady hum of her sleeping daughter's breathing before leaving the room.

She went into the bathroom and readied herself for bed. She took off her clothes and placed them in the hamper. She slipped into the white cotton nightgown that was hanging on the back of the door, washed her face, and brushed her teeth.

Once in her bedroom, she sat on the edge of her bed and lathered her arms and hands in lotion. She pushed back the covers and slid into the bed. She closed her eyes and past memories flashed in her mind.

Sending Annabel off on her first date with a boy brought back remembrances of the first day she'd laid her eyes on the man she would marry. There was nothing about that day that would lead her to believe her life would end up the way it was.

It was a sunny Saturday afternoon, three days before the Christmas of 1938. Joan was fifteen years old, sitting on her porch, when the rusty old bus made its way down the rubble road toward her house.

Her next-door neighbor, Mrs. Scully, burst out of her home and hurried down the front porch steps. "Carl's home! Carl's home!"

Lydia Baxter, Joan's mother, came out of the house and pulled Joan out of her seat. "Come on, Joanie. Carl's back."

Joan, Joanie then, hadn't seen Carl Scully in over eight months. She followed her mother down the porch steps as her heart raced with excitement, mostly from the enthusiasm exuding from everyone around her. It wasn't that Joanie wasn't happy to see Carl, but she hadn't thought of him much the last eight months. Her life had gone back to normal after he left, even though out of all the older boys in the neighborhood, Carl was the most decent and didn't tease the little kids as fiercely as the other boys did.

Blocks of neighbors made their way toward the bus to welcome their hometown boy back home. The bus stopped to a screeching halt in front of Carl Scully's house, and the family waited anxiously to see the loved one they'd been missing.

The young man stepped off the bus with his name yelled out from every direction, but he wasn't alone. Another uniformed soldier followed Carl down the bus steps, each carrying large duffel bags over their shoulders.

While bodies lunged for Carl, hugging and kissing him, the other soldier stood awkwardly off to the side. Joanie was the only one who noticed the stranger and the way his strong body filled out his uniform more fully than Carl's lanky physique filled his.

The mystery soldier was handsome and stood with perfect posture in his olive drab cotton khaki military uniform. Joanie couldn't take her eyes off him. When the soldier caught her staring at him, he smiled, lowered his head, and pulled his army cap off his head. Joanie quickly looked away and shyly moved to where she could blend with the rest of the crowd.

Finally, Carl reached out and grabbed his road buddy by the shoulder. "Mom, this is the one I was tellin' you about. This here's George Turner. We're in the same platoon. He's a good fella and home's too far for him so I brought him here." With a large grin, Carl wrapped his arm around George's neck and yanked him closer. "Don't think I woulda made it through basic training without him."

Scattered voices across the crowd welcomed the stranger to their town. Carl's mother stepped to the soldier she had never met before, took him into her arms, and held him as though he were her own son.

"Welcome," she said. "This will be your home, too."

When the embrace ended, Joanie watched as the nervous soldier squeezed his hat tightly in his hands. "Thank you, ma'am."

"You may save my son's life someday," she added.

George turned his eyes to Carl. "Nothing would make me prouder."

The townspeople formed a line as the women gave Carl quick welcome home hugs, and the men, firm handshakes.

When it was Joanie's turn, Carl smiled down at her and ruffled her hair. "How's it goin', squirt? You still tryin' to catch all them bugs?"

Joanie's eyes widened with embarrassment, and it took all she had not to kick dirt at his clean, polished shoes. She glanced at the handsome soldier standing next to Carl, hoping he wasn't looking at her, but he was.

"I ain't done that since I was nine." Joanie gritted through her teeth.

"Haven't done that," Mrs. Baxter corrected and then took Joanie by the arm. "Come on, Joanie. Let's let the boys get settled in."

As Joanie was being dragged away, she stole a glimpse behind her, and the strong soldier boy was still watching her.

JOANIE WAS RAKING hay in the barn, one of the many tasks around the farm she was responsible for, when the handsome soldier stuck his head between the half-closed barn doors. Joanie had been sweating in that barn for almost two hours and worried about how she must look.

"Hi." George stepped into the barn.

"Hello," Joanie replied.

"I've never been on a farm before. I like this. The land you have here is remarkable."

Joanie leaned against the rake and looked through the open barn doors and across the fields. "I suppose it is." She was mostly unimpressed with her surroundings. It was just a farm, and a small one at that. "It used to be better, but we lost a lot on account of the Depression."

George nodded in a way that showed he understood and then everything was quiet except for the cows' moos.

"Would you like to go for a walk? I'd like to see more of the town," George said.

The first thing Joanie thought to tell him was that there wasn't much to see. Her town was much like any other, but instead, she replied, "I still have chores to do and then I have to wash up for supper."

George looked more disappointed than Joanie thought anyone should be at a rejection to walk around her dull town, but she didn't want to disappoint the handsome stranger. "But maybe after supper I can show you."

George brightened. "You sure?"

"Yes."

"Real good. I'll look forward to that."

"I'll have to ask my pa first, though."

"Yes, of course." George peered around the barn. "I better get going so you can finish up. I'd help you but Carl and I are running errands for his ma today."

"It's okay. I been doing this so long I can do it in my sleep."

"Then . . . then I'll come over later and see if it's alright for us to take that walk."

Joanie nodded and watched the soldier walk away.

GEORGE REMOVED HIS hat before walking into the house. He charmed Joanie's parents, Edward and Lydia, right from the start with his fine manners. He wasn't a country boy and though he didn't come from wealth, he was an educated man, and Joanie's parents liked that.

"Where are you kids headed?" Mr. Baxter asked.

"I was thinking a walk, sir," George said. "I'm enjoying the scenery you have here."

"It is beautiful, isn't it?" Mrs. Baxter said.

"Yes, ma'am, very much."

"You kids better get goin' then. Joanie can't stay out all night." Mr. Baxter opened the front door.

George placed his hat back onto his head. "Yes, sir."

Mrs. Baxter followed George and Joanie to the door. "Now, Joanie, make sure you take George to the lake. Show him how beautiful the sun sets over the water."

Joanie hadn't planned on going as far as the lake, but agreed to anyway.

As they walked, George asked Joanie questions about school and her favorite hobbies, which Joanie made sure to tell him no longer included collecting bugs. They soon came upon a break in the path where the quiet lake sat, with the sunset hanging just above it. From afar, the sun appeared to be sitting on top of the crisp water while the radiant sky turned a dark shade of orange.

George stepped in front of Joanie and drew in a breath. "Sure is stunning and the air has to be the cleanest air I've ever breathed."

Joanie's laugh started out as an easy, gentle chuckle, but then quickly turned so raucously boisterous she couldn't stop.

"What's so funny? What are you laughing at?" George turned slowly in a circle, his eyes gaping all around him looking for what he had missed that was so funny.

Joanie's laughter subsided. "I'm sorry, but I was laughing at you."

"At me?" George shoved a finger into his chest and let out a good-hearted chuckle. "Why?"

"I've never seen anyone react to this place the way you are—as if it was the most beautiful place in the world." Joanie jumped onto a big rock and stood on top of it. "I don't think it's so great."

"That's because you see it every day. I don't have this." George's smile faded.

Joanie sat down on the rock. "What do you have?"

George's eyes glazed as he looked over the lake, smooth like glass, surrounded by a thick forest of trees and green brush. "Not this."

"Then what do you have?" Joanie asked again. She knew nothing different than the country scenery around her.

George sat down in the grass beside the large rock Joanie was sitting. "It's crowded where I come from. The houses are stacked so close together if you look outside your window you can see what your neighbor's havin' for supper. The air is so thick with smog it chokes you. You don't see the color green much where I come from." George fell back onto his elbows and lifted his head to the setting sun. "I like green."

"Is it your favorite color?"

"It is now." He smiled.

Joanie smiled, too.

Time passed quickly between them. George was interested in knowing all about Joanie and the things that went on in her town. He asked her what it was like being around animals all the time and how much cows ate every day. Even though she had told him she didn't catch bugs anymore, George wanted to know the kind of bugs she used to catch, which embarrassed Joanie because it was such a kid thing to do. She didn't want to appear to him as a child.

But Joanie answered all of his questions. It was strange to her to see someone so curious about the things she felt she could easily live without. At fifteen, she had seen and smelled enough manure to last three lifetimes, but George even found manure fascinating.

"Do you really think that someday you'll save Carl's life?" Joanie asked.

"I will if I can. Just like Carl would save my life if it should come down to that."

Joanie couldn't picture Carl saving a dog's life, let alone a person's life. He couldn't even save a cat stuck in a tree, let alone be somebody's hero in the midst of a war with bullets spraying from all directions. No way. Not the Carl she knew. Joanie couldn't see it, but she had no problem imagining George as a hero. He had the confident look of strength and ability that neither Carl, nor any other boy she knew, could match.

"Do you know where they're sending you?"

"They haven't told us where we'll be stationed yet."

"Are you scared?"

"Soldiers don't get scared."

Joanie watched him, believing his words because she could think of nothing capable of scaring someone so strong. Where Carl looked like a boy in a man's uniform, George *was* the uniform.

"But they do get lonely," he said. "Some of the fellas were saying how on some days all they have to look forward to are letters."

"Letters about what?"

"About anything. A place like this, for instance." George peered once again over the countryside. "There are lots of men in my platoon who'd sure enjoy reading letters about a place like this, especially in the hell of places soldiers find themselves in."

"Really? You think lots of soldiers would love to read about this place?" Joanie asked in disbelief.

"Well you can't write all the soldiers." George popped up off his elbows.

"Who said I was going to write any of them?" Joanie shot back.

"Oh." George sank back into the grass. "Sorry."

It was getting dark, and when Joanie suggested they start heading back, George stood up from the grass and offered her his hand. Joanie placed her tiny hand in his and he lifted her up with gentle ease.

"About those letters . . ." George began.

"Do you want me to write you? Is that what you're trying to say to me?"

"Yes, ma'am."

"Okay, I'll write you," Joanie replied simply.

When they arrived back at the farmhouse, George walked Joanie up the front porch. "Thank you for taking me to the lake. I had a nice time."

"You're welcome. I did, too."

"And please thank your mother for making sure you showed me that sunset. Aside from you, it was the most beautiful thing I'd ever seen."

Joanie lowered her head in a shy way.

George took a couple steps off the porch, and when Joanie opened the door, he called out, "Joanie?"

"Yes?" Joanie spun around.

He stood silent for a couple seconds and stared at her. "Um . . . I'll . . . I'll see you tomorrow."

Joanie smiled. "Yes. You'll see me tomorrow."

She gave one last look at George and closed the door.

George and Joanie saw each other the next day, and the day after that, and every day until he and Carl had to go back. Joanie had kept her promise to write, and she wrote to George almost every day until he came back home and asked her to marry him.

Chapter Eight

ANNABEL AWOKE THE next morning certain the previous night had been a dream, one fantastic dream, but for once, reality was better than any dream she ever had. She pressed her cheek into the cool pillow and closed her eyes. In her mind, she danced with Danny all over again, and the safe feeling of being in his arms rushed over her once more.

A sudden knock at the door shook Annabel from her reverie.

"Annabel? Are you up?" Joan asked.

Annabel pulled the covers over her head, shutting her mother out. She wanted to do nothing more than to fantasize about her night with Danny, but it was time to get ready for church.

"Annabel?" The door squeaked open, and Joan popped her head into the room. "Are you still in bed?"

Annabel pushed away the covers. "Can't we skip church this week? Just this once?"

"You know better than to ask me something like that." Joan sat at the foot of Annabel's bed. "I'm sorry that going to the dance has made you so tired, but your father's home."

Annabel shot up. "Already?"

"Yes, and he's getting ready for church. I've got to go downstairs and finish making the biscuits so they're ready when we get home. Please don't diddle-daddle. Also, you haven't gotten to your chores yet. You promised me yesterday you'd get them done today."

"I'll do them after church."

"Thank you. Now get ready." Joan patted Annabel's leg as she stood up and left the room.

Annabel stepped into the hallway just as George stormed from his room, a dress shirt crumbled in his hand, and barged past her as if she weren't even there.

"Joan! Joan!" George yelled from the top of the stairs.

"What is it?" Joan rushed up the stairs. "What's happened?"

"This shirt is wrinkled." George squeezed the long-sleeved white dress shirt in his hand.

"I ironed it three times already," Joan said.

"Well, iron it again." He whipped the shirt at her. "You can't expect me to go to church with a wrinkled shirt." He barreled past Annabel as she stood at the threshold of her room and slammed his bedroom door shut.

A violent tremble blasted through Annabel's body. The peace that was her and her mother's life when he was away was long gone. The thought that in less than an hour she'd be sitting beside her father for prayer in the Lord's house made her want to vomit.

Joan folded the shirt over her arm, and when her eyes met Annabel's, she tried to smile, but even she had her limits.

"He wants a crisp shirt for church," Joan offered meekly.

"Don't, Mother. Just don't." Annabel shut her bedroom door.

Annabel questioned the usefulness of religion when a person who behaved as her father did could call himself a Christian. The Turner family was Protestant Christians, as were most everyone in town, but religion didn't interest Annabel much. She didn't care what faith anyone followed as long as they were decent people. She couldn't understand why a person like her father bothered to go to church every week, only to live against the teachings of his own religion every day.

The Protestant faith taught people to follow the Bible as the supreme authority over all things and should be used as an example of how to live one's life. Though Annabel was no expert on the Bible, she had yet to read any scripture that was consistent with the way her father lived, and yet the Protestant faith required no repentance from him.

Annabel sat next to a Catholic girl in study hall. One day, the girl shared with Annabel that she had lied to her parents about being with a boy and was frantic she would end up in purgatory if she didn't repent for her sin.

"I have to go to confession," she'd whispered to Annabel. "If I die before I confess my sins, I will spend the rest of my life in purgatory."

"What's purgatory?" Annabel asked.

"It's a place you go after you die if you do bad things while you're alive that you haven't repented for. It's a dark, dark place and you can spend thousands of years there if you live a bad life. Don't you have purgatory?"

Annabel didn't have purgatory. Neither did her father, and that bothered her. Purgatory was a Catholic doctrine. The Catholic faith punished those who believed in God but hadn't lived according to His teachings and traditions. Being a Catholic meant that Man had to pay for his sins. If not through time spent in purgatory, then through acts of penance, but they had to do something, and this amazed Annabel.

Her own religion had taught her that Christ died on the cross for all people's sins and that alone was enough for a sinner to go straight to heaven as long as he was a believer, because non-believers were to spend eternity in hell.

Annabel's religion let her father off the hook. He didn't have to repent for anything. He had no incentive to change . . . ever. Maybe he wouldn't have anyway, but Annabel liked the idea of her father spending time in purgatory for all of his sins.

She'd decided that she no longer wanted to worship a religion that let people like her father stroll right into heaven. Jesus dying on a cross for mankind's sins didn't seem like enough punishment for her father. Purgatory sounded like an awful place, a place George deserved to be.

As soon as she was old enough, Annabel resolved to change religions.

ANNABEL SAT BETWEEN her parents in the pew, but if it were up to her she'd sit on the end, away from her father. Joan preferred the seating arrangement with Annabel in the middle. That seemed to be the way most families sat, with a parent on each end and the children stuck in the middle. It made sense. Not only would unruly children be kept a watchful eye on, but it also appeared as a protective position of the children, though Annabel never felt protected sitting between her parents. She only felt trapped.

Annabel glanced around the church to the perfect-looking families gathered around her. Maybe her own family, with George's perfectly ironed shirt and Joan's docile demeanor, looked just as pristine, but looks were too often deceiving.

Although George always dressed properly for work, he was never as meticulous about his attire as when he went to church. It was an overcompensation for his shortcomings.

George was a religious man. At fourteen years old he led Bible studies and headed youth Christian services. Now, as he sat in the church, beads of sweat ran down his face and dropped to his shirt collar. He was a sweaty mess sitting in his tight-fitting suit in the stuffy church.

After the service ended, Joan, George, and Annabel made their way out the wide-wooden doors to the back of the church where people lingered and chatted with the clergy. While Joan was engaged in conversation about upcoming church events, George waited impatiently near the doors and offered short, stiff nods to people who greeted him.

As moody as George was when he came home from work, it was nothing compared to when he came home from church. As much as he drank during the week, it was nothing compared to how much he drank on Sundays after church.

It made Annabel, again, wonder why he even bothered to go.

ANNABEL AND JOAN were getting breakfast on the table when they were stopped by the pounding of George's feet rushing down the stairs. Annabel immediately put down the platter of bacon she was holding and backed away from the table, certain somehow her father had found out about the dance.

George entered the dining room and glared at Joan. He was still wearing his church clothes, only now the top three buttons of his shirt splayed open.

"What are these?" He held out a handful of crumpled papers.

Joan looked at the wrinkled papers, and the color drained from her face. "George, you know what those are," she answered in a calm voice.

"But what are they still doing in this house? I told you to get rid of them. All of them." George tossed the letters in Joan's face, and the papers flew like parachutes across the room.

Annabel watched with no clue as to what those papers were that made her father so angry. Selfishly, she was relieved his fury wasn't directed at her and that he hadn't found out about the dance.

"George . . . I . . . I," Joan stammered.

He rushed for Joan and stopped only inches away from her face. "You just what? I told you I didn't want to see those letters again, didn't I?"

Joan turned her head away from him.

"Didn't I?" he yelled louder.

"Yes," Joan whispered.

"Then get rid of them!" He raised a hand as if he was going to hit her, but instead grabbed the large platter of pancakes sitting on the center of the table and threw it across the room, shattering the dish against the wall.

Annabel jumped back.

"Go to your room," Joan instructed Annabel.

"But . . ."

"Go!"

Annabel hurried out of the room.

"You don't listen to me!" George continued. "The other wives listen to their husbands, but not you, Not Joan."

Annabel escaped to her room. Not having a lock on her door, she dragged her dresser in front of it. She went to her bed, pulled a pillow against her body, and cried. She thought about Danny, certain that his Sunday was nothing like her own.

Had she enjoyed walking during the day, Annabel would have snuck to Danny's house to catch a glimpse of his life on that Sunday afternoon. But there was no dark intimacy in walking while the sun shone. The daytime was too open and left her too vulnerable.

Annabel imagined Danny's father sitting at the kitchen table, reading the paper as his wife poured him a fresh cup of coffee. He'd lean his head back, kiss her sweetly on the cheek, and thank her with a smile on his face.

She'd place the coffee pot down and wrap her arms around his neck as she skimmed the paper over his shoulder. She'd make a comment about a particular article, and he'd listen to what she had to say, valuing her opinion. Annabel imagined that was how most husbands and wives spoke to each other—just not her own.

Annabel considered her walks and the confidence that sneaking out of her house without permission gave her. In those moments she felt she could do anything she wanted, that her opportunities in the world were limitless. And yet other times, like right then, all Annabel wanted to do was crawl into Danny's arms and let him protect her from the world.

The stairs creaked and seconds later there was a knock at Annabel's door.

"Can I come in?" Joan's voice called out.

Annabel pushed the dresser back to its place and opened the door.

"Are you okay?" Joan asked.

"Should I be okay?" Annabel snapped.

"Annabel . . ."

"Where is he?"

"Eating what's left of breakfast that didn't end up on the floor."

Annabel scoffed. "Breaking plates against the wall and screaming in your face didn't ruin his appetite."

Joan circled her fingers over her temples. "I'm really beginning to regret that I let you go last night. Your father cannot find out you went to this dance. When he came down those stairs like that, I thought for sure he knew."

"Me too," Annabel responded quietly.

"We need to make sure he never finds out . . . ever."

"I know." Annabel paused. "What were those letters that made him so mad?"

"They were . . . something from another time. Something I never should have been so careless to let him see again."

"Donna invited me to her house today."

"On a Sunday? Your father won't like that."

"I don't care what he won't like. Tell him I'm in my room if he asks, he won't know the difference."

ELVIS PLAYED IN the background as Annabel, Molly, and Donna sat in a circle on Donna's bedroom floor.

"The night at the dance was like magic, wasn't it?" Molly sat crossed-legged and leaned back onto her hands.

"You got your toes stepped on, remember? How was *that* like magic?" Donna asked, with a tight smirk.

"Gosh, why'd you have to remind me?" Molly slouched forward and rested her elbows on her knees.

"How could you forget?" Donna asked.

"Well, I did and I wasn't even talking about that part, okay? I was talking about the night as a whole. Just being there felt so magical. How beautiful the gym looked and seeing everyone dressed up so nicely, especially the boys. I felt like a princess attending a fancy Ball. It was so exciting."

Annabel and Donna made funny faces at each other while trying to hold in their laughter.

"Except your Prince Charming stepped all over your feet," Donna yelled with amusement, and Annabel laughed with her.

Molly grabbed a pillow from Donna's bed and slammed Donna in the face with it. "Oh, I swear, Donna. I'm not telling you anything anymore. You either Annabel." She raised the pillow and smacked Annabel with it, too.

Donna used her hands to shield herself from more pillow attacks and crawled on her hands and knees to get closer to Annabel. "That's okay because all I want to hear about is Danny."

"Yes!" Molly tossed the pillow aside. "Let's hear more about Danny."

"But I've already told you everything," Annabel said.

"I want to hear it again," Donna said.

"Me too, especially the part about the slow dance. Did he really hold you that tightly in his arms?" Molly asked.

"Yes."

"But he didn't kiss you?" Donna asked.

"No," Annabel lied.

"I can't believe he didn't kiss you, especially with the way he was looking at you all night," Molly said.

"How was he looking at me?" Annabel asked.

"Like he really wanted to kiss you," Molly said.

Annabel felt extremely self-conscious. Even though Molly and Donna were her closest friends, she wasn't ready to share her first kiss with them. "With everything that happened that night—the car ride alone with Danny, dancing in his arms, holding his hand—I don't think I could have handled a kiss after all that."

"I could have handled a kiss after all that," Molly said with great certainty.

Donna moved so close to Annabel their knees touched. "Do you think he'll kiss you the next time you go out with him?"

"I don't know. Maybe." Annabel scooted back to give herself some breathing room from her over-zealous friends, but she understood their curiosity.

Until Molly and Donna had their own experiences with boys, they were forced to live vicariously through her, just as she would have had to do if Danny had taken one of them to the dance instead.

"Even without the kiss, your night was better than anything Molly and I have ever experienced," Donna said.

"Hey!" Molly yelled. "You don't have to rub it in."

A knock at the door silenced them.

"Who is it?" Donna called out.

The door opened, and Donna's father popped into the room. Where Donna was short and plump, Mr. Parker was tall and slim. He wore thin-framed glasses and his dark-brown hair was slicked closely against his scalp. Wearing brown slacks and a crème-colored cardigan, he looked like a nosebleed.

"Hi ya, girls." Mr. Parker smiled.

"Dad, we're kinda busy."

"I was just going to ask if you girls wanted to get some ice cream, but if you're too busy."

"Dad, we're in high school not kindergarten. We don't want to get ice cream." Donna rolled her eyes.

"I want ice cream." Molly jumped to her feet.

Donna gave Molly a hard look and said through gritted teeth, "I don't want to get ice cream with my father."

"Very good. I'll get my car keys. Meet me downstairs, girls." Mr. Parker smiled and left the room.

"Thanks a lot, Molly. Now I have to go get ice-cream with my father. Gosh, I'll die if anybody sees us."

"It could be worse," Annabel said, believing Donna was overreacting.

"How worse can it get than your father taking you for ice cream when you're sixteen years old?" Donna lamented.

Molly hurried out of the room.

"Is your dad always like this?" Annabel asked.

"Like what?" Donna got up and wrapped a blue sweater around her shoulders, succumbing to the prospect of getting ice cream with her father.

"This cheery," Annabel answered.

"Oh." Donna seemed to consider the question. "I guess so."

"Does he ever yell?"

"Sometimes. Sure. Why?"

Annabel shrugged lightly. "Just wondering. He seems so calm and quiet all the time."

"I guess he's mostly like that. My mom says he's the most boring man she's ever known. All he wants to do is read and listen to his radio, well, before I broke it. Oh, and he also likes to go out for ice cream."

Chapter Nine

THE HALLWAYS WERE mostly empty as Annabel sat on the floor in front of her locker, reading a homework assignment she was supposed to have finished the night before. But when Mr. Parker took her home after their ice cream treat, she'd gone straight to bed. Spending time with a normal family and doing normal family things like getting ice cream was exhaustingly depressing.

Annabel didn't bother going on her walk that night because no matter how many walks she took, she couldn't escape her life, and no matter how many tears she cried, she wouldn't have a father like Mr. Parker.

Annabel was hunched over her papers when Danny showed up at her locker.

"Hey, Annabel. What are you doing here so early?"

She looked up at him, with her elbows pressed against her notebooks, not expecting to see him. "I . . . I didn't finish my homework last night. What are you doing here so early?"

"We had a workout session with Coach this morning." He knelt down next to her. "I was thinking of you yesterday. I wanted to call you, but I couldn't find your number in the phone book."

"You were thinking of me?"

Danny smiled. "Well . . . yeah."

Annabel had been thinking of him too, but she didn't want to imagine the trouble she'd catch from her father if he answered the phone to a boy calling to talk to her.

"It's okay you didn't call me," she quickly said.

"Really? You mean you didn't want to talk to me?"

"Of course I wanted to talk to you. I . . . I just meant I was at my aunt's house most of the day anyhow," Annabel lied.

"How about today? Are you going to be at your aunt's house today?"

"No."

"Then can I have your number so I can call you tonight?"

Annabel hesitated, but Danny was waiting on her. She panicked and quickly ripped a page from her notebook and scribbled her number across it. "Here."

Danny took the sheet of paper, looked at it, and laughed. "You didn't have to write 'Annabel's number.' I know it's your number."

"Oh, right," Annabel said. "I . . . I wasn't sure."

"I have practice after school today. Is it okay if I call you after?"

"Sure," Annabel replied. She was both nervous and excited. She'd never had a boy ask to call her before.

The halls started to get busy as it was nearing the first bell. Donna and Molly would be at her locker soon to walk to first period together. She and Danny said goodbye, with Danny promising to call her later.

DANNY LIMPED OUT of the empty locker room. The rest of the team had left while Danny stayed to ice his throbbing knees. He'd taken a couple hard hits at practice and was now feeling it all over his body. He was heading to the parking lot, anxious to get home and soak his aching muscles in a hot bath, when someone called out his name.

Danny turned around and his teammate, Steve, was rushing toward him.

"Hey, Danny! Hold back a sec."

"I thought you left with the rest of 'em," Danny said.

"No. I was waiting for you. I need to talk to you about Saturday night."

"Oh, yeah." Danny kicked at pebbles on the ground. "I was gonna talk to you about that."

"Come on, Danny." Steve tossed back his head. "Don't back out on me now."

"I never said I was gonna go."

"But you never said you weren't," Steve countered. "So I assumed you were. I mean, why wouldn't you want to go? Mary Sue ain't bad to look at and if the rumors are true, she's pretty easy too."

Danny looked away from Steve, but didn't say anything.

"It's because of that girl isn't it? Annabel?" Steve stepped closer to Danny. "What is it about her? I didn't even know you were considering asking her to the dance until I found out you already did."

"I didn't realize I needed to clear with you who I take to dances."

"That's not what I meant."

"Then what'd you mean?"

"I just . . ." Steve rubbed his hands together. "I thought you were gonna ask Mary Sue and I'd ask Beth and we'd all go to the dance together. But because you went with Annabel, I couldn't take Beth."

"Why couldn't you take Beth?"

"Because her father won't let Beth go out alone with a boy, and Mary Sue only wanted to go with you. You asking Annabel messed up everything for me."

"What did you want me to do? Ask a girl I don't even like to the dance? Why would I do that? I wanted to take Annabel, so I did."

"Then you owe me Saturday night. Beth said Mary Sue will still go out with you even though you didn't ask her to the dance. Besides, you promised we'd double."

"That was before Annabel."

"I don't care." Steve stood firm. "A promise is a promise and you don't break a promise to a buddy."

Danny crossed his arms. "Why won't she go alone with you?"

"I told you. Her father won't let her go alone with me."

"He doesn't trust you?"

"Are you kidding?" Steve scoffed "He doesn't trust anyone. He'd make a priest empty his pockets before leaving his house. And that's just his house. We're talking about his daughter."

"And you're no priest," Danny said.

"I know. That's why I need you with me." Steve threw his arm around Danny's neck, and Danny almost lost his balance on his unsteady knees. "Help me out, Danny. If I don't score soon, I'm gonna explode."

"You're not gonna explode." Danny drew his keys from the front pocket of his jeans and started limping to his car.

"You don't know what it's like." Steve followed Danny, his feet pounding against the pavement, and then he suddenly stopped. "Or maybe you do."

"What'd you say?" Danny turned around.

"Maybe you do know what it's like," Steve said.

"What the heck's that supposed to mean?" Danny asked.

"It means, what kind of action are you getting these days?"

Danny jostled the car keys in his hands. "With jabs like that, no one will ever help you out." He turned and walked away.

"Wait!" Steve yelled.

"What?" Danny was annoyed and his joints were hurting.

"Can I have a ride home?"

Danny sighed and waved Steve over. "Come on. Hurry up, but no more hassling me about this date."

Steve ran to the car. "Okay. Okay." He opened the passenger-side door and plopped into the front seat. "Thanks for the ride."

Danny started the engine, spun the car out of the parking lot, and hit the streets.

Steve dropped his head against the headrest. "You don't understand. It's bad. I need action, Danny."

"It'll come."

"No, I need it now. My mom asked me the other day at supper if I'd been feeling well lately. I said, 'Sure mom. I feel fine, why?' You know what she says?"

Danny shook his head.

"She says, 'Because you've been spending so much time in the bathroom, I figured you were coming down with something.'"

Danny laughed hard as he beat his hand against the steering wheel. "Oh boy. You think she knew?"

"I don't think so, but my dad sure did. I was so embarrassed. So was he. I can't talk about stuff like that, not even with my dad. He wouldn't look up from his dinner. His face turned as red as the beets on his plate."

Danny brought his laughter under control. "Oh gosh. That's horrible. Funny, but horrible."

"Tell me about it. Your old lady ever catch you too long in the john?"

"No."

"Ah, so you must be a two-minute man," Steve quipped.

Danny raised a fist as if to punch Steve.

"I'm kidding," Steve said. "Gosh, take a joke."

"I can take a joke. I wasn't gonna hit you, you little girl."

Steve looked pensively out the passenger window. "But I'm serious. This whole chick thing is driving me crazy. I'm sick of dating kittens. I need a girl who's fast. She's gotta be active, Danny. And I can't talk to the other guys about this because they've gone a lot further than I have and wouldn't understand."

"They *say* they've gone a lot further than you," Danny corrected. "But you don't really know what the truth is, so no sense in comparing yourself."

"I suppose so." Steve shifted his gaze to Danny. "Listen, I know it's none of my business, but the girls you've dated aren't known for being easy and neither is Annabel. So maybe this'll be good for you, too. Mary Sue guarantees you bona fide action, and I'm not just talkin' about snogging in the backseat or coppin' a feel over her sweater. She's legit action."

Danny stared at the road ahead, but didn't say a word.

"You don't have to be embarrassed," Steve said.

"I'm not embarrassed," Danny replied with little conviction.

"I'm in the same boat. The girls I like aren't fast, either. That's the problem."

"Then go out with a fast girl if it bothers you so much."

"I tried that once. Remember Sally Brummer?"

"She graduated last year, right?"

"Yeah. I took her out once."

Danny frowned. "You took out Sally Brummer? She went out with the entire basketball team."

"What can I say? I was desperate."

"So what happened?"

"Nothing," Steve replied flatly.

"Nothing? Wait. Are you telling me the girl that made it with the entire varsity basketball team wouldn't make it with you?"

"No dipstick, of course she would've made it with me, but just as we were getting there I couldn't do it. All the guys she'd been with popped into my head."

Danny considered this. "Like Paul Chancey?"

Steve nodded. "Yeah, like Paul Chancey."

"Eric Kramer?"

"Yeah, him too."

"That guy was awful lookin'. That woulda ruined it for me, too." Danny pulled up to a red light.

"But it wasn't just that. I wasn't so sure how I'd compare, you know? I mean, I want a girl who'll make it with me, but I also want one who hasn't made it with anyone else."

Danny thought about it. "What's Beth like?"

Steve shrugged. "Your guess is as good as mine. I don't think she's made it with anyone yet, which probably means she won't make it with me, either. But, if I get her to like me, I mean *really* like me, then maybe she'll make it with me. What do you think?"

The light turned green and Danny stepped on the gas. "I think . . . I think you should stop thinking so much. Just like how I'm always telling you on the field, the more you think, the more pressure you put on yourself and you drop the ball. You always drop the ball when you think too much."

Steve let out a small laugh that snowballed into full-blown enthusiasm. "That's right. You *are* always telling me that. And I *do* always drop the ball. But when I'm not weighing myself down worrying about making the play, that's when I catch a pass for a touchdown."

"See?" Danny pressed harder on the gas and the car sped down the road.

"Okay. So that's what I'll do. I'll take her out and I won't even think about making it with her. But, man, I hope she doesn't wear a tight sweater. She's so stacked it'll be hard not to think about anything but making it with her if she wears a tight sweater."

Danny laughed. "You'll be fine."

"Does this mean you'll come along?"

"Steve . . ." Danny hesitated. "You . . . you need to ask somebody else."

Steve slapped his hand against his thigh. "Come on, Danny. I already told you that she won't go with anyone else. You're not going steady with Annabel. You took her to one lousy dance. You know how much this means to me."

"What'd I tell you before I let you in my car? No hassling, remember?"

They didn't talk the rest of the way until Danny pulled up in front of Steve's house.

Steve turned to Danny. "Look, I'm sorry I'm bothering you with this. It's just . . . I can't go to college a virgin. I just can't. I couldn't take it if a girl was more experienced than me, and college girls are different than high school girls. They're more mature and . . . knowledgeable."

Danny listened quietly.

"If you're in the same situation as me, and I'm not saying you are, but if you are, then you should consider it, too. This time next year you'll be in college and it'll be hard enough fitting into a new school while trying to prove yourself to a new team and a new coach. Do you really want the extra pressure of worrying if a girl's gone further than you have? Having a girl laugh in your face?"

"No girl's gonna laugh in my face," Danny shot back.

"Then make sure of it. If Mary Sue's offering then use her as practice. It might even be good for Annabel."

"How would me making it with Mary Sue be good for Annabel?"

"Because if you finally do it you won't pester her for it because you'll already have done it."

"I'm not pestering Annabel about anything."

"Not yet," Steve said.

"And I never said I haven't done it."

"You never said you have."

Danny turned away from Steve and peered out the driver-side window.

"Listen," Steve began. "I don't care what you have or haven't done, but we've been friends for a long time. I know how your old man is. He's got you wound up so damn tight with all his lectures about doing the right thing and taking the moral high road—all the damn time. He's been cramming that garbage down your throat since we were kids. Heck, it's the reason I stopped coming around so much. And it was a shame too because your mom stocks the best refrigerator in town."

Danny ignored Steve's attempt at humor. "What's your point?"

"My point is there's nothing wrong with messing up once in a while. I mean, what makes you so special that you always have to be so damn perfect?"

"I'm not special and I'm not perfect," Danny stated plainly.

"Exactly. So go on this date with Mary Sue, and if it ends up being a mistake, oh well, so you screwed up like the rest of us do all the time."

Danny let Steve's words sink in.

"There's nothing wrong with admitting you want action."

DANNY LAY IN his bed with his fingers intertwined behind his head as he stared at the ceiling. A sports magazine splayed open across his stomach and a small lamp burned dimly on the nightstand.

Danny thought about Mary Sue while he contemplated the prospect of going to college a virgin. Despite being a star athlete, he hadn't gone any further with girls than Steve. Since freshman year, he had been showcased in the sports section of the town's local paper. Most girls knew his name before he even had the chance to introduce himself, but his father had instilled in him at a young age that he was to work hard at football and not get distracted by anything, especially girls.

That direction had been fine with Danny while he was still young enough to find girls a nuisance—like flies buzzing around his head that needed swatting away. But once his interest in girls matured and the opposite sex started to fill out in places Danny couldn't ignore, he got distracted.

He had his first serious girlfriend freshman year. The first game she watched him play, Danny was so nervous he threw for three interceptions, more interceptions than he had thrown in his previous five games combined. Danny was forcing passes and overthrowing receivers. His team had lost badly that day, and when more games like that followed, his father confronted him.

"Danny," Mr. Winfield had said in his usual even tone. "There's a time for everything in life. I know you're curious about the opposite sex, but now is not the time for girls. You've worked too hard to succumb to distraction. You're in high school now. Colleges are watching you. You're the best quarterback in the county, maybe even the state. I'm not expecting you to ignore girls, but your priorities are to be your studies and football. That is your future. Do you understand?"

Danny had understood then just as he understood now. He casually dated, but not too seriously to ever get distracted again. Finding girls to go out with was easy for school jocks. Girls, especially the ones with reputations, naturally gravitated toward the athletes, especially the star athlete.

Danny folded up the sports magazine and tossed it to the floor. He switched off the lamp and turned onto his side. He didn't call Annabel that night as he had planned. He didn't feel right talking to her while he considered going on a date with another girl.

He was a virgin, and like Steve, he was thinking maybe it wasn't such a good idea to go to college a virgin.

ANNABEL WENT TO bed relieved that Danny hadn't called her like he said he would. She shouldn't have given him her phone number, knowing how irate her father would be if he found out, so she'd concocted a plan. Annabel didn't have a phone in her room and would need her mother's help.

"If the phone rings you must answer it before he does," Annabel had instructed Joan. "If it's Danny, you have to pretend it's Molly or Donna."

Joan had been hesitant about the plan. "I think I've kept enough from your father. Don't you?"

"What am I going to tell him if he finds out that a boy called for me? He'll flip."

"Annabel, really. I wished you'd think things through better. Why did you give this boy your number?"

"Because it's Danny. I'm in high school. I should be able to get phone calls from boys. Girls at school tell stories about how they talk to boys for hours on the phone. This is another normal teenage thing I can't do."

"Are Donna and Molly talking to boys for hours on the phone?"

"Well . . . no, but they could if boys wanted to talk to them for hours on the phone. That's the point."

"Fine," Joan had said after a long consideration. "I'll make sure your father doesn't answer the phone, but like the dance, he can't ever find out."

"He won't," Annabel assured. "Just be sure to answer the phone when I'm not around. Maybe you can convince him to put a phone in my room."

Joan shook her head. "No way. That's not a battle I'm in the mood to fight right now. If you talk in the kitchen or use the phone in the hallway while he's watching TV, it should be okay. But you can't talk for hours like those other girls."

"I won't. Besides, I don't even know what we would talk about for that long."

Joan smiled. "It'll be awkward at first, but then you'll relax and the two of you will talk about everything."

"I hope so."

For the rest of the night Annabel had jumped every time the phone rang. Joan had done a great job at getting to the phone quickly, not that George ever rushed to answer the phone, but all that work had been for nothing because Danny never called.

The next morning, Annabel rushed out of the house, embarrassed, and made little eye contact with her mother. She had all but assured Joan that Danny was going to call her, but then he never did.

She walked to school, unsure what had caused Danny to change his mind, nervous he was no longer interested in her. But those nerves were calmed when she arrived at school and found Danny standing at her locker.

"Hi," Danny said as Annabel approached him.

"Hey." Annabel clutched her books.

"I'm sorry I never called last night." Danny crossed his arms over his varsity jacket. "Football practice ran late. Then I had a ton of homework to do. Mr. Barnes is killing me in English. You wouldn't believe how many papers he has us writing."

"I've heard that about Barnes. He's supposed to be a tough class."

"He is. Plus Coach is riding us pretty hard. We have a big game this Friday and . . ."

"I get it, Danny," Annabel interrupted. "You have a lot going on. It's okay. You're busy and don't have time to call or time for . . . anything else."

"Whoa." Danny stepped closer to her. "That's not what I was going to say. Do you go to football games?"

Annabel shook her head. "Me and Molly and Donna wanted to go to some last year, but we were just freshman and didn't really know anyone . . ."

"You know me now," Danny interrupted. "And I want you to come to one of the games. We're away this Friday, but we play at home next weekend. Think you can go?"

"You really want me to come to your game?"

"I haven't asked a girl to come see me play in a while, but I like the thought of looking into the stands and seeing your face."

The first bell rang, sending students shuffling quickly through the halls.

Danny took Annabel's books from her. "Let me carry these for you. You have Kroger first period, right?"

"I do." Annabel walked beside him, her shoulder grazing his arm.

She had never felt so visible walking the halls of her school. She used to blend in with her classmates, barely eliciting a simple glance her way. Now, every pair of eyes she passed fell on her like a laser.

The whispers were audible. "They're really together?" "What's the captain of the football team doing with her?" "I thought he took her to the dance as a joke."

Danny had to have heard the murmurs and noticed the gawking, but he walked tall, and his confidence never faltered. Annabel kept her gaze to the floor as she walked, uncomfortable with her newfound popularity.

"Thanks for walking me to class," Annabel said outside the classroom door.

"Sure."

"There she is. Why didn't you wait for us, Bel?" Donna ran up behind Annabel, saw Danny, and covered her mouth with her hand. "Sorry, I didn't see you there."

"It's okay. Sorry I stole Annabel from you," Danny said.

"It's fine." Donna giggled nervously.

Danny handed Annabel her books. "I'll see you later then."

"Okay," Annabel said and watched Danny walk away.

"Oh my gosh, Annabel. He walked you to class? You walked the halls with Danny Winfield." Molly squeezed her books and leaned on her tiptoes.

"Don't flip your wig, Molly," Donna said. "Annabel went to a dance with Danny. Of course she's gonna walk the halls with him."

"That is so cool," Molly said.

Annabel and Donna laughed at Molly.

"What? It is cool," Molly insisted.

The second bell rang and they filed into the room alongside their classmates.

Chapter Ten

ANNABEL SAT ON her bedroom window's ledge and watched the sun set, enjoying one of the rare peaceful moments her home offered. She could see through her neighbor's window. Sylvia was sitting alone at the kitchen table, crying over a bowl of soup, and Annabel knew that meant Henry was on another business trip. The only time Sylvia was that miserable was when Henry was away, and she cried a lot. Annabel didn't mean to snoop on her neighbor, but the height of her bedroom window gave the perfect view into the kitchen.

Annabel opened the window and climbed down the tree. She walked around her neighborhood, looking through the windows of the homes she passed. She huddled near a tree and watched a young pregnant woman and her husband. The woman appeared only months away from giving birth, and the man rubbed his wife's swollen belly as they watched TV snuggled on the couch, a bowl of pretzels between them.

Their feet were propped up on the table in front of them, and the woman rested her head on the man's shoulder. Annabel watched as the man fed his wife a pretzel and sweetly kissed the top of her round belly.

Annabel wondered if her own parents had, in any way, resembled this happy young couple and if her own father had kissed her mother's belly when she was in there. She tried to imagine her parents this much in love, but nothing about their present marriage enabled such an image.

She watched the couple a little while longer and then made her way back home without stopping by Danny's house. She no longer needed the comfort that watching Danny through his window once gave her. She had him in real life now.

Annabel was walking toward the tree outside her window when she heard her name.

Annabel froze, believing at first that the voice belonged to her mother and that she'd just been caught, but then she relaxed knowing her mother never called her "Bel."

"Bel, over here!" the voice called out louder.

Annabel looked across her front lawn and saw Sylvia sitting on her front porch swing, under the porch light.

Sylvia waved her over.

"Bel, what are you doing out here all alone?" Sylvia's painted red lips matched the color of her manicured nails. With her eyes lined in black and her lashes curled, she looked like a Hollywood actress.

"I was walking around town," Annabel replied casually.

She didn't share her nightly adventures with anyone, but she didn't mind sharing them with her eccentric neighbor.

"Mmmm." Sylvia drew in a deep breath and leaned back in the bench swing. "I love a good walk, too." She patted the spot next to her. "Sit with me, sweetie." She scooted over. "I like having the company."

Annabel sat down.

"Do you always walk alone at night?" Sylvia asked.

"Yes."

"What do you do on these walks alone at night?"

"Look through people's windows."

"You do what?" Sylvia perked up.

"Look through people's windows," Annabel said again.

"What do you do that for?"

"To see how they live and compare it to my own life."

"That's remarkable and very insightful for a girl your age."

"Thank you." Annabel tried not to show her giddiness at the coolest woman she knew calling her remarkable.

"You're welcome."

"Can I ask you something?" Annabel tucked her fingers underneath her thighs.

"You can ask me anything you want, sweetie."

"Why do you wear makeup like that when you're alone?"

Sylvia ran a finger over her caked lips and smiled. "In case Henry surprises me and comes home early. Maybe it's too much"—she tilted back her head and touched her rosy cheeks—"but getting ready to see Henry makes me happy and I need to be happy. For reasons I don't always understand, I get sad."

Annabel got sad too, but for reasons she completely understood.

"I never liked being alone much," Sylvia said. "I'm glad I saw you tonight."

"Me too. I like being here."

Sylvia smiled. "And I like having you here, especially when Henry's gone. I would take walks alone too if it didn't make me miss Henry so. Walks just aren't the same without my Henry beside me holding my hand or kissing my forehead."

"I don't mind being alone if the alternative is dreadful company."

"You really are insightful for your age. Have you had much dreaded company in your young life?"

A conversation about her father wasn't something Annabel wanted to engage in. "No. But I've read a lot of books filled with all kinds of situations."

"That's good. Keep reading. Stay smart. Me? I never liked it. Have a hard time concentrating on all those words page after page." Sylvia pulled a pack of cigarettes from the pocket of her beige slacks and placed the cig in its silver holder. She drew deeply on the tip and a cloud of smoke rose from her red-coated lips. "I saw you leaving your house last weekend with a boy. You looked very pretty."

"Thank you. We went to a dance."

"Ohhh. How exciting. I remember the first time I danced with a boy." Sylvia paused for another pull on her cigarette. "There's nothing quite like it, is there?"

"It was the best night of my life."

"What's this boy's name?"

"Danny."

"That's a good name. Is he your boyfriend?"

"I'm . . . I'm not sure, but I think he likes me."

Sylvia laughed and knocked the ashes off her cigarette. "He took you to a dance, honey. Of course he likes you."

"He carried my books to class today, and he wants me to go to his football game next Friday."

Sylvia nudged Annabel gently in the shoulder with the tip of her elbow. "See? Sounds like this boy is crazy about you."

"But yesterday he told me he'd call me, but never did."

"Well"—Sylvia leaned back and rested the cigarette holder between her slender fingers—"boys get nervous, too. I'm sure he had his reasons."

"He told me he had football practice and a lot of studies."

"See? That's all it was. He didn't call you because he was busy, not because he didn't want to talk to you. Sounds like you have an honest boyfriend."

"I never said he was my boyfriend, but . . . why do you say he's honest?"

"Because he didn't have to give you a reason at all. He could have just not called you and have been done with it. But he considered your feelings and felt he owed you an explanation. Not many men feel they owe a woman anything. They just do what they want."

"Danny's not like that."

Sylvia inhaled her cigarette one last time, pulled the cigarette out of its holder, and tossed the butt into the bushes. "Then you better hang on to him." She tapped the top of Annabel's nose with her finger. "He's one of the good ones."

Though Annabel could have talked with Sylvia all night, she had to get home. "I have to go now. I can't stay out too late. I never know when my mom's gonna come knockin' on my bedroom door."

"I understand. But what if she's knocking on your door right now and you're not there?"

"Hopefully, she'll think I'm sleeping and won't want to wake me. You won't tell my mom you saw me out, will you?"

Sylvia smiled as her blonde hair swayed against the soft breeze. "It'll be our little secret and whoever else's you tell."

"I don't plan on telling anyone else. Goodnight." Annabel ran across Sylvia's lawn and past her own front yard.

"Hey, I thought you were going home!" Sylvia called out.

"I am."

"Then where are you going?"

"I can't walk in through there." Annabel pointed to the front door. "They'll see me."

"Then how do you get inside your house?"

"I climb a tree and crawl in through my window."

"Of course you do." Sylvia shook her head in amazement. "You truly are a remarkable girl, Annabel."

"Does that mean we can sit together and talk again sometime?"

"I'd like that." Sylvia waved goodbye to Annabel.

Annabel got back into her room and cracked open her bedroom door. She heard George's rumbling snores coming from his room. She wasn't surprised he was dead asleep given how much he had to drink at dinner.

She tiptoed down the stairs and peeked over the banister, into the living room. Joan was busy knitting on the couch, and Annabel was relieved she'd gotten away with another night of sneaking out.

She went back to her room and dressed for bed, knowing that Sylvia was right. Danny was one of the good ones.

STEVE DROVE TO the bowling alley with the windows down and Buddy Holly cranked up on the radio. Beth sat beside him in the front seat, and Danny and Mary Sue were in the back. Steve gave a side glance to Beth and zeroed in on her weighted chest.

Steve caught Danny's eye in the rear-view mirror and gave him a wink and a wicked grin. Danny knew immediately what was on Steve's mind and quickly looked away. He didn't share the same excitement about the night's prospects as Steve, and he regretted going, even if his own prospects included Mary Sue, the leader of the cheerleading squad and most popular girl in school.

Mary Sue slid closer to Danny until their thighs touched. Danny could hear her trying to get his attention but continued to stare out the window.

"Do you like my sweater, Danny?" she asked.

Danny looked at her. "Huh?"

"My sweater. Do you like it?" She leaned closer to Danny and stuck out her chest, the embroidered rose across her white sweater was almost in his face. "My mother had this made especially for me because I love roses. They're my favorite flower."

Mary Sue's long blonde hair was held back in a red headband. Her hair settled evenly across her shoulders and curled up at the bottom. Her lips were colored with bright red lipstick, and heavy mascara darkened her eyelashes.

Beth was a plainer version of Mary Sue. Her brown hair was cut in a bob. She wore a light shade of lipstick and hardly any eye makeup. Like Mary Sue, she was also a cheerleader, but was less flashy about it.

They got to the bowling alley, and Danny and Steve went to the counter to buy the shoe rentals.

"I can't believe I let you talk me into doing this." Danny slipped off his shoes.

"What are you complaining about? Did you even notice how easy Mary Sue looks tonight? That sweater's practically plastered on her. She can't wear a tighter sweater than she's wearing tonight. And that, my friend, is for you. You keep that sour puss look on your face, and I'll give you a knuckle sandwich just for being such a wet rag. It's Saturday night. Lace up your shoes, and let's have some fun."

They walked back to the girls and handed them their rentals.

After Danny's fourth gutter ball, Steve pulled him to the side.

"What's eating you?"

Danny usually had fun bowling, and even while goofing around and not trying very hard, he was usually pretty good at it. "I can't get a strike every time."

"But do you have to get gutter balls every time? You're bringing down our score, and I don't enjoy losing to girls."

Beth and Mary Sue had playfully challenged the boys to a game.

"I have a lot on my mind right now." Danny couldn't stop thinking about Annabel.

"*I'm* the one being watched by ol' creepy eyes over there." Steve motioned to a man with big wide eyes staring in their direction as he wiped down the counter.

Steve had told Danny that Beth's father knew the man who ran the place and probably had instructed him to keep an eye on Beth.

"I gotta cut out. I can't take those pesky eyes glaring at me all night." Steve fished his hand into his pocket for his car keys.

"I agreed to go bowling. That's all," Danny quickly replied.

"Quit being a drag. We don't have much time before I gotta get Beth home. Let's split."

They crowded into Steve's car and drove around town, searching for something to do.

"We can stop at the diner," Beth said.

"Or we can go to the drive-in," Mary Sue suggested and slid closer to Danny.

"Sure, I can go for a flick." Steve made a U-turn for the theater.

"I'll have to call my house." Beth pulled change from her purse. "Ask my parents for a later curfew."

Mary Sue rolled her eyes. "I'm so glad my parents pulled curfews for me after junior high."

"It's really just a formality. All I have to do is call them and tell them I'll be coming home later. It's like not having a curfew at all. My parents just need to *feel* like they're in charge of me when really I end up doing whatever I want anyway."

"How about you, Danny-boy?" Steve looked at Danny through the rear-view mirror. "You up for a flick?"

Danny felt trapped in the backseat with Mary Sue and suddenly going to college a virgin didn't seem so bad. There was no part of him that wanted to be with Mary Sue. Yet he agreed to the movie only to get the night moving along.

"A flick it is!" Steve yelled.

"What's playing?" Beth asked.

"Who cares?" Mary Sue replied.

The conversation on the way to the drive-in was dominated by Beth going on a rant about how the cheerleaders were just as important to the school as the football players. While Steve couldn't hold back his laughter, Danny kept his opinion to himself.

"How can you even think that you paper-shakers are just as important to the school as the football players?" Steve asked Beth. "While we're on the field no one even notices you girls."

"Trust me. *I* get noticed, and I am *more* than just a paper-shaker," Mary Sue said in a cocky tone. She turned to Danny. "You don't think we're invisible out there, do you, Danny? I mean, I like to think that when you boys are down, it's us who help get you up and back in the game."

"Sure, Dolly." Steve tossed a sarcastic grin her way. "You help get us up, doesn't she, Danny? In fact, I'm getting up right now just thinking about you girls in your little skirts and big pom-poms." He glanced down at his pants.

Beth slapped him across his shoulder. "That's disgusting. We work hard out there, too."

"Yeah, you should see how loud the crowd gets when we start our cheers. Like last night, the crowd was so loud we couldn't even hear ourselves," Mary Sue proudly proclaimed.

"The crowd was screaming last night because Danny threw another thirty-yard touchdown pass caught by yours truly. No cheer's gonna beat that. Ain't that right, Danny-boy?" Steve raised his hand behind him and waited for Danny to clap hands with him.

Danny sighed and slapped his hand.

"We're winning State this year, Danny! State!" Steve yelled.

Danny laughed. Steve was relaxed and acting every bit of his usual self, devoid of any of the insecurities he had expressed only a couple nights ago.

"Are you always this quiet?" Mary Sue asked Danny.

"Danny does his talking on the field and as far as I'm concerned, that's the only chatter that matters," Steve answered.

"I wasn't asking you, Steve, so just hush. I was asking Danny." Mary Sue turned her body to Danny. She pulled off her headband and ran her fingers through her soft hair. "Why are you being so quiet?"

"Am I?"

"Yes." She slid closer to him. "I can't imagine you'd be more nervous with little ol' me than over a big football game."

"I'm not nervous," Danny said.

"Really?"

"Yes." Danny avoided her eyes.

"Well you look nervous."

Beth turned around to the backseat. "Gosh, Mary Sue, let it go already. He's not nervous."

"Oh, you hush, too," Mary Sue said. "Our friends talk too much, don't they, Danny."

"Is that so, Mary Sue?" Steve asked. "Well I know a place we can go where we don't have to talk at all. We can just park our car and never say another word."

Mary Sue popped her head over the front seat. "Let's go."

"Really?" Steve asked, excitingly surprised.

Beth looked cautiously at Mary Sue. "We don't even know what place he's talking about."

"I don't care. I love surprises." Mary Sue smiled.

"I think you should take us home, Steve," Beth said.

"But don't you want to find out what place I was talking about?" he asked.

"No," Beth replied flatly.

Steve pressed his head against the seat. "We don't have to call it a night. We can still catch a movie."

Beth shook her head. "I don't feel like it anymore."

"How come?" Steve asked.

"Yeah, how come?" Mary Sue repeated. "The night's still young. There's a payphone up ahead. Call your parents. And forget about the movie. I wanna go to that place."

"Mary Sue," Beth warned. "Stop it."

"Wait a minute. I'm the head of the cheerleaders. You're not. So you don't get to tell me what to do. I tell *you* what to do."

"We're not on the field right now, are we? So I don't have to listen to you."

Mary Sue clenched her right hand into a tight ball, her body stiffened, and her shoulders straightened. "Yes, you do. The football players listen to Danny even when they're not on the field."

"Hey." Steve looked up. "No we don't."

"Oh, yes you do," Mary Sue yelled. "And I don't wanna go to some stupid movie. Take us to that place."

"Great." Steve made a quick turn. "It's this way."

"Mary Sue, I already told you—" Beth started.

"Steve," Danny said. "Forget the movie and forget that place. It's time to go home."

With a heavy sigh, Steve listened to Danny just like he did on the field and steered the car toward Beth's house without saying another word. Mary Sue, being equally as upset as Steve, also kept silent as she crumbled to the other side of the car, away from Danny.

HUGH WINFIELD WAS in the living room, sitting in his reading chair, when Danny walked into the house. He lowered his newspaper and glanced at his watch. "Home already?"

A thick bookcase was steadily mounted behind him, lined with classic literature and scholarly magazines. Hugh Winfield had brown hair like Danny and shared the same warm smile and marked dimple on his right cheek.

"Yep." Danny tossed his jacket over the staircase railing. "Is mom home?"

"Not yet. It's bridge night," Mr. Winfield replied.

Danny sighed and dropped onto the couch. "Home before my mother on a Saturday night."

Hugh let out a lighthearted laugh. "I'm sure you'll find there are worse things in life, son." He folded the paper and set it on his lap. He took off his reading glasses and gave Danny his full attention. "Everything okay?"

"Sure," Danny lied.

"Were you out with the football team?"

"No. I was with Steve and a couple girls."

"Your mother tells me you took George Turner's daughter to a dance."

"Her name's Annabel."

"Is that one of the girls you were with tonight?" Mr. Winfield asked.

Danny shook his head and washed his hands over his face. "No." He leaned forward, pressing his elbows against his knees. "I went out with a girl tonight that I don't even like."

"Why would you do that?"

"It's complicated."

"I hope it's not so complicated that it's distracting you from your studies or football."

"You know I wouldn't let that happen," Danny said.

"That's right. I do know that. You played an excellent game last night and have a big home game next week."

"I know."

"This is gearing up to be a big season. Your last year and you're looking at a State championship."

"Yes, sir."

"So tell me, is Annabel the girl you like?"

"Yes," Danny responded.

"Then why would you go out with someone you don't like and leave at home the girl you do like?"

Danny shook his head. "I can't tell you why. I have no good reason."

"Does this Annabel like you?" Hugh Winfield continued.

"Yes."

"Then it shouldn't be complicated at all, but now you feel guilty for taking out this other girl."

"Very."

"This is a good lesson for you, son." Hugh leaned back into his chair and kept his eyes on Danny. "You should feel guilty."

Danny dropped his gaze to the floor. He shouldn't have expected anything but a direct response from his father. Excuses, exceptions, nor circumstances were ever accepted as reasons for not doing the right thing. As far as Hugh Winfield was concerned, right was right and wrong was wrong, no matter what. A man's situation shouldn't affect his ability to do the moral thing.

"Son, don't look to the floor when you're speaking to someone. What have I always told you?" His voice was calm and held no hint of anger or disappointment. It was that lack of emotion that made everything he said all the more soberer.

Danny raised his head and looked his father in the eyes. "A man who cannot speak while looking another man in the eye is no man at all."

"That's right, and when you're out on that football field the ones hanging their heads are either afraid or have already given up. Do you understand that?"

"Yes, sir."

Hugh placed the paper on a small end table and crossed his legs. "If you didn't want to go out with this girl tonight, then why did you?"

"Steve wanted—"

"Already using the wrong words," Hugh interrupted. "You don't do things just because someone else wants you to. How long have I been telling you this?"

"I know, but I didn't want to let him down. You can understand that, can't you? He's my friend, my teammate."

"I understand the loyalty a boy feels to his friends, but is it worth compromising the values I've spent years instilling in you?"

"No, sir." Danny swallowed.

"I'm hard on you, Danny. I know that, but it's because I don't like seeing you the way you're looking right now—defeated and ashamed. You've let yourself down."

"I know I did." Danny stood and shoved his hands into his pockets.

"You don't have to play follow the leader when you are the leader. Remember that." Mr. Winfield slid his glasses back on, picked the paper off the table, and opened it up across his lap.

"I'll remember that. Goodnight." Danny turned to leave the room.

"Also," Hugh continued. Danny stopped. "I hope you're not getting too attached to any girl. Before you know it, you'll be packed up and leaving on a bus for college."

"Yes, sir." Danny left the room, and Hugh Winfield went back to his paper.

Even though his father had been a teenager once too, Danny couldn't tell him the reason he went on the date was to lose his virginity before he went to college, when all he could think about was Annabel.

Chapter Eleven

"WHOLE LOTTA SHAKIN' Goin' On" rocked on the radio as Annabel, Molly, and Donna danced across Molly's bedroom. They followed Jerry Lee Lewis's order to shake it one time for him and to get real low. They wiggled and shook their bodies until the song faded out and the girls dropped where they stood, giggling with all the energy they could muster.

Annabel landed on the floor while Molly and Donna fell onto the bed. They panted heavily as they tried to catch their breath.

"He's so wild." Annabel splayed her arms across the beige carpet.

"That's why they call him The Killer," Molly said. "I sure do love that song. My mother would kill me if she heard us playing it. She hates Jerry Lee."

"Most parents do," Donna said. "They know what shaking means."

"Oh my gosh, Donna," Molly said. "You're so bad."

"You always say that," Donna said.

"Because you are."

"I know." Donna laughed, and turned her attention to Annabel. "Hey, Bel. Are you gonna shake it with Danny?"

"Donna!" Molly yelled. "Annabel's not that kind of a girl. Right, Bel?"

Annabel didn't respond right away. She'd never had a boyfriend before. Maybe she wasn't sure what kind of a girl she was.

Molly yelled louder, "Bel!"

"What? Of course not." Annabel jumped up from the floor. "Why are we even talking about this?"

"But have you thought about what you'd do if Danny asked you to go"—Molly stopped and made sure her bedroom door was closed tight—"all the way."

"Yeah. Have you thought about that?" Donna sat up on the bed.

"I think . . ." Annabel didn't want to talk about that and took a couple steps toward the bed. "I think it's time . . . for a pillow fight!" She snatched a pillow from behind Molly and smacked Molly and Donna with it until they grabbed pillows, and they all hit each other with their fluffy weapons until they tired and collapsed onto the bed.

It was Saturday night. They were having a sleepover at Molly's. Annabel hadn't talked to Danny since Friday morning at school, when he apologized for not calling her. She had spent most of Saturday afternoon keeping close to the phone in case Danny called, but once again, he never did.

They sprawled on the bed as their breathing returned to normal.

Annabel stared at the ceiling. "I don't have to think about what I'd say to Danny if he asks me to go all the way with him because he wouldn't ask me to do that. He'd know that a girl like me is waiting for marriage."

"What if he asks you to marry him?" Donna asked.

"That's crazy. He's only asked me to a dance. Besides, he hasn't even called when he said he'd call me."

"Oh, Bel. He'll call," Molly said. "He took you to a dance *and* he personally asked you to be at his game next week. He likes you. You don't have to worry about that."

"I hope so."

Donna sat up and snatched a box of cookies that was sitting on the nightstand and shoved one into her mouth. "You know, Annabel," she said as she chewed. "I think you're thinking too much. I know it's overwhelming to be dating the high school quarterback and the cutest boy in school, but maybe you should try to relax and just go with it."

"Relax and just go with it?" Annabel sat up and looked at her friends. "You guys have been total spazzes throughout all of this and now you're telling me to just go with it?"

Donna set the cookies down. "It's Danny. How could we not be total spazzes about Danny?"

"I saw Danny watching you the other day in the halls." Molly sat crossed-legged on the bed. "You didn't see him, but, boy was he watching you. He didn't take his eyes off you. It's like he was in a trance. He's on the hook with you. Trust me."

"I'm not so sure about that," Annabel replied.

"Then you're not paying attention." Molly took a cookie and bit into it. "I sure hope a boy looks at me that way someday."

"He will." Annabel smiled.

"I know girls who have done it," Donna said.

"You have?" Molly jumped to her knees. "Who?"

There were enough rumors that went around school about easy girls to fill an entire night of gossip.

"I heard some of the junior and senior girls talking in the locker room about stuff they did. Do you know the difference between petting and heavy petting?" Donna asked.

Annabel and Molly shook their heads.

Donna sighed. "It's okay if Molly doesn't know the difference because she doesn't have anyone."

"Hey," Molly said.

"But you need to know the difference Annabel," Donna continued. "What if Danny wants to do those things and you have no idea how to do them?"

"Wha . . . what kinds of things?" Annabel asked.

"Come on, Bel. He's a boy," Donna said.

"And he's a senior," Molly added. "But whatever you do, Bel, don't be one of those girls who disappears for nine months and comes back and tells everyone she had to care for an out-of-state relative. We've all heard that story before."

"We sure have," Donna added.

"Whoa." Annabel leapt off the bed. "I'm not even thinking about that stuff."

"Not even a little bit?" Molly asked.

"Yeah, not even a little bit?" Donna repeated. "It's Danny. The cutest and most popular boy in high school."

"Oh my gosh. How many times do you think you have to tell me that? I know he's the cutest and most popular boy in school. You don't have to keep reminding me of that. And I know there are a lot of girls at our school with reputations, but if that was all Danny wanted he would have asked one of those girls to the dance. But he didn't, he asked me."

"Sorry, Bel. You're right," Donna said. "Maybe that's not all Danny wants."

"My mom says that's all every boy wants," Molly said.

"I bet he wants to marry you," Donna said as she brushed cookie crumbs off her sweater.

"Gosh, guys. Will you stop it with the marriage thing?"

"Would it be the worst thing to get a marriage proposal from Danny? Most girls would jump off a cliff for a chance to get that. I know I would." Molly lay onto her back and stared at the ceiling. "He's so dreamy."

Annabel rolled her eyes. "Come off it, Molly. You two are acting like there's nothing else in the world than getting married."

"What else is there?" Donna asked.

"Are you serious?" Annabel sat beside her on the bed. "There's college. Don't you want to go to school and get a good job?"

Molly and Donna exchanged peculiar looks.

"Why would we want that?" Molly asked.

"Yeah, why would we want that? I just want to get married, live in a big house, and have lots of kids. Well, maybe not lots, two or three is enough," Donna said.

"What could be more perfect than that?" Molly asked.

Annabel listened to her friends talk about how many kids they wanted and how big their homes were going to be, but she wasn't interested in those things. Her first priority was to go to college. Marriage and kids would wait.

"Remember Angela? The girl who practically had a breakdown in the hallway last year because her boyfriend took back her engagement ring?" Molly asked.

"That's right. It was a week before graduation, and she was so frosted she was going to graduate without being engaged," Donna said. "Gosh, no girl wants that."

"I'd breakdown too if I thought I was getting married and then, bam, just like that, I'm not. Is there anything worse than that?" Molly asked.

"Are you guys saying you would accept a proposal from someone you don't love just so you could be engaged by graduation?"

"Hmmm." Molly hesitated. "You said I don't love him, but do I like him?"

"Molly. We're talking about marriage here. The man you would spend the rest of your life with. Don't you want to be in love?"

"This would work better if I had some examples. Name some guys in school," she said.

"Examples? Molly, it's a straightforward question. Would you say 'I do' to a boy you didn't love just to beat an artificial deadline like getting engaged before graduation?"

"But I can't answer that without knowing what boys you're referring to," Molly pressed.

"I am referring to any boy you don't love. What's so hard about this?"

"I thought the question was more about a boy we don't really love, but we don't hate either. So we like him a little. Was that the question?" Donna asked.

"Forget it," Annabel replied hopelessly and hopped off the bed.

"Why are you getting so upset?" Molly asked.

"I'm not upset."

"You seem like it. What gives?" Molly asked.

"I just can't understand why either of you can't say that you wouldn't marry someone you weren't truly in love with." Annabel crossed her arms. "I don't see why that'd be such a hard thing to say."

Donna slid to the edge of the bed and looked at Annabel and Molly. "I don't have either of yours bodies or looks. Of course I'd want to be in love with the man who asks me to marry him, but boys aren't falling over themselves for my hand. If I get a proposal from a boy who doesn't make me completely want to vomit, I'd be a fool not to take it. If he's a decent man, I'd learn to love him."

"Why are you selling yourself short like that?" Annabel asked. "You don't have to settle for anyone."

"Oh, come off it, Annabel." Donna stood up and raised her arms at her sides. "You see me. You're looking at me right now. I'm not beautiful."

"I saw Charlie talking to you after third period on Thursday," Molly said.

"Big deal." Donna fell back onto the bed.

"What'd he want?" Molly pressed.

"He wanted to know if I was going to the football game. I told him I couldn't go because I didn't have a ride because it was an away game, and he offered to drive me."

"What. A boy offered to give you a ride to a football game and you didn't tell us?" Molly plopped down beside her. "What's wrong with you?"

"He asked me because he thought I was hanging out with Danny after the game. He wanted to use me to get close to the star quarterback because my best friend's his girlfriend."

Molly slapped her forehead. "That explains it."

"Explains what?" Annabel asked.

"Explains why when I drop something—my books, a pencil—five guys fall to the ground to pick it up, but it's not just the boys. Did you know Peggy Sue asked me what I was doing this weekend? She's never said one word to me in the two years we've been in the same classes." Molly looked at Annabel. "This is all because of you. Nobody noticed us before."

Annabel sat down between her Donna and Molly on the bed. "This is all because of Danny. Same things are happening to me."

"They're just using us," Molly said.

"They sure are," Donna added. "And it doesn't feel too good."

"You know what?" Annabel asked. "Who cares if it's not genuine? This is high school. How much of it is real anyway? If they want to use us to get close to Danny, then let's use them for what they're offering. Donna, if you wanted to go to the game and needed a ride, then you should have taken it. Listen, I don't know what's gonna happen with Danny, but I do know this is his last year here. Let's make the best of it. No more talk about proposals, kids, or anything else that doesn't matter right now."

"You're right," Molly said. "We're popular right now and we've never been popular before. Who would have thought that would ever happen?"

"Not me!" Donna yelled.

"Let's enjoy this. One for all." Annabel stuck her hand in the middle of them.

"And all for one!" Molly and Donna called out in unison as they clamped their hands together.

ANNABEL SHOVED HER books into her locker and felt a sharp nudge at her arm. She turned around, and Mary Sue was standing in front of her, a squad of cheerleaders gathered behind her.

"What are you and Danny?" Mary Sue demanded.

"What?" Annabel asked.

"Even though I can't imagine Danny would go steady with *you*." A sordid expression smeared across Mary Sue's face. "I have to ask, are you and Danny actually going steady?"

Annabel pressed her back against the lockers as she gazed at the hostile faces staring back at her. "We . . . we went to the dance together."

"Yeah. I know you went to the dance together," Mary Sue said with a harsh attitude. "But I heard you two were going steady. Has Danny actually asked you to go steady?"

"I'm . . . I'm not sure," Annabel answered quietly.

Mary Sue pressed a hand against her hip. "Does he think you're going steady?"

Annabel didn't say anything.

"She doesn't even know," one of the other cheerleaders standing behind Mary Sue shouted, and all the girls laughed.

Mary Sue twirled the ends of her long blonde hair. "Poor, Danny, he has no idea what he passed up to be with you. If I were going steady with him, I'd make sure he knew it . . . if you know what I mean." She looked Annabel over. "But you probably don't."

Mary Sue and her crew walked away, their laughter blasting through the halls. The last of their shadows barely disappeared around the corridor as Molly and Donna ran to Annabel and grabbed at her arms.

"What is it? What's wrong?" Annabel asked.

"Danny went out with Mary Sue Saturday night," Donna blurted loudly.

"What are you talking about?" Annabel shook her arms free from her friends' grips.

"It's true," Molly said. "I'm so sorry, Bel."

"Danny's a jerk and a liar." Donna slammed her fist against Annabel's locker.

"It can't be true," Annabel replied.

"We heard it in the halls," Molly said.

"Yeah, we heard it in the halls," Donna repeated.

"The halls? You want me to take something for fact because you heard it in the halls?"

"Bel," Molly somberly said. "Betsy said it."

"Betsy?" Annabel defeatedly fell back against the lockers. "Betsy said Danny went out with Mary Sue on Saturday night?"

Annabel didn't want to cry in the middle of the hallway, but if Betsy said it, then it was true. Betsy knew everything about everything. She was editor of the school paper, and if she said something happened, it happened. Her sources were as solid as her reputation was for accuracy.

"What are you gonna do, Bel?" Donna clung to Annabel's side.

"We went to one dance, right? One stupid dance." Annabel backed away from her friends. "I have to get to class."

Annabel left Molly and Donna and walked the halls alone, feeling the stares and hearing the whispers and giggles at her back. Danny had made a fool of her. He'd taken her to a dance for the whole school to see and then he went on a date with Mary Sue.

Annabel sat in her next class, a prisoner in her own mind, where all she could think about was if Danny held Mary Sue's hand, or wrapped his jacket around her cold shoulders, or kissed her lips the way he had kissed hers.

ANNABEL WENT STRAIGHT home after school, despite Molly and Donna's pleas for her to go to Donna's house. Annabel was miserable and wanted to be miserable in her own miserable home.

She didn't even mind her father's ornery manner at the dinner table as he drank more than he ate. Annabel picked at her food and kept quiet, and soon, George was settled in front of the TV and passed out in his favorite chair.

Annabel finished clearing the table and went straight to her room. Joan caught her just as she was about to shut her bedroom door.

"Is everything all right? You barely touched your food and you look pale. I hope you're not coming down with something?" Joan placed a hand against Annabel's forehead.

"I'm not sick." Annabel tilted her head away from her mother's touch. "Just a little tired."

Joan pulled her hand back and straightened the apron around her waist. "Okay, but let me know if you start feeling ill."

Annabel gave a slight nod.

"Also, do you know when that boy is going to phone here? I've been making sure I answer every call. You know how angry your father will get if he . . ."

"Don't worry," Annabel said impatiently. "Danny's not calling."

"What happened? Is this why you were so quiet at dinner?"

"When am I ever not quiet at dinner?" Annabel snapped.

"I see." Joan hesitated. "I'll . . . I'll just let you be."

"Wait," Annabel said. "I didn't mean to talk to you like that, but I can't take it when you try to pretend things aren't the way they are around here. I'm always quiet at dinner and you know why. We're not the family who talks about our day while we eat our peas."

"So that boy who didn't call had nothing to do with your somber mood?" Joan asked.

"I don't want to talk about it." Annabel turned her head from Joan, and tears welled in her eyes.

"Oh, Annabel." Joan glided her hand underneath Annabel's chin. "I'm sorry, but please don't cry. There are going to be so many other boys you'll have a hard time remembering all their names."

"I don't care about other boys." Annabel pressed her hand against her mouth to muffle her cries.

"Please don't cry." Joan wrapped her arms around Annabel and kissed the top of her head. "Everyone goes through a first heartbreak and we all make it. I promise."

Annabel quickly wiped the tears off her face. "I'm fine. Just tired. I need to go to bed." She went in her room and shut the door.

She didn't turn on the radio as she usually did. She was too heartbroken to listen to songs about love. She lay on her bed and waited for the sun to go down. When it was time, she climbed out her window.

Annabel avoided Danny's house. The sight that used to serve as her hope for better days had turned into the reason for her despair. She walked a couple blocks and was crossing the street when a car pulled up to the stop sign.

"Annabel?" Danny popped his head out the car window. "What are you doing out here?"

"I don't want to talk to you right now, Danny."

"Why not?" Danny yelled back.

"Just leave me alone, Danny. Please." Annabel picked up her pace.

"Wait! Annabel!" Danny drove alongside Annabel as she quickened her pace. "Will you please stop?" He parked the car along the curb and chased after her. "Why are you running away from me?"

Annabel spun around and faced him. "Why didn't you ask Mary Sue to go to the dance if you wanted to go out with her so bad?"

Danny stopped walking. "I . . . I didn't want to go with her to the dance. I wanted to go with you."

"Then why'd you go out with her on Saturday night?"

"It wasn't like that, Bel."

"So you didn't go on a date with her?"

"Well . . . yeah . . . sort of . . . but . . . but it wasn't like that."

""Yeah…right." Annabel walked away from Danny.

"Bel, please." Danny followed her. "It's not that simple."

"I don't understand what makes it so hard." She kept walking, and Danny kept pace with her.

"I suppose you wouldn't understand."

"What does that mean?" Annabel turned around. She wanted to see his face to know what he looked like when he lied to her.

Danny shuffled the keys in his pocket, and his expression tensed. "Bel, please. Let's not do this."

"Tell me what you meant by that." She looked him in the eyes. "Why wouldn't I understand?"

"You're not gonna let this go, are you? Geez, Annabel, most girls in school wouldn't care as much as you do. As long as they got to walk the school halls next to the quarterback they'd put up with just about anything, but not you. You really don't care about that stuff, do you?"

"Tell me why I wouldn't understand and don't lie. You've done enough of that already."

"Bel . . ." He groaned.

"Tell me!"

"Shhhhh." He pressed a finger against her lips. "You want to wake up the whole neighborhood?"

"I can scream louder," she stated flatly.

"I'll bet you can. But I don't want to make you prove it. Can we at least get out of the street and go in my car?"

"No. You tell me right here."

"Fine." He sighed and muttered under his breath about how stubborn she was. "You never dated anyone before. It isn't always as easy as just liking someone. Sometimes other things get in the way."

"Like what? Being cool? Is that it, Danny? You want to date someone who'll impress all your friends, like Mary Sue?"

Danny shook his head. "No. I don't care about that stuff, either."

"Obviously you do. That's why you went on a date with her, isn't it? The captain of the football team should date the head cheerleader. It makes perfect sense. So stick with going on dates with Mary Sue." Annabel turned away, but Danny pulled her back.

"I don't want to go on dates with Mary Sue. I want to go on dates with you," he said.

Annabel looked into Danny's eyes and tried to understand what he was saying to her. "You say you like me, but you also say it's not as easy as just liking someone. I don't know what I'm supposed to do with that, and my never dating before has nothing to do with it. Maybe you're not the right boy for me to be with."

"You can't believe that, Annabel."

Annabel wanted to tell Danny how she watched him through his window at night and that she was using him as an escape from her own unbearable life and that she needed him to be perfect. Without that, she had nothing to look forward to. Danny had to be everything she needed him to be.

"But I can believe it," Annabel said. "Mary Sue asked me about you. She asked what we were."

"That's none of her business," Danny muttered through his teeth.

"I . . . I didn't know what to tell her, but now I know I should have told her that we were nothing."

"Don't say that, Bel. It isn't true."

"Isn't it? That's what you've been trying to tell me all this time. That we're noth—"

Danny covered Annabel's lips with his.

Annabel closed her eyes and embraced his warm breath against the cool air. She let him kiss her without one worry that anyone was watching them. She wasn't far from home and would be recognized if someone was looking out their window. If word got back to her father that she was kissing a boy in the streets at night, she would catch more rage from him than she'd ever seen. But she welcomed the risk for that wonderful moment as Danny kissed her and she kissed him back.

Danny softly grazed the side of her face with his fingers and whispered, "I'll never do anything to hurt you again."

Chapter Twelve

MOLLY AND DONNA were waiting by Annabel's locker the next morning and ran to her when they saw her.

"What happened? Did you talk to him?" Molly asked.

"Did he really go out with Mary Sue?"

Annabel walked past her friends, opened her locker, and pulled out her first period books. "Yes, I talked to Danny. And yes," she faced them, "he went out with Mary Sue."

Molly and Donna let out simultaneous groans.

"How could he do that to you?" Molly fell back against the row of lockers. "He went to the dance with *you* not Mary Sue."

"I bet you let him have it, didn't you? Tell us what you said to him," Donna prodded.

"About what?" Annabel asked flippantly.

Donna and Molly exchanged flabbergasted looks.

"What do you mean 'about what'?" Molly asked.

"Yeah." Donna looked at Annabel, her face crumpling in confusion. "What do you mean 'about what'?"

"I forgave him," Annabel said quickly and then turned and started down the hall to class.

Molly and Donna followed at Annabel's heels.

"What do you mean you forgave him?" Molly asked.

"Yeah, what do you mean you forgave him? He lied to you," Donna said.

Annabel kept walking.

"How could you forgive him?" Molly yelled.

"Bel, answer us." Donna quickened her pace.

Annabel whirled around. "Because he kissed me. Okay? Danny Winfield kissed me again, and I . . . I forgot why I was mad at him."

Donna and Molly's stone-faced expressions softened.

"Danny kissed you?" Molly asked.

"Danny's lips touched yours?" Donna carried on.

Annabel nodded, and Molly and Donna swooned loudly.

"Shhhh." Annabel dragged them around the corner of the hall. "Will you two keep it down? I don't need the whole school knowing."

"Wait," Molly said. "What do you mean he kissed you *again*? When did he kiss you the first time?"

"Yeah, Bel." Donna placed a hand on her hips. "When did he kiss you the first time? You didn't tell us he kissed you before."

"I . . . I . . ." Annabel was cornered. The bell rang. "I lied. He kissed me the night of the dance but I didn't want to tell you guys." She hurried to class.

"What do you mean you didn't want to tell us?" Molly followed Annabel down the hall.

"Yeah, what do you mean you didn't want to tell us?" Donna trailed Annabel and Molly. "Didn't you think that was something we'd want to know?"

"I WANT A hundred reps of each! Push-ups *and* sit-ups!" Coach roared from across the field.

Danny and Jimmy lay across the twenty-yard line and started the round of sit-ups.

"Yes, sir!" they yelled in scattered breaths as sweat dripped down their faces.

They finished their hundredth sit-up and plopped onto their stomachs and started their hundred push-ups.

"You think Thompson's team coach is pushing his players like this?" Jimmy lowered his chin to the tip of the stiff grass.

"We'll find out Friday." Danny grunted as he pushed his strong body away from the ground.

"I already puked twice," Jimmy spat. "Pretty sure I'm gonna do it again."

Danny laughed but his sore muscles ached. "I may join you."

They spent the rest of the workout in silence while the team practiced on the other side of the field. Every practice, Coach randomly picked two players for extra side workouts. Nobody looked forward to being the one selected, always at the end of practice, when the boys were the most tired. But that was the point. Coach wanted the team physically ready at all minutes of the game.

Danny and Jimmy finished their last push-up, went to the bench, and took a drink from the water cooler.

Jimmy finished his cup in one gulp and crushed the paper cup in his hand. "Steve told me you asked Annabel to come to the game."

"Yeah. So?" Danny tilted his head back and finished off his drink.

"He said you seemed pretty goofy about it."

"Goofy?" Danny asked with heavy breath.

"Excited, anxious, eager, whatever. This is a big game, Danny. We don't need any of the guys being distracted, especially our quarterback."

"That's something you don't have to worry about." Danny tossed the cup into the trash.

"Well, I am worried about it. This involves all of us. We all want State and we're gonna need your arm to get us there."

"Annabel has nothing to with my arm so just back off."

"What is it about this chick?" Jimmy asked.

"I swear between you and Steve—the two of you were never interested in the girls I took out before or who came to watch me play. What gives now?"

"You're different with this one, and we don't get it. Of all the girls in school Annabel Turner is the chick you choose? I noticed her twice before you started seeing her. Once when she tripped over my chair at lunch and spilled apple juice all over my shirt, and the other when I passed her on the stairwell. I was going down. She was coming up, and her blouse was open just enough that I could see—"

Danny punched Jimmy in the arm.

"Whoa. Excuse me," Jimmy said. "Didn't mean to rattle your cage."

"Well, you did. That's what you talking about Annabel like that does to me. It rattles my cage." Danny moved closer to him. "Got it?"

"Fine. But why her? Like I said, I barely knew who she was before you started talking to her. I hardly noticed her."

"I know you didn't and that's a good thing because I don't want you noticing her."

Jimmy scoffed. "You have nothing to worry about my friend. She's not exactly my type."

"What's that supposed to mean?" Danny stared at his teammate.

"How much longer are you two gonna dilly-dally?" Coach blew his whistle. "Get to running."

"We already ran," Jimmy mumbled low enough for only Danny to hear and swiped the perspiration from his face with his sweat-stained shirt.

They ran side by side. Jimmy's bulky body, heavy with muscle, couldn't sustain the same stamina as Danny's lean body. He gasped for air while trying to keep up with Danny's pace.

"Tell me what you meant," Danny pressed.

"It just means what it means." Jimmy pushed out labored breaths. "She's not my type."

"That's right. She's *not* your type. I know your type—cheap and easy."

"Hey, don't insult your mother like that." Jimmy chuckled and threw an elbow into Danny's ribs.

"Oh, now you're dead." Danny tackled Jimmy to the ground.

They playfully wrestled across the thirty-yard line until Coach yelled for the team to bring it in.

ANNABEL SAT IN the stands between Molly and Donna, and anxiously watched as Danny huddled with his teammates at midfield. They were down by four with less than a minute left in the game. On their own thirty-yard line, Danny and his team needed to cover seventy yards to get a touchdown for the win. Some fans clapped and cheered, while others sat quietly—too nervous to watch.

"Boys look so good in uniform." Molly gazed starry-eyed onto the field. "They're tight in all the right places."

Annabel was too on edge to laugh at Molly the way Donna was laughing at her, but she did crack a smile when Molly blurted, "Laugh all you want, but don't act like the two of you haven't noticed either."

Of course Annabel had noticed Danny's tight butt underneath his close-fitting football pants, and she wasn't the only one. Most of the girls in school knew by then that she and Danny were together, and every so often after Danny made a great play, a jealous girl would glance in her direction with a curious look that asked, "How'd someone like *her* get a boy like Danny."

But not everyone was as rude when Danny did something spectacular on the field. Some of the boys and girls sitting near Annabel nudged her while throwing out comments like, "Did you know he was so good?" "Can you believe that play he just made?" "Did you teach him everything he knows?"

Annabel was the star quarterback's girlfriend, and everything had changed. Not only at football games, but at school, too. When she walked the halls, kids looked at her instead of past her. She had become someone worthy of looking in the eye—all because she was now Danny's girl.

Annabel's existence suddenly mattered.

Girls of higher social status than Annabel couldn't understand why Danny had chosen her over them. The ones who seemed to take the most offense at being passed up by the star athlete were the cheerleaders, especially the captain of the squad, Mary Sue.

Mary Sue waved her pom-poms in the air and led her pack in cheers for a team rally. A huge roar exploded throughout the stadium as the boys broke huddle and took their positions on the line. Danny called out a play over the crowd noise, caught the snap, and stepped back to pass. He struggled to find an open man, which only intensified the crowd's nerves.

Annabel covered her eyes. She felt every hit and tackle Danny absorbed as though she were on the field with him. The attacks from the opposing team were personal. Annabel was unable to watch as the seconds ticked away and Danny was still scrambling to find an open receiver.

Donna watched with wide eyes as every muscle in her body tightened with suspense. She poked Annabel in the side. "Open your eyes. You're gonna miss this."

"I can't!"

"Bel, oh my gosh!" Molly screamed. "I don't think he's gonna find anyone. Look!"

"I can't look!" Annabel squeezed her eyes shut and didn't open them again until the crowd screamed in celebration. Molly and Donna were jumping up and down with their hands in the air.

"What! What happened?" Annabel yelled.

Donna put her hands on her hips and peered down at Annabel, who was still seated on the bleachers. "You'd know if you had your eyes open."

Danny had just completed a fifteen-yard pass, and the receiver ran for an additional ten yards before going out of bounds, putting them on the opposing team's forty-five-yard line with thirty-eight seconds to go. Annabel stood with the rest of the crowd and clutched her hands nervously at her side.

"Relax." Molly touched her shoulder. "It's just a game."

"Feels like a whole lot more than that." Annabel breathed in deeply and smacked her hands over her eyes again.

Donna pulled Annabel's hands away from her face and pointed to the field. "You need to watch this. That's your boyfriend out there."

Donna was right. With all the pressure weighing on Danny's shoulders right now, Annabel owed it to him to at least keep her eyes open and cheer him on. She watched as Danny, once again, took the snap. This time, to her great relief, he connected with a receiver right away for a gain of five more yards.

The team was now on the forty-yard line, but the runner had failed to go out of bounds and the clock was still running with less than thirty seconds to go. With no time-outs left, Danny hurried to the line and spiked the ball, stopping the clock with twenty-six seconds remaining.

This gave the team a chance to catch their breath and go over a play, but Annabel just wanted the game to end. The anticipation was too much, and just when she could take no more, Danny had the ball in his hands again. He pumped his arm for a throw but pulled back at the last second when the intended receiver was no longer open. Five seconds went by and Danny moved across the field in search of an open man.

"Throw the ball!" Donna yelled. "Just throw the ball!"

"But there's no one to throw to." Annabel watched, more nervous than before.

"Eighteen seconds left. Let it loose!" a voice behind Annabel screamed.

"Let it loose! Let it loose! Let it loose!" The crowd erupted in chants.

All around Annabel people screamed for Danny to do something. She forced herself to watch when all she wanted to do was close her eyes again.

Fifteen seconds left.

"Throw it! Time's running out!" Donna yelled.

Annabel shot her a look. Donna wasn't helping her nerves.

An opposing player rushed toward Danny.

"Move somewhere else! Don't get tackled, Danny!" Molly screamed.

Molly wasn't helping, either.

Ten seconds.

Annabel held her breath as Danny found an open path between two of his teammates. He ran where his players blocked for him. The crowd gasped as a defender grabbed Danny by the shoulder and tried to bring him down, but Danny brushed him off with one tug of his arm and kept running.

He approached the twenty-yard line with five seconds left. Only one defender in the middle of the field stood between Danny and the goal line. Danny kicked up his speed and ran to the outside. He hustled past the defender as the opposing player reached his arms out and flung his out-stretched body into the air—desperately trying to get a piece of Danny.

The player's hand hit Danny's foot, causing Danny to lose his balance near the line. Three seconds. Two seconds. The crowd stammered into a hushed silence knowing that if Danny stumbled out of bounds with no time left, they'd lose the game.

Running at top speed, Danny raised his arms at his sides, struggling to hold his balance. This position helped him regain his stability, but it also exposed the ball.

As he crossed the ten-yard line, the defender chasing Danny knocked the ball out of his hands. Annabel screamed and covered her eyes.

"Stop it. Be strong. Danny's out there." Donna again pulled Annabel's hands from her face.

"I know. I'm sorry." Annabel winced and looked back to the field.

Danny pushed the defender away and picked up the ball just as another opposing player attempted to fall on it. Danny cradled the ball securely with both hands and ran hard past the five-yard line . . . the three yard-line . . .

Touchdown!

A blast of cheers exploded in the stands. Molly and Donna threw their arms around each other. They pulled Annabel into their huddle of screams and hugs. The team lifted Danny in the end zone and carried him onto their shoulders across the field.

The cheerleaders joined the team in the midfield celebration. Jimmy lifted Mary Sue onto his heavily padded shoulders. She was sitting even with Danny and wrapped her arms around his neck and kissed his cheek.

Danny jumped off his teammates' shoulders and clapped hands with anyone who ran toward him. He seemed to be searching the stands but was constantly interrupted by hugs and pats on the back.

Chaos enfolded around him. It was as though the entire school was on the field celebrating the victory. The coach whistled for the team to follow him into the locker room.

Danny gave one last wave to the fans still cheering the team on and ran off the field with his teammates.

Chapter Thirteen

ANNABEL WAITED FOR Danny behind the metal fence, just outside the locker room door. They were meeting up with the rest of the team at Marvin's. Though Annabel had told her mother she was going to the football game, she neglected to tell her about Marvin's. Annabel was sleeping at Donna's that night and didn't think her mother needed to know anything past the football game. George, of course, was already passed out in his chair by the time Annabel had left for the game, so she didn't have to tell him anything.

As Annabel stood alone waiting for Danny, she couldn't push away the image of Mary Sue kissing Danny out of her mind. A hand touched her shoulder. Annabel jumped.

"Sorry. Didn't mean to scare you. Thanks for waiting for me." Danny glanced around the parking lot. "Did everyone split?"

"I think so. Molly and Donna got a ride. I told them we'd meet them at the diner."

"Okay." Danny smiled. "I'm really glad you came tonight."

"Me too." Annabel tugged at the arm of his letterman jacket. "But I don't know how many more games like these I can take. I was sure I was about to have a nervous breakdown."

"You're telling me." Danny laughed as he snaked his arm around Annabel's neck. "Come on."

Annabel brushed her face against Danny's collar as they walked to his car.

"Here, you look cold." Danny took off his jacket and wrapped it over her shoulders. He opened the car door on the driver's side, and Annabel slid across the seat. Danny got in and cranked up the heat. "You'll warm up quick."

"I'm already warm." Annabel tugged Danny's jacket tighter around her body.

Danny faced Annabel. "I really am glad you came tonight. I don't know why, but I wasn't sure if you would."

"You wanted me here. Why wouldn't I come? But I'm serious when I tell you that I don't know how many more games like this I can take."

"Most people love close games like this," Danny said.

Annabel shook her head. "Not me, not anymore. Those guys on the other team looked like they wanted to kill you. I was scared you were going to get hurt and I worried about how upset you'd be if you had lost. I . . . I didn't want to see you like that."

"That's very sweet." Danny took Annabel's hand and kissed it. "No one's ever been concerned about my feelings like that on the football field. Well, maybe my mother, but she doesn't really count."

"I couldn't help it. It was just the way I felt."

Danny gave her hand a reassuring squeeze. "Did you at least have a little fun watching me play?"

"Probably not as much fun as Mary Sue did."

Danny sighed and slumped back into his seat. "You really know how to break a mood."

Annabel didn't want to bring up Mary Sue, but the girl had been on her mind since the cheerleader celebrated with Danny on the field. "Sorry, I don't know why I said that."

"I think you do."

"She's the head cheerleader."

"So?"

"And you're the captain of the football team."

"So?"

"So . . . the two of you match. I saw her kiss you."

"That's right. You saw *her* kiss *me*. Bel, there was a rush of people coming at me. It happened so fast I could hardly tell who was who. Did you see it out there? I tried looking for you, but I couldn't find you with all the people."

She felt her face flush as she looked down into her lap. "I don't want to be jealous, but this is all new to me."

Danny placed a finger underneath her chin and gently pushed her head up until her eyes met his. "Don't you know you're the only one I wanted to celebrate with?"

Just when Annabel was sure he was going to kiss her, a loud banging sound against Danny's window caused them both to jump in their seats.

"Come on," one of his teammates yelled. "Let's get to the diner. We've got to celebrate."

Danny raised his hand and motioned to his teammate that he was coming, and then turned his eyes back to Annabel. "Are you okay now?"

Annabel nodded. "I'm sorry I overreacted."

"You didn't overreact. I wouldn't like it either if I saw some boy kiss you."

Danny switched on the radio and took Annabel's hand. Her small hand disappeared in his, and she rested her head against his shoulder as he drove, while "Earth Angel" played softly in the background.

AN EXPLOSION OF cheers greeted Annabel and Danny as they walked into the diner. Danny, the object of everyone's glory, smiled as his classmates shouted about the great game he played. Annabel stood by his side, unused to so many sets of eyes peering at her.

Molly and Donna were dancing with others to Elvis Presley in the middle of the diner when they spotted Annabel.

"Bel! Bel!" they yelled in unison.

"Come on." Donna panted heavily as she grabbed Annabel by the sleeve of Danny's jacket she was still wearing. "They're playing our song."

They yanked Annabel from Danny's side and pulled her into the dancing craze of twisting bodies and flailing arms and legs moving in all directions. They swayed their hips as "That's All Right" rocked from the loud speakers.

If Annabel closed her eyes, she could easily imagine herself in her bedroom, dancing with Molly and Donna to their favorite Elvis song because they'd done it so many times before, but she kept her eyes open. What she was living was better than any memory she had.

ANNABEL DANCED WITH Molly and Donna a while longer until Buddy Holly's "Oh Boy" came on, and Danny joined them on the makeshift dance floor. Two songs in, Steve pushed his way through the crowd and turned Danny around by the shoulders.

"Look." Steve pointed to the front door, where Brett and his pack of greasers stood.

Danny looked at Annabel, who was still dancing with her friends and hadn't yet noticed the mess at the door.

"Trouble just walked in." Jimmy popped up between Danny and Steve. "I'm sick of these scumbags. We need to show 'em once and for all who's in charge." Jimmy puffed out his chest with the confidence that only a guy who was always the strongest player on the field could pull off.

"No fights." Danny gazed at the chains dangling from the greasers' jeans.

Steve and Jimmy gave Danny impatient looks.

"Come on, man. We're not backing down again. We're doing something this time," Jimmy yelled.

"What do you think they want?" Steve asked.

"I'm not sure." Danny watched the greasers cautiously.

Jimmy rolled up his sleeves. "I don't know about you pansy-asses, but I'm ready to find out."

Danny planted a hand against Jimmy's thick chest. "Not here."

"But look at 'em." Jimmy motioned to the unruly gang who strutted to the counter and bothered the girls by sticking their fingers in sundaes and burgers that didn't belong to them. "Why do you always have to be so cool?"

"Why do you have to be such a hot head?" Danny fired back.

"It's my hot head that keeps your ass protected on the field."

"Not so much tonight, did it?"

"Hey," Steve interrupted. "I'm not saying we need to go around bustin' heads. This is supposed to be a good time, but we can't let them just show up at our place and hassle our girls."

"Screw the good time and I *am* talking about bustin' heads." Jimmy looked straight at Danny. "You cowered out of fighting them that day in the halls. Then you let them walk all over us at the dance. And now you wanna chicken out of this, too?"

"I didn't cower." Danny stared Jimmy in the eyes. "And I'm not a chicken."

Jimmy folded his arms across his hefty body and returned Danny's intense stare. "You didn't fight then and you don't want to fight now. What do you call that?"

The muscles in Danny's jaw tightened. "It wasn't the right time."

"What about now?" Jimmy tossed his hands in the air. "Is now the right time?"

Danny glanced at Annabel, who, like everyone else in the diner, now had her attention turned to the greasers.

"Come on, Danny. Don't let us down again," Steve said.

"Let you down? When have I ever let you down? Did I let you down tonight? I won that game for us."

By now they had attracted attention. Jimmy grabbed Danny by his shirt and yanked him off his feet. "You think you can make all those fancy passes without someone blocking for you, especially someone like *me*?"

"Get off." Danny pushed Jimmy back.

With his face only inches from Danny's, Jimmy warned, "I'm nothing compared to what you're gonna get at next week's game when no one's protecting you. When it comes down to it, Danny, you're nothin' but a big Sally."

Danny shoved Jimmy back, and they were all over each other, stumbling over tables and falling into chairs. Jimmy's size and strength overpowered Danny, but Danny had the agility and speed to wear Jimmy down.

This was Danny's greatest asset. If he kept moving, just like on the field, the big guy tired first. Danny just never imagined a scenario where he'd have to use this strategy against his own teammate.

ANNABEL STARED IN horror as Danny and Jimmy threw punches at each other, some missing, and some connecting. They seemed to be in their own worlds because neither one of them acknowledged the crowd gathering around them, nor did they listen to their teammates' pleas to stop fighting.

Annabel found a safe spot next to the jukebox where she could watch the fight away from the gathering crowd.

She froze as the greasers stopped teasing the girls at the bar and pushed their way to the front of the crowd.

The greasers howled and banged their fists on the tables. Curtis hopped his skinny body on top of one of the tables and beat his fists against his chest and made ape-like noises.

Dennis pounded a chair against the floor like a drum, and the top of his forehead glistened with sweat. The rest of the bystanders imitated the greasers' raucous behavior and egged on the fight.

The diner was rockin' as music played loudly and a chant of "Fight! Fight! Fight!" exploded throughout the place. Annabel was sure that this was the most excitement some of her classmates had ever experienced in their lives, and it showed across their faces.

The boys positioned themselves so they could get the best view of Danny and Jimmy. The girls were just as curious, but stayed at a safer distance. The rest of the football team crammed to get in the middle of their two teammates, but neither Danny nor Jimmy seemed willing to give way.

"Come on guys. We're on the same team!" one yelled.

"Yeah, Coach is gonna lose it when he finds out!" another screamed, desperately trying to separate Danny and Jimmy.

The owner of the diner, Mario Finchero, a short round man in his fifties, wearing white pants, a white buttoned-down shirt, and a matching white paper hat on his balding head ran from around the counter with his arms flailing in the air. "Stop this! Stop this right now!" He scrambled to find a way around the rowdy crowd. "Enough! Enough!" He tried to break up the fight.

Ricky grabbed Mario from behind and shoved him onto a chair. "Have a seat Daddy-O and don't move. This fight ain't over. It's just beginning."

Ricky very coolly smoothed his hands over the sides of his grease-filled hair. He winked at a blonde-haired, blue-eyed girl, and the boy standing next to the blonde put his arm possessively around her shoulders and kept his eye on the girl.

Brett wrapped his arm around Ricky's neck, forcing his attention away from the girl and back to the fight.

"Ain't this something?" Brett watched as Danny and Jimmy punched, pulled, and rammed each other into whatever crossed their paths. "The fucking guy won't fight us, but he'll take on his own teammate. That's great! Nice team work guys!" Brett shouted and applauded.

Ricky clapped, too.

Steve turned to Brett. "This has nothing to do with you, so beat it greasers."

"You're right." Brett offered a satisfied smile. "It's got nothin' to do with us, but it's got everything to do with you." He placed his hand over his heart and feigned disappointment. "And I expected so much more from such a talented group of young athletes."

Ricky and Brett stood shoulder to shoulder as they broke into bouts of laughter. Steve pushed Brett and Ricky with all of his weight, knocking them onto their backs.

Immediately, Curtis jumped off the table, plowed onto Steve's back, and bashed him to the floor.

"Another fight!" a boy in the crowd yelled out.

The kids shifted their attention to the latest fiasco. Girls scurried out of the way as another set of bodies wrestled across the floor, turning over more tables and chairs.

One of the football players yelled that the greasers were fighting with Steve. Danny and Jimmy finally dropped their hands against each other.

JIMMY JUMPED IN to help Steve. All of the football team did, except for Danny. He didn't move. He looked around the diner and watched the frenzied scene unfolding in front of him as if he were looking at it for the first time.

Danny hadn't realized how loud the place was. The music was still playing while everyone in the diner was shouting. Whether it was screams to keep the fight going or to make it stop, everybody was yelling something.

There were just too many people fighting; the team, the greasers, and anyone else who got in the way. It was bedlam.

Danny searched for Annabel, but couldn't find her. Panic rose inside him as he imagined Annabel getting sucked into one of the fights. He frantically pushed people out of his way as he looked for her.

Finally, he caught sight of her across the room. She was alone, surrounded by the uproar. He needed to get to her and take her out of the raucous place, but his friends were calling for him.

Brett and Ricky teamed up against Jimmy, while Curtis and Dennis had their hands full with Steve and two other players. The greasers were outnumbered, but by then it didn't matter. Everyone was fighting everyone.

Most of the girls were running for the doors. Molly and Donna rushed to Annabel and tried to pull her away, but Annabel resisted. Her eyes were fixed on Danny.

Sweat dripped down Danny's flushed face and his left eye swelled. He wiped away the blood trickling down his cheek and looked down at his hands. They were bruised and they throbbed, but they weren't broken.

Danny turned to Jimmy. He was roughed up, too, from both Danny and the greasers. His teammates were spread out, throwing punches at anyone who took a swing at them.

Mario jumped off his chair, crawled across the floor, grabbed a phone from behind the counter, and frantically dialed a number.

Brett and Ricky held Jimmy down as they each gave him a blow to the face and abdomen. Steve picked up Curtis' slim-jim body and threw it against a row of chairs, and Dennis bashed a teammate's head against a table until another teammate jumped on Dennis' back and clawed at him until he stopped.

Numerous fights were scattered across the diner. By now anyone who didn't want to fight seemed to be outside and those who stayed inside did so because they wanted a piece of the action.

Danny noticed that some of the boys who stayed didn't have reputations as brawlers and were fighting in what he assumed was their first fight. The intense looks on their faces resembled the expressions of some of his most fierce opponents, but Danny didn't know those boys to be athletes. He'd never seen them relish in the glory of victory in a sport. He presumed they had never tasted the adrenaline of competing in a sport in front of hundreds of screaming fans with the game on the line. Or felt triumph by scoring the winning touchdown and being hoisted into the air for a celebration in the end zone.

Danny assumed those boys never shone like that, but imagined this was their chance. The diner was the field. Those watching were the fans. The fight was the game and this was their moment.

Danny didn't turn back to Annabel, alone across the room. He instead jumped into the mayhem breaking wildly around him and knocked Brett off Jimmy. He and Brett wrestled to the floor where Danny laid a couple hard, gut-wrenching punches, causing Brett to crunch over in pain.

Jimmy was having an easier time fighting Ricky now that the fight was no longer two against one. Dennis slammed one of the football players hard against the tiled floor and let out a loud victorious roar. Then he grabbed the next closest football player and started beating him, too.

Danny had Dennis in his sights and rushed for him. The blood of his teammates was splattered across Dennis's white T-shirt.

Mario cut the loud rock-n-roll music and the only sounds heard throughout the diner were the grunts of sweaty boys punching each other. Danny strode toward Dennis, who was busy beating up his teammates.

"Danny!"

Danny stopped and turned.

Annabel was pressed against the back wall, looking especially vulnerable in his oversized jacket as swinging fists and flailing bodies were shoved all around her.

Danny had a decision to make, and despite the fact that one of his teammates was getting a hard beating by Dennis, Danny shoved past everything standing in his way to get to Annabel. Two fighters pounded their way in Annabel's direction. Danny ignored the pain in his banged-up hands, took hold of them, and heaved them against the wall. He pulled Annabel against him and shielded her body with his as he led her through the pandemonium out of the diner.

MOLLY AND DONNA were standing outside, their faces pressed against the large pane glass window. They hurried to Annabel's side as Annabel bent over her knees and gasped for air.

"Are you okay?" Molly asked.

"I couldn't breathe in there," Annabel choked and peeled Danny's jacket off her.

"We tried to get you to come out with us," Donna yelled. "How come you didn't come with us?"

"You could have gotten killed in there," Molly yelled.

"Are you hurt?" Danny asked Annabel.

"What?" Annabel's ears were ringing from the noise in the diner.

"Are you hurt?" Danny said louder.

Annabel shook her head.

"You sure?"

"I . . . I think so," she replied, and he pulled her closer to him and turned to Molly and Donna.

"Are you two okay?"

They nodded despite looking scared. Annabel was also scared, and despite the toughness with which he had fought, Danny seemed shaken up too.

Inside the diner, the boys were still going at it.

"I have to go back," Danny said.

Annabel grabbed his arm. The cuts on his face were deep. "Haven't you had enough?"

"My team's in there," he replied.

"But you're hurt."

"Some are hurt more."

"Mario called the police," Donna said. "I saw him on the phone."

Molly threw her hands over her mouth. "Oh my God. I cannot be here when they get here. My parents'll kill me."

"But we didn't do anything wrong. They won't kill you if you didn't do anything wrong," Donna calmly said.

"It doesn't matter." Molly shook her head frantically. "I'm here. They'll assume I did something wrong."

"We'll be gone before the cops get here." Donna put her arm around Molly. "I promise."

"Nothing good will come out of you going back in there," Annabel said to Danny. "It's pointless fighting. The cops are going to show up any minute. One look at you and they'll know you were involved in the fight." She pulled at his sleeve, but Danny didn't budge.

"I can't just leave them," he said. "They're my teammates."

"Weren't you just pounding the face of one of your teammates?" Annabel threw at him, but Danny looked away from her and took a step toward the diner.

"I saw your teammates," Annabel continued. "They're the ones who wanted this fight, not you. So let them have it."

Danny peered through the diner window. The fighting had slowed. More kids were splitting. Only the greasers and the football players were left. Some were still fighting, while others were laid-out on the floor.

Sirens rang out in the distance.

"Let's go Danny, please," Molly begged.

The rest of the kids who were hanging outside ran to their cars and peeled out of the parking lot.

The sirens blared louder as they got closer.

"Fine." Danny pulled his keys from his pocket. "Let's go."

DANNY PULLED THE car into Donna's driveway.

"Thanks for getting us back in time for curfew," Donna said.

"You're welcome." Danny got out of the car and opened the backdoor for the girls. "I'm really sorry about tonight."

"It's okay." Donna stepped out of the car.

"I'm just glad we're all still alive." Molly came out behind Donna.

When Annabel didn't make a move to leave the car, Molly and Donna went to the passenger side window.

"What are you doing, Bel?" Molly asked.

"Yeah, Bel. What are you doing? We can't waste anymore time. My parents ..." Donna started to say.

"I'm gonna just head home tonight."

"What about your parents?" Donna asked. "They think you're sleeping by my house."

"I'll tell them I wasn't feeling well and that your dad dropped me off. I just feel like being home right now."

That was the first time Annabel ever uttered those words, but it was true. She wanted to be home. Molly and Donna would want to spend the night talking about the fights, and that didn't appeal to her.

The girls weren't accustomed to wild and crazy weekends. Before Annabel dated Danny, they never went to the diner on a Saturday night. Saturday nights at the diner were reserved for the cool kids, and up until recently, that didn't include Annabel or her friends.

On a usual Saturday night, Annabel would be at Donna or Molly's house for a sleepover, spending most of the night talking about boys and listening to records while waiting for everyone in the house to go to bed so they could raid the refrigerator.

Annabel watched her friends rush up the front porch steps. She folded her arms across her body and dropped her head against the headrest as Danny drove.

"Are you cold?" Danny started to take off the jacket Annabel had given back to him, but she stopped him.

Despite being cold, Annabel told Danny she was fine. She didn't want to wear his jacket. Wearing his jacket at that moment wouldn't give her the safe feeling wearing his jacket usually gave her.

Something had changed.

The first time Annabel had watched Danny through his window, he appeared tender and calm. He was different from the other boys, but that night Danny was just like them and, maybe, a little like her father too, something Annabel never thought she'd see.

"Are you mad at me?" Danny asked as he drove.

"I don't want to talk about it," Annabel replied.

"Bel, what was I supposed to do?" Danny gripped the steering wheel. "You were there. You saw that I did what I had to do."

"You really believe that, don't you?"

"You don't know what it's like. A fella's gotta protect his pals."

"The fighting. The violence. It's all the same. You're exactly like him."

"I'm exactly like who? Brett? Jimmy? Annabel, I didn't want to fight."

"But you did."

Danny jerked the car to the side of the road and threw the gear into park. "I can't stand by and watch my friends get hurt. That's not what a man does. You think I went too far when, really, I didn't go far enough. I left my teammates back there. Do you understand that? I'm the captain of the team. There's a code that says you don't leave your teammates behind, but I did that for you." He let out a deep sigh. "Why didn't you just go outside with your friends? Why'd you have to stay in the diner?"

"Are you saying this is my fault?"

"You distracted me in there," Danny said.

"You *are* saying this is my fault."

Danny washed his hands over his face. "No, I'm not. It's just those greasers showed up and I lost it." He squeezed his hands around the steering wheel even tighter than before. "But I promise this will never happen again."

"Danny, I don't want you fighting anymore, but I want that for *you*. Not just for me. I don't want you to get hurt. Look at your face." Annabel softly pressed her fingers against Danny's swollen, cut-up face, and he winced. "Sorry." She dropped her hands in her lap and gazed at the blood stains on his shirt.

"It's okay." Danny smiled as much as his sore face allowed him to. "I don't know what I would have done if something happened to you in there." He smoothed his hand gently over her cheek. "I want you to feel safe with me, always." He kissed her, and any uncertainties Annabel had held against him for fighting slipped away as she kissed him back.

When their lips slowly fell apart, Danny leaned back into his seat. "Come on, let's get you home." He shifted gears and slipped his arm protectively around her shoulders, and Annabel longed to wear his jacket again.

Chapter Fourteen

TROPHIES LINED THE walls of Coach Mandel's small and untidy office that showcased his dedication to winning. With over twenty years of experience, the man knew how to win on a football field.

Playbooks and notepads scattered the cluttered desk, and take-out containers splayed over the edges of the overstuffed garbage can beside it. The room was stifling with the scent of old socks and greasy food.

Danny sat in the chair facing Coach's desk and waited. Fifteen minutes passed before the door blasted open, and Coach barreled into the office. His military style crew cut fit his strict and principled reputation. His office may have been in shambles, but his coaching style was orderly and precise.

He brushed past Danny and situated his husky frame behind his desk. He pushed a stack of papers to the side and tossed the remainders of a meatloaf sandwich and dirty napkins into the wastebasket. He paid no attention to the pieces of food and wrappers that missed the garbage and landed on the floor. Coach scooted his chair closer to the desk and looked squarely at Danny. "I don't want to know what the fight was about or who started it. All I want to know is did you leave your teammates behind?"

Danny peered out the small window with only the football field for a view. The sun was shining on an unusually warm day for mid-October, though he was in no state of mind to enjoy it.

"Look at me!" Coach yelled.

Danny perked up in his seat and looked Coach in the eyes, but stumbled for an answer.

"I'll ask you just once more. As the captain of this football team, did you leave your teammates behind?"

Danny rubbed his sweaty palms against the arms of his chair. "I had a girl with me. I ... I did what I could but ... I ... I needed to get her to safety."

"You should have thought about your girl's safety before you fought with those good-for-nothing hoodlums."

"I didn't want to fight, Coach. I swear," Danny said.

"Did you try to stop it?"

"I tried to talk the guys out of it, but ... but everything happened so fast. They were looking for trouble. Those greasers are always looking for trouble."

"And I'm looking for a State Championship. How am I going to get a State Championship if my quarterback breaks his hand punching out some no-good thug? Or my best running-back breaks his leg getting thrown into a table? For what? To act like a bunch of tough guys who can throw punches for fifteen minutes?"

"Coach, I'm telling you, I didn't even want to fight. Those greasers started every . . ."

"I don't want to hear blame, boy. You're lucky the sheriff's a fan of our team and that he called me first. We gave the school a watered-down version of what happened. Mario complied with that story because he wants to see us win State, too. Your parents are going to hear that version of the story." Coach pointed a fat, stubby finger at Danny. "So you better make sure everyone who was there understands what's on the line. I don't like being put in this position. A lot of people stuck their necks out for you boys. They didn't have to do it, but they want a State Championship almost as much as we do. I can assure you that you won't get another chance like this, understand?"

"Yes, Coach." Danny started to get up from his seat.

"One more thing before I excuse you," Coach said, and Danny sunk back into his chair.

"You said you didn't want to fight, yet you're sitting before me looking like you just went a couple rounds with Rocky Marciano. You get all those cuts fighting with the greasers?"

Danny remained quiet.

"See, I hear a lot of things the team doesn't know I hear, but I listen even when it appears I'm not listening. And I heard some rumblings about punches being thrown within the team." Coach rested his thick arms over the desk and clasped his hands together. "Something you want to tell me, Danny?"

Danny sighed. "Not really."

"You better tell me anyway," Coach said, and Danny knew he had no choice but to do as he was told.

"Jimmy, Steve, and the rest of 'em wanted those greasers the second they walked in the diner," Danny explained. "And they got exactly what they wanted. They got a fight."

"And what did you get?" Coach's large eyes peered into him.

"I told you. I didn't want to fight."

"And yet you threw a punch at your own teammate and when the situation got to be too much for you, you left them all behind."

"I had a girl with me. I told you that."

Coach dropped his fist against the desk like a gavel. "Those guys stick their necks out for you every single game. They protect you so you can make all those pretty passes college recruiters love to watch you throw. You can't expect the boys to have your back if you don't have theirs. You're supposed to be a leader out there."

"I am a leader. I'd do anything for my teammates on the field. You know that, Coach."

"You're not just a team on the field. You need to do anything for them off the field, too. Those are your teammates with or without the uniform on."

"I don't understand, Coach. First you're upset with me because I fought and didn't do enough to stop a fight, and now you're upset because I didn't fight enough?"

"I don't want any fights, but the fights I don't want the most are the ones within my own team. If a troublemaker starts with your teammates, I expect you to protect your teammates. You see, Danny. You've presented me with a dilemma, and I *hate* dilemmas. My star quarterback, my *captain*, is no longer respected by his team—his squad. Not on the field, in the locker room, not even walking the halls. Nowhere!"

Danny stood up. "You're wrong, Coach. I did stand up for my team. I fought when I didn't want to fight. I did that for them. The whole place erupted into fights, and I stayed and fought for them when what I should have done was grab my girl and got her the hell out of there. But I didn't, for them. If I failed at anything that night, I failed at being a man, not a leader. If fighting a meaningless fight with a bunch of greasers is what you want from your captain . . . your *leader* . . . then I'm not your guy."

ANNABEL, DONNA, AND Molly were walking home from school when the loud cranking sound of an engine spun them around and Brett's car drove up the curb beside them.

"Hey!" Donna jumped back.

"What's your problem?" Molly yelled.

Ricky leaned his body outside the car window and whistled. "Want some candy, little girls? I got the sweetest tasting candy you'll ever wrap your lips around."

The rest of the greasers howled obnoxiously from inside the car and acted so wildly the car shook.

"Ignore them and keep walking." Annabel held her books against her body and walked quickly with her gaze down.

The rowdy gang jumped out of the car and the girls quickened their pace as footsteps hitting the pavement pounded closely behind them.

"Well, razz my berries look what we have here." Brett pushed a strand of Annabel's hair from her face. "It's the quarterback's girl. Tell me, where's the hero of the game hiding?"

"He's not hiding anywhere." Annabel tried to push past Brett, but he moved in front of her.

"Where's the fire?" Brett said.

"There's no fire. We just want to get away from you," Donna yelled straight into his face.

"Look at this one with the mouth." Ricky yanked on Donna's ponytail. "I guess she uses her mouth for more than just eating, even though it doesn't look like it."

The guys laughed and Brett added, "Do you really think you can outrun us with those fat-piggy legs of yours?"

"Shut up and leave her alone," Annabel shouted.

"Yeah, stop being so mean," Molly yelled.

"Your little boyfriend's not here to protect you," Ricky said to Annabel, "not that he did a good job of it the other night. Sorry we had to scratch up that pretty little face of his."

"We're not finished with him yet," Brett said. "Better tell him to watch his back."

"Tell him yourself. He's not afraid of you." Annabel backed away from Brett.

A tight smirk slowly spread across Brett's face. "But you are . . . and I like that."

Dennis wrapped his thick hairy arm around Molly's shoulders. "How 'bout we give you a ride home. There's plenty of room in Brett's backseat."

Molly shoved the chubby greaser as hard as she could, but he didn't budge, and he knocked Molly's school books out of her hands.

"You're a real creep," Annabel yelled.

"Forget it, Dennis. She wouldn't know what to do in anyone's backseat." Brett stepped closer to the girls and flashed an ugly smile. "But lucky for you chicks I don't mind teaching along the way. I'm patient like that." He ran a finger down Annabel's bare arm.

"Get bent." Annabel shoved his hand away.

Curtis pushed his skinny body between Brett and Ricky, and stepped closer to Annabel. "Girl's got a pretty face, but a smart mouth on her. You know what I like to do to girls who talk back?" Curtis grabbed Annabel by the elbow, and she squirmed underneath his grip.

"Get your hands off her," Donna yelled.

"Let her go!" Molly hit Curtis in the shoulder.

Brett grabbed Molly from behind, and the girls' loud screams sent a silver-haired man, holding a broom above his head, running down his front yard toward the commotion.

"Hey, you boys, leave those girls alone!" He opened the gate of his white-picket fence and ran out to the sidewalk.

"Look at Big Daddy comin' to the rescue. Go back to your house and mind your own business, old man." Curtis tightened his grip on Annabel.

"This *is* my business!" He pointed the end of the broomstick at them. "This is my neighborhood and I'm calling the police if you don't leave right now."

"Shove that broomstick up your ass, old man!" Ricky yelled.

Brett let Molly go and nudged Ricky's shoulder. "We don't need the fuzz on us today. These chicks ain't worth the trouble." Brett kept his eyes on the man while he backed away. "We'll be back, old man."

"Ah, go on. Get outta here." The man swatted the broom at the greasers.

The greasers jumped into Brett's car and Brett squealed the tires loudly as he peeled away.

"You girls okay?" the man asked.

Annabel, Molly, and Donna nodded even though Annabel knew that none of them felt okay.

"You shouldn't hang around boys like that," the man added before walking back to his house.

Annabel and Donna helped Molly pick her books off the sidewalk and quietly walked to Molly's house. They had planned on listening to records, but they always danced when they listened to records and no one felt like dancing anymore.

"Wait until Danny finds out what they did. I can't wait to see what he does to those no-good greasers once and for all." Molly rubbed the spot on her arm where Brett had gripped her tightly.

"Yeah. He won't let anyone get away with treating us like that," Donna said.

Annabel stopped walking and faced her friends. "Danny's not gonna do anything because Danny's not gonna find out. Hear me? No one can tell him."

"What are you talking about, Bel? You mean you're not gonna tell Danny what those greasers did to us?" Donna asked

"No. I'm not. And you guys aren't either."

"How come?" Molly asked.

"Yeah, how come?" Donna echoed.

"Because I don't want any more fights," Annabel replied. "I'm through with fights."

"We don't want a fight either, do we, Donna?" Molly looked at Donna.

"Of course not," Donna said. "I hate the fight that happened at the diner too, but those filthy greasers can't get away with what they did to us. What if that man hadn't come out when he did? What would have happened to us?"

Annabel didn't want to think about that. The greasers were crazy and they were rough and they should pay for the trouble they caused, but she didn't want Danny to be the one to hand them the bill.

"I don't want Danny to know about this. Can you understand that?" Annabel asked.

Molly and Donna glanced at each other and then gave Annabel a small nod.

"We understand, Bel." Molly slipped an arm around Annabel's shoulders and they continued walking.

"You like him a lot and you don't want to see him get hurt. And as much as I hate those greasers, I won't tell Danny." Donna hung her head and continued walking, but soon fell a pace behind Annabel and Molly's.

"What's wrong?" Molly asked, looking back at Donna.

Donna lifted her head and wiped her wet eyes. "Why do they have to be so mean? They're so cruel the way they talk to me."

Annabel rushed to Donna's side. "You listen to me. You don't pay any attention to what those creeps say. Got it? They're nothing . . . *nothing*."

"Yeah, Donna," Molly said. "Who cares what they say? They won't even graduate. They're gonna end up working at a gas station for the rest of their lives—pumping gas, checking oil, and washing people's windshields."

Donna forced a smile and wiped away the tears falling down her face. "I know I shouldn't let the things they say get to me, but it's hard because I look in the mirror and I know they're right." She covered her hands over her face and cried some more.

"That's not true," Molly said. "Don't ever believe that."

Annabel pushed Donna's hands from her face. "Underneath all that tough clothes are a bunch of scared boys who have to tease other people to feel better about themselves. Don't let them do this to you."

"I don't mean to be such a baby." Donna wiped her face.

"You're not a baby." Molly patted Donna's shoulder. "No one likes being made fun of."

"Remember that day we were talking about getting engaged," Annabel said. "And you said you won't wait to marry someone you truly love because guys won't fall over themselves to propose to you?"

"Of course I remember."

"Well, you were wrong. You don't have to only take what you can get. You're beautiful and someday the boy you are meant to be with will see that. And you'll be happy because you deserve to be happy."

"I want to believe that," Donna said.

"Then believe it," Annabel said.

"That's the nicest thing anyone's ever said to me."

"Come on." Molly yanked Annabel and Donna along the sidewalk. "Let's get to my house before she starts crying again."

DANNY WAS HEADED to the locker room where the rest of the team were putting on their gear for practice, when Jimmy met him in front of the locker room door and pulled him to the side.

"I know you think I went running to Coach about you leaving us to fight the greasers, but I didn't. Not sure who told him, could've been anyone. A lot of guys were frosted about you splitting while we were still fighting."

"I did what I had to do. I didn't want that fight, you did. Maybe you shouldn't start fights you can't finish."

"Is that so?" Jimmy crossed his arms. "For your information I did finish the fight, but then how would you know, right?"

"Are you finished?" Danny asked.

"No. I need to know what gives."

"I told you. I had my reasons."

"Your teammates were gettin' pounded. I don't give a shit about your reasons."

Danny attempted to step around Jimmy, but Jimmy moved in his way. "You know, Danny. There's been some chatter about leaving your ass out there to dry Friday night like you did to us. Some guys figured why should we block for you when you don't block for us?"

Danny glared at Jimmy, and every muscle in his body tightened.

"But don't worry your pretty little head." Jimmy smirked. "I talked the boys down. Lucky for you we're in contention for State, but if we weren't, your ass would be spending a lot of time on the ground."

"Now are you finished?" Danny stared Jimmy down.

"Yeah. Yeah, I'm finished."

Danny brushed past Jimmy and strode into the locker room.

WHILE SITTING IN a circle on Molly's bedroom floor, Annabel and Molly tried to cheer Donna up and assure her that before they knew it they'd be graduating, and the greasers would be out of their lives forever.

"We graduate in two years," Donna yelled. "That's a long time."

"But they're juniors so they'll be gone in just one year," Annabel countered.

"It doesn't matter. They'll always be boys like Brett and the rest of those jerks."

Molly sighed and leaned her back against the bed. "They live to make life miserable for everyone. I hate them too after what they did in the diner and especially after what they did today." She looked at Annabel. "You really aren't going to tell Danny?"

"No, and I've already told you why."

Molly and Donna exchanged looks.

"What was that for?" Annabel demanded.

"What was what for?" Molly asked innocently.

"Yeah, what was what for?" Donna repeated.

"Guys, I saw the look. You did it right in front of me. You think I'm blind?"

Molly sighed again. "No, Annabel. We don't think you're blind. We couldn't help it. We just don't understand. How do you think we're gonna get the greasers to leave us alone without Danny's help? You know they're gonna keep bothering us, right?"

"We don't know that," Annabel said.

"Oh yes we do," Molly replied. "Who knows, maybe Danny's the reason they pick on us. They've never noticed us before. Maybe it's you they really want. They don't like Danny and everyone knows you're his girl now."

"You're saying this is my fault?" Annabel asked.

"I'm not saying that," Molly said.

"Sure sounds like it."

"Annabel, we wouldn't blame you," Donna said. "We're just scared. I know I am. I'm starting to think it wasn't so bad when we were nobodys and no one noticed us."

"We all didn't go unnoticed." Molly looked at Annabel, but Annabel turned her head away.

"That's right. Danny noticed Annabel," Donna said quietly.

Annabel nodded and blinked back tears. "He did. And here we are. Wishing we were nobodys again."

Chapter Fifteen

JUST AFTER MIDNIGHT a car horn blared loudly from outside the house. Startled out of her sleep, Joan shot out of her bed and hurried to the window. She pulled back the curtain and saw George's Cadillac in the driveway. Its engine was still running with George slumped over the seat, his head pressed against the horn.

Joan rushed down the stairs, ran out the front door, and yanked open the car door. She pushed George's head off the wheel, and finally, the streets were quiet again, but too much noise had already been made. She turned off the car. The Chapman's front porch light turned on, and Sylvia appeared at the edge of the porch.

"Joan. Joan," Sylvia yelled in a hushed voice. "What's going on? Are you all right?" She leaned over her porch railing in a black silk robe, a look of horror across her face. "Is somebody hurt?"

George lay passed out in the front seat, his mouth opened wide. He looked like he was dead, except that he was snoring as loud as a lion. This wasn't the life Joan had imagined was waiting for her when she married the young, handsome soldier who showed up unexpectantly in her small town. But George had come back from the war a changed man, and had yet to show any semblance of the person she walked to the lake with that day.

"I'll get Henry." Sylvia tightened her robe around her waist and hurried inside the house.

Joan watched Sylvia disappear inside the house and knew she couldn't fathom the life she was living, not with the loving husband Sylvia had.

The front door of a house across the street opened, and a man and a woman huddled in the entrance, watching the commotion unfolding on the other side of the street.

Henry followed Sylvia out of the house, wearing blue pajama bottoms, a white shirt, and a thick pair of black slippers.

"Come on." Sylvia led the way down the front walk and across the lawn. "Joan needs your help."

"He fell asleep in his car, you say?" Henry rubbed his tired eyes.

"He didn't fall asleep. I think he *passed* out," Sylvia whispered as they approached the Turners' driveway.

Henry rushed to the driver's side door and then took a step back, looking shocked.

Joan tried to push down her panic as she watched Henry study George as if trying to find the best way of moving him.

Sylvia put her arm around Joan's shoulders. "Let's go inside, hon." She glanced across the street as more neighbors were either gaping from their porches or peering through their windows. "You don't need to be out here anymore."

Joan and Sylvia went inside and left Henry to deal with George.

A few minutes later, Joan opened the door for Henry to stagger-carry George into the house.

"Where do you want him?" Henry's body was hunched over and beads of sweat glistened off his forehead.

Joan pointed to the couch.

Henry shuffled across the room while holding tightly to George's body.

"Thank you." Joan stood near the edge of the couch with a hand cupped over her mouth as Henry plopped George onto the cushions.

"He'll probably be asleep for a good few hours," Henry said.

"I'll never be able to leave my house again," Joan stated.

"No one's judging you, Joan," Sylvia said.

"Oh yes they are. You saw them out there. They're judging me." Joan paused, and then continued in a soft voice, "The same way they judged you and the way you frolicked around your garden with Henry all summer."

"They . . . they judged me? But why?" She looked at Henry. "We didn't frolic, did we?"

Henry shrugged. "Maybe a little."

"Don't concern yourself with that. They were jealous they don't have that silliness and playful relationship with their own husbands." Joan gazed at George sprawled on the couch, his snores still deafening. "I know I was."

Sylvia gave Joan's hand a squeeze and smiled sweetly. "I'm sorry you don't have the relationship you want. I wish I could change that."

"Me too," Joan replied.

"But I never cared what people said or thought about me . . . and you shouldn't either. This is a private matter."

"I'll try to remember that." Joan looked at George again. "But it won't be easy. I don't know what I would have done if you two hadn't come out and helped me. I couldn't have gotten him in here by myself. If I'd left him out there, someone would have called the police and then what?" She pressed her hands in prayer form. "I don't want to think about that."

"Then don't," Sylvia said.

"And please don't be embarrassed." Henry stood in the middle of the living room in his pajamas and slippers. "George fought the Nazis and made it home. God only knows what he saw out there. I'm only sorry I couldn't go. Damn war."

"Henry, the language." Sylvia motioned to Joan.

"I'm sorry, ma'am. But I was rejected, deemed a class 4F, completely disqualified from serving my country. I never got to wear the uniform and fulfill my duty as a man. I know your husband looks down on me for that, and I can't say that I blame him. So the man takes a drink every once in a while. He deserves it."

Joan met Henry's eyes. "But I don't deserve a drunk for a husband nor does Annabel as a father." She paused and drew in a slow breath. "Thank you for your help tonight, but I can take it from here."

"Henry didn't mean to upset you, Joan," Sylvia said.

"I sure didn't," Henry said. "I'm sorry, ma'am."

"You didn't. I'm just ready to call it a night."

"Of course." Sylvia took Henry's arm and pulled him toward the door. She turned back to Joan. "Any time you need anything, I'll be right over."

"Thank you."

Joan saw her neighbors to the door and then went upstairs and checked on Annabel, relieved to find her soundly asleep in her bed.

THE NEXT MORNING, Annabel was on her way to the bathroom when she saw her parents' bedroom door closed. The door was only closed when someone was in the room, and she could hear her mother making breakfast downstairs.

Annabel walked quietly across the hall and pressed her ear against the door. George's loud snores rang out from the room. She backed away, hurried to the bathroom, and splashed cold water on her face. She brushed her teeth while wondering why her father wasn't at work

Annabel quickly finished dressing for school and hurried downstairs. Joan was on her hands and knees, frantically scrubbing the kitchen floors. A bucket of water, overflowing with suds, sat in the middle of the room.

"Eggs, bacon, and orange juice are on the table," Joan said without looking up.

"Why is dad . . . ?"

"Your father's ill. He's staying home today."

"Is something burning in the oven?" Annabel asked.

Joan jumped up from the floor. "Oh no! My brownies." She opened the oven door and a heap of black smoke seeped out as she pulled out a tray of charcoaled brownies. "These were supposed to be for tonight's dessert."

"You didn't smell it burning?" Annabel asked.

"I guess not. I've been a bit preoccupied this morning." Joan dumped the ruined treats into the garbage. "Hurry up and eat your breakfast. You don't want to be late for school."

Annabel picked at her breakfast and asked no more questions. She didn't need to. She knew why her father was sick. He hadn't made it home for dinner the evening before and that meant he was out drinking, but she didn't care. Dinner was better without her father's ornery presence, and after what had happened with the greasers that day, she had been happy not to have to deal with her father's foul mood last night.

Annabel got up from the table without finishing her breakfast, and despite her mother's pleas to at least drink her juice, she left for school.

Molly and Donna were waiting for her at her locker.

"The first bell already rang. Why are you so late?" Donna asked. "We have a test first period. We usually quiz each other before an exam. And you know this stuff better than we do. We really needed you."

Annabel tucked her books under her arm and slammed her locker shut. "You'll do fine." She started walking. "It's just one test."

Molly and Donna followed her.

"Are you okay?" Molly walked up beside Annabel.

"Sure. Why wouldn't I be?"

"I don't know. You just seem . . . not yourself. Is this about what was said at my house yesterday? Annabel, I don't wish we were nobodys. I'm glad you're with Danny. I'm really happy for you."

"Yeah, I'm really happy for you too." Donna kept up pace on the other side of Annabel. "I was just feeling sorry for myself. It doesn't matter if you're with Danny or not. Boys are always gonna pick on me so you may as well be with him."

Annabel pulled Molly and Donna to the side of the hall, bumping shoulders with students heading to class.

"I don't want to hear any more talk about us being nobodys," Annabel began. "We just weren't popular. That's all. There's nothing wrong with that. As for Danny, I don't know what's gonna happen with us. He's graduating in the spring. And with everything that happened at the diner, I don't know how much further I even want . . ."

Donna tapped Annabel's arm and pointed over her shoulder. Annabel turned around to see Danny standing behind her.

"Can we talk?" he asked.

Annabel told Molly and Donna she'd catch up with them later. They walked away, but glanced back several times before finally turning the corner to their classroom. Annabel knew the final bell would ring soon, but she didn't care about getting her first tardy slip, and Danny didn't mind either because he acted in no hurry.

"I wanted to talk to you before first period, sorry I'm so late," he said. "I needed to make sure you're okay—that *we're* okay."

"Danny, we're fine."

"Are you sure? I heard you just now with your friends, and you didn't sound so sure about us. I didn't mean to eavesdrop, just overheard is all." Danny slipped his hands in the pockets of his football jacket.

Annabel glanced down the empty hallway. "This isn't the time to talk about this. We need to get to class."

"Hang on." Danny clutched Annabel's arm. "I've been thinking about what happened at the diner and I know I messed up. Coach is ragging on me. The team's ragging me. The moment things got physical I should have grabbed you and gotten you the heck out of there. That'll never happen again. I promise."

"I know. You already made that promise in the car that night."

"I suppose I wanted to tell you again since I've been beating myself up over it these past few days."

"Well, stop. There's been enough beatings going around, don't you think?" She gave him a tiny smirk.

"Look at you, the wise guy." Danny laughed. "But definitely. I definitely think there's been enough beatings going around."

"Then give yourself a break," she said.

"I will. If you think I deserve that."

"I think those bruises on your face are punishment enough."

He brushed his thumb over the side of her face and watched her. "If I wasn't already in the doghouse with Coach I'd leave with you right now."

"You mean ditch?" Annabel asked.

"Sure, but I can't miss practice today. Coach would bench me for sure despite our run for State."

"I've never ditched before."

"That doesn't surprise me, but everyone should do it at least once. I've only done it a couple times. My father would kill me if he found out, but I'd do it again with you. You're worth the risk."

Annabel imagined her father's rage if she was ever caught ditching class, and not even Danny Winfield was worth that risk. "I could never risk something like that."

Danny laughed. Where Danny's statement of his father killing him was hyperbole, Annabel was sure given the right amount of alcohol, the act could be a reality with her father.

"We won't do it then," Danny said. "So the only other option is to go get our tardy slips."

"I can live with that," Annabel said.

"Me too." Danny hugged Annabel close to him and didn't want to let go. "I'll see you later."

"Okay," Annabel replied, not wanting to let him go either. She turned away and walked down the quiet hall to her first period class, not caring a bit about how late she was.

ANNABEL SAT AT her bedroom window as Ritchie Valens played on the radio. She watched cars pass and wondered, as she usually did, about the lives of those driving by and how those lives compared to her own.

Joan called for Annabel to set the table for supper before "Come on Let's Go" was over. Annabel switched off the radio and went downstairs. Dishes and utensils were stacked on the dining room table. Annabel thought about Danny as she set the places.

Thinking of him always made her feel better, and she was lost in her sweet reverie of him as she finished setting the last place-set. The front door swung open. George stormed into the house and slammed the door shut. Annabel drew in a breath, already knowing dinner that night was going to be worse than usual.

Joan greeted George at the door. "You're home a bit earlier today." She took his hat and hung it on a hook next to the door.

He ripped his coat off and slung it onto the back of a chair. "I had a lousy day! I got the hell out of there."

Joan quickly took the coat from the chair and hung it in the closet. "Dinner is almost ready. Annabel's setting the table now. Go get washed up."

"I'm already washed. I'm not a child. I don't need to be told when to wash up. I'm hungry and I want to eat now."

Annabel noted her father's already foul mood. When she heard his footsteps stomping in her direction, she quickly slipped into the kitchen just in time to miss him. She stood outside the swinging doors and listened to the sound of glasses clinking as George made a drink at the small bar in the corner of the room.

Joan scurried into the kitchen from way of the living room and peeked into the oven. She muttered that the beef casserole wasn't cooked to its usual time, but was good enough. She pulled the tray out, set it on the stove, and hurried to get dinner served to her impatient husband.

"Bring this to the table." Joan held out a basket of rolls.

Annabel didn't move. She just stared at the basket in her mother's hand.

"What are you doing?" Joan asked.

"I'm not going in there," Annabel said.

"He'll be better once he has food in him."

"No, he won't. He also has drinks in him," Annabel said, and was sure she heard the clank of fresh ice cubes as George poured another drink.

"I don't have time for this, Annabel. Take the basket." Joan shoved the basket into Annabel's chest. "Please."

Annabel reluctantly took the basket from her mother's hands, but only after seeing the desperation in her eyes. With the mood George was in that night everything had to be perfect.

George was guzzling a drink, his nose halfway into the glass, as Annabel walked into the dining room holding the bread basket stiffly against her stomach.

"It's about time." George exhaled deeply and slammed his glass on the table. Annabel set the basket down, and George reached his beefy hand into the bread basket and pulled out a thick roll. "Where's the butter."

"I'll get it," Annabel quickly replied.

"Hurry up!" George split the warm roll in two.

In the kitchen, Joan was mixing the salad as the beef casserole sat under foil on the oven.

"He wants butter," Annabel said.

Joan dropped the large mixing spoons in the bowl, went to the refrigerator, and took out a small butter dish and handed it to Annabel. "Get a butter knife from the drawer and then come back for the salad."

After the food was on the table, and George was digging hungrily into his plate, Annabel was relieved that for the moment everything seemed calm. Despite having no appetite, Annabel forced a couple forkfuls of food into her mouth. She didn't want to give her father a reason to point her out for anything. Sometimes he noticed her barely touched plates.

George spooned a hefty portion of casserole into his mouth. His messy bite caused portions of food to dribble down his chin, and Joan turned her head from him. He poured himself another drink and continued with his meal, oblivious to his wife's repulsion of him.

Annabel sat quietly and kept her attention on her plate as she took small bites of her dinner. Barely five minutes passed before George reached again for the bottle, already having drained his previous fill.

"Don't you think you've had enough?" Joan remarked.

George dropped his hand from the bottle and looked at Joan. "What did you say to me?

Joan nervously twisted the cloth napkin lying across her lap and looked away from George.

"Look at me when I'm talking to you!" George yelled.

Joan slowly met his angry eyes.

"I want you to repeat what you just said to me," he enunciated in a calm voice, which made Annabel very uneasy.

"George." Joan swallowed, and her eyes wandered from his.

"Look at me!" He pounded his fist against the table.

Joan pulled back in her seat. So did Annabel.

"Go to your room," Joan said to Annabel, and Annabel quickly got to her feet.

George slammed the table again. "Where do you think you're going?" He peered at Annabel with glassy eyes. "Dinner's not over with. Sit down! No one's going anywhere until your mother repeats what she said to me."

Annabel sank back down into her seat, looked across the table to her mother, and saw the regret in her eyes and the fear in her tense body.

"Why are you doing this?" Joan's voice waned.

"Tell me what you said!" George screamed.

"All I . . ." she paused. "I just don't know why you have to drink so much and behave like this."

George stared at her as he slowly rose to his feet and directed a finger at her. "You don't ever question me. I'll drink and behave in any goddamn way I choose!" He swiped his arm across the table and dishes crashed onto the floor.

Annabel shot up and ran from the table.

"Did I excuse you?" George looked over his shoulder at Annabel. "Get back here!"

But Annabel didn't stop running, and George took off after her. She made it to the bottom of the stairwell as George lunged at her and knocked her to the floor.

"George! Stop!" Joan cried out in a terrified voice just before Annabel's face smashed into the staircase banister.

Annabel lay across the bottom two steps of the stairwell, her father's body splayed over her feet. She crawled to her knees, her face aching.

"Annabel! Annabel!" Joan rushed to Annabel's side. "Are you all right? Let me see your face."

Annabel threw an arm up to protect her tender face from Joan's probing fingers.

"Don't." Annabel looked at her father, spread out across the steps, already passed out.

The side of his head was damp with blood, and the stairs next to him were spotted with dark, red marks. He was hurt too but wouldn't feel a thing until the morning.

The blood wasn't Annabel's. Her knees were scratched and her aching face hurt, but she wasn't bleeding. The last thirty seconds felt like a blur, even though she could replay every distinct moment in her head. She tried to imagine her friends' fathers tackling them to the floor like a football player, but she couldn't see any father doing that but her own.

"Annabel, I'm so sorry. Let me look at your eye."

In a slight daze, Annabel backed away from Joan and stepped over her father's body. She walked up the stairs. Her right eye throbbed like a heated heartbeat and the swelling blurred her vision. She used her left eye to see her way to her room.

She pushed her small dresser against her bedroom door and sat on her bed. She figured Joan would come soon and beg for her to let her in, but Annabel would not. She didn't want to see her. Though she wasn't the one who pushed Annabel down and hurt her face, she was the one who set her father's ire off and caused him to do what he did.

Annabel knew when to keep her mouth shut. Joan didn't. And that night Annabel paid for it. The events of the night pounded through her mind. She wished she were anywhere but where she was. The chilling look on her father's face when he yelled and the strength of his body as he grabbed her and pulled her down onto the stairs were memories Annabel hoped to one day forget, but knew she wouldn't.

Salty tears burned her eyes. Annabel wiped them away before they could leave their trail down her sore face. She went to the mirror, expecting to see half her face swollen and bruised, but surprisingly, she didn't look as bad as she felt. The bruising and swelling was mostly contained around her eye, but the pain extended to her entire face.

Tomorrow was Friday. Annabel was certain with everything that happened, Joan would let her skip school tomorrow and give her face some time to heal before Monday. Though Annabel didn't like missing school, good grades were her ticket out of that town, she couldn't go to school with a bruised face, and Danny did tell her that everyone should ditch at least once.

Annabel went to the window and looked out at the town she dreamed of leaving. She was certain no one else on her block had a face that was marked like hers. She opened the window and reached for the tree branch, knowing exactly where she needed to go.

Chapter Sixteen

ANNABEL CROUCHED UNDERNEATH a tree in front of Danny's house and looked for him through the window, but saw no sight of him or anyone else. The night was calm without even a slight breeze, so when the branches above her head shook, Annabel stood up to see what was causing them to tremble.

"Can I help you?" a voice called out behind her.

Annabel turned around, and Danny was standing beside the tree.

"Annabel? I didn't know that was you. What are you doing here?"

Annabel expected the night to hide her better than it did. She struggled to find the words that weren't the truth to explain what she was doing standing in Danny's front yard.

"I . . . I was walking and . . . and I heard the tree moving."

Danny looked up at the tree. "Oh no. Mrs. Paterson's cat's up there again. He's a housecat and not supposed to be outside, but he escapes every now and then. I need to get him back." He whistled at the cat. "Buttons! Here, Buttons!"

The cat's head peeked through the leaves and looked curiously at Danny.

Annabel smiled at the cat. "He's cute, but he looks scared."

"He won't be scared for much longer." Danny effortlessly climbed up the tree and took hold of the branch the cat was sitting on. In one swift motion, he gently scooped the animal into his arm, cradled it against his chest, and climbed back down the tree.

"Meet Buttons." Danny tilted the cat toward Annabel as though he were showing her a baby. "He's good for sneaking out at least once a week."

"He's adorable," Annabel said.

"He is, but he's trouble too." Danny held the cat in the air with two hands and brought it close to his face. "Isn't that right, troublemaker?" He nuzzled his face against the cat's soft fur and then snuggled him back in his arms.

"I better take him home." Danny stepped closer to Annabel. "You wanna come in for a . . ." He stopped, staring at her face. "What happened to your face?"

Annabel quickly turned her head from him. She had forgotten about her bruised face. "It's nothing. I fell. It was kind of a bad fall."

"Sure looks like it. Have you put anything on it?"

"It's fine. It'll go away by itself."

"Come inside. I have something you can use. First," he motioned to the cat, now asleep in his arms, "let me take this little guy home. Wait for me, okay?"

Annabel nodded, and Danny ran up his neighbor's walk with the cat huddled in his arms like a football. The neighbor, a plump elder woman with silver hair, opened the door in a pink robe and hugged Danny when she saw the cat. Danny handed the woman the cat and hurried back to Annabel.

"Now let's take a look at that eye." He started for the front porch, but Annabel hung back. "What's wrong?"

"I . . . I need to get home," Annabel stuttered.

"Right now? But we have to do something about the swelling. Come on." He took her hand.

It was easy for Annabel to give in to what Danny wanted, especially when what he wanted was to take care of her. They entered the house and walked past the couch Danny was sitting on the first time Annabel watched him through his window, reading a book with a look of extreme contentment on his face. Annabel was sure that expression had never crossed her face in her own home.

"Are your parents here?" Annabel asked.

"They're asleep."

"I really don't think I should be here. It's late. Your parents are sleeping. I should go."

"It's not that late. They go to bed early because they wake up early. Besides, I can't let you leave without doing something about that eye. Come on."

Annabel followed him into the kitchen.

Danny pulled a chair out from under the table. "Have a seat."

Annabel sat down, and Danny opened the refrigerator and pulled out a wrapped-up piece of butcher paper. He dropped the package onto the table, unfolded the paper, and held out a thick, raw piece of steak in front of Annabel's face.

Annabel recoiled in her seat. "What're you gonna do with that?"

"I'm going to put it across your eye, of course. Get that swelling down."

"Oh no you're not." Annabel shook her head. "That disgusting thing's not going near my face."

"It's not so bad." Danny laughed. "It'll help your eye. It's just meat."

"It's *raw* meat and it's disgusting, and I don't want it on my face."

Danny stood over her, the raw flesh dangling from his fingertips. "Do you want to walk around with a swollen eye for the next week?"

Annabel sighed. She assumed her eye would be better by Monday, but what did she know about black eyes? Danny played a rough sport and knew more about these things.

Annabel eyed the piece of meat and relented. "Fine . . . put it on me." She leaned her head back, and Danny gently laid the steak over her swollen eye.

"It stings." Annabel winced.

"I know. I'm sorry, but it'll work. I promise, okay?"

Annabel nodded, and despite the painful tingling sensation in her face, she let Danny hold the meat in place. She closed her eyes and tried to get her mind off the throbbing ache. "Whose dinner do I have sprawled across my face?"

"Mine, probably." Danny laughed and sat down next to her. "Mom likes to get me to eat lots of protein. I suppose she thinks it'll keep me strong."

"I suppose she's right." Annabel looked at him with the eye that wasn't covered with raw meat. He was looking intently at her face, and she felt very self-conscious. "I must look pretty ridiculous."

"It's not that. I'm just trying to figure out what it was you fell over that caused a nasty bruise like this," Danny replied without taking his eyes off her.

Annabel didn't like the intense way he was looking at her. She wiggled out of her seat and pushed the dead flesh off her face. "It's late. I should get home."

"Please don't leave yet. I . . . I like that you're here, and besides, you should keep the steak on your eye for a little bit longer. It needs it."

It was easy for Danny to convince her to sit back down because she didn't really want to leave, despite her protests. She placed the steak back on her eye, and Danny didn't ask any more questions about her fall. She was grateful for that. It wasn't easy to lie to Danny, especially when a small part of her wanted to pour her heart out to him and expose all of her wounds so he could save her, like a cat stuck in a tree.

"Can you imagine how crazy this town will be if we win State?" Danny held the steak steady in its place while he talked.

"That'd be really something," Annabel replied.

"Sure would. My father would be so proud of me for sure."

"I'm sure your father's proud of you right now."

"Of course. That's . . . that's what I meant." Danny held the meat against her face for a little longer and then stood up from the table. "That outta do it." He slipped the steak off Annabel's face. "It'll feel better soon. Keep a cold rag on it tonight and the swelling will go down for sure."

"Thanks, Danny. No one except my mother has taken care of me like this."

"It's nothin'. I just happen to know a lot about cuts and bruises." He paused and looked at her. "We better get you home."

They walked into the living room and there was a news report playing on the TV showing Vice President Richard Nixon with his wife and two young daughters at Disneyland. The news reporter commented about all the families the new amusement park was attracting.

The reporter, with thick black glasses, went on to say, while reading off a sheet of paper, "Walt Disney wanted to build a park where parents can enjoy themselves just as much as their children. Mr. Disney is quoted as saying that he wanted a place where 'people can experience some of the wonders of life, of adventure, and feel better for it.'" The newscaster took off his glasses and looked into the camera. "Well, it appears Walt Disney has done just that. It looks like the park pleases the Vice President and his family just fine."

The picture on the TV froze to a shot of the Vice President holding hands with his wife and two young daughters, who were outfitted with delicate perfection in little white matching dresses and white ribbons tied in their hair.

A majestic kingdom stood in the background, offering a mere glimpse of the splendor that was Disneyland. The park looked like something straight out of a dream, and Annabel knew a lot about dreams. Every night—on her walks and in her room listening to music—she dreamed of a different life, the life that was waiting for her after she finished living the one she hadn't chosen.

Annabel turned away from the screen. Watching a happy family standing in front of an extravagant amusement park while she stood there, bruised by her father, was too much for her to take.

Danny turned off the TV. "Come on. I'll walk you home."

ANNABEL LAY IN bed the next morning and listened to George's heavy footsteps stomp through the house, until the front door finally slammed shut. Seconds later, the hum of his car made its way into Annabel's room as he backed out of the driveway. She went to the window and watched as the car went down the street.

Joan knocked on Annabel's door. "Are you up?"

Annabel sat on the window's ledge and called for Joan to come in.

Joan entered the room. "Why aren't you in bed? How do you feel?"

"I can't go to school today because my father gave me a black eye. How am I supposed to feel?"

Joan went to her. "He didn't say anything this morning about what happened last night. I wouldn't be surprised if he doesn't even remember."

"That doesn't make it okay," Annabel said.

"I didn't say it made it okay, just that I don't think he remembers." Joan raised a hand to Annabel's face, but Annabel pulled back.

"Don't touch."

"I'm not going to touch it. I just want to look at it. Looks like the swelling is down. You'll need to ice it more today. I'll bring an ice pack up. Does it still hurt a lot?"

"Not a lot," Annabel answered.

Although her eye still stung a bit, it felt much better compared to the night before, and she had Danny to thank for that.

"Come downstairs and have something to eat."

"I'm not hungry."

"You have to eat something."

"I'm not hungry," Annabel repeated. "I'm gonna spend the day in my room. Read my books and listen to my music, and I don't want to be disturbed."

"I see. Well . . . after I clean the house I need to go to the grocery store. If you decide you want some fresh air you can come with me."

"I won't want fresh air. I don't want to see anyone."

"Okay." Joan backed away. "I'll . . . I'll leave you, but I'm right downstairs if you need anything. I'll be back up with that ice."

Annabel looked out the window at the street and couldn't wait for the sun to set so she could disappear in the night.

GEORGE TURNER SAT alone at the desk of his quiet office. In the lobby, just outside the door, the bank was readying to close. Employees dutifully carried out their end-of-day procedures as he waited for the knock at the door that would deliver the day's final paperwork.

He sat at his desk and waited. Every day, George waited. And each day he spent waiting alone at his desk, the face of a man he hadn't seen in decades tormented his mind and bombarded his every thought with memories he tried to forget. Drops of sweat trickled down his forehead, and the pace of his breathing quickened as he fought to block the reminiscences that tortured his entire being with both regret and longing.

George leaned back in his chair, closed his eyes, and tried to steady his racing mind with deep breaths. He often felt overcome with constant anxiety. His suit coat draped the back of his seat. He wore only a shirt and tie, yet he perspired so much the underarms of his shirt were stained with sweat.

He slid open the bottom drawer of his desk and pulled out a quarter-filled bottle of whiskey. He took a hefty swig and relaxed into his chair. He had a couple minutes until the expected knock would come, and he quickly swiped another mouthful off the bottle. He wiped the brown liquid that dribbled down his chin off with his bare hand.

He reached underneath his desk and peeled off a covertly taped black-and-white photograph of three soldiers taken during the war. In the photo, George was leaning against a tattered metal fence in front of a row of decrepit buildings as the sun was setting in the background.

George stood between Carl Scully and another young soldier. The young soldier was even handsomer than George. His hair was shaved into a short crew cut, tapered at the sides. With a strong jawline, straight posture, and powerful stature, the man was the optimum portrayal of a robust military soldier.

While Carl was looking away at something off-camera, George and the fine-looking soldier stood close, their gazes turned to each other. The smile they shared, as subtle as it was, was captured with the flash of a camera for all of time.

George remembered the day the picture was taken, no matter how hard he tried to forget. Earlier that morning, George and the young soldier had spent time alone together in an isolated spot in a field that assured their privacy. They would come to know that place very well in the months they spent in boot camp together, until they were stationed overseas.

George drank from the bottle once more and then tucked the bottle away into its drawer. He held the worn photo closer to his face and ran his finger along the outline of the handsome soldier's body. He peered into the eyes he hadn't seen in nearly twenty years.

"Michael," George whispered and pressed the photograph against his lips, until the knock at the door he'd been waiting for came.

George straightened in his seat and slammed the photo back to its hidden spot. "Come in," he grumbled loudly, and was delivered his papers.

He finished the review of the day's business, slipped on his suit coat, and stood up. He picked up his briefcase sitting at his feet, paused, and reached underneath the desk to touch the snapshot taken from a time in his life he bitterly missed so much, once more before he left.

A day never passed when George didn't touch the photograph of Michael, the man George loved.

JOAN LET ANNABEL eat her dinner early that night, so that by the time George walked through the door and let out his usual grumble of arrival, Annabel was already tucked in her room. She was lying on her bed, listening to the Everly Brothers on the radio, waiting for night to come.

She heard the clinking of dishes being set and felt guilty for leaving her mother alone at the dinner table with her father. Then she remembered her mother was partly to blame for what happened to her eye, and the guilt subsided.

Annabel imagined what Danny was doing at that moment. It was just after six o' clock. Danny was playing a team two towns away. Maybe he was on the field for pregame stretching, or on the team bus studying the playbook, or in the locker room engaging in pre-game pep talks about winning the State Championship the team had its sights on.

Annabel didn't know.

Night finally came, and she took a cardigan sweater from her closet and climbed out her window. She cut across the front lawn to the sidewalk.

"Another walk?"

Annabel turned around to see Sylvia Chapman sitting on her porch swing, a cigarette dangling between her fingers.

Annabel smiled and went to her.

"Don't let me stop you," the woman said. "I think it's great you go on these walks by yourself."

"Would you like to come with me?"

Sylvia leaned her head back and took a deep pull on her cigarette. She exhaled a fog of smoke and smoothed her hand over her fitted light-blue skirt. "Henry's away again. I don't feel like walking. I don't feel like doing much of anything."

"I'm sorry," Annabel said.

Sylvia patted the spot next to her. "Come on. Take Henry's place while he's not here. I hate being alone out here, but I also hate being alone in there." She motioned to the house.

"I like being alone out here." Annabel sat beside Sylvia. "I mean, I like being out here with you, but I also like being alone."

Sylvia laughed and smoked her cigarette. "It's okay. You leave whenever you want to go. I won't keep you from your walk."

"It's okay. I'd rather be here."

Sylvia smiled. "I don't know if you mean it or not, but it's what I needed to hear. You're a good girl. You're smart and you know just what to say to people. That's a good trait to have—to know how to talk to people—to tell them what they want to hear. That'll come in handy when you're married, and your husband's up for a big promotion, and his boss wants to meet you to make sure you're worthy of a promotion, too. You'll have to be charming."

"Why would I have to be worthy of my husband's promotion?"

"Would you believe that the way a woman looks can affect her husband's chances at a promotion?"

"I don't believe that," Annabel said.

"Believe it. If she's not pretty enough a wife can doom her husband's career. A man who used to work with Henry divorced his wife and married a prettier woman all to help his career. That woman was devastated. She really loved her husband, but if a man wants to become a top executive of a successful company he can't have an unkempt wife. The stink of it is men don't need to look nearly as good as women. That bar is always set higher for us ladies."

"I didn't know any of this." Annabel frowned. "That doesn't seem fair."

"Don't worry, my dear. You're pretty now and will grow into a beautiful woman someday. Men'll be fighting for your hand. Just wait and see."

"It doesn't matter. I don't care if I never get married," Annabel said.

"You say that now." Sylvia drew in her last breath of smoke and tossed the butt into the bushes. "But you'll change your mind. Women always do."

"It all sounds so degrading the way women are put under that kind of pressure solely based on their looks. You're lucky though. You're beautiful." Only Katherine Hepburn offered more defined cheekbones, but no woman could compete with Sylvia's crystal blue eyes.

Sylvia smiled modestly at Annabel's compliment and crossed her legs as she went on. "Henry's work had a picnic this past summer. I was as nervous as I'd ever been. I don't . . . I don't do well around a lot of people, especially people I don't know. I knew Henry wanted me to go off on my own and talk to people, but I stayed by his side . . . all night. I don't have what you have, Annabel. I'm not smart, and I don't know just what to say. I'd sure hate to be the reason Henry doesn't get a promotion."

"How can you say that? How can you even think that?" Annabel asked. "You're beautiful and you have a lot to offer. So what if you don't like to talk to strangers. I see how you are. I see you leave the house and drive off and it's . . . it's like you're doing your own thing. And you're always smiling and you look like you have everything under control. You have a confidence that I've never seen in my mother . . . ever. I want to be just like you."

"Don't say that. Don't you ever say you want to be like me. When Henry's at work, I bide my time until he gets back. When you see me leaving the house, I'm going shopping. That's what I do. I buy things. It gives me temporary joy until he comes home and I'm happy again. I know I'm too needy for him at times, but he's too concerned with my feelings to tell me so. He makes hints though. He's been pestering me to get a hobby. He bought me a paint-by-number set. Thinks it'll help for me to have something to keep me busy while he's away. I don't care much for it, but I do it because he wants me to. I'll do anything he wants me to."

Annabel was stunned and disappointed by what she was hearing. Everything she had thought about Sylvia, the image she had created in her mind of a strong, independent woman, was gone.

"Nights when Henry's away," Sylvia went on, "like tonight, I'll wait by the phone for him to call, and the longer I wait the more I'm sure he's not calling because he's with another woman."

"You can't really believe that," Annabel said.

Sylvia threw her hands up. "That's where my mind goes, and when I question why it took him so long to call me, the reason is always because a meeting ran late or something work-related."

"Well, he is on a business trip so that makes sense, right?" Annabel asked.

Sylvia looked to the dark sky and drew in a breath. "I don't always make sense. That's the problem. Even when I know I'm being ridiculous I can't stop.

But, really, it wouldn't matter what he does on his business trips because I'll never leave him. I couldn't."

"What!" Annabel's mind was blown. "You mean you'd stay with him even if you found out he really was with another woman?"

"Of course."

"But why?"

"Where would I go?" she asked simply. "I'm nothing without him. I'm nobody."

"That's crazy. You're Sylvia. You're Sylvia with him and you'd be Sylvia without him."

Sylvia shook her head. "I'm only me when I'm with him. You think I'm a confident woman and that I have everything under control, but you're wrong. I'm not confident nor do I have anything under control." She paused and swiped a hand over her forehead. "I take pills."

"Pills?"

"Yes. They help me feel happy when it's hard for me to feel happy, especially when Henry's gone. That's when I really need them. They don't always work though. I still cry a lot, especially when Henry's gone. I'm a hard woman to figure out. That's what Henry says. But he loves me. He's patient with me, but he wants me to be more stable—control my emotions better. I try. I really do." Sylvia lit another cigarette and took a deep drag. "But it's not easy. It's hard to control when I cry and don't cry. Sometimes I cry and I don't even know why I'm crying. Ever done that?"

Sylvia looked to Annabel, but Annabel didn't know what to say. Every time she'd cried, she knew exactly why she was crying. "I . . . I . . . don't think so."

"Hey." Sylvia lowered her cigarette and moved her face closer to Annabel, and Annabel could smell the smoke on her lips. "What happened to your eye?"

Annabel turned her head. "It's . . . it's nothing. I tripped and smacked my face into the banister."

"Here I've been going on and on about me and I hadn't even noticed your eye. I'm so self-absorbed sometimes. That's what Henry always says. Does it hurt?" Sylvia gently touched the side of Annabel's face.

"Not really. Not anymore. It's just a bruise. Bruises go away." Annabel stood up from the porch swing. "I have to get going."

"Right. You have that walk to go on."

"I don't think I'm going for that walk anymore. Goodnight."

"Good night, sweetie."

Annabel went home disappointed that Sylvia was the kind of woman who wouldn't leave a man who treated her badly. That meant Sylvia was as docile as her mother.

Chapter Seventeen

AFTER SPENDING SATURDAY night and most of Sunday with an ice pack on her eye, by the time she went to school on Monday there was nothing but a small bruise mark under her eye.

"We missed you on Friday," Donna said at Annabel's locker. "Did your fever go away?"

Donna had called Annabel after school on Friday to ask why she wasn't there and to also invite her to her house for a sleepover Saturday night. Annabel lied and told her she was sick with a fever.

"Yes, I'm much better now." Annabel pulled her books out of her locker. "Sorry I missed your sleepover."

"It's okay. We can do it again next week," Donna said.

"All we did was talk about boys. I can do that two weekends in a row." Molly giggled.

Annabel had convinced her friends that she couldn't have sleepovers at her house because her father was a light sleeper, and they wouldn't be able to talk and laugh through the night like they do. The truth was that they could have thrown a big party right outside her father's door and his passed-out self wouldn't have heard a thing.

Donna was the first to ask about Annabel's eye.

"I slipped and hit my eye on the banister," Annabel replied as casually as she could.

"Gosh, if anyone was going to trip into a banister I'd have thought it'd be Donna for sure." Molly laughed.

"Hey, I can't help it if I'm a bit clumsy," Donna said.

"A *bit* clumsy? That's all you think you are? With as many times as you're falling all over the place you're more than a *bit* clumsy, you're a hazardous sign," Molly said, and Annabel laughed with her friends as they walked to their class.

"You guys are mean," Donna said.

"Hey, I didn't say anything," Annabel said.

"But you laughed."

"That makes me a mean person?"

"Yes, you both are," Donna said, and Molly laughed again.

Annabel walked into class with them, relieved at the lack of interest in her bruised eye.

"We didn't tell Annabel what we saw in the halls this morning." Donna dropped her books onto her desk and sat down.

"What'd you see?" Annabel settled into the desk between Donna and Molly.

"Just a bunch of boys hovering around Danny's locker, absolutely losing their minds," Molly said. "They were asking a bunch of questions about football and if he'd committed to a college yet. The newspaper had an article about him this morning and listed all the colleges offering Danny full scholarships. Did you see it?"

Annabel shook her head.

"All the boys are so jealous that he's leaving this town, but I don't see what's so bad here. I like it here just fine," Donna said.

Annabel didn't say anything and acted like the news had no effect on her, even though it did a little. She and Danny hadn't talked about what happens when he leaves for college, and she never pushed the subject because she had plans of her own.

ENGLISH WAS ANNABEL'S most engaging subject and Mr. Clive was her most favorite teacher, yet when he asked the class for their thoughts on William Shakespeare's *A Midsummer Night's Dream,* Annabel positioned herself in her chair so that she was mostly hidden behind the classmate sitting in front of her.

Though Annabel adored Shakespeare and all of his great tragedies, she was too distracted to be reflective of even the works of literature she loved. She sat quietly as her classmates halfheartedly shared their uninspiring opinions of the piece some hadn't bothered to read.

Mr. Clive pushed his wire-rimmed glasses up his nose and scratched the bald spot on the top of his head. He stopped pacing the room and sat on the edge of his desk while clutching Shakespeare's book in his hand. "Is it too much to ask for some enthusiasm for the greatest and most influential writer in all of history?" He faced a sea of indifferent expressions. "This is very disheartening. A very sad day for literature."

A couple of classmates sitting around Annabel snickered into their hands. Annabel moved her head just enough so she could peek at Mr. Clive, and their eyes met for a fleeting moment. Annabel looked straight ahead, but it was too late.

"You!" Mr. Clive jumped off the desk and pointed the book at Annabel. "You always have something poignant to say about our reading assignments, what do you think of our latest Shakespeare piece?"

Annabel looked up from her desk, and every head in the class was turned her way.

"Yeah, Annabel. Let's hear what the most poignant student has to say," the boy next to her mocked and others sitting around them laughed.

Annabel tried to ignore him as much as she could, but her heart was beating much too fast for that to happen. "I . . . I . . . um . . ."

"Yes. Yes. What is it?" Mr. Clive eagerly pressed.

"I . . . I need to go to the bathroom," she said.

Her classmates laughed, and Mr. Clive lowered his head in disappointment and pointed to the door. "Take the pass. Make it quick."

Annabel left the classroom with the hall pass squeezed tightly in her fist. She didn't really have to go to the bathroom, she just needed to get out of that room. She escaped into the halls the way she escaped into the streets at night.

She walked the quiet halls and peeked into the classrooms she passed. Some students were attentive, while others slouched in their seats and slept behind hands that hid their eyes. Though she had never fallen asleep in class before, she'd had moments where she lost her concentration, mostly while thinking about her father's drunken rages.

Annabel's walk led her to the theater stage room at the end of a hallway, secluded from the rest of the classrooms. By design the theater room was built to be as far away from the classrooms as possible so classes wouldn't be disrupted by the drama and music courses taking place there.

Annabel stood at the door of the school hall. With a seating capacity of three hundred, most of the school's productions were multiple-night sellouts. The high school's yearly production was something most of the town looked forward to seeing. Joan took Annabel every year and Molly and Donna attended with their own families.

That year, the school drama class was performing *Oklahoma*. Last year, Molly had expressed interest in joining the drama club and starring in one of the plays, for all of the town to see, but thought more about it and developed a sudden case of stage fright.

Donna also had fantasies about performing on stage, being the star of the show, but never seriously considered joining the drama club. She was too self-conscious of her plump figure to put herself in that kind of a spotlight.

Annabel lingered at the theater doors and stared out at the sea of unfilled seats in the empty auditorium until a voice briefly stopped her heart.

"Don't tell me Miss Goody-Two-Shoes is ditchin' class, too."

Annabel didn't have to turn around to know who the voice belonged to. She had come to know the sound of Brett's voice very well. The greaser, wearing tight blue jeans and a black T-shirt rolled up to his shoulders, slowly made his way to Annabel.

"Tsk, tsk, tsk." Brett wagged a finger at her. "Shouldn't you be in class? I'd hate to have to turn you in." He looked her over. "Oh, look." He snatched the hall pass from her fingers. "You have a pass. Such an obedient girl. I like obedient girls. They do exactly as they're told."

"What do you want, Brett?" Annabel asked impatiently. "I haven't done anything to you. Why can't you just leave me alone?"

"Because I don't want to leave you alone." He moved closer and gave her body another long look. A tight grin appeared on his face. "I always thought you were pretty even before you started dating the darling of the school, pretty boy Winfield."

"I need to get to class." Annabel attempted to snag the pass back from Brett, but he pulled his hand away.

He nodded toward the theater room. "We're hangin' backstage, smokin' and destroying props. Join us."

"No." Annabel tried to get past Brett, but he blocked her path.

"What's so interesting in class that you have to leave so fast? You'll have more fun here. I promise." He licked his bottom lip, and Annabel pushed past him and broke into a hard run.

Having thrown Brett off balance, Annabel ran hard down the empty corridor. She could hear Brett following her.

Annabel didn't run in the same direction she had come, and soon, she was facing a dead end. Brett laughed loudly as he cornered her and yanked on her skirt.

"Don't touch me!" She backed away from him until her body was pressed against the wall.

"Sometimes a girl says no when she really means yes."

"Get away from me." Annabel's voice quivered.

"Are you scared? You don't have to be scared of me." He ran a finger slowly up her arm. "I'm a fun guy. Ask Patty or Mary Sue or . . . well . . . just about any girl in school. They all know how much fun I am, that is, most of them except for you."

"Please leave me alone," Annabel begged and pulled her arm away from his touch.

"I can't do that." Brett placed his foot on the wall beside Annabel, trapping her. He leaned into her and whispered in her ear, "You see, I don't think our star quarterback knows how to really appreciate a pretty girl."

Brett gripped Annabel by her shoulders and held her still with both hands, even as she tried to get away from him. "All I want is a kiss. One kiss and I'll let you go."

Annabel fought to break his hold on her, and he grabbed her arm and slammed it against the wall.

"You could have made this easy, but you wanted this the hard way." Brett slid his free hand down the front of Annabel's sweater, over her chest, and then slowly made his way underneath her skirt.

He moved his hand over her bare thighs, and Annabel adjusted her body so that she was directly in line with his, and with all her strength she plowed her knee straight between his legs.

Brett dropped to the floor, and Annabel ran as fast as she could as Brett's groans echoed down the empty hallway.

ANNABEL TRIED TO act like her normal self for the rest of the school day, but she couldn't shake the uneasy feeling of having Brett's forceful hands all over her body. She didn't tell Molly and Donna what had happened. They'd only pester her into telling Danny because she'd already kept so much from him, and this was something she had to keep from him too.

"Come on, Bel," Molly said at lunch. "We know something's up."

"Yeah, Bel," Donna said. "We know something's up."

Annabel tried to assure them everything was okay, but they weren't buying it.

Donna bit into an overstuffed turkey, lettuce, and mayo sandwich. "You're supposed to tell us stuff." She chewed her large bite of food. "You're never this quiet unless you have . . ." Donna put down her sandwich and leaned across the table to Annabel. "Is it your . . . *time?*" She quickly assessed Annabel. "You do look kind of pale. During my time, I . . ."

"Donna!" Molly yelled. "You know I hate talking about that stuff, especially at lunch." She tossed the remainder of her peanut butter and jelly sandwich into the garbage.

"Gosh Molly," Donna said. "I was just going to say . . ."

Molly shot up from the table and picked up her books. "We know what you were going to say because you say it every month. You get moody and genuinely fear you'll kill the person who gets on your nerves. You get bloated, yet still want to eat every piece of chocolate in your house and your feet sweat so bad you have to bring an extra pair of socks to school." She looked at Annabel. "Did I miss anything?"

Annabel pointed to her right armpit.

"Oh, that's right." Molly turned back to Donna. "Your right armpit develops a rash that you spend the entire day itching and it makes you look like a monkey. Now excuse me, but I need to get to next period early. I didn't study too hard for the exam and need to cram."

Donna giggled. "You said period."

"Ugh." Molly turned away, and Annabel laughed.

"If I didn't know any better I'd say *she* was having her time too," Donna said.

ANNABEL SET THE dining room table with her mother while trying to forget her frightful day at school, but she couldn't force the images of Brett cornering her in the halls out of her head. The arm Brett bashed against the wall still hurt.

With Brett around, the school hallways were more dangerous than the streets Annabel wandered alone at night. She'd been certain that Brett and his gang would tire of her soon, but now she worried what they might do next.

Joan trailed Annabel with silverware and set them on the napkins beside the plates. "You've been seeing a lot of Danny lately."

"Not really." Annabel set the last dish in its place and went into the kitchen to retrieve the glasses.

Joan followed her. "A dance, football games, diners. That's more than not really."

"We're just doing what all the other kids do." Annabel picked up the glasses off the counter.

"So you two are a couple?" Joan asked.

Annabel didn't want to talk to her mother about Danny, the first boy she'd ever kissed. She walked past Joan and into the dining room.

"Annabel, please," Joan said.

Annabel spun around, glasses in her hands. "What do you want to know? Yes, we go to football games, and diners, and we went to a dance. What's the big deal? Danny and I are dating. Teenagers date each other."

"A proper boy should ask permission from a girl's father before going steady. Your father did."

"And look how proper he turned out to be." Annabel set the glasses on the table and attempted to leave the room, but Joan stopped her and spun her around by the shoulders.

"Hey, I don't appreciate your sass. You don't know everything. I know you think you do, but you don't. Your father wasn't always like this. He was good." She paused, and a small smile crept across her face. "He was very good once."

"Why did he change?"

Joan took the question in and after a slight pause, she softly replied, "I don't know."

"Was he still good in that picture?"

Annabel motioned to the family portrait hanging on the wall. The youth of her mother showed all over her round face. No more than eighteen years old, Joan looked happy.

Joan's blue eyes shone in a way Annabel had never seen before. They sparkled without a sense of worry on her face. She looked healthier. She wasn't as thin as she was now. Annabel thought, but couldn't remember, the last time her mother finished all the food on her plate, despite nagging for Annabel to do so.

Annabel studied Joan's broad smile, a smile of a young woman innocently anticipating the rest of her life—a woman who didn't yet know of all the drunken fights ahead of her.

Now Joan's smile, when she smiled, was no longer that of a young woman eagerly anticipating the rest of her life. It was the smile of a deflated woman already knowing what her life was, yet trying to make the best of it. George had dulled the sparkle in his wife's eyes.

Joan was only two years older than Annabel in the picture, yet was already a wife and a mother. By the time she'd realized her husband was an alcoholic, she was trapped. Without even a high school diploma, she didn't have many options.

"He wasn't as bad in that picture as he is now, but his hardness was starting to show. I didn't know how to stop it."

Annabel looked away from the picture. "I'm sorry." She paused. "Maybe I don't know what I expect you to do. I know why you pretend like things aren't the way they are. I know it's not easy, but if you think that one day he'll just wake up a changed man, he won't. It's just a desperate attempt to get him to care, and he doesn't."

"Even though he may not ask how our day is, I like to think he wants to know."

"Well he doesn't," Annabel said softly.

Joan pressed her lips tightly together and whispered, "I know."

GEORGE SAT AT his desk and waited for the work hour to come to an end. He was tired, but was used to being tired. The struggle to forget one's past was mentally exhausting, and he had been feeling the effects of a distressed mind for a long time. Drink was his only source of solace.

George shuffled mindlessly through a stack of work papers and the phone rang on his direct line.

"Turner," he mumbled into the receiver.

"George. It's Bobby Hanley."

"Bobby. I hope you're not calling about going hunting this weekend. I don't feel much for hunting this ..."

"No, no that's not why I'm calling. Listen, I got a call from Carl Scully yesterday. Michael Feller passed away."

"Wh ... wh ... what's that you say?" George stumbled. "You ... you got a ... a ..."

"A call, George. I got a call. Feller died in a car accident a couple days ago. The service is next week. Me and the fellas are arranging to go and pay our respects. Even though he didn't keep in touch with anyone after the war, it's the right thing to do. He's out on the east coast. Think you can arrange to come?"

George sat stunned. He couldn't move. He couldn't talk. He was numb and felt nothing but the thud of his heart beating against his chest.

"Say," Bobby continued, "how come the two of you didn't keep in touch after the war? You guys were pretty tight."

There was no insinuation in Bobby's tone. He was merely stating a fact that everyone in their unit knew. George and Michael were close buddies, yet George still caught his breath. For so long he'd feared his and Michael's secret being found out even more than he feared the enemies he fought in the war. Dying on the battlefield was brave. Loving another man was unspeakable.

George couldn't attend the burial service of the man he still loved. His sorrow was too strong and would give him away. He took in a breath and made his voice strong so it didn't shake the way his hands shook.

"I won't be going," George said into the receiver. "I have no respect to pay."

"Jesus, George. What the hell happened between the two of you?"

"He means nothing to me. And I'm not making a trip to the east coast for a man who means nothing to me." George slammed the receiver down.

George sat for a while as the news settled in his cluttered mind. He pulled out the bottle of whiskey from the bottom drawer. With his eyes squeezed shut, he poured the brown liquid down his throat until the bottle emptied, and he wiped his wet lips with the palm of his bare hand.

George snatched the old photo from underneath his desk, looked at the picture, and smiled as tears wet his face. George and Michael were young, just boys in some ways, living away from home and seeing the world for the first time. George was young and naïve and believed he and Michael could live a life together. It would be a secret life, but George reasoned a hidden life together was better than no life together at all.

The night before their tour ended, and they were heading home, George told Michael that what they had between them didn't have to end there. He shared with Michael his plan for them to be together, but Michael was doubtful about their covert future. Against George's pleas, Michael went back to his hometown and married a girl he'd known since the seventh grade.

The whiskey hit George hard as he settled his lopsided vision onto the photo. He remembered everything, and it broke him up inside that he would never again feel the love he felt with Michael.

Even though he hadn't seen Michael in decades, it was now certain that George would never see Michael again.

Chapter Eighteen

AN UNEASY STIR made its way across the crowd. It was late in the third quarter, and the home team was down by eighteen points. Annabel plopped her elbows onto her knees and buried her hands over her face.

Danny had just overthrown another open receiver. His offense went three and out again. With his head down and his hands on his hips, he trotted to the sidelines and was welcomed by a chorus of boos.

Annabel blocked out the crowd's loud heckling, as well as Molly and Donna's nervous chatter about the game. She was in a zone, and her tunnel vision led straight to Danny. She watched him throw his helmet to the ground and take a seat alone at the end of the bench.

Coach soon stood over him and shouted in his face. Danny, red in the cheeks and drenched with sweat, stared at the ground until Coach took him by the shoulders and forced him to look him in the eyes. This was personal. Danny was embarrassing his team and Coach's legacy.

In sports, moments of glory and jubilation often collide with moments of agony, defeat, and humiliation. Annabel witnessed Danny experience all of these. She'd seen him hoisted as a champion, and now she watched him being derided as a failure. She felt it all as if it were happening to her. She reveled in Danny's accomplishments on the field, as if they were her own, but she also carried the heavy burden of his defeat.

And it hurt.

When Coach finished berating Danny, none of his teammates offered him encouragement, not even a supportive pat on the back. They kept their distance, frustrated over their quarterback's struggles.

The crowd was just as bad. The same people who had cheered Danny like a hero in previous games were now shouting for him to get out of the game. Annabel ignored the hypocrites. Danny may not have been giving the crowd much to cheer about that night, but as soon as he started playing like the quarterback they were used to seeing, they'd shower him with love again.

"What's wrong with him, Bel?" Donna yelled. "He never plays like this."

"Is he sick or something?" Molly shook her head. "He must be sick."

Annabel stared stone-faced at the field and stayed quiet as her friends carried on.

"Why's he playing so bad?" Donna asked.

"Time's running out! He better get it together soon," Molly said. "Bel! What's he doing?"

Annabel shot to her feet. "Shut up! Why don't the two of you just shut up!" She ran down the bleachers, her feet plopping heavily onto each step until she finally got to the bottom. She sped away from the field, the crowd, her friends, and Danny.

She hurried across the parking lot, feeling guilty for leaving Danny behind. She should have stayed and supported him, yet she kept walking until the crowd noise was just a soft hum against the evening breeze.

Annabel stopped at the edge of the parking lot and grasped onto the metal fence. She didn't want to cry but couldn't stop. The crowd's angry jeers and Coach screaming in Danny's face got the best of her.

The scene was violent, ferocious, and fierce.

The scene was her father.

ANNABEL ENTWINED HER fingers through the chain-linked fence and waited for Danny in her usual spot outside the locker room. Danny was the first player to storm out the door, and he headed straight to Annabel.

"I don't want to go to the diner tonight. I want to go somewhere else."

"Okay," Annabel replied. "Where?"

"To the meadow. I go there when I'm feeling like . . . like this," he said. "Come on."

Danny drove with his hands wrapped tightly around the wheel. He didn't reach for Annabel's hand as he often did. He brightened the car's headlights and turned into the dark gravel-covered lot of the meadow and parked the car in front of a large oak tree. A couple yards ahead, the gravel gave way to long blades of grass and fields thick with brush.

"You ever been here?" Danny switched off the engine and rolled down his window.

Annabel shook her head. "My mother would never allow me. She said it was dangerous."

"Dangerous? How?"

"She told me wild animals were back here."

"I've seen foxes, coyotes, and deer, but those things won't hurt you. The deer are pretty to watch if you're lucky enough to spot one. There's a stream up ahead, behind all the trees, that leads to the river. My dad used to take me fishing there when I was little."

"Really? That must have been a lot of fun," Annabel said, having no good memories with her own father to share.

"It was, but I'll be honest. The first time I came here I was pretty scared."

"What were you scared of?"

"Not the vicious wild deer," Danny teased.

Annabel nudged him. "Hey, that was my mom."

"I know. I know. What scared me was getting lost. I was six, and this place was so huge to me then. I was afraid I'd get lost and never see my mom or dad again. Just walking to the river was so far my father had to carry me on his shoulders halfway there. Now the place feels smaller every time I come here."

"You come here a lot?" Annabel asked.

"Not as often as I used to. We used to come here all the time—me, Jimmy, Steve, all the guys—when we were in junior high. This place wasn't scary anymore once I stopped being six. It felt like an adventure with so much land to explore. The fellas and I spent summers here swimming in the river, swinging from branches in the trees, just goofin' around."

"Sounds like fun," Annabel said.

"It was, but now I come here to relax. No more cannonballs for me." Danny leaned back into his seat and gazed thoughtfully out his window.

"Growing up stinks sometimes, doesn't it?" Annabel said.

"It sure does."

They sat quietly for a little while, surrounded by nature and all of its serenity. Danny's demeanor had eased since the disastrous football game. His shoulders relaxed, and his once tense hands that had clasped tightly around the steering wheel now lay loose and free at his sides.

There was peace to be found while sitting in the middle of nowhere.

Danny settled his eyes on Annabel. "Tell me something about you your friends don't even know."

The question made Annabel uneasy. There was much Molly and Donna didn't know about her, and she didn't want anyone else to know either, especially Danny.

"Oh . . . there isn't much," Annabel lied.

"There has to be something. It doesn't need to be anything big, just something Molly and Donna don't yet know."

Hearing Molly and Donna's name made Annabel feel bad for the way she yelled at them. The guilt was building up inside her and she blurted, "I told my friends to shut up at the game tonight."

"Why'd you do that?"

"It was at a very tense time, and they weren't exactly making me feel at ease."

"'A very tense time'? Is that code for the time I was stinking up the place?" Danny asked.

"You weren't doing that bad."

"Please, Bel. I know how I was. Were they giving me heck too?"

"No. They weren't like the others in the stands, but they were enough, and I couldn't take hearing it anymore so I told them to shut up. Then I left. Danny, I've never spoken to my friends like that before. I had no right to do that. I'm just horrible."

"You're not horrible. You know how many times I tell the fellas to shut up or to take a hike?"

"It's different with girls."

"They'll get over it."

"No they won't. They're girls."

Danny laughed.

"I'm serious," Annabel said. "We don't get over things like this easily."

"I'll remember that," he said. "But you're being too hard on yourself."

"Maybe," she responded softly and leaned back into her seat and looked out the window. "You still want to know something about me?"

"Yes."

"Though it's something my friends know about me, I don't think they know how strongly I feel about it."

"Okay. What is it?" Danny asked.

"That I don't care about getting married or having kids—at least not as much as everyone else. As though all there is to life is getting married and having kids. I'm not saying I wouldn't want that someday. I don't know, but what I do know is I really want to go to college. Live my life before I give everything up for a man and a bunch of kids."

Danny crossed his arms over his chest. "Wow. That's pretty big."

"Sorry, but it's what I want."

"If it's what you want then don't be sorry."

"It is what I want, and I won't be sorry."

"Where do you want to go?" Danny asked.

"No where. I need to be home soon."

Danny laughed. "I meant college. Where do you want to go to college?"

"Oh." Annabel felt stupid. "Right. Um . . . I haven't really thought about where I want to go. I just know I want to go somewhere that isn't here."

"Me too," Danny said softly and stared out his window.

Annabel rolled down her window, and the crisp evening breeze brushed against her face. She watched the wind overtake the trees and rustle the leaves on that perfect autumn night.

"Won't you get cold?" Danny asked.

"No. I like it like this." Annabel smiled.

Up until that night, most of their time together was spent socially with friends. Their time alone was limited, but now they sat in Danny's car without another soul in sight, and Danny's backseat theirs for the taking. Annabel thought about when her friends had asked what she'd do if Danny wanted to go all the way, and she was nervous this was the moment he'd ask.

Danny kept his gaze out the window as he fiddled anxiously with the door knob.

"Are you okay?" Annabel asked. "We can leave if you want to."

Danny turned away from the window and looked at Annabel. "Do you ever feel like you'll never get that one dream you've worked so hard for, or that maybe you'll lose that one dream you've worked so hard for just as you're about to get it?"

Annabel thought for a bit. "I suppose anything can happen. Is this about the game tonight? Danny, it was just one game. You're gonna . . ."

"It's not about the game," Danny interrupted. "It's about you."

"Me?"

"Well . . . us."

"Us? What are you talking about?"

Danny moved onto his side so he faced Annabel in a more comfortable position. "There was this guy. Eddie Capshaw. Quarterback. He played here when I was a kid. He had a rocket for an arm. My dad used to go on and on about him. He was that amazing. By the time Eddie was a sophomore every college wanted him. Not just colleges, but big universities. This town was crazy for him. Do you remember him?"

"No. I . . . I never paid much attention to sports."

"He was in all the papers."

"I guess I never paid much attention to papers either."

"Well he was everything to this town," Danny continued. "What every father wished his son to be."

"He sounds a lot like you," Annabel said.

Danny scoffed loudly. "Not even close. This guy was beyond anything anyone around here had ever seen. Coaches from towns all over fawned over him and still do. Except now it's not about what he could be, but what he could have been. Annabel . . ." Danny paused. "Eddie lost his dream because he got some girl pregnant and had to give it all up. College. Football. Life. He married a girl he didn't love and he lost everything. Can you imagine? Being so close to your dream, your *only* dream, and then the consequence of one moment in your life, one impulsive decision, snatches that all away and all you're left with is regret."

Annabel remembered the stories about girls getting caught in that way and then go away for a little while. "Why didn't the girl just go away for a while?"

"What do you know about things like that?" he asked.

"I . . . I heard stories. But I didn't believe all of them. I thought they were just stories."

"I guess we've all heard stories, but some, maybe even most, weren't just stories. They really happened. Do you know what an abortion is?"

Annabel shook her head.

"Those girls who go away for a while go to a place where they have the baby and then the baby is put up for adoption. You know that part, right?"

Annabel did.

"But not all girls have their babies," he said.

Annabel didn't know that.

"They get rid of it," Danny told her.

"How do you get rid of a baby?"

"It's done before there's a baby. They go to a special doctor who does that sort of thing. It's not legal, but it gets done anyway, but not all girls can afford to go to real doctors, and they have to go to dirty places where men who aren't even real doctors do things to them, painful things, to make sure the baby is never born."

Annabel was horrified. "How . . . how do you know all of this?"

"My dad told me."

"What?" Annabel popped up in her seat. "Why would your dad tell you something like this?"

"Because he wanted me to know the consequences. He always wants me to know the consequences."

Annabel didn't know what to say. She wasn't expecting to be told something like that. She crossed her legs tightly while imagining the atrocious things, the painful things, a man had to do to a girl to make her not pregnant anymore.

She thought about Molly and Donna, and wondered if they knew what an abortion was, but guessed they didn't since neither had mentioned it before. She decided she wouldn't let slip what she now knew. She didn't want to be the person to tell them that a baby was something you can get rid of, and she didn't want to make them wonder, as she was wondering, what that felt like.

"This is why I've only been willing to go so far with a girl. You know what I mean by that?" Danny watched her.

Annabel knew exactly what Danny meant by that and was relieved because it meant Danny probably wasn't going to ask her to go all the way. "Why are you telling me this?"

"Because I wanted you to know."

"But why? Why would you think I'd want to know something like this?"

Like a child's regret in learning Santa Claus wasn't real, Annabel regretted learning there were babies prevented from being born and consequences destroying dreams.

She needed to believe that dreams came true because she had so many of them, and she just didn't want to know the thing about the babies.

"I suppose I went too far. I'm sorry. Do you hate me?" Danny asked.

"Of course not." She leaned her head against the seat and looked at the boy she could never hate. Except, maybe, if he got her in a bad way and made her do what those other boys made those girls do to themselves and their babies. Only then could she imagine hating Danny Winfield.

Chapter Nineteen

DANNY DROVE DOWN the quiet road as Annabel sat at his side. The serenity he had felt at the meadow slowly seeped out of him. Images from the disastrous game again pounded through his mind—passes that sailed over receivers' heads, Coach screaming in his face, and the crowd jeering loudly at him.

Danny let everyone down that night, especially Annabel—the only person he wanted to please. He assumed he'd disappointed her to the point where she couldn't take it anymore, because with only minutes left in the game, and after another lousy throw, he had scanned the crowd for her, but all he saw was an empty seat between Molly and Donna. Annabel leaving before the game was over proved to him his performance was so horrible that even his own girlfriend couldn't bear to watch.

He glanced down at Annabel, as she lay against him with her eyes closed, and wondered if she was also thinking of the game and reliving his failure in her mind.

The bright headlights of a car sped up behind him. Danny clasped the wheel tightly and drove faster.

Annabel stirred. "What's wrong?"

"Somebody's coming." Danny squinted against the blaring lights in his rearview mirror as they got closer.

On a two-lane road, the fast car swerved wildly beside Danny's car.

"Hey there Danny-boy! Who you got there with you?" Ricky leaned out of the passenger-side window as Brett swerved into Danny's lane, forcing Danny nearly off the road.

"Watch it, greaser!" Danny yelled.

"Slow down, Danny." Annabel gripped the seat handle.

Danny slowed, but so did the car filled with greasers.

"Aww ain't that sweet! He's with his girl! Hey, where was the two of you tonight?" Curtis, sitting in the backseat, yelled out the window.

Ricky leaned his head farther out the window. "Annabel, I didn't know you were that kind of girl, but I like it." He made an obscene gesture with his tongue.

Danny's arm hung out the side of the car, and he pointed it to Ricky. "Watch it, greaser! And I'm not gonna tell you again."

"You're really scaring me, pretty boy," Ricky shouted. "Especially after that game tonight. I'll tie my hands behind my back and let you take a swing and you'll still miss me."

Curtis and Dennis howled loudly from the backseat and taunted Danny with insults about how badly he had played that night. Danny clenched his teeth as he clutched his hands tighter around the wheel and stepped on the gas.

"Slow down, Danny. Please," Annabel begged.

"I'm trying to get away from them, Bel. What do you want me to do?" he yelled.

Brett sped up to keep pace with Danny and leaned over Ricky. "Hey quarterback! Think those fancy colleges still want you after tonight? And tell your chic I won't forget what happened in the halls. I'm comin' for her."

Danny twisted his face at Brett. "What'd you say?"

Brett tossed him a dirty grin.

Danny looked to Annabel. "What'd he do?"

"Better keep a better eye on your girl, Danny-boy," Ricky yelled out the window. "Brett's on the make."

The raucous gang hooted and howled obnoxiously.

"Did they do something to you?" Danny yelled at Annabel.

"I don't know what they're talking about," Annabel lied. "They're trying to get you mad. Just slow down, Danny. Please."

Danny didn't slow down, and a pair of headlights appeared up ahead in Brett's lane, heading directly for Brett's car. Danny stepped on it and they sped faster down the road.

BRETT'S CAR TOOK off as the vehicle approaching head-on grew closer.

Annabel sat up and put a hand on the dashboard. "What are you doing? Slow down!"

In a trance-like stare, Danny gazed fixated on the road ahead of them.

Brett's car easily caught up with Danny's, and the two cars raced side by side. The driver heading toward the greasers laid on his horn, but it didn't deter Brett. He kept his foot punched on the gas.

"Stop this now!" Annabel pulled at Danny's shoulder. "Slow down and let them pass!"

Danny eased off the gas just in time for Brett to swerve in front of him and narrowly avoid crashing into the oncoming driver. The car filled with the greasers disappeared down the dark road.

Danny was out of his head. It was as though what just happened hadn't really happened, but Annabel's screams made it hard to ignore the reality that he had almost gotten them killed.

"Let me out!" Annabel yelled.

"What?" Danny was still driving.

"Let me out now!"

Danny pulled over, and Annabel threw open the door and stormed out of the car.

"Bel, what are you doing?" Danny shouted.

"What does it look like I'm doing?"

Danny got out of the car and followed Annabel along the side of the dark road. "Please get back in the car. We can talk about this."

Annabel spun around. "I don't want to talk about this. You almost got us killed. What were you thinking, Danny? You just . . . you . . . you . . . ugh! I can't even talk to you right now."

Danny watched her walk away. "I'm not perfect! I know that's what you want, but I'm not!"

Annabel stopped walking and faced Danny. "You think that's what I want? I just don't want to die so you can prove your ego while playing some idiotic macho game. I don't care who wins some stupid race."

"You don't care about winning?" Danny scoffed. "Yeah, sure you don't."

"What's that supposed to mean?"

"I'll tell you what that means." He put his hands on his hips and gave her a long, hard look. "Why'd you leave the game tonight before it was over?"

"What?" Annabel asked.

"You heard me."

"What's my leaving the game have to do with this?"

"Everything." Danny stepped closer to her. "Why'd you leave?"

"I . . . I just couldn't stay there. That's all."

"You say you don't care about winning, but that's not true. You do care! You care so much about winning that you couldn't even stand to watch me lose. I embarrassed you, just like I did everyone else, but at least they stayed to see me through it."

"Danny, they stayed to boo you. I didn't leave because you were losing. I left because you were hurting, and I couldn't take seeing that anymore. I wasn't embarrassed. I was weak."

"No. You left because I was losing, and you want me to be a winner. Everyone wants me to be a winner."

"Danny, that's ridiculous. Nobody wins all the time. You've lost before."

"Not like this," Danny replied softly and stuffed his hands into his jacket pockets. "I couldn't do anything right tonight, not with everyone screaming at me. Usually I'm able to block out the crowd, but not tonight. I felt defeated and alone out there. Thought I was gonna cry. Can you imagine that? Me crying on the football field in front of Coach, the guys, my father . . . the entire town."

"Danny . . ." Annabel began.

"I looked for you in the crowd," Danny interrupted. "I searched for your face."

Annabel struggled to meet his eyes, but she eventually did. "I'm . . . I'm sorry I wasn't there. You were looking for me because you needed to see a friendly face, but I left you. I'm sorry."

Danny dropped his hands from his pockets. "And I'm sorry I scared you tonight. I shouldn't have driven like that. I . . . I lost it."

"The greasers taunted you."

"I'm not using the greasers as an excuse and neither should you. I'm telling you, no matter what, that will never happen again. The way I acted. The way I talked to you. None of it will happen again. That's not me."

"You already promised me that," Annabel said.

"I promised you no more fighting. This wasn't a fight."

"No. It was a stupid car race that almost got us killed. When does it all end?"

"Now. It all ends now. I regret what I did tonight."

"Then we both did something we regret tonight."

Danny went to her, folded her hands in his, and pressed them against his chest. "I am *never* going to scare you like that again." He looked straight in her eyes. "I'm the person who should make you feel safe, always."

"You do," Annabel assured him.

"Tell me what Brett was talking about back there. What happened in the halls?"

"I don't want to talk about him," Annabel said.

"A greaser messing with you, heck, any guy messing with you is something I want to talk about. Tell me what happened."

"He's a guy who likes to torment people for kicks, and once he gets bored he moves on to the next. He's scum."

"Did he touch you?"

"Danny, please."

"Did he touch you?" Danny said louder.

"No," she lied.

Danny studied her, unsure if she was telling the truth.

"He didn't," Annabel stressed.

Danny swallowed hard. "If he ever touches you—a hair, a finger—I need you to tell me."

ANNABEL SENSED SOMETHING was wrong the moment she entered the quiet and unusually still house. The TV was off, and her father wasn't in his favorite chair. She walked through the dimly lit living room and poked her head into the kitchen. That room was empty too.

Not knowing where her parents were, Annabel went upstairs. Her parents' bedroom door was closed, but the light was on. She went to the door and heard deep groans and Joan talking on the phone, but the words were too muffled for Annabel to make out.

She backed away from the door, walked to the end of the hallway, and looked out the window. The garage door was open, but George's car wasn't in it, nor was the car parked in the driveway or on the street.

Annabel hadn't noticed any of this when she left Danny's car. Another heavy groan came from the bedroom, and she hurried back to her spot and planted her ear against the door. Seconds later, the door swung open and Annabel lost her balance and fell to her knees at her mother's feet.

Joan jumped back. "Annabel! What are you doing out here? When did you get home?"

Annabel quickly pushed herself off the floor, embarrassed she'd just been caught eavesdropping and had fallen to the floor. "Jus . . . just now."

Joan appeared anxious. She quickly closed the door behind her and stepped into the hall. Annabel stole a glance into the room before the door fully closed and saw her father lying in bed, wincing in pain. Joan took Annabel by the arm and pulled her down the hall.

"What's wrong with him?" Annabel asked.

"Your father was in a bad car accident, but nobody got hurt."

"He looks hurt."

"Nobody *else* got hurt," Joan said pointedly.

Annabel motioned toward the bedroom door that failed to keep her father's moans of agonizing pain inside. "Shouldn't he be in a hospital?"

"He didn't want to go, and the sheriff thought it best that he stay here and that we call the doctor."

"The sheriff? The sheriff knows about this?" Annabel asked.

"The sheriff brought him here. They know each other. Sheriff Brody was in the war, too."

Annabel pressed her back against the wall and inhaled a deep breath. "He was drunk."

"Annabel . . ." Joan began.

"Of course he was drunk," Annabel said flatly. "Where's his car?"

"Your father drove the car into a tree. They hauled the car to the station. The sheriff knows a place that can fix it. The sheriff's handling this quietly since no one else got hurt."

Annabel pushed herself off the wall. "No one else got hurt *this* time, but what about next time or the time after that? I used to think he was only dangerous to us because we're stuck in this house with him, but no one's safe with him around. He's nothin' but a no-good drunk."

The doorbell buzzed loudly, and both Annabel and Joan jumped.

"That's the doctor." Joan nervously ran a hand through her hair. "Stay in your room. I don't want you to see this."

Annabel glanced at the bedroom door, and despite her father's cries of pain, she casually shrugged. "Fine. I don't care what happens to him anyway."

THE DOCTOR LEFT George's room, and he and Joan went to the kitchen. Joan made coffee, and they sat down at the table and sipped their coffees while the doctor gave Joan the rundown of George's condition. His injuries weren't life-threatening, but George would have to stay in bed for a couple weeks and the doctor would visit every day to check on him.

The doctor was aware of George's drinking and cautioned Joan about the withdrawals he would experience.

"For the first time in a long time your husband won't be drinking. His body's become accustomed to alcohol, and when consumption suddenly stops, the effects can be very painful," the doctor said.

"What kind of effects?" Joan asked.

"Oh, there are many. Headache, fever, heavy sweats, nausea, possible hallucinations. If he experiences anything more serious like tremors or seizures, call me."

"Seizures? Do you think that will happen?"

"It's possible, but probably not likely." The doctor finished his coffee, stood up, and picked his coat off the back of the chair he had been sitting on. "I'll stop by every day and manage his pain. Also, try to keep him as hydrated as possible. That'll help with the symptoms."

Joan saw the doctor to the door and then went to Annabel's room. Joan watched Annabel sleep for a bit before returning to her own room, where George slept comfortably, with the help of the doctor's medication.

She grabbed a pillow from the bed and brought it downstairs. As she headed to the living room, she pulled a blanket from the hall closet and tucked herself in it on the couch. She fell asleep quickly, exhausted from the night's dramatics.

She awoke early the next morning and started making oatmeal for Annabel's breakfast.

ANNABEL WALKED INTO the kitchen, her books in hand.

"Good morning," Joan said. "The oatmeal's not ready. Take some juice."

Annabel took the jar of juice from the refrigerator and poured herself a glass. She sat down at the table and sipped her juice. "I'm not very hungry."

"You still have to eat." Joan placed a bowl in front of Annabel, and deciding that the oatmeal was cooked enough, slopped a couple spoonfuls into Annabel's bowl.

Joan relayed to Annabel what the doctor had told her last night. Annabel listened without much interest to the account of her father's condition, as she picked at her oatmeal. She cut the breakfast short by saying she had homework to do, even though it was Saturday morning, and Annabel never did homework on Saturday mornings.

Annabel called Molly and Donna, but their mothers told her neither girl was home. When she called a second time and was given the same response, she suspected the mothers of lying for their daughters, and that her friends were home but didn't want to talk to her.

Annabel was in her room, listening to the radio, when she saw Sylvia through the window sitting on her front porch swing. Other than Danny, there wasn't another person Annabel would rather have been with than Sylvia at that moment. She quickly changed into a pair of white Capris and a red cardigan sweater.

Annabel considered going out through her window, but it was daylight, and she didn't want to risk the neighbors seeing. They would certainly tell her mother if they saw her climbing down a tree through her window. That would be the end of her nightly walks, and she couldn't risk that.

Joan was putting on her jacket when Annabel went downstairs.

"I'm heading to the grocery store," she said.

"I'm heading next door. Sylvia's outside."

Joan peeked through the curtains.

"I'll be back before the doctor gets here." Joan walked out the door and gave Sylvia a wave as she got into the brown station wagon George had bought her because under no circumstance was she allowed to drive the Cadillac. He treated that car like a baby, until he drove it into a tree.

Annabel went to her neighbor. "Hi, Sylvia."

"Hello, Annabel." Sylvia smiled as she blew out smoke.

Annabel sat on the top step of the porch. "How are you?"

"I'm okay, but I'll be better when Henry comes back later this afternoon. He's been away on business. It was only three days, but it feels much longer." Sylvia pulled on her cigarette.

"I haven't seen you out here in a while," Annabel said.

"Being out here when Henry's gone makes me feel lonelier than usual. But I know he's coming home today, so I won't feel lonely for long."

Smoke rose from Sylvia's lips, and she drew deeply again on the cigarette. She tossed the stub of what was left of the cigarette into nearby bushes and pressed her fingers into the pockets of her high-waist blue jeans. She stretched her back against the porch swing, and the top buttons of her white blouse splayed open. A slight breeze tossed her blonde hair over her eyes, and she lightly brushed a hand across her forehead and pushed the strands of hair away. She leaned her head back and smiled. Sylvia was casually beautiful and serene in that moment—a result of knowing Henry was coming home soon.

"How's school?" Sylvia asked.

"It's okay," Annabel answered, then paused. "How come girls get their feelings hurt so easily?"

"Do we?" Sylvia chuckled. "Hmmm ... I suppose we do. I don't know." She looked at Annabel. "Come over here. What's this all about?"

Annabel sat beside Sylvia on the porch swing. "I got into an argument with my friends last night. I told them to shut up, and now they're not speaking to me."

"Telling someone to shut up isn't the most awful thing a person can do."

"But they aren't just someone, they're my friends. My best friends."

Sylvia slipped an arm around Annabel's shoulders. "Well, that's a big difference, isn't it?" She patted Annabel's leg. "Listen, sweetie, nobody's perfect. I'm sure your emotions were getting the best of you when you said what you did. Apologize. Tell them you were wrong and that you're sorry."

"I called them twice already, but their mothers told me they weren't home. I think they were lying."

Sylvia laughed. "Yes, they probably were. My mother lied for me when boys I was mad at and didn't want to talk to called me. You know what some of them did anyway?"

"What?" Annabel asked.

"They came to my house. They were persistent. If I wasn't going to give them a chance to apologize over the phone, they'd come to my door and apologize there. Most of them were sweet and I forgave them ... until I found another reason to break up with them." Sylvia laughed and ruffled Annabel's hair.

"So you're saying I should go to their house?"

"Why not? You have good friends. They'll forgive you."

"How do you know that?"

"Because I've forgiven friends for doing a lot worse than telling me to shut up," Sylvia answered.

"No, I mean, how do you know they're good friends?"

Sylvia smiled and picked up the pack of cigarettes sitting on the window's ledge. "I could tell. I watched the three of you this past summer almost as much as the three of you watched me." She winked at Annabel and lit a cigarette.

"How . . . how did you know? We . . . we weren't really watching you. I swear!"

Sylvia breathed in the lit cigarette and eyed Annabel as smoke escaped her lips. "You swear?" She raised her eyebrows.

"No. I don't swear. I'm sorry. We were watching you."

Sylvia laughed as she puffed her cigarette. "What are you sorry for? We were outside for all the public to see. You weren't the only ones watching. I know I don't act like most of the women here. Maybe I am a bit eccentric."

"Maybe?" Annabel asked.

Sylvia laughed. "Okay. I am. But something happens to me when Henry's near me. Everything disappears. It's just Henry and me, and I forget the world around us. I'm not sure if that's good or bad, but it's what happens."

"I don't know either, but I know we liked watching the two of you. I've never seen a couple act so in love."

Sylvia rolled the cigarette between her fingers. "It makes me happy to hear that. Sometimes I feel so unsure, even though Henry gives me no reason to do so."

"Well, that's just silly."

Sylvia laughed out loud and drew on her cigarette. "Yes. You're right. It is silly. I need to stop being so silly and be more rational. That's what Henry says. He says I'm irrational sometimes." She thought for a moment and then said, "Are you going on one of your walks tonight and look through people's windows?"

"I don't know. I'll probably go see my friends and apologize."

"That's a good idea. Hey," Sylvia tapped the ashes off the tip of the cigarette, "you ever look through my window?"

"Gosh no!"

Sylvia smiled. "I'm teasing." She raised her arms and again stretched back against the porch swing. "I'm in a good mood because Henry's coming home and Henry always says I like to play jokes when I'm happy. I guess that's true."

Annabel was relieved the issue wasn't pressed, yet felt guilty for lying to Sylvia. She had looked into her window once when Sylvia was crying while Henry was away, but it wasn't intentional, and Annabel never did it again.

"You be sure to go to your friends today. Don't lose good friends. Every girl needs her friends. Don't ever forget that. I sure wish someone had told me that when I was your age. Instead, I blew my friends off any time a new boy came into my life." Sylvia drew in the last drag and tossed the cigarette away.

"I could really use a few good girlfriends in my life right now. Your girlfriends will be there when the boys are long gone, remember that."

"I will."

"I love Henry, but I can't expect him to be everything to me. I smother him, I know. He's all I have. The other wives, I don't think they get me." She looked at Annabel. "I like your mother. I think under different circumstances we could have been good friends. Every girl, no matter her age, needs a good girlfriend."

Annabel thought about it. She couldn't imagine any circumstance where Sylvia and her mother would be friends. They were complete opposites.

"Maybe I can be your girlfriend?" Annabel asked timidly.

Sylvia smiled. "I would love that." She patted Annabel's lap and stood up. "Come on. We both have things we need to do. I need to get ready for Henry and you need to get to your friends."

Chapter Twenty

ANNABEL SAT AT the kitchen table and barely touched the tuna fish sandwich her mother prepared for her.

"Tuna fish used to be your favorite." Joan sat down next to Annabel, a glass of water in her hand. "I bought it especially for you." She took a sip of her drink and watched as Annabel picked at her food.

"I'm not very hungry." Annabel checked the kitchen clock. It was nearly two o'clock.

"You barely ate your breakfast this morning. You should at least be a little bit hungry."

"Well I'm not," Annabel said sternly and pushed the plate away.

George was still in bed. The doctor had come and gone with instruction for more rest and a prescription for the pain. Joan had more compassion than Annabel could muster, and she didn't understand how her mother could care for a man who treated her so badly.

"Can I go to Donna's?" Annabel asked.

"Have you finished your chores?"

Annabel hadn't even started her chores. "I'll finish them tomorrow."

"I want you to eat at least half of that sandwich. Then you may go."

Annabel scarfed down half of the sandwich and left the table with a mouthful of food.

"Eat like a young lady," Joan yelled.

"Gotta hurry," Annabel muttered.

She scurried up the stairs to her room. She switched on the radio and Ritchie Valens' song "We Belong Together" played. She sat on the edge of the windowsill as she listened to her favorite song.

A sunny autumn day unfolded outside her window. The sunshine made the outside appear warm, but every person who passed Annabel's window wore coats. The sun alone wasn't enough to withstand the day's brisk.

Annabel went to her closet and slid a thick wool sweater off its hanger. That would keep her warm while she walked to Donna's house. She decided to go to Donna's first because the walk to her house was shorter than to Molly's house. She could have asked her mother for a ride, but she didn't want to be trapped in a car with her for even a short distance. She was sure she'd want to talk about her father.

Annabel was about to pull the sweater over her head, when she heard a loud shriek from outside her window. She rushed to look outside and saw Henry exiting a taxi in front of his house. Sylvia ran down the long driveway, her arms extended in the air, unable to contain her excitement in seeing her husband. She cried out his name and jumped into his arms. Henry dropped his suitcase and lifted Sylvia in the air.

Sylvia laughed loudly and squeezed her legs around his waist. She smacked kisses all over his face while proclaiming how much she'd missed him. Henry held his face up to her and accepted his wife's affection with a smile.

The man in the taxi took Henry's baggage out of the trunk and placed them on the sidewalk. Henry reached into his pocketbook, pulled out a bill, and handed the money to the man. The man nodded at Henry before returning to his taxi. He looked back at the couple before getting into the car.

Annabel wondered how many times the man had seen wives greet their husbands as passionately as Sylvia greeted Henry. Did the taxi man have someone at home who loved him just as much?

As the taxi drove away, Henry carried his wife to the front door, leaving his bags on the sidewalk. Sylvia looked up to Annabel's window just as Henry stepped through the threshold of the door. She waved to Annabel and yelled, "Henry's home!"

Annabel smiled because Sylvia was happy again.

ANNABEL KNOCKED ON Donna's front door and waited until the door swung open and Donna appeared. "Oh, it's you. What do you want?"

"I called you . . . twice," Annabel said.

"I was busy."

"No you weren't."

Donna shrugged. "Maybe I wasn't."

"You can't ignore me forever."

"I'd sure like to try."

"Listen, I'm sorry I yelled at you last night. I didn't mean to. I just . . . I lost it. It was hard to take. The coach, the crowd, you, and Molly. Everyone was so angry and yelling. It was like . . ." Annabel was about to say it was like her father.

"It was like what?" Donna prodded.

Over Donna's shoulder, Annabel peered into the house and took in all the family photos that covered the hallway walls—certain that the happiness depicted in those pictures matched the actual experiences of living in that home. And she desired to know the feeling of growing up in a functional home.

Her eyes fell back on Donna. "It was like . . . it was like nothing I've ever felt before. And hope to never feel again."

"I'm sorry. I didn't know you were feeling all of that. Are you okay now?"

"Yes. Hey, can we call Molly over so I can apologize to her, too?"

"No need to call. She's upstairs."

"Gosh. You mean to tell me the two of you were that sour at me that you weren't even gonna call me over?"

"Nah." Donna pulled Annabel into the house. "We were just about to call ya."

THEY SAT IN a circle on Donna's bedroom floor, a huge bowl of popcorn in the middle. Molly accepted Annabel's apology as earnestly as Donna had, and they wasted no time falling into their regular routine of talking about boys and the latest high school gossip.

Molly took a drink from the bottle of soda Donna's mother had given each of them with careful instruction not to spill. "I think Suzy and Chuck are dating, but he's being really quiet about it because his buddies torment Suzy all the time for having a big nose, and he doesn't want to be known as the boy who's dating the girl with the big nose. He must like her some though if he's willing to date her at all, even if it is in secret."

"Gosh. I'd never let a guy date me in secret," Donna said. "I know I'm not the catch of the school, but if a boy wants to date me, then he's gonna walk the halls with me. If he's too embarrassed to do that, then I wouldn't date him."

Annabel smiled. "I'm glad to hear you say that, but stop saying you're not a catch."

Molly took a handful of popcorn from the bowl and shoved it into her mouth. "Boys are just cruel sometimes." She chomped on the snack as she talked. "Some boys are simply not nice while others are downright painful, like Brett and his followers. I can't wait till the day I never have to see the face of those rotten greasers again."

Annabel thought about the night before and almost getting run off the road by those rotten greasers. Then she recalled Danny's temper behind the wheel and her father crashing his car into a tree, and she no longer wanted to talk about the greasers.

"I think there's something wrong with Sylvia," Annabel blurted.

"What do you mean?" Donna ate a fistful of popcorn and chased it down with soda. "We know she's different, but that's what we love about watching her through your window, right?"

"Sure is," Molly agreed.

"Yeah, I know, but I've gotten to know her a bit, and she really loves her husband," Annabel said.

"No kidding." Donna giggled. "Her love for her husband was on display all summer for all to see. I don't think she could have bent over her garden any farther than she did."

Molly laughed out loud. "Donna, you're so bad."

"I know." Donna laughed even harder than Molly.

"But it's more than that," Annabel said. "It's like she can't breathe when he's not there, and she cries a lot when he goes away on business. It's like the loneliness eats at her and she's lost all purpose in life. It's so unusual. She's a grown woman, and surely a grown woman should be able to function normally when her husband is away, no matter how much she misses him, right?"

"All I know is my mom tells her friends all the time that she wishes my dad would go fishing for the weekend," Donna said, and after a couple seconds she slapped a hand over her mouth. "Oh my gosh. Does that mean that my mother doesn't love my father?"

"No, Donna. Your mother loves your father just fine," Annabel said. "It just means that your mother doesn't depend on your father the way Sylvia depends on Henry."

"Are you certain it doesn't mean she that she doesn't love him? Because some days she *really* can't wait for him to leave the house."

"Don't worry. My mom's the same way," Molly said. "One day she shooed my dad out the door with a broom. I just think she wants to talk on the phone all day about town gossip, but doesn't want my dad to hear and prove him right since he always tells her that all she does is talk on the phone all day. They bicker a lot about stuff like that, but then she makes him feel bad and he ends up apologizing."

Annabel tried to remember a time her father had ever apologized for any of the horrible things he'd done, but there was never a time.

"My dad's the same way," Donna said. "This one time he . . ."

"Guys, I think Sylvia's sick," Annabel interrupted.

Molly looked at her. "What kind of sick?"

"Yeah, what kind of sick?" Donna scrunched her face in a confused state. "She's always looked better than fine to me."

"I'm not talking about the kind of sick that makes a person physically ill. I mean the kind of sick people get in their heads."

"You mean crazy people," Donna yelled.

"Like Mr. Blacko who lives on the corner of Baker's street?" Molly asked. "He paces up and down the street all day, and his grass is so long the kids use his yard as a battlefield. They play war while army crawling through his grass and shooting each other with toy guns."

"I saw him talking to a tree one morning when I was coming out of the hardware store with my dad," Donna said. "I laughed, and my dad told me to hush, but how could I not laugh?" She chucked her arms up at her sides. "The man was talking to a tree." She turned to Annabel. "You think Sylvia's crazy like Wacko Blacko?"

"Mr. Blacko isn't crazy," Annabel said. "He's just old and senile. And I never used the word crazy. Sylvia's not crazy, but she is unstable. When Henry's home everything is fine and good in the world, but the moment he leaves, it's as I said, like she's lost all purpose in life. She told me she doesn't know who she is when she's not with him. She practically mowed him down in the driveway when he came home today. She was grinning like a fool, but I know when he leaves again she'll stay in that house and cry every day that he's gone."

"I don't care. I'd still do anything to be Sylvia and have a man like Henry touch me and kiss me the way he does," Donna said. "All I want is for a man to love me the way Henry loves Sylvia."

Molly whole-heartedly agreed with Donna.

"Despite how much you guys think Henry loves Sylvia, when he's away she thinks he's with other women," Annabel said.

"What?" Donna yelled over the bowl of popcorn. "She actually told you that?"

"Yep. She also told me she takes pills to help her be happy when Henry's away, but they don't really do a good job."

"Gosh, Bel, Sylvia sure tells you a lot," Molly said.

"She also told me she knows we used to watch her from my bedroom window."

"What?" Donna yelled again. "She knew? And she told you? Was she mad?"

"Nah." Annabel took a swig from her soda bottle. "She actually said that she likes you guys and that I had nice friends."

"That's really cool of her to know we were spying and to like us anyway," Molly said.

"She gets it, I suppose." Annabel sighed. " I just wish I knew how to help her. It's not normal to be how she is. She's up, then down, then back up again, and then back down. Just like that. Everything depends on Henry." She leaned in closer to Molly and Donna and stuck her fist in the middle of their circle. She eyed them closely. "We need to make a promise that we will never let a man dictate our emotions like that." She squeezed her fist tight until her knuckles turned white. "Promise?"

Donna shoved her fist beside Annabel's. "I promise I won't be too sad if my husband goes away for business."

"Boys still annoy me in so many ways and my husband will most likely annoy me too. I'll probably be like my mother and shoo him out the door with a broom. So, yeah, I'm in." Molly stuck her fist in the center.

"We promise to never let our love for our future husbands, if there are any . . ." Annabel began.

"Hey don't say that." Donna scowled at Annabel. "At least Molly and me are certain we want a husband."

"Fine." Annabel started over. "We promise to never let our love for our future husbands make us forget who we are because we will always be our own person."

Molly and Donna each promised as they touched fists.

DANNY WALKED OFF the practice field late Sunday afternoon, drenched in sweat. Coach had run the team hard in response to the terrible loss they endured Friday night. Jimmy, sweaty and winded, brushed Danny's shoulder as they passed each other.

"You better not throw like my grandma next week. I ain't doin' sprints again," he grumbled.

Danny ignored his moody teammate and headed to the locker room. He changed out of his sweat-stained clothes and dirty cleats. With the exception of some hostile looks shot his way, most of the team treated him like he wasn't there. The sudden disdain the team held for their quarterback was palpable.

"Hey!" Steve yelled out to Danny as he walked to his car.

Danny turned around. "What? You want to give me crap, too?"

"Nah." Steve ran to him. "I know we all have bad games."

"Then how come the rest of the fellas don't seem to know that?"

"Ah, they're still sour at you about what happened at the diner. You leaving early and all. When we're winning it's easier to overlook, but when you play like you did Friday night, not so much."

"When are they gonna let the diner thing go? I told them why I left."

"I know. I know. Forget it. They'll get over it. Have a great game this week and bring us closer to State, and it'll be like the diner thing never happened."

"We'll see." Danny stuck his key into the car door lock. "Need a ride home?"

"Nah. I got my dad's car."

"All right then." Danny opened the door.

"Wait, there's something I wanted to talk to you about."

"I don't have a lot of time." Danny started to get into his car. "I'm tired and need a shower and . . ."

"It's about Annabel," Steve said.

Danny popped out of the car, shut the door, and faced Steve. "What about Annabel?" he asked, and for the first time that day, Steve had Danny's full attention.

Steve glanced around the parking lot, making sure no one else was around. The lot was almost empty, as most of the other players had already left. "A woman who lives across the street from Annabel is part of my mom's knitting group. She told my mom some things about Annabel's father. I overheard my mom and dad talking about it. They said he recently passed out in his car in the middle of the night. His head fell on the horn and practically woke up the whole neighborhood. The man who lives next door had to carry Mr. Turner inside the house.

"Then they started talking about some other things they'd heard, something about a real bad temper and a fight Mr. Turner had with some guy in a bar, but they were whispering so low I couldn't hear much more. But he sounds like he has some real issues. Have you met him yet?"

Danny stood like a statue while taking in every word Steve said. He didn't know much about Annabel's father except that he managed the bank and he had fought in the war.

"No. I've only been to the house once and he wasn't home. I see him around town sometimes, but I don't think he knows who I am. Why would he?"

Danny used to see Mr. Turner every Saturday when he was a young boy and insisted on going to the bank with his father because the tellers handed out suckers to the little kids.

"What else do you know?" Danny asked.

"That's it. I can try to snoop some more if I hear them mention him again, but I don't know how much more they're gonna say. You gonna mention something to Annabel?"

Danny thought hard about what he was going to do and responded the only truthful way he could. "I don't know what I'm gonna do. Who else have you told?"

"Just you."

"Keep it that way."

Danny's mind raced on the short drive home. Annabel lived with a man who had a bad temper and liked to drink. Danny knew the implications of that scenario and everything that could go wrong. He remembered Annabel showing up to his house with a black eye, and he pressed on the gas, anxious to get home and confront his father.

Danny squealed the tires to a grinding halt in his driveway and bolted for the front door.

"Dad! Dad!" He entered the house and threw off his jacket. It hit the back of the living room chair and dropped to the floor.

Hugh Winfield rushed out from his study, a look of alarm settled across his face as he gripped tightly a book. "What is it? What's wrong?"

"Did you know George Turner is a drunk?" Danny faced his father with an intensity usually only felt on the football field.

"Whe . . . where did you hear this?" Hugh stammered.

"Does it matter if it's true?"

"I suppose it doesn't."

"Did you know?" Danny pressed.

"I . . . I knew of some things, but . . ." Hugh said while looking everywhere but in Danny's eyes.

"I thought you were supposed to look the person you're speaking to in the eyes."

"That's right." Hugh raised his eyes to meet Danny's. "Even when it is difficult."

"Why is this difficult? Because you lied to me?"

"Son, I didn't lie."

"But you knew," Danny said.

"I'd heard stories."

"Yet you told me nothing."

"They weren't my stories to tell."

Danny scoffed loudly. "You say it like they're some made-up bedtime tales. Whatever stories you heard were real life and had real-life consequences. Annabel had a black eye last week."

"I'm sorry. I didn't know that."

"Of course you didn't. You're not involved in her life, but I am. She said she fell. If I'd known the truth about her father, I'd have known that wasn't true."

"And what would you have done?"

"I would have asked for the truth. I would have asked if her father had done that, and if he had . . ."

Hugh stepped close to Danny. "You would have gone over there."

"That's right." Danny stood before his father with the confident posture of a soldier falling in line before his commander.

"And what would you have done?" Hugh asked.

"Whatever I needed," Danny answered.

"Whatever you needed? You're talking like a tough guy now. A tough guy with no brains and nothing to lose. This is why I didn't tell you. It's not for kids to know."

"I'm not a kid. I'll be in college in less than a year."

"That's right. You'll be in college in less than a year and I don't want you getting involved in anything that could get in the way of that. I want you to leave this alone. I didn't stop you from seeing this girl, but enough is enough. Do not get involved in her family life. That is not your concern."

Danny let out a short laugh. "You didn't stop me from seeing this girl? That's really funny. As if you could have stopped me from seeing Annabel even if you'd tried."

"I don't like the tone you're taking with me, son. You better stop right now."

Danny backed away and held his arms up at his sides. "Or else what? What are you gonna do? You gonna hit me the way Mr. Turner hits Annabel?"

"No one's hitting anyone."

Mrs. Winfield came running into the room, a red apron tied snugly around her waist. "What's going on out here? What's all this yelling?"

Hugh gave Danny a look of warning before he turned to his wife and smiled. "It's nothing, dear. Danny was just venting about his poor performance in Friday's game."

Mrs. Winfield went to Danny and took his head in her hands. "Oh, Danny. Don't beat yourself up over this." She pulled his forehead down to meet her lips and kissed him. "Everyone has bad games."

"I told him to forget about what's upsetting him. Push it to the side. Colleges already want him and college is all that matters right now. Isn't that right, Danny?" Hugh gave Danny another stern look, but Danny turned his head away and walked backward toward the front door.

"I gotta get out of here," he said.

"Where are you going?" Mrs. Winfield asked. "I just made brownies. Your favorite."

"I gotta leave." Danny twisted the doorknob, but Hugh slammed his hand over Danny's and stopped him.

"You are not to leave this house!"

"I have to go!" Danny pushed his father's hand off the door handle and ran outside

"Where are you going?" Mrs. Winfield yelled.

"Get back inside this house!" Hugh Winfield screamed.

Danny revved up the car and peeled out of the driveway and into the streets.

Chapter Twenty-One

DANNY SKIDDED HIS car to a red light, his heart pumping fast and his breath, scattered and heavy. He was out of control, and he knew it. He tried to calm his mind and steady his breathing, knowing full well all he could lose with one careless mistake, just like Eddie Capshaw.

The light turned green. Danny slammed on the gas and drove straight, despite Annabel's house being a left turn. If sports had taught Danny anything, it was that one never performed well with a scattered mind. So he drove for a while to give himself time to think about what he was doing.

He ended up at the first football field he ever played on—the place he learned to play the game he loved so much—the field where he started out as a child with a big dream, and was now only months away from achieving that big dream. College football was his for the taking.

Danny gazed nostalgically at the field, covered in memories, for a little while longer and then drove to the high school and sat in the school parking lot. He took a good, long look at the football field he now played. So far everything had worked out as he and his father had planned, and he had no reason to believe that would change.

Danny's successful path thus far had been owed to the guidance of his father, and he'd never spoken to his father in the manner he did that day, nor had he ever defied an order given to him by his father. But the demand that Danny do nothing about the possibility that Annabel was being hurt in her home was an order he couldn't obey.

Danny drew in a deep breath as he peered out at the field. He remembered coming there to watch high school games with his father when he was a little boy. The field had looked humongous to his young eyes. Little Danny couldn't imagine being big enough to ever play on that field, but now he was, and other little boys came to watch him play with their own dreams beating in their hearts.

Danny drove away from the field with a calmer mind, but he still wanted to see Annabel. He had to. He couldn't go home without knowing that she was okay. He drove to her house as the sun was setting and parked across the street.

From the outside, the house looked perfectly peaceful, but Danny knew the happenings inside the house told a far different story. The drawn shades left his imagination to roam wildly. In the time that he sat in the car, stewing over what to do, the sun had completely vanished below the horizon.

"What are you doing, Danny?" he said aloud as he tugged at his hair with both hands. "What's your plan? What's your plan? What's your plan?" he mumbled and dropped his hands into his lap. "You have no plan." He sighed and leaned back into his seat. "You were just acting like an over-confident hot head."

Danny looked back at the house, still determined to see Annabel. He didn't backtalk his father for nothing. He got out of the car and walked across the street, but a movement coming from the tree at the side of the house stopped him.

At first he thought it was a cat, but the shadow it cast was too big for a small animal, and seconds later, Annabel jumped down from the tree and landed on her front lawn.

Danny pulled back. "What are you doing jumping out of a tree?"

Annabel stopped, looking shocked. "What are you doing standing in front of my house?"

"I . . . I needed to see you." Danny pointed a finger at the tree. "Why did you just come out of that tree?"

"The tree?" Annabel wiped her hands against her pants. "Oh . . . um . . . Sometimes I sneak out of my house through my window and climbed down this tree."

"To do what?"

"To walk, mostly, and get away . . . even if it's just for a little bit."

Danny took her response in. "Tell me what happened to your eye."

"Danny," Annabel took a step away from him, "I already told you what happened. I tripped against . . ."

"The banister. Yes, I remember." Danny stood motionless in front of her, his eyes locked on her. "Do you trust me enough to tell me what really happened to your eye?"

"Wha . . . what are you talking about? I . . . I already . . . told you." Annabel backed away from him.

"Tell me what's happening in your home, Annabel."

"What are you doing?" She stared at him. "What do you think you're doing right now?"

"I'm trying to understand."

"No. You're crossing a line."

"I'm what? No . . . I . . . I want to help," Danny said.

"No, you want to be a hero. It's a role you play well."

"That's not fair."

"You're right," Annabel said after an unsettling long hesitation. "It's not fair at all." She let out a heavy sigh and washed her hands over her face. "Maybe at times I wanted you to cross that line and delve so deep in my life that you save me from everything that hurts." She glanced up at the dark sky. "What you said on the side of the road that night was true. I was looking for perfection. I made you into something no one could ever live up to, and it wasn't fair to you. I can't expect you to be the answer to all that isn't right in my life. Nobody deserves that kind of pressure."

"I don't mind." Danny reached for her hand, but Annabel turned her back to him.

"But I can't let you save me," she said, just loud enough for him to hear. "I'm ashamed of the thoughts I've had about you and me."

"What kind of thoughts?" Danny moved close behind her so that his chest pressed against her back.

"Me as your wife living a happy life."

"What's so shameful about that?"

"Because I've always wanted more, and those thoughts are just me taking the easy way out." She faced him. "What do you know about my life?"

"Your father drinks."

Annabel stared at him with a horrified expression. "How long have you known that?"

"Found out today."

"How?"

"Steve heard his parents talking about an incident with your father."

"What incident?"

"A drunken incident."

"So the whole school knows?" Annabel's voice cracked.

"No. I would have known if the whole school knew. I told Steve not to tell anyone else."

Annabel wiped her eyes. "It doesn't matter. I was a fool to think I could keep my father a secret."

"He bruised your eye?"

"Danny, I wasn't lying when I told you I tripped against the banister. I just left out the part that it was because my father was chasing me while in a drunken rage."

"You can't stay in that house another night. Come with me." He took her by the arm, but Annabel didn't budge.

"Where do you think we're gonna go? Are you going to take me home with you? Is that your plan?"

"You can't stay in that house with him."

"Then where am I gonna stay? Danny, this is my home whether I like it or not, and you can't just show up and in three minutes think you can solve everything. This isn't the football field."

"I know that. But do you think I can just go home and leave you like this? Well I can't."

"Well you have to," she flatly replied.

Danny let out a frustrated sigh and paced the sidewalk. "You say it like it's the easiest thing to do."

"Not the easiest thing to do, just the only thing we can do. This is my home," Annabel said again and watched as Danny continued to vent his frustration. "Why are you even bothering with me?"

Danny stopped pacing and looked at her. "What kind of a question is that?"

"It's a practical question. What's gonna happen to us when you go off to college?"

Danny didn't have an answer.

"See?" Annabel said. "This is my point. Why are you even bothering? You don't want to get involved in this. Once you're gone, you're gone."

"It doesn't have to be that way. You could wait for me."

"Wait for you? Danny, you barely know me. I barely know you. We went to a dance together. One lousy dance. That's all."

"We did more than that and you know it."

"I watched you play football and you took me to the diner a couple times," Annabel added.

"So that's it? You could just walk away from us?"

"What else can I do?"

"My old teammate, Jason, graduated two years ago. He's at college playing ball right now, and he's still with his girl from high school," Danny said.

"What's she doing while he's gone? Is she in college, too?"

"College?" Danny shoved his hands in his pants pockets. "Um . . . no. She's not in college."

"Then what's she doing?" Annabel pressed.

"She's working as a secretary in an office. Look, I know that's not what you want to hear."

"So she waits for him as she works some job she probably hates while he's out pursuing his football dreams. Then he'll graduate and go off in the world with all the right credentials and be anything he wants to be while she . . . she just gets to raise a bunch of babies."

"Maybe that's what she wants," Danny said.

"Bu it's not what I want. I don't want to be my mother."

"Then don't be. Annabel, I'm not trying to change your mind."

"Good, because I'm not gonna be that girl who waits for a boy."

"I know you aren't. I'm sorry I asked you to," Danny said.

"I suppose I can't really blame you. I mean, that's the expectation, right? I know Molly and Donna wouldn't think twice about waiting for a boy, especially a boy like you."

Danny looked over Annabel's shoulder toward her house. "Is he home?"

"Yeah. He's . . . he's watching TV."

"You know I left my house wanting to kill him," Danny said. "My father tried to stop me from leaving, but we got into it and I left anyway."

"Your father knows about my dad, too?"

"He's heard some stories too, but he's not telling anyone. He didn't even tell me."

"But somebody told him. So people are talking." Annabel closed her eyes and shook her head. "I can't control it. I was naïve to think that I could, but I won't let my life be the reason your life takes a turn for the worse. You just told me you left your house wanting to kill my father and you'd gotten into it with your own father. Nothing good can come from this. You have to stay out of it. My life is always going to be like this until it's my turn to leave."

"So I'm supposed to stand here and watch you walk back into that house with him?"

"Actually, I'm gonna climb that tree and go in through the window, but yes, you are." Annabel smiled, but Danny wasn't amused.

"I can't let you go," he said.

Annabel gripped a piece of his shirt and squeezed the fabric in her hand. "Danny, I appreciate what you're trying to do, but I've been living this life for a long time and you . . . you just caught a glimpse of it. You alone can't change this. So please don't try." She let go of his shirt and left Danny standing on the sidewalk.

Chapter Twenty-Two

ANNABEL DIDN'T WAIT for Molly and Donna at her locker Monday morning before going to her first period class. She wasn't in the mood for their usual mundane banter about hallway gossip while she pretended what was happening at her home wasn't really happening. She'd been doing that far too long and now she wondered who else in her school knew her truth.

Annabel was already sitting at her desk when Molly and Donna walked into the classroom.

"We waited for you at your locker. How come you didn't wait for us?" Donna dropped her books onto the desk next to Annabel and plopped down into the seat.

"Thought maybe you called in sick." Molly took a seat on the other side of Annabel.

"I had to meet Mr. Barker before class to talk about a project for extra credit," Annabel lied.

"Extra credit?" Donna's facial expression knotted into a confused mess. "How many plusses do you need after your A?"

Molly laughed. "Yeah, Annabel. That's really ambitious of you, but do you really need to bother with extra credit?"

Molly and Donna knew, just as the rest of the class did, that Annabel aced most of her exams and was the smartest student in class.

"I'm not doing nearly as well in class as you think, and besides, a little extra credit never hurt anybody," Annabel lied again.

"I suppose not," Molly said.

Donna opened her book. "I didn't read the homework assignment, did you?"

"You never read the homework assignments. Maybe *you* should be the one meeting with Mr. Barker for extra credit," Molly said.

Donna's mouth dropped open. "That was mean. I'm doing just fine, thank you very much. Maybe *you* should be the one to mind your own business."

Annabel smiled as the conversation veered into a sense of normalcy and was glad her little white lie seemed to pass until a slender, middle-aged woman walked into the room and stood in the front of the class.

"Hello, students." The woman flipped her long black hair off her shoulders. "My name is Mrs. Shields. I'm your substitute teacher. Now," she said as she made her way to the teacher's desk and picked up the attendance sheet, "when I call your name please respond with 'present.'"

Through her peripheral vision, Annabel saw both Molly and Donna staring at her. She was trapped between the friends she'd been caught lying to. Annabel parked her eyes on the substitute teacher and waited for her name to be called.

Annabel spent the class with her attention on the textbook, following intently to the teacher's lesson and avoiding eye contact with either Molly or Donna. When the bell rang, she jumped out of her seat and headed straight for the door.

"Bel! Wait up!" Molly yelled.

"Yeah, Bel. Wait for us," Donna said, and in her rush to follow Annabel she dropped her books and folders on the floor. Loose papers scattered across the floor.

Annabel took advantage of Molly helping Donna pick up her things and rushed to her next class.

Annabel didn't have any more classes with Molly and Donna until after lunch, and though she carefully avoided them in the hallways between classes, she knew she couldn't evade them forever. The lunch hour was approaching. She took her bagged lunch from her locker and sat at her usual spot in the cafeteria.

She was eating her ham and cheese sandwich when Molly and Donna sat across from her at the cafeteria table. She kept her attention on her food and didn't say a word.

"Talk to us, Bel." Molly broke the silence. "Why'd you lie to us?"

"Yeah, Bel. Talk to us. We're your friends. Why'd you tell us you met with Mr. Barker when he's not even here?" Donna asked.

Annabel dropped her sandwich on its plastic wrapper and looked up at them. "Do you know my father's a drunk?"

Molly and Donna looked blankly at each other.

"Do you?" Annabel pressed.

"We . . . we heard some things." Molly crumbled her napkin in her fist.

"What things?" Annabel looked back and forth between them. "Tell me now."

Molly gave in with a defeated sigh. "Okay. My dad knows someone at the bank and said sometimes your father leaves for lunch and comes back a little . . . different."

"You mean drunk," Annabel said.

Molly glanced down at her half-eaten sandwich and lightly shrugged her thin shoulders.

Annabel looked to Donna. "What about you? What do you know about my father?"

"My mom's cousin is a bartender at a place just outside of town," Donna said. "I heard him talking to my dad one night when they thought I was asleep, and they brought up that place. Your dad goes there sometimes and . . ."

"Gets drunk," Annabel finished, and Donna nodded.

Annabel fell back into her seat and shoved what was left of her sandwich into the paper bag. "It's a wonder your parents even let you come over to my house at all."

"They don't blame you, Annabel," Molly said.

"Yeah, and it's not as if my parents don't like your father," Donna said.

"That's right. My father actually respects your father a lot," Molly assured her.

"Why? Because they think he's some kind of a war hero?"

"Well, isn't he?" Donna asked.

Annabel thought about it. "I don't see how it's possible my father could be a hero of anything. He fought in a war. So what? Millions of men fought in wars. It doesn't make him this great human being." She paused. "Is this why you've never asked to sleep over at my house?"

"We didn't want to ask you anything that would make you uncomfortable," Molly explained.

"Yeah, I mean, we knew why we had to leave your house before your dad got home, but we never told you that because we understood," Donna said. "Please don't be mad at us."

Annabel gazed around the lunchroom and watched as kids talked and laughed with their lunch mates between bites of bologna sandwiches and cafeteria peas.

"Does everyone in this cafeteria know about my father?"

Molly and Donna exchanged dumbfounded looks.

"Bel, how are we supposed to know that?" Molly asked.

"Yeah, Bel. How are we supposed to know that?" Donna repeated.

"I thought maybe there was a secret club of people who know my personal business but don't tell me. If there were, Danny would be a part of it too." Annabel crushed the paper bag in her hands and pushed her chair so hard from the table its legs screeched against the floor.

JOAN WAS MOPPING the kitchen floor when she heard loud groans coming from upstairs. She dropped the mop and hurried to the bedroom where George was lying on his side in bed, writhing in pain.

"George." Joan lightly shook his shoulder and turned him onto his back. A look of agony swept over his sweaty face. "George, wake up. It's time for your pills."

His head tossed side to side as he mumbled words Joan couldn't understand. She patted his arm, and his breathing grew heavier and scattered.

"You really need to take your medication." Joan grazed her hand across his hot forehead. "You're burning up."

Joan stepped back, unsure if she should call the doctor, or if this was an episode that would pass. She watched him a little while longer, and when his anguish didn't subside, she went to the telephone on the nightstand.

"Michael . . . Michael," George whispered in a distressed voice, broken between heavy breaths.

She dropped her arms at her sides and squared herself to George. "What are you saying, George?"

Between groans, George again whispered the name Michael.

Joan sat beside him and listened to his soft cries for a man she didn't know. She leaned into him and whispered, "Who's Michael?"

George clutched the sheets tightly and muttered, "Miss you . . . Michael . . . my love."

Joan pulled back so fast she almost fell off the bed. She got to her feet and took in the perplexing situation as she tried to understand why her husband was calling out another man's name. She slowly maneuvered around the bed, never taking her eyes off him, and his words "my love" hit her hard.

The sudden realization of what was happening drained everything inside of her. Her legs weakened. She stumbled and grasped onto the bedpost as George longingly called out the man's name again and again.

Joan held onto the post and watched her husband squirm in bed as his deep groans filled the room, and she wasn't sure if the pain he exuded was more emotional than physical.

George started choking on his own saliva. He sat up as best he could and coughed loudly until his airways were cleared. He saw Joan standing at the edge of the bed, still gripping the bedpost, and snarled at her.

"What the hell are you doing over there?"

"I . . . I . . . was . . . just . . ." Joan's voice wavered.

"Get me my medicine," George ordered. "I need my medicine."

Joan tore herself from the sturdy post and hurried to get George's medicine from the bathroom cabinet. She brought the pills back to him and watched as he popped them into his mouth and gobbled them like candy, ignoring the tall glass of water sitting on the nightstand beside him.

"Do you need anything else?" Joan asked.

"Sleep." He rolled over and put his back to Joan. "I want to be left alone."

Joan gave a nod to his instructions and silently left the room. There were so many questions she wanted to ask, though she was frightened of the answers.

ANNABEL EXITED THE school doors with Donna and Molly at her side. They had said little to each other since their lunch period, but they walked home from school together every day, and habits were hard to break.

Donna broke the silence as they turned the corner at the end of the block. "I wish you'd stop being sour at us," she said to Annabel. "You have to understand why we didn't say anything."

Annabel held her books tightly at her side, looked straight ahead, and kept walking. "I don't want to talk about it anymore. I just want to disappear. Go to a place where no one knows that I'm the daughter of the town drunk."

"Nobody thinks of your father as the town drunk," Molly said.

"Yeah, nobody thinks of your father as the town drunk," Donna echoed.

"I think everyone assumes he has some demons he brought back with him from the war, at least that's what my dad says," Molly added as she flicked her bangs from her eyes.

"I think my dad feels guilty because he never served," Donna said, falling a couple steps behind her brisker-walking friends. "Something about his knees, but really, I think—"

"Forget it," Annabel sharply interrupted. "I said I don't want to talk about it anymore, but you guys just keep going on and on and on."

Donna slowed her pace even more and dragged her gaze to the ground. "I'm sorry, Annabel."

Annabel stopped walking and waited for Donna to catch up. Molly kept moving until she noticed Annabel had stopped, and then she turned around and waited, too.

"What are you doing?" Molly asked.

Donna stepped up beside Annabel. "Yeah, Annabel, what are you doing except yelling at us and making us feel bad?"

Annabel looked away from them and peered down the suburban street of white houses that all looked the same. "I've been awful to the two of you when all you guys are trying to do is make me feel better." She faced them. "I've already had to apologize before over my bad behavior and now I'm apologizing again. I don't want this to keep repeating."

"I know you don't," Molly said.

"I know you don't, too," Donna added.

"Thanks," Annabel said, and when she started to walk away, Molly stopped her.

"Hey, Bel, what'd you mean earlier about Danny knowing your personal business? You mean he knows about your dad, too?"

"Yep." Annabel sighed, dropped her books onto the grass, and sat down on the sidewalk. "Found out through a friend who found out through his parents. His dad then told him everything he knew." She paused. "Parents sure do talk a lot."

Donna and Molly sat down beside her, and they formed a small circle in the middle of the walkway. They smoothed their skirts over their knees and planted their books into their laps.

"My parents didn't say much, but yeah, they talked," Donna said.

"Bel, I know you probably feel like everyone was whispering behind your back, but it wasn't like that. Donna and I didn't talk about it, and we didn't hear anyone else talking about it either. There wasn't a reason to tell you we knew, because really, we didn't know all that much."

Annabel leaned back onto her hands, planted on someone's lawn, and picked at the fading green grass. "I won't have to put up with this much longer. Only a couple more years and I'm gone."

"You sure are bent on leaving," Molly said. "I admit there's something exciting about the thought of college being some kind of an adventure."

"Because it is." Annabel perked up. "I want to learn more than only what this place has taught me. I want to experience more than only what this place offers me. I want to get my hands on all those books this town has banned. I want to read Salinger and Bradbury and Ellison. Don't you?"

"I don't even know who those people are," Donna stated.

"Me either," Molly said. "So I'm fine with never reading those books."

Annabel gave them an incredulous look. "You're fine with people deciding for you which books you should read and which you shouldn't?"

Molly shrugged. "I don't like to read."

"Me either," Donna chimed.

"That's not the point. Can't you see how authoritarian it is that this town is deciding what books we can and cannot read?"

"My mom said it's good for me not to read those books and that it's for good reason that they banned them," Donna said.

"Your mother would say something like that," Annabel snarked.

"Hey, what's that supposed to mean? She said they're only protecting us."

"Against books?" Annabel twisted her face. "They're just afraid that books are going to encourage us to think for ourselves, especially us girls. And my father's one of them. He doesn't think it's important that girls get good grades. An intelligent mind is wasted on us. Ugh." She closed her eyes. "I just need to get out of here."

"Gosh Bel, we get it." Donna shot up and her books spilled to her feet. "You hate this town and everyone in it. How many times do you have to say it?"

"Hey." Annabel stood up. "What's wrong with you? Why are you talking like . . . ?"

"Like you aren't even gonna miss us when you go?" Donna directed her sad eyes at Annabel. "When you talk about leaving, Bel, you never say anything about leaving Molly and me. It's always about leaving this stupid town for something better. I know because of what's happening in your home makes you want to leave so bad, but is there nothing about this town you'll miss? Not even us?" She looked to Molly, who appeared just as rejected as herself.

Annabel wasn't prepared for such a pointed question and took a moment to take it in.

"Forget it, Bel." Donna picked her books off the ground. "I don't expect you to answer such difficult questions."

"It's not a difficult question. I just don't know why you feel you have to ask me something like that. You should know I'm going to miss you. And you." She looked down at Molly, still sitting on the sidewalk. "I assumed you both knew that all of my complaints about this town didn't include either of you. You guys are the only reason why I've survived this far." She paused and took a breath. "I wish you'd told me you knew about my dad. It would've been nice to have someone to talk to about it, help me through it all. My mom pretends things are never as bad as they are. I always felt so alone, except for when we were all together. So don't ever think for a second that when I leave here I won't miss you guys."

With her shoulders slouched, Molly slowly stood, a forlorn expression on her face. "I don't want to talk about you leaving anymore. We have two more years before we graduate. Can't we just enjoy the time we have together before everything changes?"

Annabel hadn't considered how talk of her post-high school plans affected her friends, who weren't as eager for high school to end as she was.

"Hey. I'm sorry." Annabel wrapped an arm around Molly's shoulders. "I've only been thinking of myself, and maybe I have been getting a bit ahead of myself with all this leaving talk." She looked at Donna and then back at Molly. "I'm reminded that not every moment here is terrible. I'll be quiet about that stuff until it's actually time for me to go. I promise."

THEY WERE TWO blocks from Donna's house when a car pulled up beside them. Annabel tensed at the sound of the idled engine and she slowly turned her head toward the street. She anticipated seeing a car full of greasers, but to her surprise and utter relief, it was only Danny.

Danny got out of the parked, but still running, car. "Can we talk?"

Annabel glanced uncomfortably at Molly and Donna. "Danny, I don't think now is the best time."

"Please. It's important. It won't take long."

"It's okay," Molly said. "We'll head to Donna's without you."

Donna's eyes were planted intensely on Danny and snapped her head at Molly. "Wait, what? We're leaving?"

"Meet us there when you're done," Molly said to Annabel and pulled Donna along the sidewalk.

"But I wanted to hear," Donna muttered as Molly dragged her away.

Danny waited until Molly and Donna were out of ear shot. "We already talked about it. I know. You're not the kind of girl who'll wait for a boy. And that's that. But what about now? What about where we are right now? All we talked about was where we'll be in a year, but what about *right* now? We still have a whole lot of school year left and . . . and there isn't anyone else I want to spend the time I have left here with more than you."

Annabel didn't hate where Danny was going with this, yet his plan seemed a bit self-destructive. "So we continue to date knowing that eventually we're going to break up? What's the point in that?"

"Don't think of it that way."

"Is there another way?"

"Listen, my father has been planning my life for me since I was three," Danny said. "Everything I've ever done had a purpose for some part of my future. Mostly it revolved around football and college, but would you believe my father set an age as to when I was to settle down and start a family?"

Annabel shook her head.

"Twenty-seven. He said that's long enough for a man to sow his wild oats. Bel, I'm sick of thinking about the future." Danny drew Annabel closer to him. "I don't want to think about the future anymore. I want to do what I want, what's right for me, right now, in this moment." He rolled his thumb over the collar of Annabel's white blouse. "And that's you, Annabel Turner. You're what's right for me right now."

"Your father won't like this. He can't be okay with you still seeing me, especially since he knows about my dad."

"He doesn't control me anymore. That's the point."

"He still has to be sore at you with the way you talked back to him that day the two of you got into it. Danny, I don't want to be the reason you have fights with your father."

"I apologized to him for the tone I used. It was hard for me to swallow my pride like that, but I did it. It was the right thing to do, plus my mother begged me to do it. I've done everything he's asked of me till now. I'm done. He knows it, too. So what do you say? Will you stay with me? No expectations. No promises."

Most girls in school would have hated Danny's proposition of no promises, because most girls, more than anything, wanted promises from the boys they dated, but Annabel was relieved. "Okay, Danny. I'll stay with you. We'll spend the time you have left here having fun. Then you'll go to college in the fall and I'll do the same in two years."

"I know you will." Danny brushed his fingers lightly against Annabel's cheek. "Just don't forget about me."

Danny took her in his arms and kissed her, and Annabel wondered how he could think she could ever forget him.

Chapter Twenty-Three

JOAN OPENED THE bedroom door with a dinner tray.

George sat up and leaned his back against the bed's headboard as Joan settled the tray of baked chicken, peas, and buttered mashed potatoes over his lap.

"Careful, it's very hot. Just came out of the oven," Joan said and slid the utensils that had moved from their spots while in transit back to their places.

"Thank you. But you didn't have to cook all of this. I'm really not very hungry." George didn't mumble his words in his usual moody and impatient manner. Instead, he spoke slowly with a gentle tone.

Joan sat beside him at the edge of the bed and took in the change in George's demeanor. "I figure you'll be getting your appetite back soon. Thought maybe tonight would be the night. I wanted to be prepared."

George looked down at his plate piled with food and dragged his fork over the mound of potatoes. "I don't think tonight's the night, but I'll eat as much as I can since you went to the trouble."

Joan smiled. It'd been a long time since George had given anything she'd done any consideration. "Only eat what you can. Don't make yourself sick."

George took the cloth napkin off the tray and shook it till it spread open. He laid it across his white undershirt and dug his fork and knife into the food.

A strong breeze drifted into the bedroom from an open window and blew the ivory-colored curtains back. George looked away from his plate to the window. He held his gaze there and said, "I never looked at the moon much before, but tonight I can't seem to keep my eyes off it. I don't know if it's from lying in this bed for three weeks or finally having a clear mind, but I'm noticing things I haven't noticed in many years. It's not just my body that's gotten better, but my mind, too."

George's cuts were healing nicely. Most of the bandages were removed except for the ones across his forehead, his upper left shoulder, and his right wrist.

Even though the doctor had given strict orders that George was not to consume any alcohol while taking his medications, Joan had expected a struggle with him. For the first two weeks after the accident, George was so drugged up he mostly slept, but by the third week he was feeling better, and

Joan was sure then that he'd demand his bottles. But he didn't, and Joan was happy that that was a battle she didn't have to fight.

"I'm glad to hear that," Joan said.

"Aren't you going to eat?" George asked as he nibbled at his food.

"I'll make a plate later."

"But if you're hungry you should make a plate now."

"George, I'm fine. When did you start caring so much if I'm hungry?" she asked, and their eyes locked. She was determined not to be the one to break away first, and she softly added, "When did you start caring about me at all?"

George held her eyes, but broke away from her gaze and looked down at the barely touched food. "I'm sober now. We both know it's been a long time, but I see how much you've tried to make me happy, despite how horrible I was to you."

"George," Joan began.

He lifted the tray, his head down, unwilling to look at her. "Please take this away."

"But you've barely ate a thing," Joan said.

"I'm not hungry. I'm still very tired. I just want to sleep."

"Okay." Joan stood and took the tray from his hands. "I'll put your plate in the fridge in case you get hungry later."

George rolled onto his side, away from Joan, without a response. She lingered near the side of the bed, her eyes fixed on him. His body, having lost over twenty pounds since the accident and still mildly bandaged, reminded her of how he had looked when he came home from the war.

Joan remembered him, injured from the war and appearing more vulnerable than she'd ever seen him, and the way she'd thrown her arms around his neck and hugged him so tight. He'd appeared to have been at a loss of words, with a vague expression on his face as though he were unsure where he was, even though he was home.

There was helplessness about him that day that made Joan fiercely protective of him, and she naively believed that she could fix in him whatever the war had broken. But Joan could have had no idea then that the battles George was fighting went far beyond bullets and violent deaths.

Standing beside George's bed, after everything that had happened since that day he had come home from the war, Joan had that same urge to protect him because for the first time since that day, he appeared vulnerable again.

"I'll come back and check on you in a bit." Joan stood over the bed and looked down at him.

George didn't respond and closed his eyes.

JOAN SAT AT the kitchen table with Annabel and wrapped her hands around a warm mug of coffee. She watched Annabel shove forkful after forkful of food into her mouth.

"Did you not eat lunch today?" Joan asked.

"I ate a little." Annabel looked up from her plate in between bites of chicken and watched Joan take a sip of the hot coffee. "Aren't you going to eat anything?"

"I had a little something earlier. I think I caught your father's lack of appetite." Joan set down the mug. "Your father's doing better. I know you didn't ask, but he's doing better."

Annabel laid her fork next to the near-empty plate of food. "Molly and Donna knew about his drinking. Did you know they knew?"

"I had no idea. How could I have known that?"

Annabel shrugged. "You must have an idea of who in this town knows about him."

Joan leaned her elbows on the table and rubbed her palms together. "Some of the neighbors, I suppose."

"Right. And neighbors talk."

"They do, but I didn't think they'd talk that much."

"They talked enough that my friends and Danny heard things," Annabel said.

Joan raised her eyebrows. "Danny too?"

Annabel nodded. "From his father and a friend."

"I'm sorry about that."

Annabel thought about Danny and a small smile crept over the corners of her mouth. The sensation of Danny's kiss still lingered on her lips.

"What is it?" Joan asked.

"Uh?"

"Your smile. What was that for?"

Annabel took in a breath and pushed the plate of scattered bits of food away from her. "Danny and I came to an agreement today that I like very much."

"An agreement?"

"About how we're gonna handle him going away to college."

"I see. And what's the agreement?"

"No expectations. No pressure. What happens, happens. At first he asked me to wait for him while he was away at school, but I told him I couldn't do that."

"Of course you couldn't. You have plans of your own." Joan smiled. "That's something I admire about you. You have the convictions of a woman twice your age."

Annabel appreciated her mother's compliment. "He understood and apologized for even asking. He just wants us to have the best year together that we can, and so do I."

"This boy. He makes you happy."

"Yes."

Joan stared pensively at Annabel. "I knew he would. The moment he stepped into our living room, I knew. I'm glad you're staying together. Go on dates with him. Go to dances. Go to the diner. Hold hands in the halls. Cheer him on at his football games. Annabel, if I tried to stop you from doing the things that make you happy, I'm so sorry."

"You were worried about him finding out."

Joan peered into her cup of coffee. "Very much."

"Why'd you marry him?" Annabel asked.

Joan looked up. "The same reason any woman marries a man. I fell in love with him."

"Because he made you happy?"

"Yes."

"The same way Danny makes me happy?"

"Yes."

Annabel tapped her fingers softly on the table, unsure if she really wanted to get into what was on her mind, but she needed to know. "Why'd he stop making you happy?"

"Your father was a gentle man," Joan said. "I know that's hard for you to imagine, but he was. I was fifteen when I met him. By sixteen we were married. He was nineteen, just a year in the army when he came to my town with a neighbor boy who was in the same platoon. Boy, was I smitten by him." She smiled reflectively. "After we married he went back, and I continued living at home with my parents. Your father promised a place of our own as soon as he came home and got on his feet with a job. I couldn't wait to get off that farm, though your father liked it there very much. But he wanted to make me happy, and for a little while, he did. You know he was injured in the war, right? Received the Purple Heart."

"Sure. That's why everyone thinks he's a war hero," Annabel said. "If they only knew."

"Hey." Joan squeezed Annabel's hand. "You can say what you want about the person he became after the war, but you can't take away what he did during the war. He was brave and almost died saving two of his fellow soldiers. Broke both legs. Took him a while to recover from that but he did. I know it tore him up to leave his buddies behind and come home early. There's a real camaraderie between soldiers. He spent months in the veteran's hospital before he could come home, and when he finally did, it was like I didn't know him anymore.

We'd only been married a couple years, and most of that time was spent apart, but we grew to know each other through the letters we wrote.

"But I saw the change in him right away, mostly in his eyes. He used to have the most endearing brown eyes, but they looked at me differently and then he started talking to me differently. Used harsh tones with me he never used before. I thought it was because of his injuries and everything he saw over there. I expected at some point the man who wrote those charming letters to me would return . . . but he never did."

"Does war do that to every man?" Annabel asked.

Joan caressed the back of Annabel's head. "I suppose it does, in some way."

Annabel considered her mother's words. "I hate war. I wish he never went."

"A lot of men never made it back." Joan paused. "Sometimes I think your father was one of those men." She leaned back into her chair and slowly exhaled a deep breath. "This was good. Talking like this with you."

Annabel thought so, too.

Joan stood and picked up Annabel's plate. "Go on upstairs and get washed up for bed."

Annabel got up from the table and started to leave the room, but quickly stopped. She turned back to Joan, and for the first time in a long time, she needed her to hold her.

"Mom," she said softly.

Joan went to her and took Annabel in her arms. Annabel couldn't remember the last time they'd embraced like that. Not since she was a little girl had she found so much comfort in being in her mother's arms.

THERE WAS AN excited murmur throughout the halls as the students chatted about the big game that night. Everyone was feeling the school spirit. Posters celebrating the football team covered the walls, and gold and navy blue streamers, the school's colors, decorated lockers.

Molly and Donna stood with Annabel at her locker.

"Have you seen Danny today? I haven't seen any of the football players," Donna said.

"I saw him earlier. Coach got them out of classes today. They're spending the day in the fieldhouse going over plays and things," Annabel said.

"Well that's just great." Molly leaned her back against the lockers. "Jocks in this school are treated like kings. Just because they can throw a ball, and catch a ball, and run with a ball."

"Someone sounds jealous," Donna said.

"Of course I'm jealous. I have a history exam today that I know I didn't study enough for. But Coach isn't getting me out of *my* classes, just the jocks."

"Are you done sulking?" Annabel asked.

"Yeah, Molly. Are you done sulking?" Donna repeated.

"I suppose," Molly said, and they started walking to their next class. "Is Danny nervous?"

"Of course he's nervous. If they lose tonight they don't go to the State Championships," Donna said.

"He was nervous, but I could tell he was trying not to show it," Annabel replied.

They walked into the classroom.

"My dad said he could drive us to the game." Molly dropped her books onto her desk. "He said he might even stay and watch the game. I told him he better not dare try to sit with us."

"I can't wait." Donna sat in her seat and clasped her hands together. "This is the biggest game I'll ever see in my life. Unless of course they win and go to State. Then *that* game will be the biggest game I'll ever see."

Annabel laughed at her excitement. Though she was feeling just as eager as Molly and Donna about the game, she was also nervous for Danny. She wanted him to do well, but she wanted that for him, not just for the team and the school. She wanted Danny to realize his every dream.

THE CROWD EXPLODED in a monstrous roar as Danny's pass for seventeen yards was caught and the receiver ran over twenty yards for a late fourth quarter touchdown. Annabel, Molly, and Donna celebrated their school's final quarter heroics as they went ahead by three points with twelve seconds left on the clock.

They joined the rest of the crowd in chants of "State! State! State!" Twelve seconds later, it was official. Danny and his team were going to the State Championship.

Danny was hoisted up on the shoulders of his teammates, as he had been many times before, and celebrated with the mob of students that rushed the field.

"This is crazy!" Donna threw her arms up in the air. "I've never been this excited before in my life."

Molly clapped wildly as she jumped in the stands. "Me either! Everyone is so happy. Isn't this great, Annabel?"

"Yes." Annabel smiled for a moment. She stopped clapping and dropped her arms at her sides. Her body was still as she watched Danny, laughing and touching hands with anyone who offered. He gazed across the field, over the heads of the throng of screaming teenagers. His eyes scanned the stands, and Annabel knew he was searching for her.

She stood, watching him until his eyes finally found her. He smiled at her. She smiled back. He pumped his fist in the air and let out a victorious roar, and Annabel tilted her head back and laughed. She was going to miss him next year, more than she would allow herself to believe.

Steve jumped on Danny's back and pulled him into a team celebration in the middle of the field. Coach led the players into the locker room to a huge ovation from the crowd.

"Wow." Donna sat down on the bleachers and let out a heavy breath. "That was amazing. Can you imagine how insane everyone will be if we actually win State?"

"I know." Molly sat beside Donna and pushed her skirt over her knees. "It's gonna be like nothing we've ever seen before."

"I definitely can't wait," Donna said.

"Me either," Molly replied. "And this is all because of Danny. If not for him we wouldn't be this good. So we better enjoy this now because once Danny's gone chances are slim that we'll ever experience this again."

Annabel stayed standing and stared aimlessly over the near-empty field as Molly's words "once Danny's gone" replayed in her head. She was going to miss more than just exciting football games.

She would miss the anticipation of seeing Danny in the halls and how his smile made even her worst days bearable.

"You okay, Annabel?" Donna asked.

"Annabel!" Molly yelled.

"What?" Annabel jumped and turned to her friends.

"Are you okay?"

"Am I okay? Yeah. Sure. I just got lost in the moment. Sorry."

"It's a lot to take in," Donna said.

"Sure is." Annabel looked back to the field, where scattered groups of students still celebrated their team's victory. "Come on." She turned back to her friends and smiled. "Let's find Danny. We're goin' to Marvin's."

Chapter Twenty-Four

JOAN WASHED THE dinner dishes and stacked them in the cabinets. After wiping down the countertop and stove, she left the clean kitchen and went into the living room. There wasn't much cleaning up needed in the room because George hadn't been in there for weeks.

She turned off all the lights except for a small lamp on the end table and settled onto the couch. It'd been a while since the room felt as cozy and peaceful as it did in that moment. She closed her eyes and leaned her head against the soft cushions as she took in deep steady breaths to calm her muddled mind.

Ever since George had longingly called out another man's name, the life Joan thought she was living was over. Though they hadn't been the family she wanted them to be for some time, she got through most days believing someday they would. It was with pathetic desperation that she clung to the hope that her family would one day resemble the families she saw on TV.

But George desired another man, and Joan never saw that on TV.

Throughout their marriage, as George's behavior toward Joan grew more ornery, she could only speculate as to why her husband hated her so much. Now she had the answer. George loved another man.

This was it, she thought. The secret her husband had kept hidden inside him all these years held the answer to why he was always so angry. George loved a man but couldn't be with him. It was all so simple, yet complicated at the same time. She tried to understand how two men could love each other. She never knew anyone who was that way. All she knew was that according to her church, homosexuality was the worst of sins.

Joan took two folded blankets from the hall closet and spread one of them neatly over the couch, where she'd been sleeping since George's accident. She kept the bedroom door opened at night so she could hear his calls if George should need her, but he never did. She placed the other folded blanket on the end of the couch that she would use as a blanket later. She sat down on her makeshift bed, but it was too early to go to sleep, barely seven o'clock.

On a normal night at this hour, Joan would be watching television and George would be passed out in his chair. That night she kept the TV off, not being in the mood for watching perfect television families.

Joan went to the kitchen and poured herself a glass of water. She took a strong gulp and then pressed the cold glass against her cheek. After a couple minutes she put the glass in the sink and went back into the living room.

Through the front window she saw Sylvia sitting alone on her front porch swing. She smiled. For reasons she wasn't sure, seeing Sylvia made her feel better. She pulled a shawl from the hall closet, tossed it over her shoulders, and went over to her neighbor.

Sylvia wore beige pants, a long white button-down blouse, and thick, white cotton slippers. She was looking the other way, lost in her daydream while puffing away at a cigarette, as Joan approached her.

"Hello, Sylvia."

Sylvia jumped slightly and choked on an inhale of smoke. She leaned forward as she coughed and tried to catch her breath.

Joan hurried up the porch and patted her on the back. "I'm so sorry. I didn't mean to startle you."

Sylvia coughed so hard she couldn't speak, but motioned to Joan with her hand that she was okay.

"Can I get you some water?" Joan asked.

Sylvia shook her head and let out a couple more coughs before finally drawing in a deep breath. "My God." She leaned her head back. "That was horrifying. I've never ingested so much smoke before."

"That was my fault. I'm so sorry. I didn't mean to sneak up on you like that." Joan stood over Sylvia. "Are you sure you're okay. I can still get you that water."

"No. No." Sylvia waved her off. "My mother always told me these things would kill me someday." She looked at Joan and a small smile crept across her pretty face. "Maybe she was right." She tossed the cig to the side and scooted over to make room on the porch swing. "Want to sit with me?"

"Thank you. I think I would." Joan settled into her seat. She smoothed her dress over her knees and clasped the shawl tighter around her shoulders. She glanced up and down the quiet street. "You like sitting out here, don't you?"

"I sure do. Fresh air cleanses our souls."

"If that's true then I need to sit out here more often."

Sylvia turned her body to Joan and bent her knees to her chest. "Are you okay? I've got all night if you need to talk. Henry's still away." She wrapped her arms around her bended knees and waited for Joan to respond.

Joan narrowed her eyes at Sylvia. "I think you of all people know there isn't much okay over there." She glanced over at her house. "I'm still very grateful for the way you helped me that night in the driveway, Henry too."

"You've already thanked me. Once was enough, Joan. You don't have to keep thinking about that," Sylvia said.

"Wouldn't you keep thinking about that if it were your husband passed out in his car, with his head pressed on the horn, in the middle of the night?"

"Well . . . I . . . suppose so. But I'm not judging you about that night. Neither is Henry."

"But you two weren't the only ones who saw." Joan directed her eyes to the houses across the street.

Sylvia followed Joan's gaze, took out her cigarette case, and lit up another cig. With her eyes held steady on the houses, Sylvia sucked in a deep inhale of smoke.

"They watched Henry and me over the summer with those same judging eyes," Sylvia said, the smoke creeping from her lips. "I felt their glares on me every time we were outside. They didn't approve of us. We played too loud, laughed too hard, and touched with too much affection. But look at me." She opened her arms and held out her hands, ashes falling from her cigarette. "Does it look like I care?" She threw her head back and laughed. "It's liberating not to care what anyone thinks. You should try it."

Joan dropped her gaze to her hands, folded in her lap, and remembered the times she stood at her window and watched the free-spirited couple living in a way she envied. "I want you to know I never talked about you the way they did." She raised her eyes back to the street and peered again at the houses, wondering if anyone was watching them right then. "I wanted so badly to have that with George."

"You can still have that."

"No. I can't."

"You don't know that for sure. George can get help. I had a friend whose husband also had a problem with the bottle. He went to a place and got help. It took a lot of work, but they made it. Now they're a better couple than they've ever been." Sylvia offered Joan an encouraging smile and finished off her cigarette.

Joan forced a small smile. "Yes. Maybe one day he can get help."

She turned away from Sylvia and lifted her gaze to the trees as she imagined George lying in their bed at that moment, yearning for another man. There was no place that was going to help him with that.

She looked back at Sylvia. "What would you do if you found out something about your husband that you didn't understand, but it made you realize he wasn't the man you thought he was?"

The small lines on Sylvia's forehead creased. "I . . . I don't think I know what you mean. Henry does and says things I don't understand sometimes, but I don't waste my time worrying about it. Everything always seems to come together with us just as it's supposed to."

There was no way for Sylvia to grasp what Joan was trying to ask her. Joan knew this. So she faked a smile and lightly patted Sylvia's knee and stood up. "Forget I asked."

"Wait." Sylvia dropped her feet off the bench and grabbed Joan's hand and pulled her back onto the swing, closer to her. "Is this about George's drinking? Or has something else happened?"

Their thighs touched, and Sylvia's face was only inches away as she looked into Joan's eyes, waiting for her response. Joan's personal space was intruded upon, but it wasn't without provocation. She had said too much and piqued Sylvia's curiosity.

"I'm sorry, Joan." Sylvia pulled back. "I shouldn't be prying in your life. Forgive me."

"There's nothing to forgive. I'm just tired and babbling nonsense. I should get back." Joan stood up, and this time Sylvia didn't try to stop her. "Annabel should be coming home soon."

Sylvia smiled. "She's a great girl. Wise beyond her years."

"She is and I don't know where she gets that wisdom from." Joan wished Sylvia goodnight and left her sitting alone on her porch.

ANNABEL, MOLLY, AND Donna laughed and chanted cheers with the rest of the enthusiastic students as they walked through the school parking lot, celebrating their team's victory. Danny met up with them outside the locker room.

"Great game, Danny," Molly yelled.

"Yeah, great game," Donna echoed.

"Thanks," Danny said and looked at Annabel. "What do you think?"

"What do I think? Danny. You're going to State." She jumped into his arms and he held her tight as he spun her around in a circle.

"We're going to State!" he boasted triumphantly.

Molly and Donna raised their arms and celebrated along with them. They laughed and acted silly until Danny put Annabel back down and they headed to his car.

Danny and Annabel noticed the greasers hanging around across the parking lot teasing some girls at the same time. She looked up at him. "Danny?"

He took her hand. "Don't worry. There won't be any trouble tonight." He walked quicker to his car and made sure Molly and Donna were keeping up beside Annabel. He opened the passenger-side door and pushed back the front seat to give the girls room. "Slide in."

Molly and Donna giggled as they climbed into Danny's back seat.

As Annabel got into the front seat, Danny peered over her head at the greasers. Ricky and a brunette were slipping into the backseat of Brett's car and Brett was combing back his oily hair as he headed to the driver-side door, a blonde waiting for him in the front seat.

Danny was relieved the gang's leaders had their minds set on girls instead of a fight. He watched Dennis and Curtis dejectedly standing at the side of the car, watching as Brett peeled out of the parking spot.

Annabel turned to the backseat. "Are you guys ready for some fun?"

"I know I am," Donna yelled.

Molly and Annabel laughed at Donna's excitement as Danny drove past the two stranded greasers.

JOAN STOOD BESIDE the bed and watched George sleep. His condition was improving, but if Joan couldn't tell this from his renewed sense of appetite, the decline of groans coming from the room would have told her so.

She sat on the bed beside him and gazed into his peaceful face. She slid her fingers across his forehead and slowly planted her lips over his brows and kissed him. "I know why you've been so angry," she whispered. "I know, and maybe someday you'll tell me all about him."

Joan got up quietly and left the room.

The door closed behind her and George opened his eyes. At some point, while lying in that bed, he knew he'd given himself away. He rolled onto his side, his back to the door, and cried.

He was certain he didn't deserve the wife he had.

DOWNSTAIRS, JOAN MADE a pot of tea. Blowing into a hot mug of chamomile, she went into the quiet living room and sat on the couch. She sipped her drink slowly, tasting every drop that lingered over her lips, until the cup was empty.

She set the mug on the table and lay comfortably across the couch. Just before she closed her eyes, she caught a glimpse of the clock on the wall as it approached the nine o'clock hour. Her last thought before falling asleep was hoping that Annabel was having a fun time with her friends.

THE DINER WAS jumping with happy teenagers and loud music. Annabel, Molly, and Donna danced to "Jailhouse Rock" with Danny and others, while Jimmy and a couple players scarfed down cheeseburgers and chocolate milkshakes at the counter.

After a few more songs, the craziness subsided as The Everly Brothers' "All I Have to do is Dream" played over the loudspeakers, slowing the pace. The wild dancers paired up with partners and danced to the mellow beat.

Molly and Donna were both asked to dance, and this time Molly's dance partner didn't step on her toes. Danny swept Annabel into his arms and they moved smoothly with the music.

"This night couldn't be any more perfect." Danny held Annabel close to him.

"I can't think of a more perfect night. You won the game. We're here celebrating. There wasn't any trouble with the greasers when we saw them." She rested her cheek against Danny's chest. "There truly is nothing more perfect than this."

Danny kissed the top of Annabel's head and they danced until the song struck its last note. Then, Jerry Lee Lewis came on singing about balls of fire, and the serenity of the previous ballad was gone. Annabel lifted her head off Danny's chest, and Danny dropped his arms from Annabel's waist.

They weren't the only couple in the diner who didn't want the slow song to end, but soon, bodies moving to the fast music brushed up against them.

"Come on." Danny led her to a booth. "Are you hungry? You want something to eat?"

"I'm not hungry."

"Are you thirsty?" Danny asked.

"A little bit."

"Cherry soda?"

"Sure."

"Okay." Danny glanced over to where everyone was dancing. "I'll get sodas for Molly and Donna, too. They're dancing up a storm."

Molly and Donna had yet to take a break from dancing. They were in the middle of the packed diner, taking in every song and every beat with a laugh and a spin.

Danny went to the counter and ordered the cherry sodas. Jimmy was still at his seat, attacking his third cheeseburger.

"Hey!" Jimmy wiped globs of ketchup from his mouth and sat on a stool beside Danny. He slapped him on the shoulder. "What a game, uh?"

"Sure was."

"As great as it was, you know what would have been just as great?"

"What's that?"

"Beating the shit out of those scum greasers. I saw them in the parking lot and so did you." Jimmy stared down Danny.

"You can't be serious right now."

"No better night than tonight to finally take them down. No way Coach could do anything about it now. What's he gonna do? Bench his star quarterback and best defensive player for the State Championship?"

Danny shook his head. "You really wanna fight bad enough that you'll risk breaking your hand two weeks before State? I think you've taken too many hits to the head. You're not thinking straight. I'm done with those greasers and once we win State I'll be done with you, too."

"So that's how it is?" Jimmy asked.

Danny paid for the sodas and walked away without saying another word.

THE SLIGHT MOVEMENT of the cushions as George sat down stirred Joan out of her sleep. She awakened to him sitting on the other side of the couch, the lamplight shining on half his face.

"George." Joan sat up. "What are you doing down here? You should be in bed."

George looked gently at Joan, his thinned face covered in stubble. His dim eyes broke away from hers and lingered over the knitted blanket covering her body. "I know that you know. Oh, Joannie," he breathed out and lifted his eyes to hers. "I thought if anyone could change me it would be you. The shy little girl with the pretty blue eyes who looked like an angel every time she smiled. You were young and innocent and so beautiful, I needed you to change me. Make me normal . . . but . . . ." His gaze dropped to the floor.

"I couldn't," Joan finished.

George shook his head and he shifted his eyes back to her. "No. No, you couldn't and I hated every inch of you because of it." He drew in a slow breath. "But I was too hard on you. If my own religion couldn't turn me into the man I longed to be, how could I have expected some unassuming young girl, so naïve about so many things, to be able to? Poor Joanie. She had no idea of the life she was getting herself into."

Joan thought about that fifteen-year-old girl falling for the mysterious soldier who showed up in her town without warning. It was the most exciting day in her otherwise predictable life. She needed little persuading when George asked her to marry him. She was ready to start her grownup life.

"That day you came to town with Carl, when we met. The sweet talking, the walk to the lake, that was all you trying to be someone you weren't . . . someone you still aren't?"

"I knew I was different from a young age and I knew I didn't want to be that way. I didn't."

Joan slid closer to George. "I believe you. It . . . it must have been hard living as someone else. Hiding who you are."

George looked away from her and nodded.

Joan watched him and hesitated before she asked, "Were you ever happy?"

George ran a hand over his unshaven face. His weight loss gave him back his defined chin, and he resembled for the first time, in a long time, the handsome young soldier who had stepped off the bus in her small town all those years ago.

"I was hopeful those first few years because I expected that having a wife and a child would instantly change me. That it was something that would just naturally happen. I couldn't wait to feel normal. I thought for the first time I wasn't going to feel so . . . queer. I waited for a long time, but I still felt the same. Nothing in me changed, and I could only pretend for so long before I . . . before I fell apart."

"So the answer is you were never happy." Joan pressed her lips together and let out a soft sigh. "How could I have thought there could be any other answer?"

George tilted his head toward her. "Oh, Joanie, how could I be happy knowing I could never be the man you needed me to be? You deserved a husband who could love you the way you needed to be loved. I'm sorry that husband couldn't be me. But please believe that I played the role as best I could. We moved here, and when I realized I wasn't changing and that this life was it, I panicked and became this ornery monster. I hated the way I was, but I couldn't stop. Can you understand how it would be easier to live life miserably when you hate yourself, rather than feel the way I did and try to smile every day?"

Joan understood. She understood better than any of the other wives on the block, with their perfect husbands and their perfect lives, would have been able to.

"George. Can we talk about Michael?"

"Okay. If you're sure you want to know."

"I'm sure."

George sat back into the couch. His shoulder brushed up against Joan's. "I met Michael after we married. We both knew what we were the first moment we looked at each other. He had the same look in his eyes as I did. The same look I saw in every mirror, and reflections don't lie."

"What look was that?"

"Shame. Self-loathing. It's a distinguishable look. Once you know it well you can never miss it. Michael, despite his attempts to hide it, had it." George paused reflectively. "Just like me."

Joan listened without interruption as George recapped the story of his and Michael's secret love affair. He didn't go into great detail, but told of how while on base they found places they could be alone, without anyone knowing.

Joan averted her eyes at this disclosure.

"I'm sorry," George said. "That was too much. I shouldn't have told you that. No wife wants to hear her husband say something like that."

Joan closed her eyes and gave a tight-lipped smile. "It's okay. I urged you to. Please, go ahead."

"So . . . we . . . we went to these places. We talked mostly." George let out a short laugh. "Michael sure liked to talk. But he didn't babble, you know?

Everything was well thought out. He was very precise with his words so that you knew he meant every word he said. He was the most articulate soldier in our platoon. Everyone liked him. If you were stuck on something, anything, girl problems, missing home, or just dealing with the war, Michael was the guy you went to. He'd talk you through anything. He enjoyed that, I think, being useful."

"He sounds like a wonderful man," Joan said, and she meant it.

"He was." George rubbed the palm of his hands together. "He was. But then we entered the war and we were sent overseas. Suddenly, what was happening between us took a backseat to just surviving, yet I was more concerned with his well-being than my own. I watched over him as best I could, staying as close to him as possible. If only one of us had to make it out alive, I wanted it to be him."

Joan caught her breath at this crushing revelation. She could understand George risking his life for the man he loved without any regard to making her a widow. He simply didn't love her like that. But she couldn't make right how George was so willing to give his life for Michael and risk leaving Annabel without a father.

He had put his family second.

"I was very worried about you while you were away," Joan said. "Annabel wasn't even a year old."

"I know you were worried. I got your letters." George paused and took in a breath. "I would have changed if I could have. I hope you believe that."

Joan believed what he said, but said nothing.

George slid his hand onto Joan's and locked his fingers tightly over her hand. He looked at her, and she back at him. "I'm sorry for everything I've done, all those horrible things I've done, and for the man I've become."

"I know," Joan whispered, and for the first time in a long time, she rested her head on George's shoulder.

That night was the longest conversation they had had without screaming or drunken outbursts in many years. George spoke to Joan with immeasurable patience. His gentle demeanor was something Joan hadn't seen in a long time. She pressed their folded hands against her heart, never feeling as close to him as she did in those moments when he talked about his love for another man.

Chapter Twenty-Five

DANNY WAS DRIVING Annabel home after having dropped off Molly and Donna. He switched the radio off. "I've had enough music for a night. Do you mind if we just talk?"

"Sure. What do you want to talk about?"

"I don't know. I just need to clear my head. It's been a crazy night. I haven't had a moment to really take it all in," he said. "Felt like the entire town was at the game tonight. Can you imagine what State's gonna be like?"

Annabel shook her head. "I can't imagine anything crazier than this, but I know it will be."

"Sure will. I'm gonna be busy the next couple of weeks. Coach is having us do two-a-days before and after school. I probably won't be able to think about much but the game. Even our teachers were told to take it easy on us."

"When don't the teachers take it easy on the football players?" Annabel faced him.

"Ooohhh." Danny laughed. "Is that so? I know. I know. We rule the school. Isn't that what all you non-athletes say?"

"Yes we do say that because it's true. But I get it, Danny. You're gonna be too busy for anything else these next couple weeks. So you don't have to worry about us. I'll leave you alone and . . ."

"Go to prom with me."

"What?"

"I want you to go to prom with me."

"Prom? Danny, that's like six months away."

"So? Are you holding out for someone else?"

"Of course not."

Danny pulled up to a red light. "Then say yes."

Annabel threw her head back and smiled a big smile. "So much has happened tonight. I really can't wrap my head around all of this."

"Just say yes," Danny yelled.

Annabel laughed. "Yes!"

"Well, that's settled then." Danny looked back to the road with a satisfied grin.

The light turned green, and Danny drove down Annabel's street and parked in front of her house.

"I can't believe the night I just had," Annabel said. "Heck, I can't believe the year I'm having. I feel like I'm living someone else's life."

"Tonight was something, wasn't it? You know," Danny moved closer to her and brought her hand to his lips and kissed it, "I'm glad I was able to share this night with you. It makes everything that much sweeter having someone to celebrate this with."

"I still don't understand why you picked me."

He smiled softly at her. "And that's why I like you so much."

Danny kissed her lips, and Annabel wondered what boy would be driving her home from dates a year from then, who she would be kissing goodnight, but mostly, who Danny would be kissing. It wasn't the exact thought she wanted to be having at that moment, but it was what was going through her head.

"I'm glad we have the rest of the school year left to be together," Danny said.

"Me too." Annabel smiled and traced her finger over his eyebrow. She kissed him on the cheek. "I have to go. I don't want to, but I have to."

"I know."

The wetness of Danny's kiss still lingered on Annabel's lips as he walked her to her front porch and kissed her goodnight one last time.

She watched from the front porch as Danny walked away, and when his car disappeared down the dark street, she went into the house. The shock of the scene that awaited her in the living room almost made her fall backward.

Joan and George were asleep together on the living room couch. Her head slumped on his shoulder, and their fingers were intertwined together in their laps.

Annabel walked slowly across the room while keeping her eyes planted on her parents, not yet believing what she was seeing. The floor creaked beneath her light footsteps, and Joan opened her eyes.

"Annabel." She picked her head off George's shoulder. "What time is it?"

Annabel was too confused to respond, and Joan smiled.

"I suppose the time doesn't matter." Joan glanced at George's pleasant face as he slept and turned back to Annabel. "We can talk about this now or in the morning."

Annabel was still too stunned to speak. She needed more time to take in what was happening in her living room. There wasn't a time she could recall seeing her parents cozied up together on the couch. She slanted her head and narrowed her eyes at her father. "Is he dying?"

"No." Joan gave a short laugh. "He's not dying."

"Then . . . what?"

"Come." Joan stood up, and Annabel followed her into the kitchen, glancing back at her father.

"Want some milk?" Joan went to the refrigerator.

"No."

"How about a piece of pie?"

"I don't want pie. I want to know what the heck's going on. Why were you snuggled with him on the couch like that, and why were you holding his hand? How could you even want to do those things after everything he's done to you? To us?'

Joan took Annabel's hand and pulled her to the table. They both sat down.

"Your father hasn't been drinking."

"And that turns him into a man you now want to cuddle up with on the couch?"

Annabel thought of the way her father looked sleeping so peacefully, appearing starkly younger than he did just a month ago. Despite his thinner frame and near-angelic face, she couldn't imagine him being any different from the monster she'd known him to be most of her life.

"Your father opened up to me about the war. He told me things about himself that I never knew."

"What kind of things?"

Joan tapped her fingernails on the table. "Let's just say I understand your father better than I ever have before."

"Are you saying whatever happened in the war is the reason he was like this?"

"The war brought a lot of . . . complexities in your father's life, and I'm going to try to help him through it."

"Is he gonna stop drinking?"

"I hope to lessen his need for drinking."

Annabel pushed herself away from the table and stood up. "You can try to help him through whatever it is he's going through, but unless he stops drinking, it doesn't matter."

She left the kitchen and went to her room. She sat on her bed and tried to make sense of what was happening. Joan knocked on the door and entered the room without waiting for Annabel to call her in. She sat on the bed, with a subtle resolve in her demeanor.

"I can't expect you to suddenly care about your father after the way life has been here. Things are confusing right now. I wish I could tell you that once you become an adult life gets easier, but it doesn't. And you don't always know what the right choices are. I'm set on doing something that I'm not completely comfortable with, but I truly believe is the only way to handle this certain situation."

"This certain situation? Is that code for dad's a drunk?"

"It's not code for anything. This is what marriage is. You make sacrifices to give troubled situations the best chances of working out."

"I'm never getting married if marriage means you have to make sacrifices for a husband who treats you as badly as dad treats you. Forget it."

"You'll think differently about marriage someday."

"No. I won't," Annabel answered adamantly.

"Annabel, I know you think a woman's life has to be lived a certain way—get married, have kids, be a wife and mother. I know you struggle with trying to fit that role—with *wanting* to fit that role.

"Did you ever struggle with that?"

"No. I always knew I wanted to be a mother. Not because it was what was expected of me, but because it's what I always wanted. It's important to me that you know that, Annabel. That I married your father and had you because that's what I wanted to do, not because I thought it was something I had to do. So don't ever doubt that being here with you is exactly where I want to be, because it is."

"That's what I'm afraid of. That I'll get married and have kids and hate them the way dad hates us."

"Hey, hey. Your father doesn't hate you or me. What you don't realize is that some men struggle with the expectations set on them, too. They have certain roles they're expected to fulfill as well. They're expected to settle down, get married, and have a family, just like women. Sure, it's socially more acceptable for men to be bachelors longer than women, but eventually marriage and family are expected of them, too.

"Women are the caretakers and men are the providers. Men are supposed to get a good job and provide a home, food, and everything a family needs to live. You see? Everyone has a role. But in the same way that you don't want to fulfill your role of housewife and mother, some men feel the same about fulfilling their role as husband, father, and breadwinner. But they do it anyway because it's what's expected of them."

"So you're saying dad didn't want to get married or have a family?"

"I'm saying your father didn't have the option to be the man he wanted to be. You know, live the life he felt fit him best."

"You mean he didn't want to settle down?"

"Not like this," Joan answered.

Annabel thought about it. "Maybe he wanted to travel and go places, like I do, instead of being stuck in this town."

Joan pressed her lips together and offered a small smile. "Maybe. But this was the life he thought was his only choice."

"Is that what you're gonna help him with? Help him to live the life he really wants?"

Joan ran her hands over her lap. "I don't think I could give him the life he really wants. But maybe I can make this one good enough so that he doesn't need a bottle to get through the day anymore."

Annabel sat with her legs folded on the bed and looked up at Joan. "Is that what happens when you choose the life you don't want? You drink every day?"

"I don't know what everyone else does, but that's what your father did. I suppose being drunk makes it so you don't feel your pain as much."

Annabel looked down and twirled her thumbs in her lap. "I've thought about marrying Danny, and those thoughts scare me. Maybe because I fear I'll eventually regret it, and what if I have to drink every day to help me forget it? Just like dad."

Joan put her arm around Annabel. "You won't have the same regrets as your father. I can promise you that. You won't marry someone until you really want to, and marriage isn't something to be scared of if you really want it."

"But how do I know if I really want it?"

"You'll know. Trust me. You'll know." Joan kissed Annabel's forehead. "Now go to sleep."

GEORGE WAS AWAKE on the couch when Joan went downstairs later that night. He looked at her, his eyes dark and vacant. "Where do we go from here?"

"We're still a family, George."

"How can you still feel that way? After everything you now know."

Joan walked across the room and sat beside him on the couch. "How else should I feel?"

"How should you feel after I told you that I loved another man? I don't know, but not like this. So calm. So understanding."

"Oh, I can't say I understand this because I don't. But we still have a daughter upstairs, and I have to make decisions that are best for her."

George stared out the window for a while. "I've been a terrible husband, but an even worse father."

"It isn't too late to be a better father, George. I know in certain ways you can never be like other husbands, but that doesn't mean we can't have a good relationship. A decent marriage."

"You mean you want to stay married?"

"Are you saying you want a divorce?"

"Well ... I ... I just assumed."

"A divorce? George, we can't get a divorce. What would my family say? I'd be a disgrace. And the church? I could never go back to the church again if we got a divorce."

"So you'd rather stay married to a man . . . like me?" George gave her an incredulous look. "How does that work?"

"You stopping drinking would be a good start."

George leaned back against the couch. "I can't take any of what I did away, all of those horrible things."

"I know," Joan answered.

"Would you believe me if I told you I don't even want to drink anymore? Would you also believe me if I told you that I'm relieved you know my secret? Oh," George groaned and covered his face with his hands, "you have no idea how hard it's been, carrying this burden with me every day, hating myself a little more every day. You have no idea." He tore his hands from his face and looked at Joan.

Joan placed a hand on his knee. "You're right. I have no idea what that was like for you. I understand why you needed to drink. I really do. Now that I know and am willing to help you and be here for you, I believe you when you say you don't want to drink anymore. If you're willing, I want to make it so that this life is at least bearable for you so that you no longer have to hate yourself a little more every day."

"Why? Why would you want to do all of that for me?"

"Because we're still a family. You're still Annabel's father. And you can still be a good father. And us . . . well . . . I'm hoping we can at least be friends and talk to each other like we're talking right now. I can live with that because at least this is a whole lot better than the way we were living before."

"I can't believe that you mean all of what you're saying."

"But I do. I really do." Joan paused. "Did you drink to forget him?"

"Yes," George answered softly. "But it didn't work."

She placed her hand over his and squeezed lightly. "You don't have to try to forget him anymore."

Tears fell from George's eyes. Joan wiped the tears off his face as they sat on the couch, and neither said another word as they both fell asleep.

GEORGE AWOKE FIRST, just after seven a.m. Joan was asleep on the other side of the couch.

George covered a blanket over Joan and quietly walked to the front window. He peered out into the street, and it was as though he were looking at his neighborhood for the first time. There were trees in front of his house, with leaves of changing colors, that he didn't remember seeing before. A fire hydrant stood just off the curb, a spot where he had often parked his car, yet he hadn't been aware it was there until just then.

Everything that he hadn't noticed before, with eyes altered by drink and a mind over-burdened with guilt and regret, he was now taking in. He looked up at the clouds, and even though there was nothing spectacular about that late-October morning sky, it was the first time in a long time he had even bothered to notice it.

George watched Joan sleeping for a bit and then gazed back out the window. The morning sunshine, despite the crisp cool breeze, was absolutely inviting, and he had a sudden desire to go for a walk. It'd been a long while since he had wanted to do that.

He went to his room and changed into black slacks and a white long-sleeve shirt. Back downstairs, he tried to be as quiet as he could, but as he opened the front door, Joan woke up.

"George?" She squinted her sleepy eyes at him. "Where are you going?"

George stopped at the open door and turned to Joan. "For a walk. It's a beautiful morning."

"Hmm." She smiled.

"What? What is it?"

"I don't think I've ever heard you utter those words, 'It's a beautiful morning' before. But I like hearing it."

"I suppose I didn't notice those things before."

"Yes, I suppose you didn't."

"Would you like to come with?"

Joan smiled. "Yes, I think I would."

THE WIND BLEW against George's baggy clothes, hanging loosely off his body, as they walked along the sidewalk.

"We need to get you new clothes," Joan said. "Even with a belt your pants look like they're about to fall off."

George inspected his attire and laughed. "Yes, you're right. They do look like they're about to fall off. Maybe it was a bad idea to go for a walk. Maybe we should go back."

He turned and started to walk back, but Joan grabbed his hand.

"No. Wait, please. It's been so long since we've walked like this. Do you remember the last time we took a walk together?"

"Sure. When I came to your town, and we walked to the lake. I still have yet to see a more beautiful sunset than the one I saw that day."

"I'm surprised you remember that day."

"I have so many days to be ashamed of, but that's one day I'm glad to remember."

Joan held onto his hand. "Can we still walk? Don't worry about your pants."

"If you say so."

They held hands as they walked. To a stranger's eye they would appear as a typical happily married couple rather than a married couple holding hands for the first time in years.

They walked in silence for about a couple blocks.

"How many men have you loved?" Joan asked.

"Just Michael."

"Do you still desire to be with a man?"

George dropped his hand from Joan's grip and stopped walking. "If I could take that desire away I would have done it a long time ago."

"Of course. I . . . I know you would. I shouldn't have asked you that. It was an intrusive question. I'm sorry."

"Don't be sorry. You're free to ask me anything. You've earned that."

They went on walking and George scooped Joan's hand back in his. "Walks are better when holding hands."

"I agree." She smiled and let her hand fall into his.

George watched her. "Did you ever imagine we'd be doing this?"

"Walking down the street hand in hand?"

"Yes."

Joan shook her head, a tight smirk on her face, and sighed. "No way. How could I have imagined this? We couldn't get through a simple dinner without a fight."

George slowed his walk and looked away from her. "I can't take any of that back."

"I know." Joan patted his hand and tugged him along. "Come on. We don't have to talk about all of that anymore."

But George didn't budge. He stood in place with his eyes locked on Joan. "Are you happy now?"

"I'm happier than I've been in a long time," she answered.

"And you're satisfied with that? With being happier instead of happy?"

"What are you saying, George?"

"I'm saying you could be happy, really happy, whole-heartedly happy with a different husband, and you know why."

Another soft sigh escaped Joan's lips. "George. I told you we can't get a divorce. I can't take the judgement. Being a divorcee is harder for a woman than it is for a man."

She turned away from him and started walking.

"Joan," he followed her, "people would understand. Everyone knows I'm a lousy drunk. They'd appreciate how a good woman could only take so much. You're still young. You have a whole lot of life ahead of you. Don't you need the kind of love I can't give you?"

"Probably not as much as you need the love I can't give you." She turned to look at him. "You want passion."

"Don't you want that, too?"

"It would be nice, I admit. But men aren't clamoring to marry a divorced woman with a child. Besides, I can't get married in the church again. Where do I go from here? I wish this didn't have to be so difficult." Joan started to turn away.

"Hey." George gave her hand a light squeeze and pulled her back to him. "We don't have to decide on everything right now. My priorities need to be to stay sober and figure out how to be a father, though I imagine it's too late for that. The damage I've done is irreparable."

"I wouldn't say irreparable. Annabel is an intelligent girl. She'd understand . . ."

"Wait, you're not saying we tell her about Michael."

"No. We absolutely do not tell her about Michael. I was going to say she'd understand that alcohol was the reason you were the way you were. She'd give you a second chance because she desperately wants a father, but you need to have taken your last drink for that to happen."

George drew in a deep breath and eyed the skies again. It was a beautiful, cool fall morning. A kind of day George would have never bothered to take in before, but he intended on noticing those beautiful days more often. To do that, he could never drink again.

"You have my word," he said. "I've drunk my last drink."

Chapter Twenty-Six

JOAN KNOCKED LIGHTLY on Annabel's door and poked her head into the room. "Are you awake?"

Annabel was still in bed, but she was awake. It was Saturday morning, and Joan didn't usually bother her on Saturday mornings.

Annabel popped her head off her pillow. "What's wrong?"

Joan walked into the room and shut the door behind her. "Nothing's wrong." She sat down on the bed. "I was just checking if you were up."

"Why?" Annabel sat up. "Did something happen?"

Joan rubbed her hands together. "I suppose you can say something happened."

"What? What happened?" Annabel asked, horrified that her father had gotten drunk and had again done something to publicly embarrass the family. She shoved the covers off herself and jumped out of bed. "When is this going to end? He drove his car into a tree. What more has to happen for him to—"

"We went for a walk," Joan said.

Annabel jerked her head at her mother. "You did what?"

"We went for a walk," Joan said.

"A walk? The two of you went for a walk? Together?"

Joan took Annabel by the arm and pulled her back onto the bed. "Since the accident, your father hasn't been drinking, and since he hasn't been drinking he's been acting differently. He's been himself. It's been a very long time since I've seen this person."

"So that's it? Just like that he's a different person?"

"His drinking made him behave in ways he normally wouldn't have and turned him into someone he wasn't."

"How long is he going to be this new person?"

"He said he's done drinking forever."

"And you believe him?"

"I do."

"Well, I don't."

"I understand your reluctance to believe him," Joan said. "He has a lot to make up for and has so much to prove. I'm only asking that you give him a chance."

JOAN AND GEORGE'S voices carried into Annabel's room, along with the smell of greasy bacon and homemade pancakes, as they casually chatted about the headline news of the Saturday paper. Annabel imagined the scene happening in her kitchen, a husband and wife talking about newspaper articles over pancakes and coffee, was just an ordinary Saturday morning in most people's homes, but in her own home it was an anomaly. She didn't know what to make of it.

Joan had called Annabel down for breakfast twenty minutes ago, and even though her stomach craved the thick, buttery pancakes her mother always made to perfection, she wasn't ready to face her father. She didn't know what to say to him, which had never been a problem before because most of the time they didn't talk to each other.

There was a knock at the door, and Joan entered the room.

"Aren't you coming down for breakfast?"

Annabel leaned against the dresser and faced her mother. "I'm not ready yet. This change is too much, too fast."

Joan dragged her fingers across Annabel's pink bedspread as she made her way to her. "At some point you're going to have to talk to your father."

"I know. But not right now. Not this morning. I'm tired. I had a big night last night. We won and did a lot of celebrating."

"Yes. I saw pictures in the paper. There was a big write-up about Danny and the great game he played last night. I'll put it aside for you."

"Thanks, but I don't have to read about it. I was there. I saw it all. Danny was amazing."

"The article sure made it sound like it. I'm glad you're having such a fun time with Danny and your friends."

"It's been a lot of fun, but it's all gonna be so different next year."

"Hey." Joan pushed Annabel's hair behind her ear. "Just enjoy this. Okay?"

"I am."

"Good." Joan tapped Annabel on the nose with her finger. "I'm going to the grocery store. Your father wants to come with me. Can you believe that? I don't think your father has stepped into a grocery store in fifteen years." She shook her head with a smile on her face. "I'll put a plate of pancakes and bacon on the oven for you if you get hungry later."

Joan gave Annabel's hand a quick squeeze before leaving the room.

ANNABEL SAT ALONE at the kitchen table and ate the last of the buttered pancakes topped with thick maple syrup. She swiped a dishrag from the counter and wiped away the sticky sweet liquid dripping down her chin and then finished off her cold glass of milk.

She pulled up the sleeves of her blue sweater, placed the dishes in the sink, and rinsed them under the faucet. She wiped her hands on a towel and leaned against the counter and thought about the prospect of her father never drinking again. It was a hard image to maintain because she had no solid memory of what her father was like when he wasn't drinking.

Annabel went into the living room, and through the window, saw Sylvia smoking on her front porch. She went outside to see her.

The sun shone bright with hardly a cloud in the clear blue sky as Annabel made her way down the front walk.

"Hello, Annabel!" Sylvia yelled from her place on the porch swing. "Isn't it a beautiful day?" She smiled as Annabel approached her. "When Henry's away only a day like this can make me happy. How're you doing, sweetie?"

Annabel sat down on the top porch step.

"I'm okay. Danny won his game last night. The team's going to State. He threw three touchdowns."

"He did? Well that's great." Sylvia took a pull on her cigarette. "Touchdowns . . . that's football right?"

"Yes. He's the quarterback and he's so good. He's going to college in the fall on a full scholarship."

"A full scholarship? I suppose he has to be amazing to get a full scholarship." Sylvia drew again on her cigarette and kept her eyes on Annabel as she slowly exhaled. "And how do you feel about him leaving in the fall?"

Annabel looked up at the beautiful sky. "What can I do about it? He's a senior and he's leaving for college. It's okay, though. It's his time to leave. I'm not waiting for him. In two years, it'll be my time to leave."

"You're taking this better than I did," Sylvia said.

"What do you mean?"

"When my high school boyfriend left for college he didn't ask me to wait for him either. We broke up, and it broke my heart."

"But you had your whole life in front of you to do whatever you wanted," Annabel said. "You were just a teenager."

Sylvia tossed her cigarette away. "I wanted to marry him."

"Oh. I'm sorry."

Sylvia smiled. "But things worked out. I found my Henry. So don't worry. Just because Danny didn't ask you to wait for him, life can still have a way of working itself out."

Annabel got up from the step and sat next to Sylvia. She pulled the sleeves of her sweater down to her wrists. "Do you think people can change?"

"Of course. People change all the time. Nobody stays the same always. Change is a part of life."

"Can people just stop drinking?"

"What?" Sylvia asked.

"You know my dad is a drunk."

"I know he has his problems with alcohol."

"My mother thinks that those problems are over. That he's not a drunk anymore. Can people change, just like that?"

Sylvia leaned back into the porch swing and thought about it. "I . . . I don't know. Maybe if they really want to, but they'd have to really want to. How badly does your father want to stop drinking?"

"I'm not sure. I guess I'll find out soon. We're supposed to talk later. He went grocery shopping with my mom. He's never done that before."

"That's a good sign. He's already starting to change."

"I guess so." She paused and stood up. "I better get back. They'll probably be coming home soon. Bye."

"Bye, sweetie."

"Oh," Annabel turned back to Sylvia. "Danny did ask me to wait for him, but I told him I wouldn't. I have plans of my own. Sylvia, I think you need plans of your own, too. I know you love Henry, but you need to live for yourself more. Don't find happiness only from Henry. Life shouldn't stop just because Henry's away. You're stronger and more capable than you know."

"Wow. Thank you, Annabel. I needed to hear that, probably more than I should. I wish I was more like you when I was your age. Actually, I wish I was more like you right now. I admire you. You're strong in ways I've never been, but I'll try to be."

"You can do it."

"You are a special girl, Annabel, and I'm so glad Henry and I chose this house to move into. If I have only two more years to know you before you leave here and go off to accomplish all the amazing things I know you will, I hope to spend a lot more time out here on this porch talking with you because I know I won't meet another person like you again."

"I know that I won't either."

Sylvia held out her arms and Annabel stepped into her embrace.

JOAN ADDED THE last of the ingredients to the green bean casserole and put it on the oven rack next to the roast. She set the timer and went into the living room, anticipating that night's family dinner wouldn't resemble any other past family dinners.

George was on the couch. The TV was on, but he wasn't paying much attention to what was playing.

Joan went to him. "Go talk to her, George. She's waiting for you."

George drew in a shaky breath. He leaned forward and pressed his elbows against his knees and intertwined his fingers tightly together. "What do I say to her?"

"She's your daughter."

George looked helplessly at Joan. "But I've never talked to her before . . . not in the way I was supposed to."

"George, you're not that person anymore. It's you doing the talking now, not the booze, not the regrets, not the guilt. Just you."

"I'm not sure I know who that is."

Joan pushed a small decorative pillow to the side and sat beside him. "This'll take time. We're all going to have to get to know each other all over again. So go upstairs, George, and meet your daughter."

GEORGE WALKED UP the stairwell one step at a time. Even though he'd spent an hour on the couch reciting exactly what he would say to her, he was still unsure.

All of the vicious drunken incidents the bottle let him forget, Joan and Annabel held clearly in their minds. George knew this, and it made trying to make up for his horrible behavior dreadfully impossible. For everything he did remember, he knew words couldn't take any of it away.

George stood in front of Annabel's bedroom door for at least a minute before he knocked. Annabel called him in. George opened the door. She was sitting at her window.

She stood up as he walked into the room, her fingers tugging nervously at the edges of her skirt. "Hi."

"Hello." George took a couple more steps forward and then stopped at her dresser. "What were you doing?"

"Looking out the window."

"Is that something you do often?"

"Look out the window?"

"Yes."

"Sure. Sometimes."

George glanced around the room to all of Annabel's posters on her walls, and books and stuffed animals on her shelves until his eyes landed back on her. He smiled tensely as his arms pressed stiffly at his sides.

"How . . . how's school going?"

"Okay."

"I think it's great that you do well in school, despite what I may have told you before."

"Do you really mean that?"

"I do."

"Good because I really like school."

"That's what your mother tells me." George stood awkwardly in the middle of the room. "Do . . . do you want . . . is it okay if we sit down?"

"Sure," Annabel replied.

George sat at the foot of Annabel's bed and Annabel sat parallel to him on the other side. She crossed her feet at the ankles, and they dangled over the floor.

George looked at the floor and everywhere but at Annabel.

"Mom told me you like walks," Annabel said, breaking the incredibly awkward silence between them.

"That's right. I didn't know how much I liked walks until just now."

"I like walks, too. I go for a lot of walks."

"You do?"

Annabel nodded. "Almost every night."

"You go at night?"

"It's best to go at night."

"Why is that?"

"Because the darkness covers you, and you can hide in the darkness."

"Do you like to hide?"

"Sometimes."

"What are you hiding from?"

Annabel didn't answer right away. "My life."

George understood, better than Annabel could have known, about hiding from one's own life.

"Was I the reason for that?" George asked, and when Annabel didn't answer, he knew he had his answer. "Of course, I was. That was a stupid question."

"Mom told me you didn't want to settle down. That you didn't want to have a family."

"Mom told you that? I . . . I wish she hadn't told you that. It . . . it really isn't that simple."

"It's okay. I don't want to have a family either."

"You don't?"

"No." Annabel shook her head.

"Then don't."

"You mean that? Because you said I didn't need to be good at school because I was to get married and be in the home. That mine and mom's place was in the home. You said that."

George sighed and glanced at Annabel before shamefully looking away. "I suppose I said a lot of things I wish you'd forget. That's just one of them."

"I don't think I know how to forget all of this."

George set his eyes back on Annabel and held them there despite how painful it was to look at her, knowing the horrible way he'd treated her. "I'm sorry for the way I was. A father shouldn't be that way to his child."

"Maybe that's the way a father is with a child he never wanted."

"No, no, no." George frowned as he looked at Annabel, desperate for her to understand. "Don't ever think that. You're not what made me the way I was. You weren't what was wrong with me. You were the only thing that was right."

"It didn't feel that way."

"I know. I'm sorry for that." He paused. "I'm going to do better."

"Mom said you aren't drinking anymore."

"That's right."

"I didn't believe her."

"I don't blame you, but you'll see."

Annabel peered out the window.

"You like looking out the window," George observed.

Annabel drew her attention back to her father. "Yes."

"What do you see when you look out there?"

Annabel thought about it. "Possibility."

"Possibility," George repeated softly under his breath. "I like that."

"What was the life you really wanted?"

"The life I really wanted?"

"Yes. You didn't want this life. Mom said that's what made you drink. What life wouldn't have made you drink like you did?"

"Annabel, I . . . I don't want to think about that anymore, and I don't want you to either. I don't like you thinking of this as the life I didn't want."

"But you didn't."

"I meant it when I said you were the only thing right in my life. It isn't you that was wrong"

"Was it Mom?"

"It's not as simple as blaming one person. Nothing was her fault."

Annabel crossed her arms. "I don't understand."

He smiled sadly. "I know." He leaned his head back, looked to the ceiling, and sighed. "I want to finally be the father to you I never was, if you'll let me. I want to. I really do. Is that something you can understand?"

"Maybe."

"Then can you stop trying to figure out why I was the way I was and instead concentrate on the way I am right now?"

Annabel uncrossed her arms and dropped her hands into her lap. She looked again out the window.

"I didn't always know what I wanted in this life, but now it's clearer than ever," George continued. "I want to know you. If you think I deserve as much, will you let me know you?"

Annabel directed her gaze back to George. They looked at each other, and what felt like an honest and raw moment passed between them.

"I take my walks after supper," Annabel said. "Would you like to walk with me after supper?"

A corner of George's mouth lifted in a smile. "I would like that very much."

GEORGE WAS SHOWERING while Joan and Annabel set the dinner table.

"Did you have a nice talk with your father?"

Annabel placed the forks and knives in their spots, atop the folded cloth napkins. "Yes."

"How does that make you feel?" Joan walked ahead of Annabel and set the plates on the table.

"I'm not sure. I don't feel like this is real yet. I've only known him to be this one person and now I'm to believe he's someone else."

"This'll take time."

"How much time?"

"As long as it takes for this to be our normal, everyday life so that maybe someday you'll forget how he used to be."

"I'll never forget."

A screen door slammed outside. Through an open window, Annabel and Joan watched Sylvia light a cigarette on her front porch. She leaned against the rails and looked out into the street.

"She must be waiting for Henry to come home. He's away again," Joan said.

"I saw her today. We talked. We talk a lot. I think it's weird the way she waits on him while he's away. She puts her life on hold for him. I don't know why she'd want to do that."

"Sylvia needs Henry in ways you can't understand because you haven't had her life experiences. I'm sure there's a reason she is the way she is."

"Like dad has his reasons for being the way he was?"

"Well . . . yes. There's usually a reason why people do the things they do."

"But if dad can change, maybe Sylvia can change too."

"Only if she wants to."

"I told her she needs to live for herself more. Not rely on Henry so much."

"That's very good advice."

Annabel sat down at the table and looked at her mother. "I was hard on you. I had no right to be so hard on you. I thought you were just a submissive housewife. But I know now why you did it. Why you pretended everything was okay. That was for me. You wanted to make things here as good as they could be, despite how bad it was. You're a lot stronger than Sylvia, and for so long I thought you weren't. I'm sorry."

Joan walked around the table and knelt down beside Annabel. She brushed her hand through Annabel's hair. "You don't have to be sorry. You were right to feel the way you did. I should have taken you far away from here as soon as your father's drinking got worse. But I had nowhere to go. Your grandparents had lost the farm by then and were living in a one bedroom ranch. I had no education. I had no choice but to try to make this life as tolerable as I could. At least, that's what I thought I had to do. I felt stuck. But you, Annabel, you're going to have an education and a good job and you'll never be stuck living a life you don't want. There is no man you will ever have to rely on. I'm sorry I wasn't more than what I am, and wasn't able to take you away from here."

"You did what you had to do. I know that now. You don't have to blame yourself anymore."

GEORGE WALKED INTO the kitchen as Annabel and Joan prepped dinner, his hair still damp from the shower. Joan dropped the bowl of salad she just made at his unexpected appearance.

"Oh no," Joan yelled as the vegetables hit the floor, and she quickly dropped to her knees and cleaned the mess.

George stood awkwardly in the doorway. A few strands of hair fell over his eyes that he didn't bother to brush away. "I'm sorry." He knelt beside her and helped to clean up the fallen lettuce and carrots. "I didn't mean to startle you. Just wanted to know if you needed help in here."

Annabel and Joan exchanged peculiar looks. Never once had George asked if he could help. On a usual night, George would have gone straight to the dining room, mixed himself a drink, and waited at the table for the food to be served. The longer the food took, the drunker he'd get.

"We're fine in here. Right, Annabel?" Joan looked to Annabel, who was standing at the counter where she'd been slicing a loaf of bread.

"Yes," Annabel replied, not taking her eyes off her father. It was a sight to see—him, on his knees, beside her mother, cleaning up the floor. The image of that moment was the start in her belief that things were actually going to change.

They sat down to dinner that night, and for the first time that Annabel could remember, their family dinner resembled all of the perfect family dinners she had enviously watched through other people's windows. There were no drunken outbursts. No reason to keep her head down. No reason to be fearful.

The roast and green bean casserole sat in the middle of the table, beside the basket of sliced bread and a bowl of salad that Joan remade.

"This dinner looks marvelous." George took the serving spoons from the casserole dish. "Shall we?" he asked and filled their plates with food.

Annabel smiled as she watched him serve the food. It was the first time she remembered smiling while sitting at a dinner table with her father.

Two Weeks Later

ANNABEL LOOKED HERSELF over in her bedroom mirror and redid her ponytail so that it was tighter and smoother. She pushed the sleeves of her white cardigan sweater down to her wrists and pulled the waist of her light blue Capris up to her belly button.

"Stop fidgeting. You look great," Molly said.

"Yeah. You look great. Danny won't be able to keep his eyes off you," Donna said.

"Sure, while Danny's playing for the State Championship he won't be able to keep his eyes off her," Molly said with heavy sarcasm.

"I meant after the game, smarty pants, when we're celebrating winning State."

"I can't even imagine the fun we're gonna have tonight when we win this thing," Molly yelled.

Little Richard's "Good Golly Miss Molly" came on the radio and Molly turned up the volume, and she and Donna twirled wildly around the room.

Annabel sat on her bed and watched her goofy friends celebrate a game that hadn't yet been won, and though she was just as excited as they were, she didn't join in on their fun.

She sat on the bed and took in the moment, not wanting this time in her life to end. It was all so good. She had two great friends. A sweet boyfriend. A mother she didn't resent anymore. And a father she was no longer afraid to talk to.

She wanted this moment to last forever, but the song ended and the girls settled down.

"What's wrong, Annabel?" Molly asked and sat on the bed, catching her breath from the dancing.

"Nothing's wrong. Everything's just right." Annabel smiled. "Come on. We have to go. My dad's gonna drive us to the game."

Alicia Joseph lives in the Midwest. Her published works include, *Her Name*, *Loving Again*, *A Penny on the Tracks*, and *Annabel and the Boy in the Window*. When she isn't writing, Alicia enjoys volunteering with animals, reading, rooting for her favorite sports teams, and spending time with her friends and family, including her many nieces and nephews.

Learn more about Alicia at https://aliciajoseph.com